After...Happily Ever After

Nature of Desire — Vampire Queen — Knights of the Board Room — Daughters of Arianne

To fans of Joey W. Hill's work, these series have special significance, because they contain many of her readers' favorite characters. Because they are her favorites too, Joey doesn't like saying good-bye at "The End" any more than her readers do. So here for your reading pleasure, at last available in compilation form, are novellas and shorts revisiting these characters. Poignant romantic moments, erotic encounters, holiday celebrations...wherever daily life might take them.

These stories have become a way for Joey to take a breather and simply immerse herself in the pleasure of spending leisure time with past characters. We hope you will enjoy the same experience when reading them!

Cantrips: Volume #1

Copyright © 2016 Joey W. Hill

Cover design by W. Scott Hill

SWP Digital & Print Edition publication November 2016

The following material contains graphic sexual content meant for mature readers. Reader discretion is advised.

Digital ISBN: 978-1-942122-51-7

Print ISBN: 978-1-942122-52-4

Cantrips: Volume #1

Minor Magics Crafted to Amuse and Entertain

A Collection of Vignettes by

Joey W. Hill

Table of Contents

Foreword

"Cantrip" has several meanings. What amused me initially, due to my "storywitch" moniker, was that the first one I read was the Scottish source, "A witch's trick." But the definition that applies the most to these volumes is "minor magics meant to amuse and entertain."

My first vignette, a short story written around 2008 revisiting Mac and Violet of *Natural Law*, was offered to readers who wanted more about these two. I didn't have an idea for another full-length book for them, but the idea of revisiting them in a short story format was a lot of fun for me, and the readers received it enthusiastically. I enjoyed the breather from deadline pressure and a full-length storyline arc to instead do a slice-of-life moment with favorite characters. So the definition of Cantrips above resonated on multiple levels.

Since we have been repeatedly asked about offering the vignettes in print and ebook compilation volumes, your wish is our command, and these volumes are our answer. Going forward, as long as there is a demand for them, we will release a new volume of vignettes when we have enough to make a book. Volumes 1 & 2 of *Cantrips* are only the first two of what we hope will be more "vignette volumes." Currently they represent all vignettes written through 2016.

Now, these vignettes come with several caveats, as follows:

1. **The individual, digital download versions of these stories have always been—and will**

continue to be—offered for free. Right now they reside at the JWH Connection, a wonderful fan forum run by a handful of very enthusiastic ladies who independently promote and support my work. To find the forum and the vignettes, visit storywitch.com/community for more information.

2. My readers have told me all of the stories can be enjoyed even if you haven't read the books, but you may get plot spoilers or miss some emotional nuances between the characters that were developed in their specific book(s). However, when needed, each vignette is prefaced by a short explanation to help you figure out what the vignette is about, and to identify the series/books from which it originated. This will help you seek out these titles if you decide you'd like to read some of them first.

3. Many of the vignettes were written as serials (a different segment every couple of weeks), and then compiled into one download at the fan forum upon completion. As such, you may notice a little redundancy in these segments as certain concepts are "recapped." We could have edited that out, but we wanted to keep them essentially as they were written.

They say the best gifts are handmade. As the number of my loyal readers have grown—an amazing and humbling thing—writing these vignettes has turned out to be the best way to say a heartfelt thank you for the insights and wisdom, laughter and smiles, you all have offered to me. You enrich my life greatly, and I thank you for that.

I appreciate all you have done, do, or will do, to support my work! And I hope you enjoy your Cantrips.

The Baby Shower

A vignette featuring Violet and Mac of Natural Law *as well as some other characters from the* Nature of Desire Series *who refused to be left out!*

Originally Posted September, 2008

Background: *In this vignette, Violet is pregnant and a host of the* Nature of Desire *series characters decide to throw her a baby shower. Also special appearance by Sarah of* If Wishes Were Horses, *because we've always considered her and Justin's book part of the NOD anyway. After all, the first mention of Violet happened in their story, right?*

Additional note: *When this vignette was written, I offered readers a chance to participate by suggesting "gifts" for the shower. So some of the names referenced in this vignette are/were fan forum members. Violet and Mac were very appreciative!*

§

Violet laid her hands on the firm basketball of her abdomen, stroking there to soothe, and perhaps to soothe herself as well. "He's fine, daisy-girl," she murmured. "Your daddy's tough. Toughest, strongest cop around. Smart and fast, and he wants to meet you more than anything. He's fine."

"Violet?" The front door closed and she heard the movement of booted heels through their small kitchen and

3

the sitting room. "Where the hell are you?"

"Just like a police chief," she called out, turning away from the back screen porch view of the Florida marsh. "Too lazy to do her own detective work. I'm out here."

Sarah peered out, her face wreathed in a smile. "Hey, why wear the chief hat if you can't order minions to do the shitwork?" But when she focused on Violet's face, her blue-gray eyes narrowed, proving that the Chicago cop who'd become a small town police chief still had well-honed investigative skills. "What's the matter?"

"Nothing," Violet shrugged. "Just mommy hormones fucking with my head. Mac had a fairly big drug bust going down today. I haven't heard from him yet."

"You know how those things go. The wrap-up onsite can tie you up for hours—"

"I know. Really, I know." Violet sighed, rubbed her hands over her stomach again, then laughed at herself. "It's like a Buddha's bald head. I keep rubbing her for luck."

"Well, here, I'll add a rub." Sarah cupped the cocooned life beneath Violet's pretty gauze maternity top and stroked gently. "He'll be fine. I wouldn't want to be the thing standing between Mac Nighthorse and seeing his daughter come into the world. Come on. We've got plenty to keep the mommy hormones occupied."

"Oh yeah?" But Violet could now hear the sound of other car doors closing, women's chatter and laughter. While it did make her feel better, a part of her remained coiled tight, wanting to send them all away and closet herself in worry. But Sarah wouldn't let her. Her friend slid an arm through hers. "Come on, Tinkerbell."

"You're only brave enough to call me that because you know I won't throw down with you while I'm carrying the little alien here."

"And you're not armed," Sarah added with a grin. "Hey, I didn't know they sold maternity tops in kid sizes."

"Just wait, beanpole. When this baby pops out, it's on." But Violet let herself be led by the tall, blond-haired woman who'd been her friend since they'd met at an Illinois gun show and discovered they were both in law enforcement.

During her pregnancy, Violet had been doing desk duty. Today she was off, and Sarah, visiting Tampa from Lilesville, had organized a baby shower. While men typically weren't invited, Violet found herself almost desperate for Mac's presence. As his Mistress, she had tied him up, flogged his broad shoulders, caned his beautiful ass and made him beg to brush his mouth over just the arch of her foot. But when he was away like this, everything inside her begged for *him*. Maybe it wouldn't be so bad if he hadn't almost died in the line of duty nearly two years ago, but she still had a hard time shaking it when he was going into a potentially deadly situation like this operation.

Well, she needed to. This is what they both did, damn it. *Get a grip. Go do girl things, or he'll laugh at you when he gets here, you worrying like some civilian wife.* Of course, since she'd married Mac, she'd developed a much greater respect for those civilian wives. It was indescribable, letting the center of your world walk out your door every morning, knowing that, as tedious as police work could often be, the odds were still greater than for most that you might not see him alive again.

"There she is!" As she came into the living room, she was amazed to find, in such a short period of time, the room had been transformed into a party. A festive tablecloth decorated with a stroller pattern was tossed over the coffee table. Several trays of gooey hors d'oeuvres, perfect for a pregnant woman's appetite, were spread out next to plastic tumblers for punch and sodas. A pile of gifts had been mounded on the sofa, several larger ones off to the side. And the room was filled with the small circle of women she now counted as her closest friends.

While Sarah had been in her life the longest, Violet's best friend—before Mac— had been Tyler Winterman, a fellow sexual Dominant who'd considered it his responsibility to give Mac the once over before approving his pairing with Violet. Fortunately, murder hadn't ensued. A smile touched her lips in remembrance.

In the past year, Tyler had fallen to matrimony. Marguerite was taller than even Sarah. With silky white hair and pale blue eyes, as well as a lean, riveting figure, she was striking enough to cause traffic incidents. Remarkably, Marguerite was also a Dominant. Tyler's courtship of her had been an intriguing and volatile example of the odd pairings created by the D/s preference.

Marguerite ran a tea room, and her employees, Chloe and Gen, had also become favored friends of Violet's. Though not active in that lifestyle, they were apparently more aware of their boss's preferences now. Violet had heard that Chloe was dating Brendan, a former submissive of Marguerite's, which her woman's curiosity hoped she'd hear more about while they were here.

She was delighted and surprised to see Lauren in the group, because Violet hadn't expected her to be able to make the trip. The pediatric surgeon was another leggy blonde, but since Violet barely hit five feet, she'd learned to tolerate that any friends she had over the age of puberty were going to be taller. Lauren lived on an island off the coast of Florida with her artist husband, another submissive, who was a friend of Tyler's. So once she met Josh's wife, Violet had secured her friendship for herself.

Looking around the small assembly, seeing the effort they'd put into it, she was determined to put aside her fears. If there was one thing a cop knew, worry did nothing but steal away the present moment, which was always too short. She lifted a brow.

"Should I be worried? I know the tastes of this crowd, and the baby may be too young for some of the gifts you've brought."

"Now, they make St. Andrew's crosses in all sizes." Lauren tucked her tongue in her cheek. "And I did have it fitted with monogrammed fleece restraints."

"Oh, God..." As Violet rolled her eyes, they shepherded her to a chair, considerately making sure she was close to the food. Chloe, her eyes sparkling under a mop of hair, brought her a cup of punch, as a piece of celery obscured by gouda cheese and smelling of a heavenly spice was tucked into her other hand. "Let's just hope you don't arrest us all for corrupting a minor in the womb," she said.

"I think that deed's already done, given whose womb the poor kid's in," Sarah rejoined. "Can you imagine what she's witnessed in that bedroom in just these past few months? Or the kitchen, this living room, the dock outside..." She dodged Violet's swat, laughing. Then Lauren reached her. Bending down, she kissed Violet's mouth warmly in welcome, cradling her face.

"You look beautiful," she pronounced, with both the eye of a doctor and a friend. "Pregnancy agrees with you."

"Well, we're only agreeing once, that's for sure. I'm not going through the bionic bladder and ankles thicker than my waist again." Violet squeezed her wrists fondly.

"Everyone says that," Gen remarked. "My neighbor said it, and she now has five. Her green footprint is the size of the Jolly Green Giant's. I told her she can stop now, before her offspring consume all the resources in the greater Florida area."

Violet laughed and reached over to take Gen's hand. As the oldest of the group, nearing forty, Gen was likely present to help Marguerite keep Chloe's younger antics firmly in hand, though she didn't seem above joining in the fun.

"How is Josh?" Violet directed her next question back to Lauren.

"Oh, he's lovely." Lauren's smile softened, her eyes reflecting her feelings for her husband as clearly as a lighthouse beacon. "We're staying at Tyler and Marguerite's, so he's sculpting in that workshop Tyler converts for him whenever he comes to stay. He's started a whole new line I think you'll like." She cocked a brow. "Want a preview?"

"Absolutely. Tell us your favorite piece."

"Well, I guess none of you are going to run off and give the idea to a competitor," Lauren decided.

"Unless they pay us enough," Gen put in.

Lauren rolled her eyes and crossed her legs in the chair she'd taken, but she was visibly thinking over the question. "Okay, my favorite piece. It's a bronze, where the male nude is on his stomach, hogtied."

"Ankles and wrists chained and all four connected to one another over his back," Marguerite added, at Chloe's curious glance.

"Right," Lauren nodded. "You can see every muscle straining, because it appears his Mistress has commanded him to keep his head up, his eyes on her. She's squatting on her stilettos, wearing nothing but them, right in front of his face. Josh made her hair long, so it's curling down over her body, naturally hiding everything the sub most wants to see. She has one hand gripping the man's hair, and her other hand is sliding down the inside of her thigh, just hinting at what she might do next to torment him...and I better stop there."

"I wonder where *that* idea came from?" Marguerite arched a perfect brow. She was sitting on the sofa, while Chloe had snugged down on the floor in front of her like an ebullient younger sister.

"I can't imagine." Lauren's eyes twinkled.

"Well, I'll definitely come see the pieces before they're shipped off, because I know I won't ever be able to afford any of them," Violet said.

"Just depends on whether Mac shoves some drug money under his vest." Sarah sat down on her chair arm with a soda and stroked a hand over Violet's auburn curls.

"Let's see if we can save him some money. Come open some of this stuff before I decide to keep my gift." Gen pushed a gift wrapped in yellow, with a tassel of pink and blue ribbon on the top, toward her. "This one is somewhat from Marguerite and me, because she came up with the idea."

"No, Gen did all the work, so she gets 100% of the credit," Marguerite amended. "Tyler and I found you something different."

When Violet reached forward, she found herself stuck. The chair she'd been pressed into was Mac's recliner and, with its deep seat intended for his long, rangy frame, she was now off balance for pushing herself forward over her belly. "It's like watching a Weeble," Sarah noted, but gave her a helpful push in the lower back that propelled her to the seat edge, with Chloe and Gen tugging on her hands.

"If you ever get pregnant," Violet threatened, "I intend to make fun of you the entire time."

"Justin won't let you," Sarah sniffed. "I'll tell him any

teasing might upset the unborn child's aura."

"Yeah, right. I don't think being a Wiccan priest makes him brain dead. Plus he knows I'll just pistol whip him if he tries to stop me. Fuck his aura up three ways to Sunday."

"Just don't get his face," Chloe protested. "You wouldn't want to mar a work of art like that."

"Forget the face. It's what he carries around in those pants that should be insured."

Sarah leaned over and shoved at Lauren. "Hey, no lusting after my husband. I'm not going to allow friend-verbal-adultery-by-proxy here."

"That doesn't even make grammatical sense," Gen protested.

"You all understood well enough."

"If you're going to marry a moveable feast, you can stop the snacking, but nothing's going to stop the salivating." Chloe's nostrils flared and she took a dramatic inhale. "One whiff of the guy—he even smells fuckable..."

There was a chorus of giggles, drowning out Sarah's threats. Violet interrupted them as her fingers came in contact with a blanket so soft it felt like the down of angel wings. "Oh, my. Gen, this is beautiful."

The crocheted baby throw was a soft white. In the bottom right hand corner a satin and velvet motif of two teddy bears faced one another inside a large heart. There was a monogrammed "V" and "M" on the outside of each bear. A baby bear slept in the center of the heart. The card read: *Made with love, given with love.*

"Oh, Gen. Come here." She gave the attractive brown-haired woman an enthusiastic hug as Marguerite looked on with quiet approval. "We'll treasure this. And it's perfect. I can wrap her up to keep her warm when we go sit on the dock at night."

Gen smiled. "I'm so glad you like it. My friend Maryde helped me with the embroidery work. And I thought it would bolster you to have something nice and *appropriate*, to brace you for Chloe's gift." She thrust it at Violet as Chloe made a noise of protest.

"What I bought might not be as sentimental, but I think it's perfectly appropriate for the occasion, and the recipient."

Chloe's wrapping paper was a pattern of laughing cherub babies somersaulting through a blue sky with white clouds. Some were whimsically holding their toes. Inside the paper was a big case of diapers, on top of which had been taped a flatter, slim package.

"Hey, everyone needs diapers, and on a cop's salary..." Chloe was defending her choice, and Violet waved down the catcalls.

"She's absolutely right. On our salaries, I was considering just holding her over the dock edge until she was potty trained, but Mac pointed out that was likely against environmental regulations."

Violet opened the slim package and lifted out an infant pajama set. An object wrapped in it fell into her lap with a rattling sound, but when she lowered her gaze to it, they all burst out laughing.

It was a baby rattle, but one shaped like a tiny flogger. The rattler was in the handle, and the straps made a slapping noise as they were jostled back and forth. When she raised her gaze to the pajama set, she found it was a pretty lacy thing with pink fabric and white lace cuffs. However, in the center of the shirt was a small female devil, one with long eye lashes and a tall pitchfork twined with flowers. Beneath the depiction, three words were printed:

I like *spankings.*

"I have completely incorrigible friends," she decided, as the women giggled and passed the items around. Even Marguerite's normally somber expression looked at pains to remain that way.

"Here, these are safe. These are the ones Mac had us pick up from the station earlier this week." Sarah directed her to the pile.

The next package revealed a wonderful contraption, a pouch-like seat in which the baby could be placed, and the seat hung in a doorframe. Sarah opened the card. "It's from Terry at the precinct. She said to tell you this is a Johnnie Jumper, and it's great for when you're showering or somewhere else where you want the baby close, but don't want to lug a portable crib."

"Maybe when you go to the club. You could take her to The Zone to provide early education." Lauren lifted the tiny flogger rattler in thumb and forefinger and flicked it. "Okay, baby V, this is the proper way to strike Daddy's butt to make it flex in just the right way—"

"You are sick, demented, twisted. What is it about baby showers and bachelorette parties that can turn a group of otherwise mature women into overly hormonal teenagers?" Violet lunged for her awkwardly and a couple of the women caught her before she overbalanced, though they were all laughing so hard they almost upset the table. Violet secured the tiny flogger rattle, however, and collapsed back into her chair, trying to look at all of them sternly. "If she can hear you, she'll come out needing therapy. No child wants to know *anything* about her father's backside."

"Normally that's true," Lauren agreed. "But that's one hell of a backside."

"One hell of an everything," Marguerite offered thoughtfully, her mind obviously dwelling in pleasant areas. "Combine that with the fact he likes to be on his knees to a woman as often as possible, and he's damn near irresistible."

Marguerite had seen Mac naked and on his knees quite often, since they did a great deal of their play over at Tyler and Marguerite's. Because she knew Marguerite was completely absorbed in Tyler, it didn't bother her, but Violet managed a glare for form's sake.

"On his knees only to this particular pregnant woman, thank you very much. Does Tyler know you have this obsession with my husband?"

"No obsession." Marguerite tilted her head, the blue eyes glinting. "Just happy to work him out if you're too tired to keep him in proper training. Least I could do, Mommy."

"I'm getting my gun," Violet decided.

"No, no—not until you see what she and Tyler gave you." Chloe pushed it at her.

"You realize that biblical adultery includes thinking about it, right?" But Violet settled back, accepting the next gift.

"Well then, every girl who's been exposed to that husband of yours is going straight to hell," Sarah observed.

"I think it's a medical condition," Lauren said practically. "God won't hold a medical condition against you, else He or She wouldn't have created a man that fine. Though you're a fine one to talk, Sarah. When Justin saunters across the street to pick up his morning paper, you probably get ten traffic accidents in that one-stoplight town of yours."

"Justin does not saunter," Sarah defended.

"Oh, he *sooo* saunters. That sexy ooze of motion." Chloe got up and demonstrated, to a new wave of giggles and shouts of laughter. "Can you imagine coming into his shop? He says, 'What may I do for you today, ma'am?' and three illegal acts run through the head of every customer, whether she's eighteen or eighty."

Violet elbowed her exasperated friend. "Sarah took care of that. She's put up a sign outside that says 'Beware: Proprietor guarded by cop wife, aka woman with gun.'"

The girls cackled again while Lauren screwed up her face. "Ooze of motion? That makes me think of pustules. Open the gift, Violet. Christ, and we didn't even bring alcohol. Think how out of control we'd be if we had."

"They'd probably be raiding Mac's underwear drawer," Violet responded dryly.

"That's a thought," Chloe crowed, but Gen yanked her back down to the sofa.

"Behave," the woman reproved, with a smile playing around her mouth.

"You're assuming he wears any," Violet said. While their banter continued, she turned her attention to the tastefully wrapped small box. The wrapping paper was a series of ducks marching back and forth in haphazard patterns, complimented by a soft blue bow. She wasn't surprised by the endearing packaging. Marguerite's tea shop regularly hosted little girls' tea parties. Though Marguerite couldn't have children, she enjoyed being with them. Violet removed the wrapper, revealing a velvet pink box inside. She cracked it open.

"Oh my..."

It was two silver bracelets. Each bracelet looked like a pair of overlapping angel wings, the feathers detailed out perfectly.

"There's an inscription," Marguerite put in, as the women craned their necks to look into the box.

Violet tilted the bracelets. Inside the band of one, she read "My daddy". The other one read "My husband."

It reminded her that when she'd met Mac, he'd worn a pair of slave bracelets given to him by his first Mistress, Lisette. Even after he and Lisette had amicably parted ways, he wore them at the clubs to designate his submissive status, because nothing else about Mac Nighthorse suggested he played that side of the field. But Violet hadn't needed the bracelets to know. The first time she'd touched him, she'd known, because that essential part of him, underneath the tough cop exterior, had called to her nature as a Mistress. She'd loved every minute of removing his shields and getting him to surrender to her fully.

He'd put Lisette's bracelets away out of respect for his new Mistress, so Marguerite understood the significance of providing her a replacement set, tailored to their specific relationship.

"We had Mac come by the house one day for a measurement, so they should fit his wrists perfectly, and won't interfere with the bracelet you gave him," Marguerite added.

"These are absolutely beautiful, Marguerite." Violet blinked. Damn mommy hormones. Despite her diminutive size, she was known as the most intimidating state trooper in her division, but now she was in danger of becoming a puddle. If she had any ability to move with grace instead of like a bowling ball knocking over pins, she would have hugged the woman. Of course, Marguerite wasn't much on hugging and touching, so Violet's lack of mobility was probably a relief to the woman. Which was why it was a shock when Marguerite came to her. Sliding her cool arms around Violet's back, Marguerite gave her a warm hug and a press of lips against her cheek.

"Now you can make those other ones disappear," she murmured in Violet's ear, winning a smile. While Lisette was a friend to both, they understood the possessiveness of being a Mistress. Lisette would have understood it as well as either one of them.

"This is just so marvelous." Violet shook her head. "Where did you get them?"

"Another one of Tyler's friends." Marguerite took her seat and shot a smile at Lauren. "You know how he likes to patronize the arts. Her name is Laura, and she's an exceptional silversmith and artist. But I think it's time to open Sarah and Justin's. I'm sure they found something even more wonderful."

"You're just sucking up, because we haven't raked your husband over the coals yet," Sarah threatened, but handed Violet her package, a shoebox-sized package. This one had a silver wrapping marked with tiny mice dressed as babies. They held rattles and displayed varying comical expressions, from bawling displeasure to fist-chewing contentment.

"I know you didn't wrap this, because the corners are perfectly overlapped. It's a good thing your husband runs an erotic shop that specializes in wedding gifts."

"Justin only *helped* me wrap it," Sarah sniffed.

"Correction, she tried to wrap it, and he was so horrified he rewrapped it," Lauren pointed out. "Weren't we going to talk about Marguerite's husband?"

"Absolutely..." Chloe sighed. "I work in paradise. I get to see him every day."

"You seduce him into the tea room with free dessert. If he gets a weight problem, I'm taking it out of your ass," Marguerite noted darkly. "And the dessert out of your paycheck."

"It's totally worth it." Chloe slid an arm around Marguerite's calf, since she was back to sitting on the floor next to her crossed legs, and squeezed with affection. "The least you could do is leave your door cracked in the morning when you spend the night above the shop, so I can see him naked."

"Just consider it an employee benefit," Gen suggested.

"I'll replace your healthcare with it, since you obviously don't value *that* perk," Marguerite rejoined sweetly.

"Since I'm the pregnant one," Violet interjected, "and therefore inviolate, I can get away with saying it. After Mac, Tyler is the finest man that has ever been crafted. If only he didn't have a head like a rock..."

"Hey, as long as other parts are just as hard—" Chloe spluttered as Gen put a hand over her mouth and Marguerite gave her a fond swat on the head. Her relaxed expression said she had no problems with the admiration, however. As Violet knew from being close friends with Tyler, he had an unexaggerated universal appeal to any straight woman. Also, as one of the most exceptional Dominants she'd ever met, he had an uncanny way of winning over any submissive he chose. But there was only one woman he'd wanted to keep, and it was the woman who was a match for him in all ways. Violet knew that when The Zone—the fetish club at which many in this room had memberships—indicated that a public room was going to be used by Mistress Marguerite or Master Tyler—or thank the gods, both—the bartenders stocked up, expecting a standing-room-only crowd.

When she opened Sarah and Justin's gift, she found a little wooden rack of police issue revolvers. Smaller than the real thing, and made of molded plastic, like toys. The rack bore the badge number Violet wore, the other side showing Mac's detective shield.

"They're containers," Chloe realized, crouching by the table. "Oh, how cool. This one holds baby oil, this one lotion, this one"—she lifted it, squinted at the end—"freaking cool. This one has a sifter. It's for baby powder." She pointed to the labels on the rack. "And look, it says 'to protect, serve and freshen.'"

"You're insane." Violet looped an arm around Sarah and squeezed. "Now I'm sure *you* picked this one out."

"Well, Justin knew it should be a gift that reflected both of us. His creativity and my special handcuff-you-if-I-don't-get-my-way charm." Sarah smiled. "Seriously, we found it in this catalog of police-related gifts, and thought it would be perfect. Though we worried it might feel strange to point even a toy gun at your child."

"I don't know about that. When she's going through the

terrible twos, it might relieve some frustration." Violet laughed. "Stop that tantrum *now*, or I'll powder you."

The final gift was the largest. As her friends positioned it on the floor and pulled the paper away, a foolish grin wreathed Violet's face. It was a collective gift from the whole of her division. An enormous basket, filled with every conceivable item the baby might need. Baby wipes, thermometers, spoons, bowls, bibs, extra socks...it might take days to go through it all.

"The card is from Crystal, at the dispatch desk," Sarah read. "She says some of the things might not seem as practical as others, because Hank, Rick and a couple other of the guys came shopping with her. She said, 'it was worse than taking two toddlers to a candy store'. Apparently they had differing ideas as to what a baby might need."

"No, it's perfect. Look at these ribbons." Violet oohed over a brace of baby hair bows and lace-edged socks. "It will be fun figuring out which ones Hank picked out and which ones Crystal did."

"I think he went because he has the hots for Crystal, and it's the first time in ten years he's been able to get that dispatch desk out from in between them," Sarah pointed out. "He probably had a diabolical plan to ravish her in a big pile of stuffed animals at Babies R Us."

"Good luck on that. I think she had her uniform made out of body armor and surgically adhered to her skin years ago." Violet chuckled. "But then again, we use Hank as a blood hound when the dog's on vacation. He's hard to shake off the scent."

As the women cleaned up the wrapping paper and Gen offered to make up some coffee, Chloe turned on the television to find a suitable music station on cable. Now that the gift giving was done, Violet remembered she'd intended to take care of some special business today. She met Marguerite's gaze and, in silent understanding, the woman came to help her up, with Sarah's assistance. "Sarah, I need to talk to Marguerite a couple minutes, okay? Can you keep everyone entertained while we're on the docks?"

"Sure," Sarah said, but before she could turn away,

Violet's brow furrowed and she swung toward the television.

"Chloe, stop." The sharp command made the girl freeze before she could turn the channel. "Rewind that."

Sarah turned with her as Chloe scrolled back on the news program she'd been bypassing.

"*...drug deal in the downtown area has been broken up, but not without cost to local police. There are two bodies on scene and, at this time, we are waiting to find out who the casualties are and what has happened...*"

Violet was not a fainter. She'd stood toe to toe with perps when they took a shot at her, and hadn't lost her cool. Which was why the black rush covering her eyes, making her sway on her feet, had to be happening to someone else. This was ridiculous. It was preliminary information only. It wasn't him, no matter that the tears welling up in her eyes, the sobs choking her throat, told her it was. *Oh God, oh God...not again, I can't lose him again...*

There were gasps and sounds of women scrambling, something knocked over. She was caught in someone's arms. Marguerite's she realized, Sarah a close second. As they eased her down to the couch, Lauren's voice was there, calm, professional, the doctor staying collected in crisis. She was having everyone else move back, and sending Chloe for a cool washcloth. But it was Sarah's voice that brought things into focus.

"Dammit, Violet, stop being such a damned girl. Wake up, snap out of it."

She blinked back the black haze, which turned to gray. Focusing on the worried faces around her, she saw all were standing back as instructed except Sarah, admonishing her, and Marguerite, whose hand Violet had retained in a death grip. Lauren was taking the wet washcloth from Chloe to lay it on her forehead. "Sarah..." Violet turned her gaze to her. "I'm sorry, but...oh, God..."

Sarah dropped the tough routine, apparently understanding she wasn't dealing with the normal Violet, and took her other hand, cupping her face. "Sweetie, they don't know anything yet. He's going to be fine. You know him. The Oak, remember? That's what they call him. The casualties are likely the dealers. You know the fucking media. If it was a cop they'd be screaming it on every station right now. They're just drawing out the suspense to up the ratings. If I had my way, I'd shoot every one of those camera-toting idiots. Just settle down, now. You're upsetting the daisy-girl. She's wondering why her mommy is freaking out."

"You're right, I know. God, I feel like such an idiot." Even as her eyes couldn't stop leaking and she felt fury take her. Where the hell was he? Why didn't he call? She was pregnant, for Chrissakes. Why hadn't she told him he had to do desk duty at the same time she did?

Because she wasn't a weak-willed candy-ass, and what they did for a living helped people, it made a difference. And he was okay, dammit. She accepted nothing less.

"Okay." She nodded, squeezed their hands. "I want to get up, let me get up."

"Easy now," Lauren counseled, but they helped her to a sitting position. Marguerite stroked her back in reassurance. Violet turned her attention to her. "I think you and I were going to go outside and talk."

"Why don't you all do that right here? The rest of us will go in the kitchen and get the coffee ready. You can come get us when you're done." Sarah squeezed her shoulder and rose, glancing at Lauren for confirmation. The pediatrician nodded.

"Marguerite, just call out if anything seems amiss. You too." Sarah glanced at Violet. "Don't worry about overreacting, okay?"

"Okay." Violet didn't know if she was talking about any symptoms she might experience in the next few moments, or the television program, which Chloe had shut off, but either way, it helped. She drew some steady breaths, and then realized she was still holding Marguerite's hand. "Oh, I'm sorry."

Rather than letting her draw away, Marguerite simply tightened her grip, reinforcing the affection before letting her go. "It's okay."

She noticed Marguerite didn't reassure her that Mac was fine, probably because Marguerite understood better than most that, all too often, things didn't turn out fine at all. However, the somber, steady gaze didn't borrow trouble either. Marguerite's expression was neutral, the tranquil surface of a slow moving stream, and Violet drew strength from that pale blue gaze. Many people made the mistake of thinking Marguerite was cold, but no one who'd won the rare chance to get close to her did.

"What did you need to ask me?" She prodded Violet gently before Violet could get distracted by the call of the silent and dark TV screen again.

"Oh, well..." Violet shrugged. "You know Tyler's already agreed to be Daisy's godfather."

"He was tremendously honored. He's already setting up an investment fund to cover her college tuition to an Ivy League school." A smile played around Marguerite's serious lips. "So one less worry."

"Wow." Violet knew enough about Marguerite's scant sense of humor, and Tyler's personality, to know it was likely true. It gave her a moment of shock. "Yeah, that would be one less worry. I'll need to talk to him about that. It's overly generous."

"No." Marguerite shook her head. "We won't have children of our own, Violet. We thought about adopting, but because of...well, how things are with me, my memories, and Tyler's...we thought we might not be best suited to the day-to-day raising of a child. So we enjoy our children charities and mentoring. Don't talk him out of it. He would love to do it."

"I'm going to just stand outside, paint myself gray and become one of those fountains," Violet decided, taking the tissue Marguerite offered her. "Okay. I'll raz him the requisite amount, but leave him be about it. Send him the world's biggest thank you card. But here's the thing. I don't know if Tyler told you, but the way we've worked the jobs is that I'll be home for the first six months, but once she's weaned off breastfeeding, I'll go back to the job. Mac's going to take 0-6 years, then when she enters school, I'll go to part-time for 6-11 years, and he'll go back to work. We want her to have a full time parent at home until she enters middle school."

"Sensible, and admirable," Marguerite observed, though she kept studying Violet carefully, either because she sensed something momentous coming, or was keeping tabs on Violet's color.

"We hope so. I think he's really getting a charge out of the idea that his only job will be taking care of the two of us for awhile. I mean, he's worked on the job since he was eighteen. But on the other hand, I'm a little worried about him. He was really torn about it. He wants me to have a career, because I've only been doing it a few years, whereas he has twenty years under his belt. However, staying home, while I go out and risk my life, is brutally hard on him. I know it doesn't make sense, but I think somehow, when he's out on the job too, taking similar risks, it's easier on him.

"So if something happens to me"—she met Marguerite's gaze—"I need to know she'll have a mother. I want you to agree you'll be her godmother, the same way Tyler's agreed he'll be godfather. I know what you just said, about you not being suited and all. But you've faced down nightmares no one should have to. The person that's made you, that's why I know you'd be the best mom for her. You'll fight for her like a tiger, but teach her to appreciate the gifts every day brings, and how fleeting those gifts can be. And if something happens to me," she repeated, "Mac and Daisy will really need you both."

As Marguerite said nothing, Violet knew she was thinking it over in that quiet way of hers. However, as the minutes stretched out, Violet cocked her head. "You know, a woman in her last trimester gets everything she wants. I'm pretty sure it's a state statute."

The taller woman relented, with a somber nod. "All right. I'm honored, Violet."

Violet squeezed her hand, but Marguerite dispelled the weighted air between them with an arch look. "I'll do it for a price."

"A price? Mercenary."

Marguerite's blue eyes twinkled. "Two prices. One, you must do everything you can to make sure that nothing happens to you. Tyler would be devastated to lose you."

Her tone softened and her knuckles brushed Violet's cheek in a rare gesture of affection. "I might miss you some as well, even if I was bequeathed the care of Mac."

"Bitch."

Marguerite smiled a true smile then, warming Violet's heart. "Second price. Tyler has a birthday coming up. Once you're more flexible physically, you have to help me figure out how to get him chained up. I have a very special present for him."

"Do I get to watch?"

"No."

Violet pursed her lips. "Double bitch. Fine, then. Done. But I want video."

Chloe poked her head out of the kitchen, her face wreathed in smiles. "Violet, your cell phone's ringing. And the display says it's Mac."

§

The wrap up of the messy bust did take a while. Two dealers going to the morgue, three cops going to the hospital with fortunately minor injuries. It had been a long day. Violet could tell as Mac's motorcycle pulled into the driveway and he dismounted, pulling off his helmet and rubbing a hand over his curling hair. Her party goers had cleaned up, enjoyed coffee and sugar and carbohydrate overload with her and then headed out with hugs and a few tears. Not all of them hers. Such rituals made her glad she was female, particularly if her gender had gained her the prize coming down their front walkway.

When he turned, she noted the cut along his cheek, the bruised eye. And he was moving stiffly. But he hadn't been one of the hospital casualties, so he'd apparently just gotten into a scrap during the melee.

She thought she had herself under control, but she couldn't help but stand back behind the sheer panel of the window and drink him in like a hard shot of whiskey to bolster herself. That straight nose contrasting with a rugged, resolute face. Nothing pretty about Mac Nighthorse, but he was pure sexuality on the hoof. Over six feet, broad shoulders, body built like a football player's, though it was his steadfast nature under pressure that had given him the nickname Sarah had recalled. The Oak. Gray eyes under dark slashes of brow, his silky hair a white, black and silver mix. He noticed everything around him with the alertness of a lifetime cop. His attention to detail made him a liability to criminals, but a joy to a wife with an endless supply of sensual demands. He was all hers, in a way most—except those who'd been at her shower today—wouldn't expect. He'd had a lifetime of holding the reins, commanding operations, protecting and serving. And yet in their quiet world, he served and protected her, while *she* held the reins, on her irresistibly powerful sexual submissive. Maybe that was one of the reasons she had such a hard time letting him out of the house. He was one of a kind.

She made herself move, come out on the front porch to meet him. He'd stopped to get the mail and now he looked toward her, his eyes crinkling with his heart-stopping smile. "Hey, sugar. How was your girl thing?"

"You're going to love the gifts." She'd managed to stay together on the phone, because he'd been on scene and talk had to be short. But she knew he'd known. He knew everything about her, heart and soul. It was in the way his eyes covered her now, taking it all in, him understanding enough to wait until she pushed the door open with her toe, inviting him home.

As he stepped in, she reached up toward his face. He laid aside the mail. He'd read the cues right and wouldn't touch her until she said he could, but she could tell the big hands were itching for the privilege. She'd been initially concerned, like most women were, about the changes in her body from pregnancy, but he'd quickly dispelled that worry, cherishing each change as if they made her all the more sexy to him. She smoothed a finger over the cut, the bruise.

"And who dared to touch what belongs to me?" She pitched her voice low. She watched carefully, wanting to be sure he wasn't too tired out from his day, but his silver eyes glinted in pleased response.

"One of the dealer's girlfriends. I was trying to subdue her without breaking her damn neck. It was tempting."

"No, it wasn't." She cupped his face, a familiar exasperation filling her. "You've always had trouble putting a girl down. You're lucky one hasn't killed you by now."

He shrugged, and she couldn't resist any more. Catching hold of the shoulder harness for his gun to lift herself on her toes, she put her mouth over his. Oh, God...the male heat of it, along with the taste of blood, perhaps lingering from his cut, despite the fact he'd washed up. He was wearing a black T-shirt and matching jeans, his badge still clipped to his belt, and it dug into her distended belly. She missed pressing herself flush up against him. Those damn hormones had their uses, however, for now they funneled up like a cyclone, demanding him.

"Mistress," he groaned against her mouth, "Let me touch you."

"Just my waist," she managed, and closed her eyes when his fingers took the liberty of sliding along her pregnant belly, caressing, before he found her hips, dug in. The answering raging need from his body told her just how close today had been, no matter that he said it all went okay. On a normal day, he might come home tired, and she'd sense it, backing off and giving him time to just be her husband. Eating dinner, telling her about his day and watching some cable sports, easing into flirting banter that might become lovemaking. Or just a restful falling into dreams, wrapped in his arms, his hands spanning her belly as he spooned in behind her, his breath teasing her cheek, her ear. But the instant response, the erection he now rubbed with erotic disobedience against her swollen abdomen, told her how much he needed, that he'd been too close to the line between life and death today. She could hope it wasn't him directly, that he'd just rubbed elbows with someone who'd had a brush, but even then, it was still too close.

She pushed him back with the flat of her hand, though it took a few seconds for him to react, because he wasn't always malleable, her sub. One of the things she liked best about him. "Go get a shower," she ordered. "Ten minutes.

Then come back to the bedroom and kneel at the foot of the bed until I tell you otherwise."

"Sugar—"

"Obey me, Mackenzie," she said, and the bite she put in her voice was sharp, because she had a tsunami of need tied up in her as well. The way she'd felt when she heard the news program, hormones surging with the knowledge of how close he could come, every day he walked out the door... Was she going to be able to get past this unbalanced reaction, hold it together until she had a normal perspective again, which was difficult enough to manage? Sometimes she teetered so close to the edge with these hormones, she was sure she was going to knock him out in his sleep and chain him in the basement. She could get Tyler and Marguerite to help her, she was sure.

He released her but, because he was her husband as well as her submissive, he put a gentle hand along the side of her face. A brief touch only, then the fingers slid away, knuckles caressing her mouth. The love and desire in his eyes was tempered by tenderness, a reassurance she wasn't sure she could handle right now. She took it in both mental hands, though, as he walked into the house. He offered her a pleasurable view of his tight ass in those jeans as he moved down the hallway, the breadth of his shoulders and ripple of back muscle as he removed the harness and pulled the shirt over his head, tossed it in the hallway laundry.

"Stop," she said abruptly. When he did, she was sure he knew already what she wanted, but he would wait until she commanded it. "Take it all off right there."

"I was going to use the outside shower."

"I know." Cocking her head, she leaned against the front doorway as he looked at her over his shoulder, slanting a wry grin her way. "Ms. Ford loves when you slip out to the shower naked. She's our only neighbor in view. You don't want to be unfriendly, do you? In fact," she considered him, head to toe in just the jeans, her gaze lingering on his erection, held behind straining fabric, "keep the shower door open when you wash. And take a particularly long time with your cock and balls. Not enough to come. That's for me." She told him the obvious, just to see the flush build in his cheeks, the fire in his eyes. "But give her something to fantasize about tonight. Then come back to the bed. I'll be watching from the window."

He nodded, then bent to untie his boots, toe them off. Followed by the socks and the jeans. She'd been telling the truth to Chloe, unbeknownst to the younger girl. Often she didn't permit Mac to wear any underwear, loving the knowledge that when the fabric shifted over his ass or cock, it was sliding against bare, muscular skin. Knowing that when he was having a busy day at work, it wasn't enough to distract, but when things were uneventful, he was very conscious of that state of undress.

He was long, sweeping planes of muscle, scattered with some scars, incurred in the line of duty. Her gaze lingered on them, unpleasant memories but part of what made him the man she loved and admired so much. He was terrifyingly fearless, had worked undercover in drug rings for years, and then immersed himself in Homicide for a few years after that. Since the near fatal shooting, he'd been working a variety of cases in both areas. He was an asset everywhere he went, because he was as tenacious and unflinching as a pit bull. But she could make him flinch. And beg. And come like a horny teenager, in a hundred different ways.

She grasped the power of that and let it dispel all the terrible worries of earlier in the day, and moved into the house to position herself at the lower level window, where she could see the outdoor shower positioned beneath the upstairs porch. He left the door open as she required and proceeded to wash with the soap and shampoo he'd brought down. That gorgeous, muscular body—chest, legs and arms layered with a light dusting of coarse dark hair, making him look like the sensual animal he was. Lathering up his hands, he went to work on the heavy cock and testicles, the crease of his ass, just as she'd required. Slow, circling rubs that had her lips pressing together and moisture trickling between her thighs. His gaze stayed on the marsh view, as if oblivious to her attention or Ms. Ford's, but the increasingly turgid state of that erection said differently. She was throbbing with need, her fingers itching to ease herself, but she was willing to deny herself for a different form of satisfaction.

When he at last turned off the shower, she went to their room and stripped, maneuvering onto the bed and laying out the items she wanted, relaxing, at least in a surface way, while everything thrummed beneath. She ran her hands over her engorged breasts, the ones that had fascinated him in typical male fashion ever since they started to swell, preparing for Daisy's arrival. Then down over her sensitive belly, to the mons she could no longer see but she could feel, the lips slick against her fingers. He came in when she was like that, idly twitching a nipple with one hand, the weight of the breast in her palm, her other hand working between her legs.

He swept her with his gaze, but then went to his knees by the bed. He was still somewhat damp, drops of water on his neck, beads glistening on his chest hair.

"I didn't tell you that you could look at me, Mackenzie."

"No, Mistress."

"I also didn't tell you that you could touch my stomach when I said to put your hands on my waist."

"It's kind of hard to avoid it, Mistress."

She narrowed her gaze at him. He was angling for punishment, obviously, and she was more than happy to deliver. With one bare foot, she pushed the harness, cuffs and collar off the bed. "Put those on." Then she pushed the other item off. "And that inside you."

His gaze flitted up, startled. It was a sizeable, lifelike dildo that would go into the back fitting of the harness, to hold it inside. It was the largest one she had, the one she used when he was most disobedient, or when she most needed to feel her reins taut on him.

She waited to see if he would try to get out of it, knowing from his body language he was struggling. In about two more seconds she would tear into him. But anticipating the timing of her patience, he began to put everything on.

A collar, the inner pronged kind, fitted to hold his neck snug and make him feel the bite of those teeth. The strap running down the back attached securely to the harness he worked around his hips. She'd already well-lubricated the dildo, but even so, as he put the harness on and positioned the phallus he had to work it in, his lips parting, fist going to the floor to brace himself as he strained at the awkward angle. Usually she put it in, but she wanted to watch him struggle to do it, see his hips leave his heels to twitch and gyrate, impaling himself.

"Sugar—"

All the way to those soft silicon balls, Mackenzie," she breathed. "God, I could come just watching you. And if you don't hurry and get it all on, that's exactly what I'm going to do, make you watch only."

With a grunt, he slid it the rest of the way in, his trembling fingers working the front of the harness. He cinched it in hard enough to pull a guttural groan from his lips that shuddered through her.

"Tighter. I want that cock staying deep in your ass, reminding you who you belong to, next time you let a girl nearly take you down."

He found the tightest fitting his muscular waist could accommodate. His cock was leaking, making her lick her lips, craving the salty taste. He put on the cuffs last and she propped herself on her elbows.

"Come here. Put your wrists behind you and turn away from me."

"Violet, I want to touch you. Need to touch you."

God, it was that vulnerable side that could break her, because she understood the knife edge of what he wanted, versus needed, even better than he did. And he was probably the same way about her.

"That's up to me. You forget to call me Mistress again and I'll make you leave that dildo up your ass until tomorrow morning. Come here. Now."

He complied, and she relished the way he walked. Now his stiff, awkward gait was because of the movement of the dildo against his prostate, evoking pleasurable gasps from his lips as he managed a shuffle, at odds with his normal, graceful predator's movements. When he reached her, she swiped her fingers over the tip of his cock, earning a jerk, and licked her fingers while his hungry eyes watched. He looked like he wanted to devour her alive, his fists clenching. When her eyes went deliberately there, he made a visible effort to release them, hold them loose at his sides.

"Turn," she reminded him.

He did, though his gaze swept over her naked body, making her tremble. When he completed the turn, she closed her hand on one wrist, then the other, though he briefly caught her fingers with his, a needy gesture she didn't punish. She wanted him, too. She locked the cuffs together, binding his arms behind his back, and teased the base of the dildo, earning a hard shudder, another gasp.

"Mistress, please—"

"Don't make me gag you, Mackenzie. Turn back to me."

When he did, she ran her hand liberally over his distended cock, purring in approval. "You would have liked the conversation at my party. Seems all those girls would like to fuck you. In fact, I think I should have had you there. Stretched you out on the table like a party favor." Her gaze slanted up to his face. "Keep your eyes down."

When his lashes lowered, she indulged a look at the taut face, the twitching jaw muscles, the cords standing out on his powerful neck. "I wouldn't let anyone fuck you, though. Just play with you, pleasure themselves with touch and taste."

"Anything you want, sugar," he managed hoarsely, testing her again. She suppressed a smile. "What'd you all talk about?"

"The usual." She let him get away with it a bit. "Work, family, the comparative size of our husband's dicks."

"Who won?"

"Tyler, as always." She didn't miss a beat as he made a noise halfway between a resigned chuckle and a growl.

"Mistress, you're killing me here. I want to move in your hand. I want to fuck you. I want to spill my come on your belly, those beautiful large tits of yours."

"You want to mark me, because that alpha brain of yours has to have its say, even when your cock wants me to keep you in your place. God, I love you, Mackenzie."

His gaze snapped up to hers, briefly, and this time it held. She stopped her stroke of his cock, managed to get up to her knees with some trouble, but brought her mouth to his again, a hot, needy kiss. He pressed hard against her, but with his hands bound, he had to pretty much let her do as she wished, tunneling her fingers in his hair, biting his lip, tangling with his tongue, feeling that huge organ prodding her belly, wanting in.

Gasping herself, she pushed him back a pace. "Your turn, Mackenzie. I'm going to lie back down, and you convince me why I should allow you inside my pussy, since you're doing your damnedest to get punished."

She eased back to the pillows, watching him consider that, consider her motives. She blessed that harness and dildo as he awkwardly maneuvered back down the bed, but she closed her eyes as, with perfect balance, he bent over and placed his lips on her foot.

Detail-oriented, as she said. He suckled on each toe and ran the tip of his tongue up the inner arch of her foot to tease her ankles. He mixed nips of his teeth with clever flicks of tongue, the pressure of lips, and he took...his...time. Never staying too long in one place. With his hands behind his back, and that phallus shoved up his ass, he had to be careful with his balance, but that just made his moves even more carefully planned, methodical and slow. Ohhh...he'd moved up her ankle to her calf. He knew her knees were ticklish, so he was careful there. The man had the firmest, warmest lips, and the brush of his neatly trimmed beard was like a slightly coarse fur glove, gliding over her skin. She was free flowing now, and when he closed over one of those trickles of desire, a few inches above her knee, it took all she had to not loosen her thighs. Instead she crossed her ankles, made him work for the privilege.

Light flicks against her skin, suckling, a bite here or there. He used all the persuasion he had in that mouth to get her to spread her legs. She reached down, managing to graze her fingers over his hair, curl some of it around her fingers and tug. His enormous cock was sliding along the edge of the bed, like some distended beast, waiting for a chance to join in the play. She wanted to taste him again, put her mouth around the meat of that monster, feel him pulse against the demand of her tongue, the snap of her teeth. But for now, this was what she wanted more.

Relenting at last, she eased her legs apart and he worked his way up, up. She quivered as he reached that heated opening and then waited, as he knew he should, though she felt the puffs of heated breath like a bull waiting to charge. She idly played with her nipples some more, squeezed her breasts, brought them together and knew he was watching her out of the corner of his eye, over the mound of her pregnant belly. Thinking of what the women had teased her about earlier, she couldn't help thinking.

See, daisy-girl, this is the way you tease a man to raging...until he can't think of anything but wanting you... There was no more incredible rush, particularly when she was doing it to the man she loved more than the whole universe, ten times over.

"Now, Mackenzie." She spoke with soft firmness. "And since I can't see you down there, I want to hear how much you like eating my cunt."

"It would be my pleasure, Mistress," he said, those silver eyes flashing at her. He bent to the task. She arched up, despite her weight, and he easily put a shoulder against her, holding her steady so she didn't roll as he went down on her. That tongue slid like butter between her labia, working in and doing a sensual undulation that had her crying out. He nosed her clit, alternating between tongue and lips to manipulate it, then covered her completely and dove deep again, making loud, suckling noises of desire as he licked and drew on her, raw, primal sounds that proved how drenched she was. She imagined her fluids smearing his lips, making them glisten.

Oh...her body shuddered, so close. She wanted to come. She could, and then make him suffer, not give him any release, punishment for what he had and hadn't done today. While all of it had been commensurate with who he was, who she loved, she had to remind him he belonged to her like this, so he would always take as much care as possible.

And conversely, it was in his devotion he reminded her of the same thing, before she went out on the job. They were the perfect pair of meshed pieces, two parts of a whole, and now, in this second, she didn't want to be anything less.

"Come onto the bed," she whispered.

This time she helped with his balance as he put one knee up and then the other. Turning her body, she rose, and took his arm, maneuvering him. Her hand closed around his cock so when she pushed him forward and his body came down on the mattress, that hard organ was at a more comfortable angle. Didn't get stubbed, she thought with a smile, but a tight one, for her body was heavy with need.

There was a time he would have resisted being this vulnerable with all his strength. She would have had to employ more restraints. Sometimes he was still like that, for sometimes it was hard to let old demons go. However, even if he felt too helpless, he would do nothing to resist her now, anything that might strain her fragile body. Pregnancy did have its advantages, though she admitted she enjoyed their more spirited bouts as well.

She held him there, a hand on his lower back, just out of reach of his bound hands as she ran her fingers over him, over the taut buttocks. Loosening the harness, she began to work the plug in and out, fuck him with it as his buttocks clenched and he resisted the movement she was trying to create. He was such a large animal, the body lying diagonally across their king-sized bed still close to the edges at the head and the feet.

She forced him to give in to the movement, making it a command. "Pretend you're fucking me, Mackenzie. Show me how you want to fuck me."

His hips lifted and lowered, helpless not to obey her, and her mouth dried up at the sight of it, the powerful haunches rising and lowering, going faster as she went faster, his hard cock sliding against the bed, a friction that began to be so rapid she was afraid she might give him a rug burn on the coverlets, but he obeyed her pace, even as he groaned. "Mistress...don't let me come...outside of you. Please."

"So you've learned who your Mistress is? Who owns this ass? This cock?"

"You do. Goddamnit...you do. Violet...please, sugar..."

The strangled desperation told her she'd waited for the right second. In one movement, she pulled the dildo free and unlatched the cuffs. "Roll over, Mackenzie. You better not come until I do, or there will be hell to pay."

He rolled and, as he did, he caught her waist. Using all that magnificent strength, he lifted her over him so she could straddle him, and brought her down on his cock, taking it in deep, so deep, so hard...oh, God, yes. She closed her eyes at the pleasure of it, nearly screamed when he held one hand anchored on her hip but reared up to capture a breast with the other. He put his lips over it, suckling the hypersensitive tip, her swollen abdomen pressing into his hard, flat one.

She hadn't told him to do any of this, but sometimes, she got so lost in all of it, she couldn't remember if she'd spoken aloud or he'd simply heard the demand of her body, so loudly he responded as if it came from her lips. But even through the maelstrom of desire, she caught his hair in her hand, yanked his head away from her and met him eye to flashing eye. "I need you too much, damn it. Don't you dare get yourself killed. Never, you hear me? If that means you have to punch a damn high school prom queen in the face, you drop her like a brick, you hear?"

Oh, hell. On top of the desire, the earlier feeling rose, and her tears were spilling down her face. "Don't stop...please..."

"No, I won't, sugar. I'm here. Feel me. I'm here." He brought her down hard then, earning a keening gasp that darkened his silver gaze, tightened his lips, but his other hand remained cradling her face, his thumb catching every tear on that side. "I love you, Violet. You are everything. Fucking everything. Sshh, I'm sorry, I should have called as soon as those damn cameras showed up. I love you, sugar..."

She slid her arms around his shoulders then, and he banded his around her ample waist. He began to rock in and out of her in earnest, the broad shoulders flexing, biceps hardening, the lower back working it, pistoning his cock, which might not be as large as Tyler's but was still more than any woman would expect, and was perfect for her. Her tissues caught on fire and she started to release, a full body orgasm that tingled like electricity through her nipples and the veins through her breasts, down through her lower belly, below the sweet cushion of liquid in which the daisy-girl tumbled and played.

Oblivious to the carnal goings-on, but perhaps enjoying the rock-and-roll, baby-in-a-washing-machine tumble that was likely resulting. It made her think of Chloe's wrapping paper, the cherubs tumbling through the heavens, holding their toes.

Learn to roll with the pleasure, sweet baby. That's what it's all about. Because life is often too short to worry about how rough the ride will be. And if you're anything like your mommy and daddy, you'll find the rougher it is, the better you like it.

It made her smile through her tears and pleasure both, as she clasped her arms around her husband's back. She cried out as he released with her as well, giving the gift of himself, his full surrender. Everything she demanded of him, and more than she'd ever expected to be given.

§

After they'd cooled, Mac held her in his arms and dozed in that endearing state of male post-coitus, probably due as much to his demanding work day as the mind-blowing sex. She traced his brow, the firm lips. She'd stripped everything off him, so they lay flesh to flesh, the breeze from the marsh coming in the screens of the now open windows to play on their skin. Running her hand down his flat sectioned stomach, she tangled in the trimmed hair, closed on his cock.

His hand came up, closed over hers. Without opening his eyes, he mumbled, "Best leave that alone. That belongs to my Mistress and she's a scary woman."

"You don't seem that scared of her." Violet smiled as he opened one silver eye and glanced down at her.

"Well, sugar, that's because I think she has a soft spot for me."

"Hmm..." She ran her fingers over his wrists, now

wearing the bracelets Tyler and Marguerite had given them, as well as the linked bracelet she'd given him long ago. "I like these."

"Me, too." He brought them up to eye level as he cupped her face with both hands, lifted his head to take her lips in a sweet, lingering kiss. He pulled back, just far enough to gaze at her, eye to eye. "But I've still got work to do."

"How's that?"

"Well, I only got so far." His gaze swept down her body, stopping for a moment on the new baby blanket she'd spread out for him to see, and then he'd tugged up on her legs to keep her from getting a chill. "I wanted to put my mouth on every inch of that beautiful belly, spend more time with those amazing breasts of yours. Then turn you over and work my way down your spine, your pretty ass...all the way back to your feet. With my Mistress's permission of course. And if I remember, you kind of like it on all fours right now, with me coming in behind you..."

Violet felt her body tighten, and was amazed to see his cock beginning to twitch, his eyes to spark. In a tender gesture, he tangled one set of fingers with hers and stretched their joined arms in an upside down V over their heads, the palm to palm point swaying back and forth in some unheard melody, except by them. "I'll give you anything you beg for, Mackenzie. You know that."

Despite the humor she tried to inject in her voice, she felt something more intense as he rose up on an elbow, bringing the linked hands down to rest on her hip. As he stared down into her face, it felt like when he'd kissed her feet, as if he was memorizing the feeling, the vision, against the day when it might not be there for him to look at or touch. A possibility they would forever know was too close for both of them. But perhaps that was what made them savor the time they had together so much more fiercely.

"Just as I'll never deny you anything," he responded. "Not as long as I have the pleasure of serving you, Mistress. Let me serve you now."

And she did, letting herself be swept away by the love they shared, in the unique way they shared it.

Tyler Tied Up

*A vignette featuring Tyler and Marguerite of Ice Queen
and Mirror of My Soul (with guest appearances by Mac
and Violet of Natural Law) from* the Nature of Desire
Series.

*Originally posted from July through November,
2009 in serial format.*

Part 1

"What do you need, baby?" Tyler squatted on his heels,
wiping a sweaty arm across his forehead. Jesus, the Florida
spring was stifling this year. "I've hand fed you, mercilessly
destroyed your enemies, told you that you're beautiful...a
woman is allowed to be this difficult. Life's too short for a
rose to be this standoffish." Stroking a finger over the
leaves of the bush, he noted how tight and green the buds
were. "You see this fuchsia floozy next to you? She's
spreading her petals for the whole world to see. I know,
maybe you don't want to be a tramp like her, but that's why
you coming out now will be so classy and coy. You'll be the
Audrey Hepburn to her Jezebel."

"This is just sad. Or biblical, I'm not sure which. You
don't often get to see a man on his knees, begging a bush to
do anything."

Turning, Tyler saw Violet standing a few feet behind
him, fully rigged out in her state trooper uniform. It always
made his lips twitch, because she was barely five feet tall
and, despite having had a baby in the last few months, still

a pixie. But since she was also the second toughest Mistress he knew, and mean as a Georgia snake when riled, he managed to stifle the smile that would expose how cute he thought she looked.

"Who's protecting Tampa if you're here?"

"All the criminals decided not to commit any crimes today, in honor of your upcoming birthday. Wasn't that nice of them? And you can wipe that 'You look like Tinkerbell in uniform' smirk off your face. I have a Taser and a gun. As well as a baton I won't hesitate to telescope up your ass."

"You can't prove I was thinking that and, despite your threat of police brutality, the justice system is still 'innocent until proven guilty'."

"Boy, are you behind the times. It's innocent as long as you get a stupid jury or a high priced attorney. And you have enough to buy both." Violet unsnapped her handcuffs and shook them out with a metallic click. "I'm here to take you in."

Tyler blinked. "The last time I had a woman in uniform say that to me, she started stripping. It was at my bachelor party." Straightening, he picked up his Heineken, took a swallow and leaned his hips against the brick retaining wall, finding a small bare patch where his yellow climbing rose wasn't sprawling, bursting with blooms.

"I brought reinforcement, though I don't really think I'm going to need him." She nodded, and he saw Mac coming around the corner. The homicide detective was built like a brick house, his relaxed stride emanating easy power. The jeans and T-shirt he wore obviously came from the same store where the Tampa Buccaneers shopped for clothes, needing a special fit for broad shoulders and powerful thighs. But it was the anticipatory grin playing around his features as he met Tyler's gaze that gave Tyler fair warning he was in serious trouble.

"This is about my birthday, isn't it?"

"It is."

"Not a surprise party. Marguerite knows I hate surprise parties."

"I'm sorry, sir, but it's not our place to explain the

charges against you. We just cuff 'em and deliver 'em.'"

"I'll go along quietly," Tyler decided with a resigned sigh, though he was puzzled. Marguerite had infallible intuition with respect to his desires. While she might plan a get-together with their closest friends at the Tea Room to quietly celebrate his birthday, he doubted she'd go all out like this. "I don't need the cuffs."

"I don't recall making that a choice." Violet's eyes sparkled. "Are we going to have to take you to the ground, or are you going to turn around and put your hands on your head, fingers laced?"

Tyler glanced between the two of them. Mac had come to a halt, one hip cocked, fingers hooked in his armpits, the smile settling into a faint curve on his firm mouth. Damn if the bastard didn't look ready and willing for a sparring match. At the very sweaty, testosterone-laden gym they both frequented, eschewing the brightly lit yuppie co-ed workout hangouts, they were pretty even, but they knew if Violet jumped into it, it was game over. No way was Tyler going to wrestle her. He didn't care how accomplished she was; he didn't fight with girls. The last time he'd told her that, he'd earned a nice uppercut that had rocked him on his heels, but he'd taken the blow and held to his guns. A Southern gentleman did not raise a hand to a woman.

"I think this is why you like being in law enforcement. It's the chance to restrain men and order them around."

"Makes my nipples hard, baby. Now turn around, lace your fingers on your head, and let me see that fine, fine ass."

Tyler choked on a laugh and his beer, but the gleam in Violet's eyes still gave him a ripple of unease. It wasn't that he didn't trust her. Until his marriage to Marguerite, he counted Violet his best friend. He'd helped her embrace her Dominant nature as a Mistress, and had enjoyed a front row seat when she met Mac Nighthorse and discovered the tough detective was the ultimate paradox. A strong alpha who needed a Mistress's firm hand in the bedroom.

But precisely because of what she was, a smart man would think twice before being cuffed by her. Particularly when he had no idea what she was up to. However, given that Marguerite was behind this, he could do nothing more than give in. For the time being.

Because as strong a Mistress as Violet was, he was a stronger Master, and he knew it would take more than a set of cuffs to make him relinquish control.

Part 2

He'd have been surprised to know how closely Violet's thoughts reflected his own on the matter. Even with all her experience in controlling males, professional and personal, her lower belly still did an amusing little flutter when Tyler put down his clippers, slowly pivoted and brought his hands up, lacing them behind his head. It emphasized the width of his shoulders, the beautiful play of muscle, obvious even under the storm gray T-shirt he wore. And she hadn't been kidding about his ass. She wondered if Marguerite would mind if she got a little enthusiastic with the role and frisked him thoroughly. Tucking her tongue in her cheek, Violet figured what Marguerite didn't know wouldn't hurt her, but Mac, who could be a tad on the possessive side about his own Mistress, might have a few issues.

Plus, Tyler would tattle, and she'd have to worry about Marguerite asking for quid pro quo next time they were at the club. Whatever Marguerite's boundaries might be about Tyler's body, Violet knew exactly how *she* felt about another woman fondling Mac's fine ass.

Still, she was too much of a Mistress not to feel physical pleasure when she clipped the cuff on his left wrist, and guided his hands down behind his back to secure them both, his knuckles resting on the rise of his buttocks. When he gave her a sidelong glance, he was too much of a Master not to register her reaction. His lips quirked, and she arched a brow at him in return.

"Don't get cute, or I'll use that Taser after all."

Tyler grinned. "You're just looking for any excuse."

Mac had stayed at the corner of the house. As Violet guided Tyler around the large stand of oleanders, he could see why. Mac needed to keep a clear line of sight to the circular driveway and the transportation that was parked there, because the vehicle had a very important occupant. The hum of the running engine, underscored by the blowing sound of air conditioning, confirmed it.

"I'm being kidnapped and transported in a mini-van with infant sunscreens in the windows," Tyler observed dryly. "I wonder why the CIA hasn't thought of that. Perfect cover."

"Welcome to where the D/s lifestyle meets the reality of transporting tiny people," Violet agreed, unperturbed. As she took him to the van, Mac fell in behind them, lifting his hand in a farewell to someone inside the house, probably looking through the tall living room picture window.

"I assume you informed my housekeeper that you were doing this?"

"Actually, Sarah's been in on it for some time. She asked me if I'd blindfold you so she could come out and beat you like a rug, anonymously. You know, payback for every time you left your dirty boxers on the floor. I would have agreed, but I promised Marguerite I'd deliver you in pristine condition."

"You know, speaking of payback—"

"I'm just following orders, sir," Violet said in her official cop voice. "Take it up with your legal counsel."

"I get legal counsel?"

"No," Mac said amiably, sliding open the door for him.

Tyler had a suitable and colorful response to that. Violet punched his arm, hard enough he was pretty sure it would bruise.

"Language," she said. Her tone had changed again, this time to the "mother" voice, a new dialect that had amused Tyler as it developed without any plan or effort, apparently something that attached itself to her DNA once she'd conceived. "There *is* a child in the car."

At that, his tingling apprehension about their destination temporarily dissipated, pure affection taking over. Daisy was in her car seat, the five-month-old infant playing unperturbedly with a soft fabric mobile of flowers dancing over her head. She didn't appear the least concerned about being left in the car alone, but she'd emerged from the womb remarkably self-assured. Mac thought it was because she'd inherited her mother's terrifying fearless streak. Tyler was pretty sure it was also because Daisy knew she had an indomitable father who would move Heaven and Hell if necessary to keep a moment of distress from touching her.

Even now, having been in the vehicle ostensibly by herself, she looked like a tiny princess welcoming them into her throne room. Her violet-blue eyes turned toward them in calm curiosity. One curlicue of her fine dark hair sat up, tied with a pink ribbon.

Mac guided him onto the seat beside her, cupping Tyler's head to protect it as he ducked in. It was an easier feat for him than Violet, since Mac was closer to Tyler's height.

"Daisy was very excited about coming along for this." Violet slid into the front passenger seat. "She even had me dress her up special for the occasion."

For Violet's baby shower, Chloe—Marguerite's irrepressible baker and hostess at the Tea Room—had provided Daisy an applicable, if somewhat inappropriate, gift. It was a pajama set, a pretty pink and white thing that depicted a small female devil with flirtatious lashes and a pitchfork laced with flowers. Beneath the cartoon were printed the words: "I *like* spankings." Dressed in that, Daisy also had Chloe's other impudent gift, a rattle shaped like a tiny flogger. Attached to her wrist, she was vigorously shaking it even now, the rattler in the handle making a pleasant bell noise while the straps slapped together.

"I think her participation in this is illegal," Tyler noted.

"She's only assisting in transport." Violet cooed at her daughter and touched the little fist as she leaned through the opening between the seats. Mac came around to take the driver's side. "She gets to go to bed when she gets home, so the pajamas made sense."

"She still appears better dressed for the occasion than I am," Tyler responded.

"I don't think you're going to have to worry about that for long," Mac observed, with far too damn much smugness for Tyler's peace of mind.

Even so, he couldn't resist leaning over, despite his restrained hands, to tease his goddaughter's perfect nose with a puff of air. She gurgled at him, smiling, then kicked her arms and legs vigorously, whapping him several times with the flogger.

"That's my girl." Violet laughed. "Take us back to the highway, Mac. As happy as Daisy is to see Tyler, there's another woman who's even more eager to get her hands on him."

Part 3

They didn't take him into Tampa as he expected. Before they got started, after he'd said his hellos to Daisy, Violet pulled a blindfold out of the glove compartment and turned around in the seat, balancing on the center console with the long practice of a woman used to wiping a nose or handing out a cookie. Or to check on a suspect and threaten his life with a mere pointed look.

"Marguerite doesn't want you to know where you're going," she explained. "If you start to feel car sick, though, let me know. I don't want you to get there and throw up on her shoes." She gave him a steady look. "But if you'd rather just close your eyes, I think I can accept your word that you won't peek.

He had been a CIA operative, not a cop, but Violet understood that all those in law enforcement had difficulties with being rendered helpless, even in the company of trusted friends. Ironically, though, it was that sensitivity that helped.

"No, I should be fine. You're not driving, so I feel reasonably comfortable."

"Wise guy. Daisy, we might just stick your pacifier in his mouth before this ride is over." But Violet was still pretty gentle as she guided the blindfold over his face, adjusting the strap behind his ears and making sure it was comfortable.

He inhaled, and a faint smile touched his lips. "Marguerite gave you this."

"Yeah. Don't tell me what you're smelling. I'm sure I

don't want to know where that's been."

"I wouldn't mind hearing a little bit more about it," Mac offered.

Tyler heard the grunt as she punched her husband in the arm. Giving Mac a hand, he shoved his knee against the back of her seat, hearing a satisfying thud as it moved on its track. "It's the fragrance she puts on her wrists. Gutter-mind."

It was something he'd bought her, one of those customized scents that cost a ridiculous amount of money but was supposed to be aligned with the woman's body chemistry to make it uniquely hers. She'd smiled at the notion, indulging him, but they'd both been surprised by how tantalizing a touch of the oil on her pulse points had been to his nose. Not that it took much to tease his senses where Marguerite was concerned.

"Are Daisy and I going to have to separate you two?" Mac quipped, and then they were on their way.

By instinct, Tyler tried to keep track of the number of turns, the distance between them. Violet kept up an easy flow of conversation, with the obligatory interruptions to respond to Daisy's spontaneous gurgles, coos and various baby noises. He figured out they'd gotten onto some type of rural road, headed in a westerly direction, which would take them to the Keys if they stayed on it way longer than he assumed they would be. He found he was correct, because after about twenty minutes, Mac turned off and they were bumping up a gravel road.

Violet had opened one of the windows, and he smelled cut grass, distant marsh. Something else, musky, animal-like. Horses. They were somewhere that had horses. Confirming it, he heard a distant whinny and snort, the thud of hooves as they found some energy to play, despite the late afternoon Florida heat.

But something else was in the air as well. When Mac braked, a sudden still readiness settled over Tyler. Marguerite was nearby. He could sense her, waiting for him. Despite his banter with Violet, and the seemingly entertaining nature of what Marguerite had asked them to do, all that changed in this moment. That strong current of need and want that could rise up and take him over when he needed to let her know exactly how much she meant to him, surged forward now, making him as focused as he'd ever been before a mission.

Being with her defined everything he was, underscoring what he'd always been, as well as creating something new and stronger. Whenever they came together like this, Master against Mistress, it was as if both the predator and mate in him awoke, ready to do battle and seduce at once. Marguerite Perruquet Winterman was many things, but few of them were easy. Whatever it was she had planned, preparation for it coiled in his lower belly, making his cock harden and all his other senses go on alert.

Though she was a female Dominant, she'd surrendered to him, a unique scenario even in the unpredictable world of Domination and submission. She wasn't just any Mistress, but a living legend at their preferred club, The Zone. Since being a Mistress was in her blood, situations like this were intended to challenge him. She needed to be a submissive with him, to find that emotional balance her very difficult childhood had almost stolen from her permanently. However, it took both a strong and delicate hand to hold the reins on her. His lips twitched, wondering if the choice of a stable had been intended or unconscious. Either way, his blood stirred, ready for both the gauntlet and the gift she'd prepared for him. It was a fair description of the woman herself.

His wife. Something he never got tired of saying, thinking, or murmuring in the shell of her ear. Particularly after a hard climax, when he was holding her shuddering body and knowing that, by some miracle, she was all his.

§

Violet was the one who took him out of the van. As if sensing the change in his mood, she said little, merely guiding him along a gravel path. When he realized they'd stepped inside a building, he recognized it as a barn, the smell of hay and old wood filling his nostrils.

"I'm uncuffing your right wrist. I want you to move your

hands in front of you, and then I'm going to recuff them."

He complied without a word, and her small fingers tightened over the bracelets, binding him again. Her knuckles brushed his groin, inadvertently he was certain, because Violet didn't play with him like that. But he was sure she couldn't help but notice he was getting hard.

"We can't help it, can we?" she murmured. "Like pit bulls getting ready to go into the ring. Good luck, champ. Kick her ass." Then, in her cop voice, she added, "Stand right here."

She left him, her shoes crunching on the stone. The haze in the air was disturbed by a fan mounted somewhere on the wall, so that the sweat that had collected on his shirt when he was gardening cooled. Despite the pleasurable tension he was feeling about what might be ahead, it was peaceful here, quiet. Earthy. Marguerite chose her settings quite deliberately, and so had known this would be a good balance for him, too.

"Lift your hands over your head."

Had she been standing downwind from him, remaining completely still so that he couldn't detect her? Since he was already expecting her arrival, she'd managed to cloak her presence cleverly in that anticipation.

As a Dom, he knew that sensory deprivation, anticipation and denial were the three potent ways to drive up desire and need, heighten all other sensations. So he shouldn't have been surprised that those few syllables, said in the unconsciously sultry voice he most wanted to hear, could tighten his lower abdomen muscles as if he'd just driven himself into her. His cock responded accordingly with a hard jerk that made him wince, because he was definitely in need of adjustment. He hadn't thought it appropriate to ask Violet for help with that, and he sure as hell wasn't going to ask Mac.

"Don't make me tell you twice." That core of authority that made so many submissive males cream themselves, slid into her tone. In his case it stimulated more than that, an urge as primal as that which drove the first male wolf to follow an elusive female scent.

Baring his teeth in a smile, he lifted his hands and felt

the hook waiting there, just within reach of his wrists.

"Thread the cuffs over it."

"Whose gift is this, angel? Yours or mine?"

"You won't have to ask that when I'm done."

"Come here."

Her breathy soft laugh made him want to lunge at her, but he held his position, knowing she was circling him now. Her feet were bare, because he knew the sound of her smooth, slender soles padding against the wood of their bedroom floor. "You shouldn't be barefoot in here. You could cut those pretty feet. The ones that belong to me."

"You still haven't followed my instructions."

He would do anything for her, and she knew it. Tyler guided the chain connecting the cuffs over the cool steel, and immediately heard a whirring noise. Before he could consider the idea of freeing himself, the hook had retracted, stretching his body upward. She kept it going until he was fully extended, his muscles taut, though his heels remained on the floor. Barely.

"Come here," he said again. A Master's demand, one he knew would send an electric surge through her blood that matched his own, and create a gloriously unpredictable reaction. The sense of waiting was over. He was ready to handle anything she had to offer.

Part 4

Marguerite knew the significance of the tone her husband used. It never failed to send a strum of sensation coursing through her thighs. She was already pushing him and, while that was what she wanted, she knew the danger of it. He could take her over like no one else, and she was determined to give him this. She'd owed it to him for so long and, though he would argue with her about that, she had her own code of honor. She would do this, see it through, even if she was already trembling at the way he looked, his arms stretched up high. She could imagine, too well, how he was going to look when she was done with him, when she did all the things she wanted, all the things he deserved.

She took her time responding to his command, knowing he would be following every footstep, marking the deliberately provocative saunter. He was the consummate hunter, using all his senses to profile his prey. He didn't need sight to run it to ground. Testing the theory for her own pleasure, she slid her fingertips down her sternum, into the neck of her blouse to give her breast a light caress.

He tilted his head. "Want me to do that, angel?"

"In good time." She moved closer, inhaling. He'd been in his garden. She could smell earth and rose petals lingering on his skin, as well as healthy sweat. As she came closer, she pushed the tip of the riding crop under the hem of his T-shirt, and drew upward. The cotton gathered and lifted, showing her the diagonal slide of muscle over his hip bone. The temptation to touch was more than she was willing to deny herself. He was hers, after all.

She placed her palm on that heated expanse of skin, her thumb tracing the waistband and then dipping beneath to find his hip bone, graze over that. Coming even closer, she put one bare foot on the inside of his loafer, aligning their feet precisely so her knee pressed against the inside of his leg.

"What are you wearing?"

She had her moonlit-colored hair down, the way he liked it best. She scooped it up in one hand, letting the long mane of it slide over his shoulder and tease his neck as she drew back, carefully out of reach, when he turned his head in the hair's direction.

"A white silk blouse, very thin. A pair of riding breeches, very tight. The two grooms got impressively hard, watching me walk from my car to the stables. I had them arrange this area for me and indulged a few fantasies of my own as they said 'yes ma'am' and 'no ma'am.' Then I sent them to an early lunch so they could go to some quiet place, put their hands into their far-too-baggy jeans and have their own fantasies."

"Nothing under your clothes?" A muscle flexed in his jaw.

She pressed against his chest, a brief, taunting contact, and let him feel the soft give of her breasts, the tight arousal of her nipples. "What do you think...Master?"

His muttered oath, the overt sensual threat, made her want to push him even harder. When she lifted on her bare toes, she brought her mouth so close, her breath whispered against his face.

"Do you want to know what I was fantasizing about, when I was ordering those two grooms to do my bidding?"

"Not if it involves them." He tried to bring his mouth to hers. She expected that, averting her face so his lips cruised down her cheek to her jaw. He was an excellent improviser, turning that into a slow rub of his lips, a teasing caress of his tongue along the erogenous zone just below the hinge of her jaw, where her pulse beat the hardest. She gave him that, feeling everything below her neck tighten and roll in slow pleasure.

He said nothing else, waiting on her, his silence a palpable demand all by itself. As he probably well knew, it increased all her suppressed desires, making them push against the boundaries she wanted to maintain. If she were an ocean, she could create another Great Flood by unleashing them here. She could never get enough of him, and she had ceased trying to understand why that was, why he could do for her what no one else could.

"I imagined it was a couple hundred years ago. You were the plantation owner, lord of the manor, with that sexy Georgian drawl of yours. I had persuaded those two grooms to ambush you on your morning ride, tie you up and bring you here, hang you on this hook for me. You were wearing those old-fashioned, snug, ivory-colored riding breeches." Her palm dropped and cupped straining denim. Her pulse leaped under his mouth at the size he was already, the heat that blasted from his confined cock. "That feels terribly uncomfortable."

"Cruel Mistress. It makes you wet, knowing I'm that hard."

"Would you beg me to make you more comfortable?"

"You know I don't beg, angel."

"Well then, I'll continue." Digging her nails into him, she dropped her thumb to idly trace the generous weight of testicles that filled out the jeans so perfectly. And the way these jeans fit his ass...

Not more than a few days ago, she'd enjoyed that very view while watching him rearrange border plants in the garden. Curled up in the hammock chair reading, she'd come up with an even more pleasant occupation. He'd turned around to find she'd put her hand beneath her gauzy white skirt to stroke her pussy. Rocking back and forth in the hammock chair, slow and easy as the breeze, she'd indulged myriad fantasies about him while the cicada song rasped in the morning heat. She'd known he would notice in his own time, no rush. It had pleased her to be doing it so close to him, without his knowledge. His reaction when he did discover what she was doing had been just as pleasurable, a different form of sharp anticipation.

He'd punished her for starting without him by threading her arms and legs through the holes in the hammock hemp ropes, which held her thighs open and kept her hands out of the equation. Then he'd knelt and put his clever mouth and agile tongue to work on her pussy, bare because he hadn't permitted her underwear that morning. He'd commanded her to remain completely still. An exercise for her own considerable control, because it had been an excruciatingly long build up to the climax. When she was on the cusp of orgasm, he'd drawn back and opened his jeans with an impatient hand. He'd pushed that thick, steel and velvet cock with a salty wet tip between her lips, stretching them, filling her mouth while her pussy wept for him. Holding the top of the hammock chair in one strong hand, he'd rocked her back and forth against him, just as slow and easy, as she tried not to beg.

He could turn a Mistress into a slave. She wanted to give him the pleasure of that kind of surrender. Wanted him to trust her with it.

When at last he'd pulled free, he'd tilted her up, all those strong muscles rippling across his chest, and driven into her. Clutching her through the rope fibers, he'd used them and the rasp of his fingers against her hips to pump into her, her body entirely at his mercy, the climax pulling her up and throwing her out into waves of sensation that had led to screams she couldn't bite back.

Such thoughts wouldn't help her keep control in the present, but the air of the stable was already saturated with sex, and she'd been contemplating his arrival for well over an hour. If his hands were free, she knew he could make her climax with barely a touch.

"Isn't it odd," she said, keeping her voice low so it would be steady, "how back in those plantation days those breeches so clearly showed the line of a man's cock, when they were all so supposedly modest and pure in thought..."

His breath huffed out in a half chuckle. "No man can be pure in thought around you, Marguerite."

Same goes to any woman within a mile of your scent, your power. Your sheer male beauty. She drew back out of range again, though she kept her body close. Allowing both of her hands to slide beneath the T-shirt, holding the crop on her wrist, she spread her fingers and traveled up that terrain that should be so familiar, and yet was always such a new thrill to her sensitive palms, the nerve-rich ends of her fingers. She covered each ridge of muscle, the silken arrow of hair down the center of his stomach, following it up to the pectorals, the fine mat of masculine hair there.

For so long, at the club, she'd had her share of pretty, pretty boys, like those two grooms. All smoothly sculpted muscle. Tyler's body was that of a rugged, mature male, the landscape occasionally marked by a scar, a memory of risk that could have taken him from her before she even knew he was her salvation.

There was a time she couldn't afford to show tenderness, or her own deep needs, but it was not with this man, not now, not ever again. So she permitted herself to lay her cheek on his chest, over his beating heart and rub there. She intended to make him mindless with lust, but the joy of being his wife, of him being her husband, was that she could also take the time for this.

He bent his head over hers, his lips grazing the crown of her head. "What is this all about, angel?"

Lifting her face, she caressed his mouth with her hand, liking how the blindfold emphasized the firmness of his lips and slope of jaw, the fall of hair on his forehead. He kept it cropped short on the sides and back, but she liked it a little longer on the top, and he indulged her preferences.

"Do you remember when you first started pursuing me—so relentlessly—you agreed to submit to me for one night?"

"It was a memorable night."

"Yes. It was a shameful night."

"No." His head came up then. "It was the night you started learning to trust me, Marguerite. There was no shame in that. If you think that, you and I will have a problem." Though she couldn't see his expression beneath the blindfold, his tone left no doubt of his intent. "And if you think I can't slip a hook, you'll find out differently."

She was a tall woman. Though he was taller, it didn't take too much of a stretch to follow his arms with her hands, grazing the straining muscles until she clasped his forearms. She took the T-shirt up with her, baring his chest and shoulders, pushing the neckline over his face and then past it, up to the wrists, securing the folds of the shirt in the cuffs, so the garment would stay out of their way.

She let her gaze travel down again, because it was impossible not to do so. All that bare male skin. An upward stretch like this loosened the jeans' waistband, made them drop a little lower, hint at the curve of his excellent ass, the architecture of muscle sloping to the groin area.

He had his sweaty combat and gym sessions where he might lift a couple hundred pounds, punch a gym bag, do grueling reps and sparring matches. But she could do yoga moves that would make the jaws of his fellow weight pumpers drop and their imaginations go wild.

This wasn't one of them, but it was a palpable reminder. Lifting her left leg, standing with easy balance on the right, she coiled it high around his hip, letting her calf brush his taut ass and rub a teasing circle on it before she braced her foot on the back of his calf to balance her in the modified tree pose.

"Tough guy." She whispered it against his ear and caught it in her teeth. "You know I'm not intimidated by you." She'd never admit it if she was. There'd been times he'd scared her to death, because of the things he could make her feel and want, but he already knew that well enough. No need to give him a better opinion of himself than necessary. As Violet was fond of saying, Tyler's arrogance might be fully justified, but there was no need to give a Ferrari an additional wax job.

She suppressed another soft smile at that thought, but, remembering what answer she needed to give to him, she sobered.

"That night was shameful because of what I did to you."

Whatever he'd been about to say in their escalating sexual fencing came to stillness as his brow creased above the blindfold. "No, angel."

"Yes," she said quietly. "That night was about something far different, true, but I want to give you what I should have given you that night. I want you to let me take care of you, trust me with everything you are, the way you've taught me to trust you. I want to give you that gift, the way I didn't, all that time ago. Though I know we're past that, it's bothered me. I want you to know you can trust me, like this."

"I do. And I trusted you that night, angel. I never faltered in that trust. Not once, and not once since."

How he could draw tears from her so easily, when she had gone years dry-eyed, was another mystery to her. But she guessed it was understandable. When you were lonely and unable to trust any softer emotions, tears would not come. When you trusted in love, you could celebrate it with laughter or tears. He'd brought both miracles into her life. A woman's kind of miracles.

Now she wanted to bring him a man's kind of miracle. A fantasy that would make him hard whenever he recalled it, whether it was tomorrow or years from now, when he was in a rocking chair, thinking he was far beyond such things.

"I thought about keeping those two male grooms around. Have them strip you, put you in those tight, tight pants. A pair of black boots. They were fine-looking young men. All lean muscle and hair like horses' manes. Eager colts. I'd have made them kneel and polish your boots while your muscles gleamed with perspiration. Your shoulders"—her palms grazed over them—"would have been knotted, a Dom's tension at being touched without permission. I'd have stood back, watched your cock getting harder as you imagined the ways you'd punish me for it. You know that I'd have them do such things to you again and again, just to get the same response from you every time."

Her fingers whispered high on his thigh. "They were eager colts, but you're the dangerous mount in the stable. I'd take care of your discomfort, open your pants to stretch your cock out, but only to put some tack on you. A cock harness with a stimulator, and then I'd put you back in those tight pants so they would get damp in front. Your cock showing your intent to fuck me, to take me down beneath you and prove who's Master."

This time, when he whipped his head around, she didn't try to evade. She met him, welcoming the hard, open kiss with a sound of helpless desire caught in the back of her throat. His tongue swept down over hers, tangling and shoving, his lips closing over her mouth as if devouring it, letting her feel all the power and lust he had to give to her.

Marguerite cupped his skull, fingers pressing into hard bone to convey how tightly her own arousal was leashed, how wet for him she already was. She leaned into his body, letting him feel every inch he couldn't touch with his hands, what she wouldn't let his cock have, until she did what she intended.

They had so much further to go. She just hoped his considerable ability to derail her from her plans, sweep her away on a tide of her own personal desires, wouldn't overwhelm her before she got him there first.

Part 5

Catching his bottom lip in her teeth, she held him there as he stilled, his hot breath caressing her face. She gave him a tiny flicker with her tongue, then drew back.

"I'm going to strip you now. I want to see all of you."

"Your voice isn't steady, angel. Why don't you let me go?"

"So you can rob me of speech entirely?" She smiled, but took several steps away to open the cabinet where extra tack was kept, only she'd placed some different equipment there. She was sure he was acquainted with the snick of a well-oiled switchblade, so she wasn't surprised to see his head come up, a delicious tension running through his upper body at the sound.

"Where did you get that?"

"From your desk, of course." Coming back to him, she laid her palm on his chest to feel the thud of his heart. "Hope you're not fond of that shirt."

"I'll use the strips to tie your hands when I get loose from here."

"Threats, promises." She leaned into him, using the firm brace of his body to reach up and slice smoothly through the seam and free the shirt from the cuffs. She knew as long as she was leaning against him, he'd hold steady. Taking care of her, as always.

She'd intended to drop the shirt to the side, but she gave herself a moment. Adjusting so her shoulder was propped against his chest, she brought the fabric to her nose and inhaled. She had all sorts of sexy lingerie that Tyler had bought her, but she'd noticed they both seemed to prefer it when she wore one of his shirts to bed. The sense of claim, and being claimed. If something awful ever happened to him, she suspected she'd just lay all of his clothes on the bed, use them as her linens for as long as she could last without him. Or simply sleep in his closet.

Because such a thought was unbearable, she pushed it away and let the shirt go, moving to his waist band. Using the tip of the blade, she traced that delectable diagonal line of muscle from groin to hip bone, revealed by the low ride of the jeans. She made a fine red line, just short of drawing blood.

"Sometimes I've wanted to brand you, the way I did Brendan that night," she mused. "Something that said you were mine, that I could reach over and touch at night, as if it were a magical symbol that would always keep you with me." She raised her gaze to his firm mouth, the attentive cant of his head. "And sometimes I want to give you pain, as if it's somehow more permanent than pleasure, like cauterizing a wound to heal it. Does that make sense?"

"You do whatever you need to do, angel," he said in a

husky voice. "Just touch me."

She drew the knife up, then down, a flourish that did draw blood, another thin line. Pressing her palm against it, she felt the essence of him dampen her palm, make it sticky like his other fluids could.

Setting the knife aside, she slid the button of the jeans free and worked the zipper down, moving carefully over the sizeable impediment there. He had lean hips, long thighs. If he were a club submissive, she would have had him toe off his shoes himself, enjoying his struggle to do it while maintaining his balance against the give of the suspended hook. But he was her Master, and she liked the dichotomy of it, having him at her mercy while she knelt at his feet, leaving his jeans open as she slid off the loafers. She suppressed a smile at the dirt in them from the garden. In her position, it was easy to rub her cheek over his confined erection, inhale the damp musk of his arousal.

"While you're down there..." There was strain behind the humor, and she managed a breathy chuckle.

"You wish." She curled her fingers in the jeans and worked them down his legs, scraping his thighs with her nails, giving his knees a passing caress, knowing the backs were slightly ticklish. The beauty of eroticism and domestic bliss mixed. She wondered that anyone ever tired of their spouse, thinking the terrain too familiar, the mind too well plumbed. Maybe because she was a Mistress, she knew that the male body was infinitely responsive, the mind never fully revealed. And for a complex man like her husband, she could spend ten lifetimes with him and still not have it all.

He wore his preferred boxers underneath the jeans, the snug knit that emphasized the hips and thighs, the large cock stretching the fabric. She took the underwear down next, making a pleased purr behind her teeth as his organ stretched up toward his belly, hard and enthralling, the testicles a heavy, virile weight between his thighs. Her pussy contracted, weeping into the thin stretched fabric of the riding breeches, her thighs already loosening in response to his cock's proximity, the implied demand of it.

How often had she woken in the middle of the night to

see the shelter of his broad shoulders over her, the wide chest? Felt his knee insinuating between hers, her legs already spreading for him, body automatically welcoming him?

Controlling her body's learned and eager response, she finished removing the jeans and underwear, then stepped back to survey pure art. Lean, long muscle in his arms and chest, thighs and stomach, cock aroused and at her mercy. She walked around him, dropping the clothes in a pile to the side, and studied a back like that of a powerful Roman god's, tapering down to firm, high buttocks and spread thighs. Moving casually as if considering him from all angles, she picked up something else from the cabinet without pausing or giving away what she'd acquired. When she came back around, one step, two, she laid her unoccupied hand on his lower back, caressing the rise of his ass. Shifting onto her toes, she put her lips on his nape, bit down.

"Are you mine, Tyler?"

"Yours and no other. You're killing me, Marguerite."

"Really?" She bit him again, suckled the place hard, wanting to leave a nice imprint of teeth. Why was it so many sensual things had such silly, demeaning names? A hickey. It sounded juvenile, harmless, rather than a mark of pure erotic possession.

He let out a growl, responding in kind, and she brought her tongue into it. Pressing her body to his bare side, she slid hard nipples over the expanse of his ribs. Her pubic mound rubbed against his flank, telling him how snug her riding breeches were. The seam bit into her labia, making the friction of his hard heat a pleasurable gift.

Considering him sufficiently distracted, she made her move. Before he had time to react or tighten, she positioned the slim probe between his buttocks and slid it through the two rings of muscle in one economical movement. The slick lubricant on it made it sink swiftly into the dark channel and her fingers followed, delving between the buttocks to tease and caress the now stretched rim.

"Son of a—"

She'd never placed anything there. It really wasn't something a submissive did to her Master, was it? Unless she happened to also be a Mistress, who knew the kind of pleasure it could bring, how it could reduce a male to mindless orgasm.

"Easy," she crooned, placing her hand on his shoulder, her fingers caressing his throat. "You have such a tight ass, Master. One would think you were a virgin."

His strangled sound might have been the closest thing to a threat she'd ever heard from him. It only made her anticipate his revenge. But that would be later. She wanted to savor this now. She worked the probe, stroked him inside, and was rewarded with a jerk of movement. She'd had four mirrors placed fore and aft, to the left and right, so she could see his every reaction. His lips were stretched back, breath coming through his teeth as he tried to suppress his response to the stimulation.

"I want you harder than you've ever been in your life, Tyler. I want you to beg me to let you come."

"Not...happening."

He was probably wondering once again how this qualified as his birthday present, but she knew he didn't know how to think like a submissive. He didn't know the release that came with full surrender. But she was going to take him there, because she was the only one who could. She wanted to take him where he had taken her, countless times before.

Fitting the harness around the base of the probe, she threaded the straps through his legs, coming forward to work the cock ring over him and tighten the straps for it, constricting the testicles. She couldn't resist bending down after she did it, pushing her hair back onto one shoulder to keep it out of the way as she took him fully in her mouth. She went all the way to the base, teasing those metal rings and tight strap, the flesh constricted under them, before withdrawing with painful slowness, savoring every considerable inch of him. He was hot steel beneath her tongue and lips. Flicking her tongue over the slit at the end, she tasted salty male fluid.

When she straightened, the muscles in his jaw were

drawn tight enough to break. "I want to feed you now," she decided. "I know you haven't had lunch, because we were going to have an early dinner."

"You bringing your cunt up here? Because that's the only meal that interests me right now."

The raw crudeness made her shiver. Even in his most aroused moments, he had polish. But she'd opened the door to the beast beneath. It was a good thing she'd brought a whip *and* a chair.

Part 6

"If you don't mind your manners," she observed, "I'll eat these treats that Chloe made, all by myself." Sidling closer, she held up the tiny finger-shaped pineapple cake, one of Chloe's specialties. It was filled with a light, sweet cream cheese, so the fragrance of that, plus the irresistible smell of recently baked cake and pineapple so fresh they could have been in Hawaii, couldn't help but reach his nostrils. Tyler had an incorrigible sweet tooth, particularly when it came to Chloe's baking.

"Take it gently, now." She placed one end of it in her mouth, laid her hand on his chest and leaned in, bringing it forward until it brushed his lips. He curled them back like a wolf, but opened his mouth. Clever man that he was, he didn't close his mouth until he reached her lips, so he not only got the largest possible piece, but a taste of her lips flavored by the pineapple and sugar as well. He chewed without moving back, then flicked cream cheese off her upper and lower lip with his tongue as she held her portion inside her mouth. It made her glad the treat practically melted in the moist heat, because she didn't want to chew and disrupt his oral seduction.

She was fairly expert at nuances herself, so was thrilled with his rough, urgent edge, telling her the probe and her other tactics were working as she wished.

Bolstered by that, she reluctantly backed off in mid-kiss and picked up the other container, which was more of the same whipped cream cheese, only without cake this time. Taking up the switchblade again, she dipped it into the cheese and then drew a stool up close to him.

"Don't move a muscle," she instructed. "I wouldn't want to cut you."

When she started with his left nipple, letting him feel the edge as she pressed the cool icing upon him, he gave a quiet grunt. "Which explains why you're using the sharpest blade you can find."

His wry comment was cut short, replaced by a strangled noise as she pressed the button on the remote she also had sitting on the stool. It activated the heat and vibration of the probe. If his reaction was any indication, she'd seated it right where she wanted it.

"Remember," she said. "No movement."

She curved the blade in a sweeping motion around his nipple, painting the cream there, then made a serpentine trail down his rib cage, over his upper abdomen and lower, dipping back into the bowl a couple times until she reached his bound cock. Then she made one sliding stroke from base to the flared head, and set the knife aside.

"I like the filling best of all," she observed.

"Marguerite..." He swallowed, his upper body jerking as the vibration ratcheted up.

"This is one of the newest acquisitions at Justin's store. It's a programmable vibrator. If you know your lover very, very well, his ability to control his release, you can plot a program that will take him up, up...until he's almost sure he'll release, and he wants that above all else. Then it will rein him in, teasing and massaging him, so he's pulled back and forth toward climax until he can't think of anything else but how hard his cock is, and how much he wants to come."

"Is there anyone *not* involved in my birthday celebration?" he demanded. She watched the muscles stretch and tighten in his powerful shoulders, his head drop back as he tried to contain what couldn't be contained—his body's erotic response. "As far as I can tell, you have everyone from an infant to my housekeeper involved."

"Well, I called the White House, since they seem very much into promoting stimulus packages." She smiled. "But they weren't available to send a representative."

"Cute."

But all vestiges of humor disappeared from his face when she placed both her hands on his rib cage and brought her mouth to his nipple, licking the cream away delicately, scoring him with her teeth.

"Would rather...suck that off...your nipple."

"Soon," she crooned. "Let me finish here first. I don't want to leave a mess, after all."

"You keep doing that, angel, we're going to have a mess."

"Oh, no. I know my Master. He's very, very stubborn. He'll consider it a point of pride to hold out as long as he possibly can. I'm counting on it."

Because the longer it took, the more he held back, the more intense the climax would be. She wanted to see it happen, because she'd feel it in the deepest contraction of her womb, his pleasure connected to her, whether his cock was sunk inside her or not.

She worked her way down, savoring every inch of the firm skin beneath her lips and tongue, making sure she got up each bit of cream cheese, even licking the stickiness away, sucking on the skin. When she reached his cock, she went to one knee, gripping his upper thighs, scratching them with her nails. Slowly, slowly, she slid her mouth around him, taking the head in first, working her tongue under the flared head.

He jerked in her grasp, the stimulation in his ass making what she was doing to his cock even more difficult to endure, particularly when she took her fingers between his spread legs and teased that stretch of skin between testicle sac and cock base, massaging that hyper erotic area.

"Fuck..."

Victory. Tyler rarely let go of his Southern manners around her. Since their volatile courtship, she could count on one hand the number of times he'd cursed around her. He treated her like one of his delicate roses...except when she pricked him with enough thorns to tell him she wanted rougher treatment. If that was the case, right now he probably felt like she was wrapping him in a net full of thorns.

Right on cue, the probe's intensity changed, shooting up from mid-level to a high, heavy-hitting vibration that would flail his prostate like a tiny, madly flapping tongue. Given she'd also lubed it up with an aphrodisiac, he should—

He snarled, pulling against the chains, a violent movement, and she let the motion thrust him deeper into her mouth, where she captured him with the suction there, the clamp of her teeth. He froze, a shudder running through him as she flicked the pounding pulse of the underside vein. He was so thick and hot, she couldn't help indulging the pleasure of sucking on him some more. It brought more pre-cum onto her tongue, mixing with the lingering flavor of the cheese.

He swore again, and a glance upward showed that light sheen of sweat was starting to glisten. But then the vibration sank to a more gentle, teasing stroke. It had been a near thing, but she was satisfied to see she knew her man.

Rising, she brushed her mouth close to his ear. "Close only counts in horseshoes and hand grenades," she reminded him. "Do you need a little pain to keep it reined in, Master?"

"This is torture enough, angel," he muttered. "Christ, you are so going to pay for this."

"Only after you pay first." She caught his earlobe in her teeth and let him feel the flick of the flexible crop she'd retrieved from the floor, brushing it on the inside of his knee.

Because she *did* know her man, she knew he wasn't turned on by being flogged. But the audacity of her doing it to him was a different matter. Not to mention knowing how it affected her...

"I'm going to whip your ass with this now," she whispered, her breath hot on his mouth. She inhaled the lingering scent of the cake. "Not because you enjoy that, but because it will make *me* so hot and wet to do it. To see this crop striking your ass, leaving a red stripe, watching you flex against it. I'm going to take the tail at the end, use it to tease your rim, push against the base of that probe. I'll make you take it in just a little deeper a push you onto your toes, make you strain upward because your body has nowhere else to go."

She moved behind him, her hand trailing his side again, then resting high on one buttock. The crop flicked down, followed the channel between his cheeks, teasing that probe, as she'd said, manipulating it. "Then you know what I'm going to do?"

He was trying not to do what she said, his toes gripping the ground so hard that his calves flexed.

"What, angel?"

"I'm going to be so, so wet then, I'm going to unzip these tight pants, push them to my knees. Then I'm going to put my hands on the stool in front of you and back slowly, slowly onto your cock. I'll tighten the cock harness before I do, though, so you'll feel that restriction, and know you won't come until I'm all done with my own climax, serviced by the all-too-proud lord of the plantation. Then maybe we'll hose you down and give you a good currying."

He cocked his head. His breath was coming through his flared nostrils rapidly enough he sounded like a fractious stallion in truth, but when he spoke, his voice was heavy with intent, unbridled lust.

"You promised I could suck some of that cream cheese off you first. Let me taste you, angel. Or are you worried I can talk you out of doing all that with just the feel of my lips on your tight nipple? Make you forget everything but letting me off this chain."

"And what would you do if I did?" she asked in a low voice, reveling in the dangerous tone of his voice, the way his hands clenched in the restraints.

"I'd take you to your hands and knees and cover you like a mare, ramming into your sweet ass until you'd never again think you could get the upper hand on your Master."

"Mmm. Doesn't sound like a reasonable plan. In fact, sounds like I'd have every incentive in the world to try to get the upper hand again. And again." She cocked her head, listening to the hum of the probe. "Better hang on, Master. This one's going to be at maximum power."

"Son of a..."

As the motor's sound increased, she unbuttoned her shirt, watching him with her lips parted, her body humming along at the same high frequency. His cock constricted, moving in that quick jerk that preceded more viscous fluid, his thighs trembling with the effort of holding himself back. He let out another snarl, a long, drawn out one, a way of focusing his energy, keeping himself from letting go completely.

The higher frequencies in the probe's program would get shorter and shorter, adjusting for his shorter and shorter fuse. When she slid her cunt back on him as she described, he would start coming the second she engulfed the broad head. She'd timed it that way.

As excited as her own body was, she expected his climax would knock her over into hers. Unless she enraged him further by letting herself go first.

Picking up the knife, she wiped a generous gathering of the cream cheese on her left nipple and drew in her breath at just that one sensation, her lower belly tightening, anticipating his mouth. He was panting, his biceps knotted as she drew the stool directly in front of him. With grace and a perfect balance that belied her internal unsteadiness, she propped herself on her knees and slid her hands over his shoulders to hold her there.

"My breast is right in front of your mouth, Master. All you have to do is reach for it."

He pushed against her hands, insistent strength, but just the tip of his tongue came out, making the barest contact with the cream, not even putting pressure on the aroused nipple behind it. Still, it made her sway forward, her fingers digging into his flesh.

"I'm going to make you come, angel. Just from doing this."

"Only if I let you."

"You're not going to give yourself that choice."

Part 7

She slid her hand from his shoulder, up to cup the back of his head, her fingers burrowing in the short, layered hair there on his skull, at his nape, bringing him in closer. He might very well be right, because even as aroused as he was, he was always far-too-aware of how high he could drive her. It wouldn't be the first time he'd proven he could Master her while he himself was fully restrained. It was more than the physical that gave them power over one another, though. She had a gift to give him, and she fully intended to hold onto enough control to accomplish it.

Closing her eyes, she braced herself as his heated mouth sealed over her nipple, his tongue flicking the beaded tip, taking away the sweet spread, suckling it thoroughly, and then laving her with slow, massaging rolls, a teasing glide that he knew how to do so well. Not too much or too little stimulation, just enough to make her brain liquefy and leave her leaning into him, her breath speeding up. Her pussy ached, wanting to press against that hard bone in his hip, so close. Knowing it, his body was straining forward, trying to make contact. Her hands slipped back to his taut shoulders, curled over them so her bare abdomen slid across his as she kept her back arched for his mouth's ministrations. Her nails dug inward and then moved up, raking him slow and deep, earning a bite from his teeth that made her gasp, arch harder into him, asking for more of the same pain.

Instead, he changed tactics, letting go of the nipple and swiftly shifting. Before she could draw back, he'd set his teeth to her throat, precisely capturing the large artery and depressing it so it affected her pulse. *Oh God.* It wasn't a matter of underestimating him; she knew he could sweep away her will. But it was always such a miracle to have that control taken away, to experience the secure joy of letting herself fall into his keeping. That ruthless clamp of teeth made her so aware of her mortality, while the eroticism of constricting her breathing or blood flow brought all sorts of physical and emotional reactions rushing to the forefront. It was a feeling she was only permitted to indulge when he imposed it, and he used it now as one of his most potent weapons. She swayed.

You're not going to give yourself that choice...

It was Justin's device that saved her. The modulation

changed once again to that high frequency, and it jerked his body upright, his cock sliding across her stomach, leaving a wet trail across her heated flesh. She pulled back, sliding off the stool, trying to get her breath back. As she did, she let her fingers drift across that same track across her abdomen and then brought the salty taste of him to her mouth. Her neck throbbed, the bite hard enough that the teeth marks would be visible for several days afterward. That in itself brought her back on track, the delicious anticipation of what she intended to do.

He was quivering, fighting the vibration bringing him perilously close again. She saw his cock convulse and it made her breath catch anew, such that she let him hear the arousal full blown in her throaty voice.

"I may change my mind," she purred. "It would be a real temptation to watch you spurt out on the stable floor. What if, rather than fucking you at my leisure, I whipped you with the crop, then set the probe on high? Sat on this stool and watched my Master come, helpless from what I've done to him."

"Marguerite." His hands flexed in the chains and the beam let out an ominous and impressive creak. From the sudden ripple of muscle that coursed with breathtaking power across his chest and shoulders, she wouldn't have been surprised if he ripped it free on the next attempt. "You don't want to find out the answer to that. I can promise you."

"No?" She rose as the probe modulated down again. The relief almost emanated off of him, telling her how near the falling point he'd been yet again. "I can make *you* a promise, Master."

He stilled, as much as he was able, at the soft sound of the zipper teeth releasing when she opened the side of the riding breeches. She took them all the way off and let the shirt slip from her shoulders. Bringing the blouse up to his face like a veil, she trailed it over his eyes and nose, the wet heat of his mouth, before dropping it to the side, leaving her completely naked. Turning, she leaned back against him, brushing her buttocks against his restrained cock and earning a low, deliciously menacing sound from him. Even so, she indulged the feeling, turning her head to nuzzle his jaw and getting his mouth instead, a powerful kiss. So strong that, even without his arms free, she felt as if he were holding her back against him with the pressure of it, keeping her head securely in the crook between his jaw and shoulder as he plundered her mouth, long and thorough.

As the kiss drew out, she became aware their lower bodies were doing their own sinuous tango, a serpentine series of slow movements and rubbings, his cock against her ass, teasing the seam as she used the flex of her feet to make infinitesimal caresses against the thick length of him. The ridge of the broad head, the steel of the shaft, fitted itself in the channel between her buttocks and she tightened on him there.

Finally, he lifted his head, enough to speak against her lips. "And what promise was that, angel?"

The crafty bastard. It took her a moment to remember. Despite the fact he was pulsing with the type of violent lust equaled only by Vikings on convent raids, his firm, irresistible mouth curved in a satisfied smile.

But she'd employed that blindfold for a reason. She still had the advantage of surprise. Moving out of the shelter of his body, she slid the stool in front of her to give her the leverage she wanted. With him stretched the way he was, she hadn't needed to manacle his ankles. His hips would have only a certain range of motion and control.

"This is what I promise you. That the moment I start pushing my cunt down on your cock, you're going to need to come, worse than you've ever needed to in your life. You won't want to do it, though. Not until I come, at your command. But I'm not going to come, Master, not until you do. And that's going to push you even further. When you get free, you're going to want to take the most extreme measures to make me understand who serves whom."

He cocked his head, a weighted stillness settling between them. "You're baiting me, angel. Why?"

Reaching up now, she removed the blindfold slowly, dropped it to the side and met his amber-colored eyes. Having deprived herself of his beautiful gaze, she couldn't hide the tremor that swept her at the way his expression devoured her. No one, especially her, would ever be fooled into thinking he could be rendered powerless by something as simple as chains.

Yes, he could make her do anything, but there was one way she could make him helpless. His love for her would convince him to do anything she wished, if it really mattered to her. And now she called on that, because it was the last weapon she intended to use to take him where she knew the deepest part of him truly wanted to go.

Next she unbuckled the cock harness, working it carefully off his engorged cock. Moving around him, she removed the probe, caressing his tempting muscular buttocks as she did so. She let all that fall away so he was now unencumbered. Then she returned to his front, turned her back on him and leaned down again. Putting her elbows on the stool positioned her ass within several key inches of his cock. At the sharp clank of chains, she tossed her hair back so it swept over her opposite shoulder and gazed back at him.

"Can't quite reach, Master?" She shifted, spreading her legs enough so he could see the pink folds of her pussy, glistening with her arousal. She backed up, one inch, two inches, one pale cheek teasing his cock. She slid her cunt across his broad head, neatly evading as he thrust forward, so he only rammed the fleshy part of her buttock.

"Damn it, Marguerite." He gave a half laugh, half groan, but his eyes were so vivid, so fierce. "Tell me why."

She shifted her attention to a point behind him.

His brow creasing, Tyler turned his head as much as he was able, looking over his upstretched arm. Toward the very back of the long stable, she knew he'd see another source of the heat that had him glistening with sweat. And understand why he'd been getting the occasional whiff of smoke. A brazier, with what appeared to be a half dozen branding irons resting in it.

He turned his gaze back to her. She saw understanding hit, and two reactions warred in his expression—lust and denial. It told her she was close to success, but it would take a reminder to get him past the denial. That, and going forward with her plan to mercilessly take her pleasure of him, breaking every rule a Master could impose.

"You remember that night, when we were out on the Keys in your boat?"

He held her gaze. "I remember."

"You were deep inside of me. Had me spread-eagled on the forward deck, my wrists and ankles tied to the stanchions with soft nylon." She cocked her head. "I had my head dropped back, looking at the reflection of the moon on the water, all those stars above as you pushed me to climax." *And his soul in that moment had been laid out, raw and bare in the darkness.*

"You whispered"—*so fiercely that she almost felt the heat of the iron then*—"that if you were a less civilized man, you'd want to brand me, make it clear that I belonged to you, that I was your property, your possession, everything that meant anything to you."

She kept her eyes locked with his. "In the morning, you were actually embarrassed. You, who never lets anything fluster you. You made a joke, saying how the right woman could turn a man into a caveman. You missed how utterly, completely the idea overwhelmed me. I haven't forgotten it. I can't forget it."

Tyler's jaw flexed, that same raw emotion returning, gripping her with quiet victory. "Angel," he murmured.

"Everything I've done, will do in the next few moments, is intended to make you forget *everything* about being a civilized man. I want to make you so full of lust, so full of a need to possess me, remind me that I'm your slave, your property, your possession, that you won't hesitate to take one of those brands in that brazier and mark me as yours. The way I know you want to do, way deep down inside."

She made sure she let him see the resolve in her own eyes. "And I want you to know, in that same raw part of my soul, that I want you to do it. Because I truly am yours, in every way. Happy birthday, Master."

Part 8

Holding his gaze, she shifted her stance, so that she realigned herself with his cock, as large as she'd ever seen it. The combination of taunts, promises and images had focused every zone of his mind and will on one thing—taking her. Which was exactly what she wanted.

She moved back until she was against that thick, virile column. He was too erect, and he didn't have the ability to lower himself, angle his cock to thrust himself into her. He was dependent on her mercy, and there were plenty of subs who knew mercy was something Mistress Marguerite doled out with the smallest of teaspoons, if at all. Now she rubbed her slick cunt downward, going from beneath the broad head all the way to the base of the cock, and then up again, pushing up on her toes to tighten her long thigh muscles, her buttocks, knowing his eyes would be glued on how his cock looked, rubbing up and down that slick channel, so slow. Then she reached between her legs, gripped him with sure fingers and began to lever him downward, tightening her hold, sending the message that it would be at her pace, under her control.

"So help me God..." The muttered oath made her lower abdomen contract violently. However much she'd made him want her, her own body was on a deceptive simmer, covering a cauldron of heat waiting to explode at the moment of penetration. She knew she should divert her thoughts, anything to cool herself down, because she wanted to hold onto this as long as she could, but as she guided his head, wet with his own response, into the hot mouth of her sex, she couldn't stop herself. Her inner labia sucked involuntarily around him, her breath catching in her throat. With deliberation and supreme restraint, she backed down on him, a millimeter at a time, closing her eyes as the shudders that began in her lower belly and upper thighs moved closer together, zeroing in on the sensation between her legs. There was nothing in her life that felt as perfect, as complete, as having Tyler inside of her, joined this way. Depriving herself had been a double edged blade.

It took a moment before she could fight past her own reaction to focus on his. When she did, she knew instantly she'd made a critical mistake. That distraction was the only opening he'd needed.

She'd pushed him as far as he was going to allow.

Just a shift, and his cock thrust in hard, past the grip of her fingers, wresting a cry from her, and he was solidly on his feet, his body curved over hers. His hand came up beneath her arm to close on her throat, pull her up against his shoulder. Putting his teeth to that tender area beneath her ear, his other hand slid down, holding her against him, stilling the movement of their joined bodies, pulsing with unreleased—and in his case— near-violent need. The handcuffs dangled from the wrist at her throat, the cold metal a pendulum over her breast, teasing the nipple.

"You are in a great deal of trouble," he said, easing his bite to tease her carotid with a lazy flick of his tongue. Her survival and sensual instincts weren't deceived by the caress, recognizing the ominous heat emanating from the wall of tense male muscle against her.

"You cheated," she returned, and gave a soft moan as he withdrew part way then came back into her, letting her feel every increment of friction between their bodies. Her clit quivered, so close, but he knew her body so well, holding the climax just out of reach. In return, she contracted purposefully on him. His hand on her throat tightened in admonishment, constricting her air and driving her arousal up further.

"Be still," he breathed into her hair. But he nuzzled her with a sudden shift into tenderness that melted her body into him. She was still aroused past insanity, but he was adept at activating that connection between them, the emotional undercurrent in everything they did, a reassurance and a reminder of their bond.

"You thought you could arouse me to the point I would hurt you, angel. Protecting you is the most important part of being your Master."

She closed her eyes. "But I want you to do it. I'm...begging you to do it."

The sigh expanded his chest, and she slid her hands behind her, over his hips to the curves of his ass, digging into the muscle, making him flex against her grip, and moving him within her. She let out another whimper as his palm pressed harder against her abdomen. She was aware of where every finger rested, from the middle finger's position on her pubic bone, a scant space above her clit, to his thumb, sliding over her hip. He had large, strong hands. Hands that could break a neck or hold her fast during their wildest lovemaking, but they were always gentle, except when he knew being rough would drive her to greater heights of pleasure. He put limits on that, knowing her desire for pain could sometimes cross into unsafe areas. As he said, he took her protection, even from herself, more seriously than anything. But she knew he wanted this.

"Tyler..."

"You know what to call me right now."

"Master." She breathed the word, the last syllable elevating as he slid his hand lower, that middle finger now so close above her clit it registered the pressure, the tiny pulse fluttering in response. "Oh, Goddess..."

"You're ready to come all over me, aren't you?"

"The same way you're ready to spurt into me like a geyser."

"Just can't stop pushing it today, can you?" Taking her head back to a more precarious angle on his shoulder, he held that constriction as he brought her to her toes, dropped a tender kiss in the pocket between her collar bones. "Look at how hard your nipples are. You need to be well and truly fucked, angel. Over and over again, until you realize you don't trick your Master into doing anything. You ask him, beg him, and you do it pretty, sitting on your heels with your thighs spread, your tits out where I can fondle them, have access to your cunt as you beg. Stroke your hair and wind it around my hands so I can pull your head back and put my cock in your mouth."

She'd gone still as he spoke. The meaning behind the words, the power and desire behind them, made her wonder and hope...

"I have something to ask my Master, then," she ventured.

"In a moment. Bend over, take hold of your ankles, and bring your head to your knees. You hold that position until I tell you otherwise."

He paid close attention to her morning yoga, and there

wasn't a single position he hadn't evaluated with the wicked and delightful tendency of the male mind to consider all sexual possibilities. He knew this position would put her clit out of reach of his strokes, but still stimulate her to near mindless arousal, without allowing her a climax.

She understood his intent, but he added to it with the verbal command. "You don't come, angel. Not until I say."

Bending forward, feeling the fullness inside of her pussy adjust as she folded her body downward, she let her hair sweep the stable floor. She earned a gratifying exhalation of male breath as she performed the flexible movement, sliding her hands behind her calves and pressing her forehead all the way to her shins.

Without further warning or preparation, he took hold of her hips and began to thrust. Full, stretching penetration, deep, and using her body without giving her any relief, just taking the desire she'd stoked in herself up to screaming need. He only made it worse with the psychological impact, demonstrating a Master's right to give himself release and leave her craving. She was crying out, unable to help herself because it felt so damn good, even though she couldn't reach that pinnacle point. She was amazed at his own restraint, that he didn't come at the first few strokes. However, it wasn't the first time his Master's will had impressed her. She had a similarly indomitable endurance with club submissives, but with him...she'd finally admitted, at least to herself, that she couldn't hold out as long.

She'd managed well enough here, enough to get him truly worked up, such that he intended to repay her in spades. It made her body shiver in anticipation and longing, torn between her complex emotional and physical needs.

As much as she wanted to give him this, and nursed the hope that he would give in to his own desires as a result of her efforts, he was her Master, of heart, soul and mind. Something in her had to surrender to him to feel complete and whole.

His fingers flexed against her ass, his thrusts becoming

harder and more punishing. Her hair swept the floor, back and forth, her fingers tightening on her calves, anchoring herself against the impact, though if he hadn't been holding onto her, his power would have shoved her forward. Two more thrusts and he came, making her moan, a needy, plaintive noise she couldn't help as he jetted thick spurts of heat in her. Once he pulled out, it would trickle down her legs, dampen her sex and thighs. She knew he wouldn't allow her to clean it off. He'd want his marking of her with his release to dry upon her flesh.

Visceral satisfaction swept through her at how long he came, though. As well as at the guttural, animal noises he made, showing how aroused she'd made him, how intense her teasing had made that ultimate release, even as her own body yearned for the same. So much her flesh was damp with perspiration and all her muscles shaking when he finally came to a stop.

Slowly, he withdrew from her. Her pussy spasmed and, as she'd anticipated, a warm dollop of his cream came out with him and slid over her vulva, taunting her further.

Backing up to the stool, he propped his fine ass on it. Picking up a towel she'd left hanging near it for her own uses, he ran it over his cock, down his upper thighs. In this position, she could see bits and pieces of such ablutions. When he tossed it aside, she knew he was sitting back, looking at her in the folded over position. Watching his come run out of her, the heart shape of her ass and pink slit of her pussy displayed for him.

He put his jeans and shoes back on. She was glad she'd made the shirt unusable by cutting it with the knife. Particularly when she heard the threading of his belt into the jeans, the tantalizing sound of a buckle. It was a message, telling her she wouldn't get his cock for awhile. While she ached at the loss, she might have a consolation prize. She meditated on the significance of his words, wondering if they meant what she anticipated they did. *You ask your Master, beg him...*

At length, he straightened and came back to her. "Go to Child's Pose," he ordered, his voice still the stern tone of a Master, but with that sensual undercurrent which rippled over her skin. "Do it slow. You're bound to be light-headed."

She released her calves and let her knees bend, feeling his hands steadying her. Child's Pose folded her knees beneath her, her body lying flat over them, forehead pressed to the floor, the spine elongated, arms stretched forward. As she settled into it, feeling the stretch in her hips, he dropped to one knee beside her. She was a tall woman, but he was taller, and with her in this pose and him kneeling over her, she was acutely aware of the differences in their sizes, his strength. She stilled as his fingers settled on her spine. Specifically, on the scars aligned on either side of her spine, the dual row of cigarette burns that started at the nape and went to the dimples of her buttocks. He'd offered to have them removed, repaired with plastic surgery, but they were part of who she was, too intrinsic to her identity, for good or ill. But she understood the significance of him touching her there now.

"Master..."

"You think I would burn you, mark your flesh, because of a passing fantasy?"

She swallowed. He was devastating when he combined a husband's tenderness with a Master's harshness, but she knew his heart, knew his needs as well as he knew hers. "No, Master. You wouldn't. Even if it was an obsession, not a fantasy, you'd strike off your own hands before causing me pain. But this is something I want, too. Those marks were forced on me. I want yours, willingly."

Closing her eyes, she pressed her forehead deeper into the *asana*. Vulnerability slid into her voice, a gift she was only capable of giving to him. "I want a scar I can touch that's yours. That will arouse and overwhelm me, because I know it's your permanent mark. Something that I'll remember gave you deep, primal satisfaction when you did it, and that makes you hard when you touch it, because it's a claim you know I understand, all the way to the bottom of my soul."

He stroked up and down her spine, a light movement of his fingers. He was thinking. She went silent, letting him muse upon it. She forced herself not to dwell on his decision, instead enjoying being quiet and submissive under his touch, her mind free of anything but his will, for at least this second. It was late afternoon now, and she heard the cicadas talking in the nearby marsh, the occasional snort of a horse, the comfortable, rhythmic tread as they moved into another part of the pasture.

"I love you," she said softly, for no other reason than the desire to say it, the heartfelt treasure of being able to say it.

"I love you, too, angel." He cupped her buttock, thumb moving over the crease in a caress, then back up, following those scars to her nape, stroking through her hair. Then he wound his hands in the strands and put pressure on them. Obeying the unspoken command, Marguerite lifted her upper body. As she did, she sat back on her heels, spreading her knees. Deliberately, under his hot gaze, she straightened her upper body, arching her back and linking her hands behind it, knuckles brushing her buttocks as if she was bound, her breasts and pussy available to his touch.

"Please, Master," she said, a tremor in her voice. "Your slave is begging you to brand her."

He was silent again for many long moments. She continued to keep her eyes down, her body upright, vibrating. She'd never have thought it possible, but there were times in this submissive posture she could almost come, merely from having his attention on her, feeling the heat of his pleasure from her surrender to him. It made her understand the freedom of submission better, of allowing her body to tremble with involuntary need and desire for her Master's slightest touch, a stern command. A brand.

"Please," she repeated in a whisper. "Give yourself what you deserve, Master. Let me love you the way you love me."

He'd straightened and returned to the stool when she assumed the submissive pose. With her eyes lowered, she saw the long legs, braced out, and expected he'd have his arms crossed over his broad bare chest, watching her with an unreadable expression in his amber eyes. His firm mouth would be taut, even as he'd already be half hard again, just from seeing her like this, smelling her arousal, knowing how hot and ready to climax she was.

As if he read her mind, he spoke.

"If I'm going to brand my property, I won't let her come until the minute the brand touches her flesh. The pleasure and the pain will be wrapped together, intimate the way we are when I'm inside you. Where we don't know where one of us starts and the other stops."

Her heart rejoiced. "Yes, Master."

Part 9

Tyler crooked his finger at her. "Come over here. You can lower your arms, but stay on your knees. Keep your pussy off your calves. I don't want anything touching that but me."

She slid the couple of feet to him, his hand cupping her head to guide her forward. When he brought her inside the span of his spread knees, she laid her cheek on his inner thigh. She was facing inward, which gave her a tempting view of the curve of testicles and cock beneath his jeans. Flaring her nostrils, she inhaled the aroma of his recent release, and her fluids on him, even under the denim. She wanted to touch, to mouth him there, but she settled for curving an arm around his calf, holding it pressed against her ribs.

He'd begun stroking his fingers through her hair, slow and deep. Finding her scalp, he massaged it down to her nape, caressing the sensitive occipital bone. Her pussy contracted on the open space between her slightly spread folded legs, needy for him. But she could wait. She could always wait for him, because she knew how much pleasure it gave him, making her mindless with lust.

"You know that song, angel? The one that asks if the captain of the Titanic cried?"

She nodded, rubbing her cheek against him. "'Someday We'll Know.'"

"That's the one. Whenever I listen to that song, I think about how rarely people ask the right questions, the really important ones." He gripped her hair, tilted her head back to look up into his serious face. The amber eyes had the relentless intensity of a pure Master now. It made her left nipple tighten further where it brushed against his leg, her fingers curve harder into the fabric of his jeans. "We know about asking the right questions, though. You and I. Dominants. We know that's what unlocks the secrets a submissive keeps, even from herself. So you're going to tell me what this is really about."

Leaning down, he increased his grip, tilting her head so her temple pressed into his thigh, exposing the side of her throat, holding her still as his breath rippled over her pulse. He apparently didn't want her answer right away, but then he rarely did. He knew she wasn't likely to offer or reach the answer immediately, not until he aroused her to the point that truth could rise to the surface like the cream of her arousal. She resisted on instinct, even knowing in the end she would give him all of it.

His tongue was tracing her carotid, making its way down to her collar bone. She closed her eyes, soaking in the sensation, making a soft noise when his teeth bit that bone gently, then harder. His other hand dipped, his knuckles passing over her nipple, then coming back, catching it between the middle and forefinger knuckles. He didn't pinch. He had a delicious way of gradually increasing the pressure of the clamp, so it created a slow wave of sensation that made the nipple ache for more. He'd hold that clamp for a time, and then, with a tiny twitch of those long-boned fingers, he'd send a jolt of electricity through the breast and down directly to her cunt. As he did it now, she made a soft cry, jerking involuntarily over her calves. She wanted to rub so badly, but she wouldn't. She wanted his touch there, his mouth, his cock. His command.

"I told you...it *is* about you." She gave him her best answer, the only one she could offer. Then let out another whimper as he did the twitch in another, unexpected direction. His mouth moved up behind her ear, as he pulled her head back now. Back away from him so she was staring up at the barn ceiling, at the I-bolt that held the hook that had held him. He shifted his head, moving to the front, suckling on her jugular, his hair brushing her chin. Cupping her breast fully, he kneaded it, his thumb caressing her sternum. He never forgot an inch of her flesh.

Unlike so many men, obsessed with the prurient parts of a pin-up magazine, Tyler could—and would—arouse any part of her body. It wouldn't surprise her if he made her come from touching her eye lashes.

"Yes. I believe it is about me," he said, that soft Southern male voice stroking and tightening her nerves at once. "You're always far too generous, angel, giving me things you should give yourself first. But this is also about you. So before I'll do it, you'll tell me what it is you want. Why you want this. If you don't"—he brought her up onto her knees with pressure under her right breast, cradled in his hand, and lowered his head to slide a moist, hot tongue around the areola—"I'll have to take you over my knee and give you the spanking you so richly deserve."

There were crops hanging throughout the barn, and he wore a belt that could smart like hell, but early in their relationship, he'd said he'd never strike her with anything other than his hand again. He'd only broken that promise one time. A night both terrible and beautiful, because it was the night she'd told him she loved him for the first time, and the night she'd learned she had the power to destroy him.

Still, despite the emotions that gripped her with the memory, and the lust that clogged her throat at that clever tongue lapping at her nipple now, she managed to put a sultry tease into her voice. "You're going to do that anyway. You like to make me wriggle on your lap like an errant school girl."

If he'd ever decided to be a school headmaster, she suspected the girls old enough to discover sexual yearning would have lined up for their spankings. As well as the female teachers. Cafeteria workers... She decided to keep that one to herself, though. As a Georgia gentleman through and through, Tyler would be mildly scandalized at such a thought.

"Ah..." Her breath left her as he began to suckle in earnest, and his hand in her hair descended to her buttock, gripping there and delving between the cleft to tease her rim before curving beneath. Finding her wet pussy, he eased two fingertips into the opening of the damp channel.

It folded his strong body over hers, so she had her face pressed into his upper abdomen. Her hands dangled loose at her sides to keep them out of his way, as she trusted him to hold her up and bend her whichever direction he chose. But it was so difficult, when she wanted to touch him so much.

"I've ordered you the short plaid skirt," he promised, a smile in his voice, but then he shifted, rising and bringing her up with him, swiftly enough she swayed, the blood rushing through her. He steadied her, though, and slid her onto that stool, guiding her feet so they hooked under the lower rails on the left and right sides, spreading herself for him. She automatically straightened her back, watching his gaze pass over her aroused nipples, the slope of her abdomen.

"Maybe I'll put your brand here." He touched the pale expanse of skin above her navel. "And buy you a double piercing for this area. A topaz and diamond barbell would go through the rim of the navel. I'd connect a chain between that and a silver cuff pierced through the bottom of the brand, emphasizing who you belong to."

"I'd like that," she whispered, and his gaze flickered up to her face. Though his eyes were filled with desire, the stern set of his mouth told her she hadn't yet answered his question to his satisfaction.

"Keep your eyes on my hand." Passing his left palm over her thigh, up and up, he pushed three fingers inside of her drenched pussy, following the contours of her slick channel unerringly.

"Don't you move an inch, angel. You stay still."

The urge to rock forward against him was almost unbearable, but she modulated her breathing, short, tiny expulsions, feeling herself grip his fingers with involuntary need.

"Put two of your fingers inside yourself, Marguerite. Over mine. Hold onto my arm with your other hand if you need to do so."

Even if she didn't, she wouldn't pass up a chance to touch him. She gripped his biceps, registering the muscle and damp, heated skin as she lowered her other hand.

Using her middle and forefingers, she traced his palm, outlining his life and heart lines, detouring up to caress the base of those fingers that were inside her. Then, when he made a quiet noise of command, she turned her hand over into the cup of his and followed his angle to slide her fingers inside her own heat. It was a tighter fit now, but the feeling was excruciatingly pleasurable, the fullness close but not quite like his cock.

Giving her a look that was both promise and threat, he used his free hand to fish into his pocket. Ripples of response fluttered through her chest and lower abdomen, knowing what he sought. Ruefully, she realized she should have searched him when she undressed him.

Not long ago, they'd been to a premier of one of his erotic movie productions. In the darkness, his colleagues only a couple seats away, he'd matter-of-factly removed a small bullet vibrator from his pocket and slid it under her skirt, into her pussy. While they watched, he'd put his hand on one of her knees, applying firm pressure to make sure she kept her legs slightly spread throughout the feature. With the tiny remote control, he'd tormented her for two hours as she got more and more stimulated by what he'd helped create, and the vibration he had going on silently beneath her clothes. They'd barely gotten out of the parking lot that night in the limo before he'd had her straddling his cock, mouthwateringly enormous from watching her. She'd come so hard she'd almost passed out afterward.

Since then, he tended to carry it around as often as his keys or wallet, and she never knew when he'd use it to tease her. Like now.

"Put your thumb against your clit, angel."

Keeping his other fingers deep and still inside her, pressed against hers in that dark, heated place, he lowered the bullet, positioning it under her thumb so it held the device against that quivering bud of flesh. When he clicked the tiny remote in his pocket, it began its silent vibration against her, a wave of pleasure that instantly shot her up toward a peak, given how aroused she already was.

"Tyler... Master..."

"Tell me what this is about, angel," he said again, his hand catching her chin to make her look at him. "You hold perfectly, absolutely still, keep that bullet against your clit, and you tell me what it's about."

When she didn't immediately reply, he increased the speed. She let out a low cry, her body shuddering hard as she tried to stay still. Goddess, she couldn't think when he did this... How did he do this so well? She should be able to stay detached. With all the subs she'd brought to this level herself, she should know how to play this game. Except it wasn't a game. There was no fighting a Master who knew exactly what he was doing, who already knew the way into her soul.

"I can't..." she said, though the truth of it was welling up into her, hard and ruthless as a climax at his hands. "I can't..."

"Tell me, angel." Amber was becoming burnished gold, reflecting the fire that was always burning inside of her, her unending need for him.

"I love you so much," she gasped it. "Too much. I can't contain it. It hurts...I need..."

"You need the pain to handle it. To release it. So it doesn't overwhelm you."

"Tyler, I'm too close... I can't..."

It turned off, a mere second before she was sure she would have been seized by the violent orgasm. As it was, it was a near thing, her body vibrating, making tiny spasms as she clutched his arm, her head down. He tilted it back up though, making her look into his face. His own was inscrutable, but she felt his reaction. His strongest emotions often went underground, as if he thought they should detonate where they could cause the least amount of harm to civilians. But she wanted this explosion of feeling.

"I love you too much," she repeated, her voice shaking with nerves and need.

"It's all right to love me, angel. You know that, right? I'm not going anywhere. It doesn't have to hurt to love someone."

"But it does. It's the best kind of pain I've ever felt. And I wake up at night, and look at you, and I can't get close enough. I can't ever get close enough."

"You think it's ever enough for me?" His voice dropped low, rough, and he moved his hand, thrust in deeper, sliding the pads of his fingers along the dense, nerve-rich zone that made her moan, toss her head back like a fractious horse. With the movement of his hand, his knuckles pressed into the tender bending point of her own penetrating fingers. She wanted to move against him, but he still hadn't told her she could. He brushed his thumb lightly over her clit, where she still held the bullet, and she arched, she couldn't help herself. If she got any hotter, she would be on fire.

"Please, Master..."

Slowly, he withdrew his fingers, leaving hers in with a quick squeeze of her wrist. A shudder racked her from that, even as he added to it by removing the bullet, dragging it across her swollen tissues. "Move your fingers inside of you. Thrust in and out, slow, like you'd want me to move inside of you."

She complied, her breath panting shallow and hot. He reached up to the hook, figuring out how to lower it until it was within her reach. Taking her other hand from his biceps, he pressed a kiss to the palm, delicately teasing the crevices in between with his tongue. By the time he folded her fingers over the hook, every nerve in her body was begging for release. But he picked up a coiled strap she'd laid out, wanting to have a variety of restraint options, and looped it around her wrist. He secured her one hand to that hook, then retracted it back toward the ceiling until her arm was stretched out, her side arched, hair spilling over her opposite shoulder. Her ass just barely touched the stool, but her legs held her upright, spread and threaded through the lower slats. She lost rhythm, so overwhelmed by the additional stimulation, but his sharp eyes missed nothing. "Keep fucking yourself with your fingers. Do you want my cock?"

"Yes."

"Do you want it in your cunt?"

"Yes. Please, Master."

"Do you want my brand? Wherever I decide to put it?"

"Yes. Goddess, yes."

He leaned forward then, brought his mouth over hers, teased her lips apart and used a hand on her jaw to hold her still as he traced them, dipped inside and stroked her tongue with his. His eyes were on hers as he withdrew. "Then you keep that pussy nice and wet, while I go choose the mark I'm going to put on you."

Part 10

When Tyler left her, moving across the floor to the brazier, Marguerite blessed her foresight, placing those four mirrors at different angles around the area where she'd teased and tormented him. Because though he was behind her, she could watch him walk away, the sinuous movement of upper body muscles, the tight ass and long thighs shifting beneath the jeans. He'd always moved in a way that drew attention. The controlled power and grace of a sexually confident, more-than-a-little-bit dangerous man was irresistible to female eyes, and she was no exception.

From the first time she'd seen him at The Zone, she'd been hyperaware of him, though she'd denied it to herself, and they hadn't come together for months. The attraction had made no sense to her, because he was a Master, she was a Mistress. But it had continued to grow.

It had started with her noticing any occasional sighting of him at the club. Then she'd found herself dwelling on how he sounded when he spoke a courteous word to her as they passed one another, his murmured "Mistress," in his cultured Southern voice. He'd flick those amber eyes over her, appraising her in a way she told herself to ignore, but the regard lingered like an unexpected caress.

On the rare occasions when she'd mingled with other Mistresses and Masters, he'd initiated short conversations, innocuous shop talk over a punishment or restraint type she'd employed during a session with a submissive. She'd noticed how closely he listened to her responses. He'd offered her a standing invitation to his home for his famous private parties, but she'd declined every time, denying herself for reasons she didn't care to face.

In hindsight, she knew he'd been a sensual predator, circling closer and closer, pretending interest in the gazelle herd surrounding them, when the entire time he'd had his eye on the lioness hunting the same game. She had been his target.

She'd hated him for it at first, hated what he could do to her. But he'd opened a part of herself that had been a festering, cancerous wound. He hadn't flinched, hadn't backed away. He'd weathered the fallout, helped her begin to heal, and become a vital part of the cure. In every darkness she now experienced, Tyler's light was there. Warming her, guiding her, giving her comfort and faith. She needed him more than she needed anything else in her life. And what had taken her all the way across that bridge to acceptance was finding he felt the same way about her.

Now she watched him, standing over the brazier, his feet braced, head slightly tilted. She followed the appealing line of his skull, canted toward his broad shoulder, which led her attention to his curved biceps, taut waist and cocked hip. When he reached forward, shifting the irons to determine what shapes and designs she'd left for him, his back muscles rippled. Great Goddess above, everything spiritual and needy aside, he was the sexiest fucking man she'd ever seen. Not a single pretty thing about those hardened muscles, the directness of the amber eyes, the lines carved into his mature, handsome face. The firm lips.

She was playing right into his hands, staring at him like this when he'd already made her so aroused. And was keeping her aroused, by ordering her to maintain that slow thrust and withdraw motion of her fingers into her soaking flesh. Her cunt convulsed every time she pushed in deep and came back out. Her clit ached for any contact—her knuckles, her thumb. She would go off in seconds if she gave it just a few swipes of friction. But she'd restrain herself, and not just because he'd ordered it. She wanted it to happen with him inside of her, after he'd placed his mark on her.

She knew what he was seeing. Simple shapes for strike branding. As an experienced Master, he knew how to do it, but he'd only done it at the request of submissives he'd been training. He'd never done it to a woman that belonged to him. And she was secure in the knowledge he'd never wanted to do so – until now.

Apparently having chosen the one he wanted, he rolled the cart holding the brazier back to her. When he did, he saw her watching him in the mirror, not bothering to mask her avid pleasure in the view coming back, the wide chest, the prominent arousal beneath his straining jeans. He made a tsking noise as he reached her. One hand reached up to wrap in her hair, draw her head back as he captured her mouth, plundered, the brazier so close to her body she felt the heat, but his mouth was even hotter. He kept kissing her until she was straining into him, her one bound hand clutching the hook, her other trying to keep that rhythm he'd mandated, and getting all the closer to climax.

He pulled his mouth back to stare hard into her eyes. "You keep going, Marguerite. You tell me when you're close, when you can no longer hold back, when you want to come for your Master."

"Tell me when to come, Master. That's what I want. Tell me when to come, and I'll do it."

His jaw tightened, his hand shifting to cradle her jaw, raise it higher, putting her neck at a straining angle. "I want my cock inside of you, Marguerite. I want to put it in there and never take it out, fuck you every second of the day. That's the brand I'd put on you if I could. In your mouth, your ass, your cunt. When I do this, for the next day or so, you won't be wearing anything around our house except panties, so you better be prepared to call in sick to work. Because I'm not going to let anything touch your flesh until it's healed. Except me."

Thank Goddess. She swallowed, her pulse ratcheting up higher. "Master, please..."

"Come for me, Marguerite. Prove you serve your Master. Prove you belong to me."

She began to come as soon as he spoke, so the next two commands were harsh whispers against her temple when her head jerked right, pressing into his mouth, as she was overcome by the power of that long denied climax. It rolled over her so hard, she didn't know how she would have stood if he'd not given her the stool, but as it was, she jerked enough it wobbled beneath her.

Placing his foot on the bottom rung, he anchored it. It let her hook her heel onto his calf, his thigh pressed against her bare hip. Reaching around her back, he closed his hand around the upper arm of the hand that was inside of her. To steady it, keep it out of his field if she flinched.

Then he lifted the brand from the fire. She saw the orange-hot color of the metal, a blur in her lust-hazed vision. She didn't tense, didn't do anything but let herself surrender to that climax, to him, embrace what he was about to do, so he could see that willing acceptance in her face. His attention passed over it, one last assurance, before he pressed it exactly where he'd said he would. The soft flesh just above her navel.

It only took several seconds to do a strike brand. Even aroused himself, Tyler was precise and controlled. The pain seared through her nerve endings, but the brand was already gone. Metal hit metal as he tossed it back into the brazier, then he had both hands on her face, and was kissing her again, saying "I love you" against her mouth.

The orgasm had stuttered from the pain, but he was already pushing her back over that cliff edge. She moaned as he closed his hand over her wrist and withdrew the fingers she'd obediently kept moving inside of her, even through the branding. Bringing them up to his mouth, he tasted her honey. When he let them slide down and curved her fingers over his hip, she clutched, begging him to come closer, to press his need against that mark, against her spasming flesh.

The feel of his cock, so hard beneath his jeans, made her cry out into his mouth. Tears were part of that moisture, too, her reaction to what he'd done, what he'd given himself as well as her. She wanted him to be inside of her, but she also wanted him to come, spill his seed on the brand he'd made upon her. He'd chosen a circle, as she knew he would.

He was the beginning and the end, and he'd made it clear on her flesh.

He pulled back too soon, keeping space between the brand and himself, but he compensated her by continuing that kiss, and closing his hands over her breasts. All he had to do was squeeze the nipples with those clever, sensitive fingers, and the climax that had receded just out of reach suddenly swamped her again, tearing a cry from her throat. It renewed her convulsions, her body bucking and arching in a way she couldn't control. As she got even more violent, he dropped his hand, curving it under her ass to hold her up and make sure she didn't pull too hard against the hook, putting too much strain on her shoulder.

It took a long, long time, but eventually the climax, denied and then allowed, pushed back by pain and then brought back by his demand, ebbed. Or she should say the hardest, most ruthless waves of it did. She was still in the surf, her body shuddering in cycles that seemed to please him intensely, if the way he watched her, how helpless she was in her reaction to what he'd done to her, was any indication. She couldn't move or think, didn't want to. But then, she didn't have to.

Picking up a horse blanket, he draped it over his shoulder, then released her hand from the hook. He ducked his head under her arm before the tired, depleted muscles let it drop. It rested limply on his shoulders as he slid his other hand under her knees and guided her feet out of the slats of the stool. Then he lifted her in his arms.

Despite her height, he always made her feel like Scarlett O'Hara going up the staircase in Rhett's arms when he carried her. A faint smile touched her lips despite the arousal, the throbbing skin under the brand, the need coiled so tight in her she couldn't speak. But he saw the smile.

"What, angel?"

She told him, and though his eyes warmed, he didn't smile. As he looked at her, raging need and conflicting emotions were behind his eyes. But he cleared his throat, deepened his drawl. "Well, Southern men like carrying our women. Harder for them to run away."

Closing her eyes, she let her head rest on his shoulder. He pressed his lips to her temple. At the touch of the wind, she opened her eyes to see he'd taken her outside, to the back of the barn, where they were looking down a rolling slope of green pastureland and the distant marsh. Sleek horses grazed in the foreground, completing the picture.

He let her feet touch the ground, but kept a hand securely around her waist as he shook out the blanket. Letting her go only to spread it out properly, he turned to her, his eyes on her face, seeing everything, the way the nerves still made her tremble, her breath so short, the aftermath of the arousal and the branding, pain and pleasure mixed, but there was still something missing, something she craved. She didn't have to know or understand what it was, because he knew. He always knew.

"Lay down on the blanket, angel. On your back. Arms over your head and your legs spread, shoulder width apart. Keep them that way, no wider."

His steadying hand was there, of course, because her knees wouldn't stop shaking. Her teeth were almost chattering with it, those tiny little shudders that, despite her climax, seemed to originate between her legs and keep her in a mindless state of need.

Subspace. She took subs there all the time, but he'd plunged her deep into it, and she didn't want to let it go. She'd obey and do all he wished, holding onto that moment of absolute closeness, when he was everything. Masters as well as Mistresses fed on it like ambrosia of the gods, seeing their submissives deep in that well.

As she lay back, seeing blue sky and her Master's amber gaze on her bare skin, she closed her eyes, giving it all up to him. Her right to see, to breathe, to be. It was all his. Her knuckles brushed the blanket above her head, feeling the prick of the grass beneath the soft fabric.

"What do you want, angel? Tell me."

"You. Just you."

A rustle of clothing, and she didn't have to see to know that he'd opened the jeans, pushed them down, removed it all. Then he rested a knee between her legs, taking himself down upon her.

She made tiny formless noises as he guided his cock to her pussy and pushed slowly into that welcome, wet grip, her tissues clutching all along his length as he came into her.

Any contact on a brand while it was healing felt like fire, but the breath she sucked in as he lay down between her legs was acceptance, preparing for it. He was still mindful of her care, though. Gradually, he brought his body down upon hers, until his muscled abdomen hovered just a space above throbbing, inflamed flesh. His elbows braced on either side of her neck, his hands closing over her arms as he rested there, and her eyes opened.

"Please, Master."

He gazed down at her, his face so serious it had that sternness to it that always made her want to trace his mouth, seek his teeth to bite her fingers, remind her of how he could take control. But a lot more was going on, so she remained still.

"I love being your Master, angel. And you're right." He glanced down her body, allowing himself a leisurely look at her breasts, the aching nipples, before he moved his attention to the circle burned into her pale skin. "Seeing this mark on you makes me fucking hard all over again. But it also destroys me inside, to cause you any pain. To know why you need that, to know the simple fact I love you can tear you apart. It fucking kills me."

She swallowed, her gaze holding his. She had no answer for that, only needed what he could give. Hungered for it. "Please," she whispered. "You and no other."

"Damn right." He allowed the seriousness of it to be overcome by something a little less intense, but then he lowered his body that fraction, closing the distance.

Fiery heat radiated out from the brand point like a sun, goading her overstimulated nerves, making her arch and twitch beneath him. Her pussy contracted on him in a way that had his eyes flaming as if that sun had reached him, too.

"I'm not going to move, angel. I want to feel your body shake and quiver, get wetter and hotter from the lack of motion, until your pretty pussy is squeezing me harder than any other part of you could, a climax you can't stop, because your body knows what I require."

Limiting the abrasion would also prevent a much higher level of discomfort or infection risk while the brand was still fragile. She let out a half sob of acceptance and crazed need both. He curled his hands in her hair, making her look up at him. "You remember the night you branded Brendan?"

She nodded.

"You taunted me that night, didn't you? Rubbing yourself against his back with your bare breasts, stroking those new brands you'd given him with your loose hair, this waterfall of moonlit silk." His fingers stroked it as well. When his thumbs found her mouth, the corners, she parted her lips, let him tease that hinge, put pressure there.

"You talked about rubbing me down like a fractious stallion. I have my own equine fantasies, angel." His eyes gleamed. "I'd take two roses, facing in opposite directions. I'd place the stems in your mouth, push them up against the corners of your mouth like a horse's bit. When I made you bite down, you'd feel the prick of the thorns on your tongue, against the sides of your mouth, at the same time you'd smell the blossoms brushing your cheeks like silk. You'd hold them while I put my mouth between your thighs to make you come, your legs spread wide and cunt gushing for me."

Her breath had moved from soft gasps for air, managing the pain and arousal, to tiny pants of need. His cock moved inside of her on its own, telling her he was getting harder, seeing her arousal accelerate, or maybe also from the picture he was painting. She made a quiet, panicked noise, but her gaze didn't waver from his, from the knowledge in his eyes of what he was doing to her.

She was lost in amber fire, and wanted nothing more than to obey him. To come without any movement at all, because what was churning inside her was turbulent enough to realign the universe.

Part 11

He combed out her hair on either side, letting her feel the tug on her scalp, a hint of his strength. The pressure of his body on the brand made her think about how long she would have to wait before he'd agree to do that navel piercing he'd described. Knowing Tyler, he'd have the barbell and cuff custom made, set with a diamond, and inscribed with his initials. Present it to her as her birthday gift, a few months hence. She shuddered, imagining him touching that piercing and the connecting brand.

"How does it feel?" he said, his intent gaze on her face.

"Like I'm yours. Thank you, Master."

His eyes softened, a rueful tug to his mouth. "I'm still seriously tempted to turn you over and spank you for all of this."

"I'll take that as proof you liked your birthday gift."

He snorted, but then he wound his fingers into her hair, until his hands were framing her face again. He lifted his upper body so that the pressure on the throbbing skin was released. A quiver ran through her as he adjusted his hips so he was seated at a different, deeper angle. When she let out a moan, humor left his gaze, and he bent to her breast. As he scraped the curve with his teeth, he traced it with his tongue, making lazy circles toward the center, the jutting nipple that fairly vibrated with need. Her legs twitched and he gave her a warning look.

"You keep them spread and your ankles on the ground, angel. As far as you're concerned, I have you tied out here with stakes and rope. In fact…" The tip of his tongue made another pass around the areola, evoking another whimper. She was becoming a symphony of needy sounds again, but she knew that would please him, make him harder. "I think that's the perfect way to make sure you keep from abrading the burn. Tomorrow, when I'm working on my roses, I'm going to take garden stakes and soft rope and stake you out on the grass while I prune. And maybe I'll use that bit I described, those two roses, to keep you quiet and focused only on everything going on inside of you. Put that small vibrator into your sweet cunt, let you come as many times, and as often, as it takes me to do my gardening. Sara will bring us both water when we need it, snacks. I'll feed you, of course, tip the water to your lips. Run the ice cubes along your nipples, over your clit, if you're getting too hot. Would you like that, angel?"

She quivered, her breath shortening. "Sounds like a lot of work for you."

"I'm willing to make the sacrifice." He placed a single, dragging lick over the right nipple and she cried out, but remained perfectly still, as still as a trembling body could stay. "Plus, if I get too hard watching your pussy cream over that vibrator, I'll just feed my cock into my sweet slave's mouth, have you take care of me."

"Tyler." Her breath shuddered deep as he closed his mouth fully over the nipple this time, drew deep, making the suckling noises he knew could drive her crazy.

Her pussy rippled over his length, and he put a hand between them to caress her clit in a slow, sensual circle, flicking back and forth over the engorged flesh, teasing rather than stroking it, making her body quiver harder. It didn't seem possible that she could be close to coming again, but the way that brand seared into her flesh, keeping her hyperaware of its presence and meaning, along with his stimulation, made her think she was still riding the waves of the last orgasm.

"Want you...to come with me," she gasped, too close for finesse and teasing. "Please."

"You know when you say please, I can't resist you, angel." Tyler clamped down on the other nipple, suckling hard. Despite his earlier edict, he'd apparently decided he did want to feel the friction of her wet pussy gripping him, because he pulled half out and slid back in to the hilt, giving an extra thrust to take him that much deeper. It wrenched an animal sound of pleasure and effort from her throat. He kept his stomach off of hers, though.

"It...if you abrade it...it makes a deeper mark," she said, but he gave her a quelling look.

"Not happening, angel. You'll have to be happy with it as is."

"I am if you are. Thank you, Master. Thank you, Tyler."

"Christ, you kill me." Another retreat, then the slow surge back in, with that extra twitch, sending a jolt through her nerve endings. "You keep talking to me. I want to hear your voice, know when you're about to go over. I love it when I break you down like this, when you give me everything."

"You already have everything," she whispered, her fingers clutching the grass where her spread arms lay. "Everything I am. I like...what you want to do tomorrow. I want to be still, and yours, and feel the sun... Hear the birds... And not worry about anything."

"Not worrying about anything now, are you, angel? You've given it all to me." Those clever fingers flicked her clit again and Marguerite gasped over a tight spiral of response, searing a path up from between her legs, a near orgasm. If he did that a few more times, she'd be unable to hold back, and from the intent look in his amber eyes, he knew it. "Keep talking."

"Pretty horses here...can you...ride?"

"Every Southern gentleman can." His mouth was on her again, cruising down her sternum, his body performing that slow penetration and retreat that made her ache to lift her legs, clamp them around him. He knew how devastating it was to have an orgasm this way, with him controlling the build up. There'd been nights he'd strapped down her legs from hip to ankle, completely immobilizing her, so that not even a twitch of her lower body was possible. He'd licked her clit with that devil-blessed mouth until she'd come, so intensely she'd blacked out. She'd woken in his arms, him caring for her, massaging her legs, cleaning her. Though he was so aroused his cock was an iron bar pressed against her side, he'd insisted on caring for her first.

"Will you wear...those tight pants? Boots?"

"Wanton woman. You'd just be staring at my ass."

"And your big...riding crop."

He chuckled against her flesh, but she felt the flex of his hands in her hair, knew he was getting close to peak as well. She wanted to go together, and lifted her head slightly, capturing his attention. His hands slid beneath her neck, supporting her, tilting her head so her mouth was so close to his.

"Together...please." She was lost to the desires of her body, but this, this was pure emotion. She wanted to be together, melded together by that flood of release. He saw the need in her gaze, for he didn't tease her, as he might otherwise.

"Together, angel. Always. Ready?"

She nodded.

"Then come for me. Let me hear your cries."

That clever hand stopped making those light circles and instead stroked her with purpose, setting off a charge of reaction through her clit and pussy. As he did, he began to stroke harder within her, and with less defined thrusts, his own need coming up and over him, so that the leash of control broke. As her voice rose in the cry of release, he put his hands to her hips and increased his strength, hitting her labia and clit with every stroke, replacing his fingers with the overwhelming demand.

She wanted to touch him, wanted to wrap arms and legs around him, but she obeyed him, leaving her limbs straining and straight, because it made the orgasm so much more intense. The cry became a tearing scream. It overwhelmed her, took over her motor control such that he shifted and held her legs and arms pinned with his hands and hips, his feet hooked over her shins. As he did, he rose and plunged, rose and plunged. She felt the heat of him spurt into her, renewing the assault on her tissues. She caught a glimpse of his face, seized by the powerful paralysis that a universe-changing orgasm could invoke, and loved it. Loved him. Loved the deep, masculine cries of release, somewhere between a shout and growl of a savage animal.

A savage animal that slowly settled into repletion. His climax had been so intense, his hands had bruised in their grip on her arms, but she reveled in that loss of control. When he finished, he was lying full on her again, her body still twitching from aftershocks, tiny cries coming from her lips with each one.

"All right?" he asked after a long while, his voice a rumble against her ear.

"As long as you never move."

"You need to breathe, angel. And that's all the pressure we're going to put on this brand for now."

With a groan, he made it to his knees, reluctantly sliding from her. Shifting beside her, he propped himself on an elbow and regarded her pale, trembling body, from her painted toenails to the crown of her silky hair. "God, you're beautiful. The way you lay there, still obedient to me, your arms and legs spread. Who'd have thought a Mistress could surrender so utterly? You're a jewel. My wife."

It gave her an inner glow she was too proud to ever admit. Unless he seduced it out of her. But her voice had a betraying break as she spoke. "I want to touch you now."

He nodded, and she turned on her hip, her depleted body and the ache of the burn making it a careful movement. Glancing down, he traced around the burn area, not touching the skin, and slid upward to her breast. He ran his knuckles along the curve before bringing his hand to rest on the nip of her waist, his thumb close to the mark. She noticed, with satisfaction, the way his eyes kept straying to it.

"Violet thought I should do the same to you one day. You know, kind of a double D ranch brand on your haunch."

His gaze flicked up to hers, lazy amusement in it. Laying his head down on his arm, he let his knuckle descend, do another circle around the brand area, then brush her mons and her damp labia. Her legs automatically adjusted for him, letting his fingers slip inside. Her muscles gave a final, exhausted contraction, an incoherent sound coming from her as he stroked the liquid silk inside with tender fingers.

"And what does my beautiful Mistress think?"

"I think this is enough for me. Though I haven't been able to practice my hog tying in awhile."

"I should tell you something that happened to me the other day, when I was in town. It involved two young, beautiful women."

"Really?" Her brow arched.

"Mm-hmm. You know that gallery near you, the co-op for aspiring artists? I saw a sculpture in the window I particularly liked. It was a bronze of a naked female angel. It looked as if she'd been playing above stormy ocean waves. She's in a twisting motion, and a merman has surged up from the waters to take her mouth in a kiss, his hand closing on her wrist. One wing is angled down, as if she's about to pull away, but there's something about the arch of her throat, the tension in her body, that tells you she's aroused by the merman's boldness, his attempt to hold her." He let his fingers slide out, painted their combined fluids on her upper thigh and then closed his hand over her fragile wrist, bringing the hand to him so he could nuzzle her fingers with his mouth.

"I thought it was exceptional work. Figured I could buy it, take a picture of it and send it to Marcus, tell him I found it in Somalia at a street bazaar. He'd probably spend months scouring the area to get the artist under contract with him."

"You have a mean streak." Her mouth curved. "And you underestimate Marcus. I bet he'll figure out your game in no time and retaliate by putting your name and photo out on the Internet as "Gay male, single, who likes being spanked by Daddy.""

"Oh, he already did that one."

"Yes, but it was a classic."

"He prides himself on being original." At her shiver, he noticed the sun was starting to go down. "I think we probably need to get you home."

She glanced down at herself. "You said..."

"I meant it. Nothing but panties until it heals." A twinkle went through his amber eyes. "I'll put this blanket around you, but better hope we don't get stopped on the way home."

She shook her head and lay back, giving him an amused look as she draped her arms over her head in a provocative pose. "You're driving, so you'll have to explain it. But I'm not going anywhere with you until you tell me about the two beautiful women."

His eyes creased in that handsome way that never failed to make her heart lurch. "Didn't forget that, did you?" Still, before he continued, he rose, pulling his jeans back on and fastening them. He disappeared briefly into the barn. Marguerite watched the rose and gold colors paint the sky until she heard his feet. Lifting her head, she saw him crossing the ground back to her, her blouse in his hands. He helped her slide it onto her shoulders, though he left it open. "I won't let you be cold," he said, in explanation of the sudden revision to his earlier mandate. "I don't want you uncomfortable."

"Women?" she prompted, though her heart squeezed a little as it always did at his unfailing care for her.

He grinned, recapturing her hand, but continued. "When I went into the gallery, two young women were there, the owner and one of the artists. As you know, I have exceptional hearing, and I heard the owner talking about me. You know, the usual. How incredibly sexy I was, the things she'd do if she could get her hands on my ass..."

"I can think of a few things to do with your overinflated opinion of yourself," she retorted. When she tried to pull her hand away, he held her fast.

"Ssh, be still." His voice softened, his eyes sobering as he touched her face, keeping her other hand firmly in his grasp. "I could sense the artist watching me, not saying anything, but then she told her friend not to bother. That I was taken, in every sense of the word."

Marguerite pressed her lips together at the expression in his face. "I wondered, because it sounded like she meant more than being married, even if she'd noticed my ring. So I stopped by the counter on my way out and asked her point blank why she'd said that."

Marguerite could imagine it. That direct look, the firm tone and yet sexy Southern drawl that could seduce and command a woman at once, even when he was being entirely appropriate, as she was sure he was. She imagined the owner's discomfiture, knowing she'd been overheard, and the artist's clear, steady gaze as Tyler repeated her words.

"She smiled at me, and gave me a quote by the novelist George Moore: 'Other men it is said have seen angels, but I have seen thee and thou art enough.' She told me that was the look I had about me, so she knew I already had my angel." He shifted. "It was uncanny, given what I call you, so I wanted to think about it awhile before I told you. I'm glad I waited, because I couldn't think of a more perfect time to tell you."

He drew her forward, bringing his mouth to hers for a sweet, lingering kiss. Marguerite let herself get lost in it, in the scent of him, in the familiar yet arousing pressure of his lips. Every inch of him was hers.

When he lifted his head at last, he spoke. "Thank you for my birthday gift. Though you'll always be enough for me, every birthday."

In answer, Marguerite put her hand on the side of his throat, her forehead to his, holding him close. "I'll give you a quote," she said softly. "'Love has no desire but to fulfill itself. To melt and be like a running brook that sings its melody to the night. To wake at dawn with a winged heart and give thanks for another day of loving.' Kahlil Gibran."

She met his gaze, their faces so close. "Thank you for giving my heart wings. Thank you for giving this birthday to me, and every one after it."

Visibly moved, he put his hand back over her wrist and gripped her there hard. "I love you, angel. I always will. What do you say you let me take you home, and we can watch the sun set over the water?"

"I'd say that would be a perfect end to the day."

"That's every day that ends with you, angel."

One Night Only

A vignette featuring Lady Lyssa and Thomas from the Vampire Queen Series.

Originally posted March, 2010 in serial format.

These characters are introduced in the first book of the series, Vampire Queen's Servant, *and reappear throughout the series.*

Background: *This vignette is a prequel to Lyssa and Jacob's first book,* Vampire Queen's Servant. *In this story, Lyssa's servant is still Thomas, the celibate monk who later trains Jacob to take his place. Despite the carnal nature of vampires, Lyssa honored Thomas's celibacy vow, with one notable exception. He started his service as a second mark, but when he agreed to forever bind himself to her as her third marked servant, she required a loyalty test. He had to give her his body for one night only. This story is about that night.*

Part 1

Thomas circled the chamber for what felt like the hundredth time. He'd prepared her bed as he did every night. He'd turned back the cotton sheets the way she liked, arranged her pillows, and cut one perfect white rose, the bud not quite open, to lay on the linens. Though it was something she required, tonight it seemed as if he did it by his own will, for his own purposes. His fingers lingered on the petals as he imagined trailing the bud between her breasts, down a silken abdomen...

He swore, something he rarely did, but the moment seemed to call for it. He attended her in the evenings when she first rose, and she often laid out her schedule for the nighttime hours while choosing her clothing, calling for his assistance to lace a corset or tie a garter. He'd seen her naked plenty of times. He helped her bathe, after all, pouring water over that slim back, massaging oils into her skin. He washed her dark hair, a web of temptation all its own, the way it fell in twists and curls down to her flare of her hips, teasing the crease between her bare buttocks.

She was a descendant of Lilith, of Jezebel, of every woman who knew exactly how to use such beauty to confound a man's mind. Despite the fact it was a more enlightened time, almost 1852, there were still some of his monastic brethren in England who considered women Satan's agents, either deliberately or through female weakness for sin. But he didn't. Even after a year in the service of a vampire queen.

That year had brought him far from the monastery, geographically at least. Her decision to leave Europe for the young United States of America had been surprising, but she'd felt the position was strategic. It spoke to her desire to see the European vampires take a new, more enlightened view of their relationship with the human world. She'd purchased this plantation house outside of Atlanta, and, though they hadn't been able to stay here as often as she liked, she'd at least managed a prolific rose garden. She never lived anywhere she couldn't have roses. A quirk that always reminded him of the vulnerability of the woman beneath the queen's exterior.

Turning away from the bed, he moved to the fire and added another log. She didn't really get cold, but she liked warmth, the way it pressed against her skin like a lover's touch. He didn't give himself to such sensual poetry, of course. She'd told him that once, and he'd remembered it. Such words were thorns she drove into his flesh, tormenting him, goading his resolve.

He was an intelligent man. She'd told him his brilliant mind was why she'd brought him into her service, and possibly his intellect was the reason he'd been drawn to it. However, though he'd left his monastery to serve her, he had not set aside his vows as a monk. His brothers might consider him no longer one of them, but his oath had been made to God, not to them.

Because he *was* an intelligent man, he'd been able to look beyond his fear of his own weak impulses to the mind of the woman he served. It put his to shame, particularly when it came to calculation, testing a man's mettle. Lady Lyssa needed a full servant, and the past year had been a never-ending audition for it. Yes, she'd tested his resolve to honor his vow of celibacy, and though the woman in her had taken pleasure and amusement in it, her intent had been far more serious and politic. And because he'd understood that, he'd stayed.

Though she'd tempted him mercilessly in those first three months, there was some invisible cessation point where her taunts became almost affectionate barbs, no longer such a test of his will. While his soul had breathed a sigh of relief, it had been rocked back on its heels by one simple command, given two months ago.

I am ready to give you the third mark, Thomas. It will make you my full servant, your soul bound to me forever. Before I do that, you will take the Ritual of Binding to a vampire queen. And you will lie with me, to prove your loyalty to me can exist in the same heart that holds your loyalty to God. I will ask it of you only once, but your heart and body must be given to me freely, like the rest of you. If you cannot do that, then I will release you to return to your monastery. She'd paused then, those green eyes vibrant, but she wasn't done. She was thorough, his lady, and never left any stone unturned.

On that night, I will also demand to hear what you have never spoken. Why you have chosen to serve me.

Even though she could read his mind, she knew that forcing a man to say such a thing to a listening ear made it far more binding and concrete, not just nebulous wisps of thought, like clouds scudding away.

She'd not been willing to negotiate or argue her terms. In their travels, they had debated many things, even argued heatedly like two scholars. But there was a tone that entered her voice when she assumed her queen's mantle. Those jade eyes had been cool and remote, making it clear there was either acquiescence or departure. Both would be permanent. Forever.

Had she known he would need two months to decide to stay or run? The thought made him chastise himself. Why did he think of it that way? If he hadn't been able to reconcile himself to it, he would have left, not run away. He'd come into this relationship with his eyes open.

She was not like other vampires he knew, and he'd met many since their paths had crossed. Any other vampire mistress would have demanded this act long before tonight, because sexual demands of servants were closely integrated into all aspects of the vampire world. However, part of it was his lady had spent her year up to her slim neck in conflict, addressing the guerilla tactics from those he feared eventually would cause outright war between the vampires. There'd been plenty of vicious brutality and bloodshed going on in the shadows of the oblivious human world, but he already knew they were minor moves on the chessboard for what might come. His lady had a vision for the future, and he could see the knowledge in her eyes, what the cost would ultimately be. She would face it unflinchingly, as she did everything else.

But he believed there was another reason she hadn't pushed it before now. She respected him. When he'd come into her service, she'd needed his intellect, his companionship. The reasons he'd found himself here were complicated and simple at once, as much intuition and gut as reasoned thinking. He knew he was an oddity, a monk who wished to be a monk, yet serve God in a way that seemed inconsistent with those vows. She was a vampire equally as unique in her world. Another thing that drew them together.

At the beginning, she'd made him a first marked servant, the geographical locater merely a protection from the other vampires they might encounter. It was a sigil of her service. As his duties became more involved, he took the second mark, so she could speak in his mind and he in hers, though he did not have the same free access to her thoughts as she did to his. He had told himself it did not concern him. After all, God could be in his mind at any time, so it would be an additional test, to ensure that everything in Thomas's mind reflected his devotion to His will.

While he knew his order would scoff at such things, she never did. Nor did she do anything to reassure him what he was doing was right. She left it entirely between him and God...though everything else was subject to *her* will.

His faith was predicated on the belief that other men were ordained to know better than he what God demanded—priests, cardinals, the Pope himself. The Bible spoke of sins and betrayed faith. Thomas knew all that, but he could not deny what his heart had told him, the first time he had met her.

She'd been seeking an ancient manuscript, a history of the Crusades. Specifically, a reference to a knight who had fought in it. The reference had been obscure and vague, no way to tell if it was the man she sought. Even so, Thomas remembered the way she'd placed her fingers on the line of text, her eyes closing, her mouth softening in a way he had not seen since. However, it had been a blinding light into her soul, showing him who she was, this mysterious, dangerous and powerful woman, like no other he'd met.

After that, she'd engaged him in a lively dialogue about the other histories and texts he had. She spent three days there, apparently to increase her knowledge by testing his. By the time she prepared to leave, he knew what she was. She told him she would take him into her service, if he went willingly. He'd been at the monastery nearly twenty years, yet it took him only one night to decide to leave it, as if all his training and preparation had been for her eventual arrival.

His place was at her side, not as an abandonment of his faith, but as a reinforcement of it. He'd been sure of it, had rarely doubted it. Tonight, however, that belief would be tested as it had not been before, because it was the first time his service to her would so definitively trespass on promises given to Another.

He usually laid out a filmy silken gown for her slumber, one that clearly showed her body beneath it. It was her preferred nightwear, a woman of no shame when it came to her sexual beauty. Tonight, though, she'd told him to lay out only a robe.

"It's all I'll need tonight," she'd said. She'd mentioned it in a careless offhand way during their quarterstaff training. She'd spent time in Japan learning the intricate staff work, and in turn she'd trained Thomas so he could spar with her, though she of course had to slow her movements. He'd missed a step, and gotten his knuckles wrapped for his trouble.

Not by a flicker did she acknowledge the significance of her words, but he'd felt the impact beyond his smarting knuckles. It had seared through his gut and lower, in parts not even given the relief of his hand for nearly twenty years, let alone the heated silk of a woman's body.

Would he shame himself like a boy? Surely not, for she'd tested him so often this past year that restraint should be second nature. But there was a keen difference between her honeyed words, her casual touches, and being bare together by the light of this fire, his body between her legs, his cock... Ah, God help him, he hadn't thought so much about his cock over two decades as he had in the past two months. All monks figured out ways to get past the involuntary urges, accept and eventually quell the desires that came in the middle of the night, the churning need of the male body to spend. To deny it made one stronger for God, that energy channeled into prayer and service. Tonight, he was going to channel it into its animal purpose. As the moment grew closer, he was more desperate to understand if he was acting on his desires or God's.

Realizing his pacing was wearing a hole in the Persian rug, he dropped to his knees on the stone near the fire, putting his head near enough to the heat to feel the burn through his hair. *Dear Father, I have prayed about this so much. I believe it is Your Will that I serve her, to the extent you will overlook this one night, but forgive me, I do not know if an overly developed intellect masquerades as divination of Your Purpose, to have what my man's greedy soul might want...*

He could remain her second mark servant. After all, he served her well in that capacity. But he'd known his destiny was to be far more to her. As her third mark servant he could help her in ways he would never be able to do as a second mark, giving her strength and support she would need in the days ahead. No one else in her retinue was as close to her, understood her mind the way he did. That was not a boast – it was a tricky, dangerous path every day, something that drove his conflict to even deeper levels when he saw he had a knack for it that no one else did. She knew it, too. Why else would God have brought him into her life?

He knew what others of his order would say. The Devil was equally as capable of bringing such influences into a man's life. But he'd long ago faced the truth—that every choice and decision lay in a man's heart. No other man or institution could bear the responsibility or blame for it. There was no one between him and God on this. He had to follow what his own soul told him to do.

"Thomas."

He hadn't heard her come in, so deep had been his contemplation. Or perhaps she'd chosen to move as a vampire, so silent that no man could see her when she did not wish to be seen. He lifted his head, tilted it so he could find her in the corner of his gaze, though for the first time in their relationship, he found it too difficult to look at her directly. "My lady."

Her gaze passed over the bed, lingering on the rose. "White, the color of death. Or of endings. Is this your answer?"

"No, my lady. But I am..." She would not tolerate prevarication. He could not assuage his soul by justifying his actions to her. So he stopped before he started. He made himself get to his feet, turn and face her, meet her gaze. "No, my lady. White can also be the color of beginnings. Or a reflection of your fair skin."

"So it can. Though a monk should hardly be considering a woman's fair skin."

"Well, the night seems to call for a certain amount of

gallantry."

A faint smile touched her lips, but he was absurdly touched by the seriousness of her gaze, an acknowledgment of what this might cost him. She would not mock or tease him tonight, not that way. Pulling the sticks from her hair, she let it tumble down her shoulders, all the way to her hips. That glory of ebony silk would soon be filling his hands. It was much easier to resist when he knew it was not his to touch. Now, when it would be required, it was almost impossible not to feel it already sliding over his palms.

If he unleashed this longing growing in his breast, would he ever leash it back again? Could he serve them both?

"You've never been nervous in my presence. Even when you understood what I was. You are different from most monks. You fence my sharpest wit like an expert swordsman, you endure my subtle taunts with a resigned smile and a dry humor that makes me laugh, when nothing else can. I'm in your mind, I've seen you quell your desire, the way you quell hunger or any other natural impulse. You have more discipline than any human I have ever met. But you're nervous now, aren't you?"

No use denying it. "Yes, my lady. I am."

"I like it." She leaned in the door frame, accentuating her hips in the men's trousers she'd donned for her practice, pants that hugged her body indecently. But nothing about her had ever seemed indecent to him. She seemed above such rules.

"Did you talk to your God?"

"He is your God as well, my lady. But yes."

"Hmm. If you have spoken to him, made what peace you are going to, then we leave Him outside this door." Turning, she closed it with a significant click, shot the bolt home, then gave him a glance, filled with sensual power and yet amusement that could be tender and merciless at once. "That leaves just you and me, doesn't it?"

Thomas wondered. He couldn't imagine even God denying Himself the pleasure of seeing what would happen next in this energy-charged room that suddenly seemed much warmer. *God have mercy on my soul.*

Her lips curved. She'd heard the thought.

Ask Him for mercy, Thomas. Because I shall give you none. Not until dawn.

Part 2

"You are taking unseemly joy in this, my lady. Like a man given a virgin to defile."

Her eyes gleamed. "My intent is not to defile you, only ensure myself of your loyalty."

"Practically, I'm not sure how this proves that. Very few men could resist your charms." In fact, if Jesus had met Lady Lyssa in the desert instead of Satan, Thomas was sure Christian history would have turned out far differently.

Because she was inside his mind, that surprised a chuckle out of her. But her voice softened. "You are an exceedingly devout man, Thomas. If you defined your faith only by brick and mortar and holy texts writ by men, you would have given in to temptation a hundred times by now. I have certainly tested it." In her gaze he saw the sensual reflection of it, every time she'd bade him bathe her, dress her hair, lie in her bed so she could curl around him, absorb his warm and companionship while she slept. "Your order has shut the door against you. But you have not abandoned your oath to God."

Until tonight. He couldn't help the thought, but of course she heard it.

"You have the sense to know better. Don't become mindlessly pious on me." No softness in her voice now, a cue he'd learned to read well. His spine automatically straightened, his senses sharpening. She arched a perfect brow. "Show me the scars I put upon you."

Two nights ago, he'd taken the Ritual of Binding to a Vampire Queen. She'd used a whip, striped him with it fifty times. She'd soaked the single tail in her own blood so the lashes would leave these permanent scars, despite a second mark's advanced healing ability. As a third mark, he would never have another scar except this, an intentional branding.

I am sworn to your service. Compelled by absolute loyalty, I safeguard your well-being before my own or any other ties of family or friendship. I swear it by the giving of my blood to you and before all of Divinity, may my life be cursed and my soul be damned if I speak false or ever betray the vow.

The ancient vow he'd said to her echoed in his mind. Had the words required he put her above Divinity, he wasn't sure he could have done it, because he'd gotten this far believing the vows were not in competition. *Until tonight.*

That phrase was going to be branded on his mind like those lashes, though Lyssa's faint tone of scorn had told him she wouldn't tolerate false guilt. The fact he was going ahead with it said so. Even if she wasn't in his mind, he expected she'd never let a man hide from the truth of his soul, however base or noble its intent.

She made a noise, reminding him she'd given him a command. He was wearing a coarse linen shirt over workman's trousers and boots. It was clean and modest, neat, something over which he could easily don a jacket and dress up if she had guests, but which worked well otherwise for his work around the plantation, tending the garden, helping the staff with repairs or reading in the orchard.

Now though, stripping off the shirt was like taking off his skin. It was another mystery, why he felt self-conscious at this point. While she was entirely immodest with him in her bath and dressing areas, she had no compunction about invading his privacy the same way. Many times, when he'd been bathing, she'd come to watch him.

She hadn't cloaked it in a pretense of conversation. She'd sat on a chair in silence and studied his naked male form in detail, making it clear it was her right to do so, to take whatever pleasure she wished in the sight of his hands cupping and lathering his genitals, the stretch of his body, the length of an arm as he rubbed soap over the firm expanse of skin over his rib cage and the indentation of arm pit, the curve of biceps. The first time she'd ever come upon him like that, he'd practically leapt out of the tub like a squealing girl and taken refuge behind a bush.

"You startled me, my lady," he'd stammered. *"What*

may I do for you?"

"What you are doing. I will watch you, Thomas. Whenever I wish. Come out of there."

Her eyes had stayed fixed upon him, as intently as they were now, until he stepped out from behind the foliage. Lord in Heaven, his stomach had been quaking. There'd been a tremor through his legs, but it wasn't that reaction which caused him the most mortification. He'd continued bathing even as he became fully erect in front of her. Because of that and a wealth of other reasons, he hadn't washed his cock and balls. He had absolutely no intention of doing so. Not in front of her. However, not for the first time, she reminded him how clever she was.

"You missed a spot, Thomas. A substantial one. If you will not clean it yourself, you'll goad me to do it. I won't suffer an unclean servant."

"I think you're the one goading, my lady."

"Testing. Whether you pass or fail is entirely up to me."

Now, returning to the present, he considered her. "You've watched me bathe before, my lady."

Her gaze touched his chest, the muscled lines of his arms and abdomen. He helped with the manual labor, tending horses, clearing brush and making repairs, not liking to be idle when she didn't need him, or he wasn't at prayer or study. Vanity was a sin, but he couldn't help the way the obvious pleasure in her regard uncurled warmth inside of him, tightening his lower abdomen and hardening his cock even further. She noted that, the increased constriction of the pants revealed to her.

"Yes, I have. I've required you to strip quite a few times when you weren't expecting it. In my library, to give me the pleasure of looking at you while we were both reading. In the gardens, while I tended the roses. I like seeing your backside flex as you dig or plant. The way your knees press into the dirt, your testicles so heavy and touchable, swinging between your legs."

He closed his eyes. The fit of the pants was getting decidedly uncomfortable. He was also certain fluid was leaking from his organ, likely staining the front of the thin cloth with a damp kiss. "Why would you do that? Tempt yourself with nakedness but not touch?"

"Because I like the look of you. Pure and perfect, a creation of God. So sexual. You got hard, every time I required it of you. Just as now."

"And I've told you that men cannot help what their cocks do. Only what they do with them."

"So you have." A light smile touched her lips, but didn't reach her eyes. "Thomas, turn."

He did, and knew she was looking at those fifty raw stripes, the ones that had kept him moving stiffly this past day, though his healing ability had turned them into closed scars. In his world, the healing powers of a second mark would be considered a miracle. In her world, it was simply part of being a vampire's servant. When she drew closer, that first touch was like a lightning strike, the way her fingers trailed down his shoulder. He closed his eyes again, and his fists. Throughout the ages, men of God had flogged themselves. For penance. To show their devotion by giving up comfort and immersing themselves in agony. To resist temptation.

Father, forgive me...

Could a man ask for forgiveness before he sinned, knowing that he was going to do it, even if it was wrong? Of course not, not unless he was hypocrite. He was worse than that. A scholar, a thinking man. She was right. In his heart, he didn't consider this a sin.

She let those fingers drift down his shoulder and rest on the line of scars. The pain during the lashing had been excruciating, such that he'd cried out during the last twenty. Afterwards, he'd lain down naked on the cold stone floor of her small chapel. She hadn't required that. He'd done it to underscore what he was choosing to do, praying for guidance. He'd fallen asleep that way. When he woke, a blanket had been laid over him by her own hands, and his head was in her lap, her fingers stroking his temples. She'd let him into her mind in that intimate moment, and he saw her considering the dusting of silver in his hair, a reminder he was no boy. He was a man. He'd been taught they were all children of God, but he'd often wondered why God would want a world full of creatures who never matured and grew up. Even infants could learn enough from their parents to be guided by their wisdom in making their own decisions. Why couldn't adults do the same from God's Wisdom?

"Do you really consider lying with a woman a defilement?" She could purr like a cat, stroke a man with her voice, but sometimes that would fall away. He'd hear a trace of vulnerability it seemed only his ears were allowed to detect. Such evidence of her trust was a gift he valued beyond comprehension.

"Not this. Not with you. God help me."

She laid her cheek between his shoulder blades, her lips grazing the nearest one. He thought her eyes might have closed now, because her hands slipped around his waist, her knuckles curling to trace the muscles in his abdomen, then down, around the hip bone, along the line of hip and upper thigh. At last, she plucked at a crease in the strained fabric of his trousers, like a string in a violin tightened to near snapping. His testicles contracted at the thrum of incidental contact all along his groin.

"I told you I would want to hear it tonight, Thomas. Why you want to be my full servant."

"You asked me that the very first day, my lady."

"Yes. You said you felt it would serve the Lord's purpose. I laughed at you."

"You did more than that, my lady. You said, 'That's a convenient male excuse.'"

"And you hid behind your wit and impertinence. You said, 'No man would willingly choose to serve such a demanding taskmaster. Only a monk, used to serving God, would be up to the task of serving you as you demand, my lady.'"

She straightened, her body sliding against his as she pushed up on his left arm so she could pass beneath it and settle herself on him so her breasts rested on his chest, her thigh brushing the inside of his. Their mouths were so close. It wasn't often that he was so directly reminded of how much shorter she was, a petite doll of a woman. One who, standing so close, had to tilt her head to look up into his face. As he had to bow his own to see hers.

Her hair fell in curls down to her hips and teased his fingers there. "You amused me, because it was a challenge," she said. "You were an enigma. You still are."

"I doubt that. You are inside my mind, my lady. If you honor me with your final mark, you believe you will have ingress into my very soul."

"I have seen a squirrel dance across a branch that should snap beneath his weight, fling himself in the air and land without fear on a tree limb fifteen feet away. I know squirrels can do that. It doesn't make the mystery of how they came to be what they are any less. Your greatest sin is speaking the truth, embracing your own wisdom, believing that it can be inspired by God's. And that sin has endured, despite a lifetime of self-deprecation, of being nurtured on the idea that man is hopelessly weak, ignorant and misguided. You try to flagellate yourself with it, and yet your skin bears no scars. Not until mine." Her fingers passed over them again. "Do you want to touch my hair, Thomas?"

"Yes." He swallowed, but kept his hand hovering in the air where she'd pushed it, the other in a clenched knot at his hip.

She nodded, but didn't give him permission to do so. Instead, she outlined his collar bone with one long-nailed finger, scraping enough to leave a mark. "That first day, I thought you a man of God led astray by your lust. But your gentleness intrigued me. And when I looked in your eyes, I saw something far more than lust in your gaze. So now, you must tell me the truth, whatever it is. Why would you turn from God to give yourself to me?"

Now her expression sharpened in that way she had that took a man off guard. All playfulness gone, no games or tricks. Her gaze was as piercing as a monarch's, and her voice was clear, demanding truth. Though he hadn't been quite sure how he would say it, it came from him concise and immediate, the way she had trained him to react to her commands.

"Because I feel I am turning toward Him, not away." He swallowed and made himself hold her gaze. There were times she didn't allow it, but this was not one of them. She waited, wanting more, because she knew as he did there was more truth to be told. She wouldn't break the lock between their eyes until she had all of it. All of him.

"The history of my church, of men in my church... Monks, cardinals, priests, popes...we've often engaged in earthly matters. Politics, wars, scheming. Acts of deceit, to secure power or privilege for the Church. Such men have stood next to kings, influenced the direction of countries." He swallowed again. "They believed power was an acceptable weapon to secure faith. And sometimes it was. Though sometimes, to our shame, it wasn't."

He only had to look into her slanted eyes and at the abundance of her black hair to know they would have burned her alive during those shameful times. Being a vampire would have been the least of it.

She nodded. "I have been alive for nearly nine hundred years, Thomas. Such a time span gives one far less respect for religion, and far more for the Divine."

Despite the tension of the moment, the conflicting reactions of his body and his heart, he couldn't help but smile. As beautiful as she was, he sometimes thought it was her clever, irreverent mind that truly bewitched him.

"I do not seek to compare myself to such men," he continued, "though I pray I am not misguided as some of them have been. But I see what you are trying to do with the Vampire Council. And if I may be so bold, my lady, I will say that perhaps I have seen what others have not about your intentions. You may not consider humans equal, but you do not think that gives you the right to take advantage of the power God has given you. You think like a predator, not a human. You take what you need, and you demand respect, but that is all. You do not kill or subjugate merely for the power."

Her other hand still rested on his back. But now her fingers dug into one of the scars, enough to have him draw in a breath. "You may be wrong about a part of that," she murmured. "Sometimes I do subjugate...for the pleasure *in* the power. But you haven't finished your explanation, have you?"

This was the more difficult part. He almost had to close

his eyes again as her hand came back to his neck, slid down over the pectoral to tease the nipple. Her clothing was thin, and he could feel the press of her body. He wasn't a virgin. He'd come into the monastery after sowing a few wild oats as a stable boy, so he knew what it was to feel a woman's arousal through her breasts, the hardening tips a reflection of his own body. It was a heady feeling, one that made him dizzy, but she was holding him, steadying him.

"I think what you are doing will save lives. It will make it possible for two species to live in relative peace. From what I can see, you are alone at the head of a small army, standing against a far more savage one. One that wants no law but blood. I...feel what you are, my lady. I know there is a savagery inside you as well. You have the strength of will to use it for good...but you are also alone. If you will forgive me for the presumption, I can give you what others cannot – a quiet place, a confessional, a place to rest. A place of understanding. A reminder of why you are doing what you are doing."

Despite the urges of his body, the conflict in his mind, something else took hold of him now. He spoke without flinching, his voice gaining in strength, resonating with the attentive look on her face. "I think I can be a way to hold onto your compassion and mercy. I can help you retain your belief in balance, that it is more important than power for its own sake. It is ambitious for a humble monk, and I have prayed upon it. Scorn my humility if you will, and though it could be my ego, pride or truth that guides my feeling in this, I know I feel it. As surely as I feel my love for God." He took a breath. "And my love for you."

At the flicker in her gaze, the press of her lips, he allowed himself to twine a finger in one ebony curl. Not to touch, but to affirm. "In the end, we answer to God. But I know by serving you, I serve him. I've made that peace, and this moment is as much about that for me as it is for anything else."

He stared directly into those jewel-green irises, the darkness inside of them. As her fingers came to rest on his face, near his lips, he spoke again. "Whether I burn for it or find my way to the Heavenly Gates, it is what I have decided. May God have mercy on us both if I've chosen wrongly."

"I think you are burning now," she said after a long moment. "Your skin is so warm. Just a light gleam of sweat."

"It's from the fire. You like it far warmer than most would find comfortable." She would be comfortable in the bowels of Hell itself. Lucifer would offer her a comfortable chair and a glass of wine, if she ever graced his gates. A creature of all worlds and none.

After another long pause, she spoke. "I accept you as my servant, gentle monk. Tonight I will mark you as I take your body. Give yourself to me generously, this one night. Every ounce of your heart, soul and body. If you do that, you will have done my bidding."

She smiled, and the soft pleasure to it dropped the bottom out of his world. It was several moments before he could speak. When he did, he knew he'd stepped out of the world of books and theology, and left his eloquence there. Now he could only say what he was feeling. This primal place was her world.

"I'm nervous," he admitted. "Nervous that I will not please you."

"Now that *is* shameful pride." Her eyes glinted and she teased his mouth with her fingers again, such that he couldn't help himself. His lips parted and he tasted her. In the reflection of her eyes he saw the look of concentrated wonder on his face, amazement at himself. Lifting up on her toes, she brought her lips within a breath of his and spoke in that sensuous whisper she did so well.

"Thomas, I promise you, you are incapable of not pleasing me. Before this night is over, you will kiss my throat, my breasts, between my legs. You will taste every inch of my skin, and I will taste yours. As well as your blood. No more waiting. As much as I have enjoyed our dialogues, until I bid you otherwise, I bid you silent." Her eyes grew close, taking over everything as the whisper became a breath, taking the air in his lungs.

"Kiss me. Use your body to talk to me."

Part 3

"I know you've thought of touching me with your mouth, these hands." Closing her fingers over his right hand, she lifted it so they were palm to palm. She widened her slim fingers, watching as he slowly slid his in between the spaces, down those narrow valleys. His expression reflected his wonder at the feel of her skin moving against his in just that small way.

That reaction made something inside her go still and quiet. Lyssa teased him often, and she wouldn't deny a certain amount of feminine satisfaction in having this night with him. But he was right. She did respect him. She'd never met a man of such singular conviction, who so trusted his intellect to teach him God's will, rather than faith alone. She'd never met a man so close to God, and she'd walked with cardinals, shared at least one dinner with a pope. Back in the...fourteenth century, she remembered. He'd chewed with his mouth open and explained to her, in great detail, the edict he'd issued against the practice of witchcraft.

Thomas was also right about his purpose in her life, but he couldn't know how accurate his word choice had been. Confessor. There'd been times, in her darkest hours, she'd wanted to go on her knees to someone, have him lay a comforting hand over her hair, give her absolution, tell her that her sins were forgiven as long as she regretted them in her heart. That was not her life, not who she could be. But Thomas understood. Those nights when she'd sit with him by a window, studying the moonlight or the rain, the way the wind moved through the trees, she'd speak her thoughts to him in a random, unguarded way. He would listen, and that was as close to confession as she'd ever come, to any man or God.

He was still studying their hands, the way they fit together, and it both amused and moved her to see how he was lingering over it. Not delaying, but simply marveling at what he'd never experienced. She spread the fingers of her other hand out on his shoulder, then slid her knuckles along his throat, moving up to his face. He often wore the wire-rimmed glasses. The second mark hadn't improved his eyesight, oddly, or perhaps he did so much reading he just found the glasses a comfort and support. She liked watching him read in them, the way they accentuated his serious gray eyes, the set of his mouth. At first, his hair had been shaved short, but in his travels with her, she'd required him to grow it out, so he blended more with the styles of other servants. It was best not to attract too much attention, and a monk who traveled in close attendance on a single woman of her looks and bearing would attract attention. A servant, however, would not attract as much.

She unhooked the wire fitting over one ear, and then freed her other hand to do the same with the other side, removing the glasses and setting them to the side. He had beautiful gray eyes, long-lashed and intent, the kind of eyes that any woman with a heart could see had strength to them, and courage.

She ran a finger over his lips, enjoying the feel of them. He had such a pleasurable mouth. How would he pleasure her with it? "You know, you've never thought about it, not when I was listening," she murmured. "I assume I am not, in fact, deflowering a virgin."

He shook his head. And though he obeyed her directive not to speak, she saw the image in his mind. When he'd worked as a stable lad, an orphan taken in by the monastery, those gray eyes and lean young body had caught the attention of a village maid. One with an ample...very ample—bosom.

A smile curved her lips at his rueful look. But after that, there'd been nothing. Once he'd taken his vow, he'd not given himself any form of release, even by his hand.

"Then perhaps we should deal with that." She cocked her head at his startled expression. "I can order you to spill your seed first, then I'll spend the night building you back so you can spill it inside of me."

He held her gaze. *I beg of you, my lady. Let me be inside you when that happens. Make me hold out until then. Make my torment your pleasure.*

He surprised her, the ferocity of that desire, welling up inside of him. He'd watched her tease and torment others, making them wait, and wait, and wait. He'd seen how it heightened her pleasure. That knowledge was in his gaze now, and she felt that tightening around her heart again. Her monk who saw so much, understood so much. Even this, which in so many essential ways revolved around him, he'd turned back to her...as a gift.

"Very well," she said, keeping her voice steady with an effort. "But I may make you do the other later. Afterward. This one night, you will give yourself to all the pleasures I demand as your Mistress. Do you understand? You will not question or refuse me. So I will know that forever forward, you can do what I demand of you as my third mark.

When he nodded, she gave him an arch look, changing the tone. "And now, I think I told you to kiss me. To use your body, not your voice *or* your mind, to speak to me."

But my lady...you've told me often that a man has to use both his mind and body to please you. That rueful look became his quiet smile, but before she could seek a suitable reprimand for impertinence, he lifted both hands to her face, that intent expression on his own as he cupped her jaw and settled his fingers along it, framing her face. He passed both thumbs over her lips and, when they parted, he traced the fangs, holding a finger under one until she pressed down gently, drew several drops of blood that fell on her tongue. His eyes registered those bright red drops, and then he dipped his head. She kept her lips parted, still, as he touched his to her mouth, and his tongue slid over hers, over that blood, sharing it between them, sending heat through her. She held back her reactive desire, though, too titillated by what her monk was doing, how he would try to please her.

His lips settled fully over hers, sealing in the heat, and his tongue was stroking hers, slow, thoughtful and teasing caresses as his arms slid around her body. Thomas was lean and tall, but not overly so. Though she'd curled around him in bed she'd never had the experience of him holding her like this. She knew he was strong, but it was different to feel it, to feel that lean, long-limbed frame pressing in against the length of hers, his arms closing over her body, bringing her flush to him, his palms flattening on her back, one traveling under her hair to find her nape and investigate the fragile neck there, the other following the valley of her spine to the upper curve of her backside. He paused there, a finger stroking along the tailbone to the indentation at the top of her buttocks.

His touch was so deliberate, and yet so meticulous, exploring every detail of each inch of skin he covered. Her reaction accelerated beyond the scope of his hands. The skin tingled all along her buttocks, down the backs of her thighs, and sent a hard pulse through the tender skin in between, anticipating. She wanted his hands cupping her buttocks, wanted him to take a firm grip, kiss her harder, but at the same time, she wanted him to continue doing what he was doing because it was raising her core desire, a flame that would build into a fire hot enough to melt the center of the earth.

His fingers at her neck tangled in her hair, and slowly he tugged, tilting her head back. She gripped his arms, nails digging in as he left her mouth to trace her jaw, then reached her throat to trace the pounding artery there with his tongue, a deceptively leisurely descent, tasting and suckling her even as he painted her with that heated, moist and far too clever muscle.

She pressed her lower body closer, felt his cock had thickened under the workman's pants. Letting her hand glide up his bare back, she dragged her nails along that flesh. His cock leaped at the stimulus of pain. He had that in him, too. Most of the men who'd served her had possessed that secret craving. There was a release in pain, she knew, a sense of sacrifice that appealed to that deep thing in men. They might not know how to show a woman—or their God—their love, not with words. But they could bleed for both of them.

He dropped to one knee now, so her hands glided up to his neck and rested on his shoulders as he parted the robe in the front. The silk gave way easily, though he didn't yet touch the sash that tied it. She watched his face as he drew the two sides back to reveal her nipples, tight points against the areolae. His lips were already wet from kissing her. Now they pressed together, and she could feel the saliva gathering in his mouth, his desire to taste her. She wanted that, too.

Suckle me, Thomas. I need that clever mouth of yours there. It will make my cunt wetter for you. Can you smell my arousal now?

He nodded, his eyes on those two weighted curves displayed before him.

"What does it smell like?" she murmured.

"Heaven's gate," he said. A response straight from his heart, one that he spoke without forethought. Nor did he castigate himself or reflect. Instead he closed that distance, his lashes lowering as he put his mouth over the right one and drew her in deep.

Lyssa pulled in a breath, a small moan escaping her throat. That captured his attention, his gaze flickering up to her briefly in amazement. She tugged at his hair, goading him onward, and he returned to his task, driving up her arousal as he made small succulent sounds at his feast, savoring the taste of her flesh, the way the nipple could be squeezed between his lips, lashed by his tongue, then teased and tickled by the tip of it until she was moving restlessly against his abdomen, pressing her pubic mound insistently against him, a nascent rhythm intimating what was to come.

But when he might have moved, she held him there, made him lave her nipple until it was achingly hard in his mouth, until her hand was flexing with bruising strength on his shoulder. She moved him to attend the other as he got harder and harder in response to her arousal. The smell of it was fascinating his mind as well as his senses, such that the hand not occupied dropped to her knee. He found his way through the overlap of her silk robe, already loosened from what he was doing above. Though he stayed at her knee, his fingertips whispered up, a bare inch, and met the tiny trickle of fluid marking her flesh, its sensual track down her flesh. He pressed his finger upon it, marking it there as the slippery liquid pooled in that tiny indentation. Then he was moving upward, following it further even as his other hand continued to hold her breast firmly for the reverent attention of his mouth.

Lyssa had been attended by vampires and humans alike who had great skill and experience as lovers. Humans who'd known quite well the pleasures of submitting to her Dominance, who knew how to goad her desire for interweaving unbearable pleasure with edgy levels of pain. Dominant vampires who warred with her in the bedroom, a delicate dance of power and control that was a pleasure all its own. But this...this monk, who'd not touched a woman since a village maid with ample bosom, was making them pale in comparison. He did everything with such intensity and focus, it superseded even the wonder of her taking a virgin, whether a virgin to sex or a virgin to the type of sex she liked. Because though his sexual experience was limited, his experience of *her* was vast. He watched, listened, heard...he knew what her body felt, what her mind craved. In his celibate attentiveness he'd learned far more of her than men who'd shared her bed for whole seasons until she tired of them or their paths diverged. And it was so obvious, it could not help but drive her lust even higher.

Now, since she would not let him rise, he descended, the heat of his mouth moving down her upper abdomen. He slipped the tie of the robe, and she took the sash in both hands, sliding it free as he spread the garment fully open. Sitting back on his heels, he took a weighted moment to let his attention move from her milk white throat, all the way down the perfect cream color and firmness of her body, the pale, naked petals of her sex, then back to her breasts, aching and swollen from his attention, marked with the damp impression of his mouth.

She didn't expect it, but when she felt it, she couldn't deny it. She was shaking, a tiny tremor in her belly that quivered through her legs. She didn't know if he noticed or not, because he was shaking as well, nerves and pleasure warring in him. But as he lifted his gray eyes to her face, pausing over the sash wrapped over her hands, he lifted his own to her, crossing his wrists and giving her what she wanted. An offer of surrender.

She wasn't sure if God had created him, or the Devil, because she'd never seen such temptation in one gesture. In a flash, she wondered what would happen if she refused to honor his vow after the sun rose. If she forever made him serve her this way, a monk devoted to her *body*, soul and mind in truth, not just the soul and mind. Thomas, laid out in her bed, night after night, marked by her fangs, her whip, spread out for her pleasure in whatever way she'd restrain him...

And he'd then be fair game for any other vampire whose company she shared. It was a code among them. Their gatherings always required it. The only thing that had spared him was her position among them...and his celibacy she openly honored. Losing that would destroy him. Whatever lay between them, whatever made this night possible...it was only meant for her, and only for tonight. A gift that could be reduced to nothing by her greed.

Firming her lips, and her resolve, narrowing the intensity of her pleasure down to these few hours, she held his gaze as she wound the sash over his wrists. She made the wrap snug, then pulled his arms out before him, watching the fold of his shoulders, the flex of the muscles.

Leaving her robe on but open, she closed her hand on the joining point between his wrists, the satiny fabric soft beneath her grip. Stepping to the side, now she took his arms up, up, until the elbows were alongside his skull and his arms formed a temple over his head. Then she moved around him and tugged, giving him time to shift back to his heels before taking him down flat on the floor, stretching him out so his knuckles rested on the floor above him. She tied the sash's slack to the heavy foot of the bed behind him, keeping him fast. Then she knelt beside him, studying the body of the man laid out before her. All hers.

All yours. Just as you commanded, my lady.

She lifted her gaze to his. *Forever.*

Forever. He nodded.

Baring her fangs, she bent forward to give him that final mark.

Part 4

He lifted his chin, giving her access. Though she saw he was sure of his decision, it didn't stop a tremor from running through those strong arms, holding tight to the bonds. She paused, running a palm up the smooth biceps to his forearm. "Ease your grip, monk. You are in your bed, dreaming. You will not resist me, your body flowing to my will like water. Do not tense against me. That is my command."

Slowly, he complied, taking one deep breath that expanded his bare chest, then another. She nodded as his fingers slackened, letting go of the sash, and he was all hers, whatever she wanted to do to him. As he realized the power and truth of that, it did add rigidity to one part of him, the part she wanted straining with all its might toward her. For now, she kept that pleasure as a peripheral awareness as she pulled her loose hair to one side, tumbling it over her left shoulder, and brought her mouth to his throat.

One had to be a vampire, or perhaps a surgeon, to understand how vulnerable the human throat was to a mortal attack. A simple depression on the windpipe for the proper number of seconds, or one puncture on the carotid, and life would slip away like a dust mote through desperately grasping fingers. The body understood that, so it took a great act of will to do what Thomas was doing now. Obeying her, refusing his instinct to protect himself in any futile way. Putting her mouth over that artery, she heard the rush of sweet blood through it, could smell it through his skin. Aligning her fangs appropriately, she let them sink in, with slow, savoring pleasure.

Many human vessels had supplied her blood needs, but all vampires knew the gift of a third mark's blood. That very first time, when the marking happened, was sweetest of all. It was stepping across a gateway into a world heretofore unknown. The territory of Thomas's soul would be open to her, to explore and cherish for all eternity.

She released the serum with a press of her tongue behind the fang, and felt his jolt at the tingling fire of it. He was used to feeding her. On occasion, he'd even fed her intimately from his throat or wrist when circumstances didn't allow him to drain his blood into a wine glass for her. When that had happened, she'd usually released pheromones into his blood to ease the pain as well as to test his resolve. She didn't do that now. He was already intensely aroused, but more than that, she wanted to know every reaction was his own tonight.

During the second mark, the mind unfolded before the vampire, but this was like going from an anteroom in Heaven into the full spread of Eden. She saw more than memories and fleeting emotions. She saw the tangled, miraculous tapestry that made Thomas everything he was, every experience, thought, feeling, instinct and unconscious need. That unconscious level was a limitless ocean for her exploration, filled with jeweled colors. She didn't look too closely at it right now, just enjoying the feel of that energy coursing through her. It was as if she were a Fate with her fingers on the loom, feeling those strands quiver under her touch. It was the ultimate bond, something Thomas had probably thought was only possible in the afterlife, this sense of total connection to another. She let the strands tighten in her grasp, strengthening their binding, even as she absorbed the feeling herself, a warm tropical wind on her soul that would never die, so long as he lived.

But it was not done yet. There was a part he'd never experienced. As her second mark, he'd remarkably not yet had an injury severe enough to need her blood. She gave him a parting nuzzle from her lips and tongue, and then raised her hand to her own throat. She wore a sharp-tipped cover over one finger, a pretty but lethal-looking silver and jade bauble that allowed her to pierce her artery cleanly when needed. She did it now and slid her hand under his head to cup his skull. Lifting it as much as his bonds would allow, she made him feel the strain in his arms as she closed the distance between her throat and his mouth.

Drink, Thomas. Take what I am offering, and seal the bond between us.

When his mouth closed over the puncture, her body reacted with a near-climactic intensity, her thighs tightening and the tips of her breasts hardening anew. Her heart accelerated with the pleasure of conquest and willing surrender at once. He was pulling against the bonds now, his body bowed up toward her, not out of tension as before, but a begging need for her.

And there it was. She closed her eyes as the flash went through her, a powerful wave that emanated out from the bite area and swept through the bloodstream, injecting heat through all her veins and spreading fire briefly over her skin. That tapestry became fully illuminated, no more shadows or twisting tunnels. It was a garden in truth, and she could partake of every inch of it. Now, though, her body was humming for only one thing, and it told her urgently that it didn't want to wait much longer.

Still, she knew the benefits of inflicting anticipation on herself as much as on her servant, who had almost abandoned any notion of civility. He was now pressing his teeth into her flesh. Something fascinatingly like a growl was simmering in his throat. The male animal was breaking through all those layers, the ones created by his vow and absurd notions of human civility.

Using her hand, fingers spread wide on his chest, she pushed him down with irresistible strength until he was flat on the mattress again. She met his gaze, the command in her eyes, the set of her mouth. Watching his face, the tense lips, the heated gray eyes, she slid her forefinger under the waistband of the straining trousers. With her other hand, she cupped the prominent evidence of his erection, giving herself the delight of touching that rigid column. He was a very impressive size. From his bathing, she knew he had an attractive shape and weight, typical for a well-made man. But his arousal tonight had taken him far past the size she would have expected. It pleased her, on many different levels.

My lady, what are you doing to me?

Whatever I wish. Where is my calm and gentle monk? All his famed control? Was I wrong in agreeing not to let you release for me earlier? Will you come all over my hand now, before I can put you inside of me?

She reveled in the fiery struggle inside him, but he shook his head, a sharp shake.

I await my lady's pleasure.

He was her pleasure. Beginning and end. She opened

the front of the pants, removing them and his undergarments, stripping him bare to her gaze. He'd been barefoot when she came in and, on impulse, she bent and let her hair brush his sensitive arches, smiling when his toes twitched and the feet jerked. She wound a lock around one, tickling it further until he huffed at her, a light snort at her antics. Then her gaze traveled upward and amusement was replaced by something far more serious.

His cock was high and tight, brushing his belly, already leaking so that the head was slick with that viscous white fluid. When she touched it with one fingertip, slowly massaging the semen around the slit in idle circles, he groaned, another animal noise. His thighs trembled. The restraint was impressive, because she could see the white-hot need in his mind. Anticipating her, he'd even resisted the idea of reciting Bible verses in his head to distract himself. He knew she wanted to test him, wanted a hundred percent of his attention upon her.

I was wrong. His thought was a hoarse whisper in her mind. *You would not* visit *the devil in Hell, my lady. You are* her.

"If it's possible God is a woman, why not the Devil? We all know women are far more likely to be arch enemies." Sliding her nail down the pulsing vein below the glans, she tilted her head. "What was that, Thomas? Speak what you are thinking now."

His jaw tightened. "I will die if you do not fuck me, my lady. I want to be inside of you, thrusting...hammering... Please do it, before you shame me further."

Hearing those raw words fall from his cultured lips gave her shivers in all the right ways. "There's no shame here, Thomas. Not now, not ever. You are never allowed to think of this in shame, or I shall be very angry with you."

When she closed her hand around the root of him, a tight manacle, she noted the way his eyes were clinging to the movement of her breasts, the slope of her abdomen down to her naked thighs. His gaze sought the treasure hiding in between as she sat next to him with her legs folded. "I am so very wet, Thomas. I will slide down your cock like cream over a butter churn. When I am done, I will straddle your face, and you will lick me clean."

"Yes, my lady. Please..."

She let the robe fall from her shoulders and stood, aware of his intent regard, that way he had of studying every detail so closely, missing nothing, not an inch of her flesh, or the aroused state of her body. Pleased with him and heavy with the sensual power of it, she stepped over him with lazy grace so she straddled his hips. "You will not move, Thomas. I shall put you inside of me, and you will not thrust until I give you permission. When I do, I want to feel every ounce of that male strength you possess."

He nodded. Something steadied in him then, something that made everything in him zero in on what she was about to do, wait on that precipice in anticipatory silence, both body and mind. Like a warrior, facing that last moment before battle, when all anticipation had to be focused on the objective. All senses honed to razor fineness for the split-second life and death decisions that lay directly ahead on the path of his fate. Lowering herself so her knees pressed to the outside of his thighs, she brushed her cunt over his cock, a passing stroke along its length. Gathering up her hair, she stretched above him, using only the strength of her thighs and balance to flirt with that organ, tease it with her undulations. Her dance offered him sinuous arches of her spine, provocative thrusts of her breasts. His gaze was riveted on her, his tongue touching dry lips with hungry need that made her think of that clever mouth between her legs again.

"I will have you quote Dante while you clean my cunt," she whispered, knowing from the heat washing through her that her eyes had flickered to near crimson among the jade lights. "I want to feel the vibration of those words against my skin, my scholar."

'Here must all distrust be left behind; all cowardice must be ended.' His gray eyes were molten steel, and her lips parted at the fervency behind the quote she heard in his mind. She would deny herself no more.

At the next upward roll of her hips, she captured his broad head in the mouth of her sex, took it inside just an inch and squeezed down on it, letting him feel the kiss of moisture and heat. His hands clenched into fists, holding himself back, and she watched the ripple of very non-monkish muscles, from powerful shoulders to striated abdomen and flexing thighs. Thank the Goddess her monk liked hard, physical work. He was lean, but there was no soft spot on him. Except his heart.

Slowly, she let herself glide further down. His engorged organ penetrated deep, stretching her until she came to a rest against his pubic region. The wet petals of her sex kissed him fully, pressing into that intimate area. In the sensitive region between her cunt and buttocks, she could feel the give of his heavy testicles.

She met his brilliant, lust-filled gaze. *Show me your strength, Thomas. Unleash that third mark and do as you will with it.*

Even though she could see it coming, it took her breath, how it possessed him. She had expected him to thrust into her from his current position on his back, take her on a hard ride on his loins. However, that expectation was gone in a flash. Instead, he tore the sash loose from the foot of the bed with a rip of fabric so decisive the strip unraveled from his wrists as he moved. He flipped them, put her under him, one arm locked strong and sure about her waist so he did not tumble her. As he brought her to her back, he reseated himself with a thrust so intent that it wrenched a cry from her own throat at the thrilling rocket of sensation that went through her. His bare body pressed down on hers, his chest against her breasts, his pumping buttocks underneath her heels. She locked him to her, arms and legs clasped with unbreakable strength around his body.

He was moving her with his thrusts, and he cupped his hand under her neck, tilting her head back and returning to her throat, sealing his mouth on that bite mark. Not to drink this time, but to put the impression of his teeth there again, his breath hot and rasping, moist against her sensitive flesh. The hair at his temple brushed the side of her face, his biceps flexing against her arms as he held her just as tightly.

Yes, Thomas. I'm all yours, sweet monk. For tonight, I am as much yours as you are mine. That is the gift the third mark gives us both.

He was beyond words, but as in all things, he amazed her. Though he was a man with no more than a stable lad's experience, he'd learned a great deal from watching her with other lovers. *I will...not release...until I bring you...pleasure.*

It was overwhelming, to hear the thought in his mind against the rutting savagery in his face, in the powerful movements of his body. The way his fingers clamped upon her. Every stroke inside of her was torture and heaven at once. Inside his soul so deeply now, she could feel how it felt to him, the wet silk of her sucking along his length, pulling and drawing on him, demanding his seed. Yet every hard smack when he surged forward brought him against her clit, already well stimulated to swollen need before she'd ever brought him inside her. As she arched up, ready to go with him, he left her throat and bent, taking her left nipple in his mouth, drawing hard, demonstrating a devilish knowledge of the workings of a woman's aroused body.

The shudder of the climax spread through her lower abdomen, making her thighs tingle with heat, and she gave him another gift. She let him into her mind now, let him feel and see it coming, increasing the power of the climax that was about to crash over them both.

"Now, Thomas," she whispered in a thready voice. "Give yourself to me now. All of you." Her whisper escalated into a sound of pleasure as her clit rippled, her sex clutching him hard, demanding he obey her. Riding the power of that wave, she turned the tables on him, flipping them back over with her vampire strength. Taking him to his back, she collared his throat with one hand, holding him to the ground as she worked herself atop him, slamming her hips down on his cock as it began to spurt seed inside of her. One of his hands gripped her hip, the other closing on her rigid forearm. As his eyes met hers, it wasn't clear who was in control...or who wasn't. She knew it didn't matter.

She jerked back against his hold, a cry tearing from her throat as the new angle pushed her up over a higher edge. The jet of his semen increased that pleasure, and she fed herself on his guttural roar of completion. He was as much animal as any man was in such a moment. Yet he was also so much more, her monk.

He went for a while. It had built up in him for a long time, of course, but she knew it was more than that. The carnal intensity of a third mark gave him an increase in stamina and duration. All the things that would bring a vampire mistress greater pleasure, when she used him for her needs.

Only in this case, that knowledge would not be put to use. She already knew he wouldn't break his oath to God again, unless she pushed him to breaking. She might make him pay for his restraint with various little torments, but she had too much regard for him to take it further than that. In the end, they would *both* be tested for the decades ahead.

When he met her gaze, she knew she'd left her mind open to him for that. Though not intentional, she didn't regret it. As the climax slowly ebbed, she eased her grip on his throat and gave him a rueful smile. Her limbs shuddered as she slipped off to lay at his side. She was pleased when his arm came up and around her, gathering her close so that she could rest in the shelter of his body.

"God bless you, my lady," he murmured.

§

He would doze some now, as most men did. She'd turned away to give him that breather, but backed her body into his, encouraging him to curl around her. She liked the feel of his bare chest pressing against her shoulder blades, her long hair spread over both of them, tangled in their limbs. His damp cock pressed against her buttocks, his thighs cupping hers. He had his arm over her, holding her close, his mouth against her neck, which kept a thrum of sensation cycling through her. Every now and then, she made small movements against him, tiny presses, enjoying the feel of his body and wanting to move against it like the ocean, a tidal rhythm of teasing strokes.

He was breathing deeply, yet after a time she knew it

was not the even breath of sleep. She turned in his arms to face him, sliding one long nailed finger along his cheek, her thumb against his mouth. His eyes were stark with emotion and, when she reached into his mind, it was a tangled garden of reaction, thorns and petals, rich soil and the blaze of the sun. "You're all right, my quiet monk?" she asked.

Nodding, he laid his fingers over hers on his mouth, tracing her knuckles. "Though I sometimes doubt my faith, my lady, I am glad I have it. Because if you were my faith, I would follow you through a dozen lifetimes to always be at your side. If you ever gave me your heart as freely as your body, I'm not certain there's anything I wouldn't do for you. It makes me realize that it will take a very, very brave man to dare to love you fully. And," he added with a touch of a smile, "it makes me relieved and yet sad not to be that man."

Tilting her head into his hand, she pressed her mouth to it. "You are brave enough for me, Thomas. I will be glad to have you at my side in this life, as many years as your God is willing to loan you to me. I will consider it singular evidence that He has in fact blessed me."

Then she tilted her head back and gave him her usual devilish smile. "Or cursed *you*."

Thomas gave a half laugh, then a groan as her hands closed on his cock, stirring to life again. "It's still some time until dawn, monk," she said, that relentless glint staying in her eye. "You will serve me until the sun rises."

"As you wish, my lady." *But after the sun rises...*

"If ever you abandon your celibacy, I will gladly welcome you to my bed. But I will never require it of you. While I do not share your view of what God is or demands of his servants, I know the love and faith you carry in your heart. As my third mark, I see how deeply that penetrates you. In truth, I already knew that."

A sad smile touched her lips, but she rose to her elbow, locking her gaze with his. She felt how her next words surprised and moved him, and knew she'd tuck that reaction into her heart, along with everything else about this night. It helped her strengthen her voice, let him hear the promise in it, the oath of a vampire queen.

"Hear me now, before I take you again. When the dawn comes, it will be my privilege, my regret and my torment to honor that part of you. For the rest of our lives together."

Taking The Gloves Off

A vignette featuring Mason and Jessica of Beloved Vampire *from the* Vampire Queen Series.

Originally posted from April through August, 2010 in serial format.

Part 1

Jessica paused in front of the heavy oak door, studying the wood panels. Any other human would simply see a random pattern in the grain, a variety of textures, rough and smooth. But with her third mark, she could take it much further than that. She could see how the wood was smoother, shinier on the area several feet above the ornate doorknob. Where a man, over six feet tall, might put one hand flat to give the door a healthy shove as he turned the knob with the other. Reaching up, she laid her hand over that area, moving it back and forth in a drifting stroke, imagining his palm pressed there.

She'd been coming here a lot lately. Well, in stages. And only when Mason was traveling on Council business, where he was far enough away he couldn't tap into her mind and know what she was doing. She hadn't asked Enrique and Amara, his other servants, to keep it from him, but they seemed to understand that this was her personal battle, and respected her privacy.

Every day he was away from her, he called right before dawn. At his command she was always in his bed, wearing only the covers that bore his scent. He would tell her to touch herself, order her to imagine her touch as his own. Fingers running along her throat, over her mouth, such that her eyes closed, lips parting for him the way all of her body submitted at his merest touch. Then down, trailing over her sternum, moving over to cup a breast. He'd pinch and tease a nipple, ordering her not to move any other muscle of her body as he did it, no matter how restlessly her legs wanted to move, or how she wanted to press her buttocks into the sheets, imagining his body holding hers down, spreading her thighs. The way his long copper hair, unclipped from its usual tie, would trail over her skin like a horse's mane, his muscles flexing, slipping under her fingers as her nails bit into that hard strength.

He would keep it going until her hand was between her legs and she was glad they had a phone with an earpiece, so her trembling fingers weren't required to hold the receiver. He would make her stroke herself until she was so close to climax her voice was breaking. Then he would tell her to roll over on her stomach, hands out to either side like wings. He'd have her legs spread wide, so that she felt the barest flutter of the sheet against her wet cunt where the linen pooled in that triangular area between her thighs. He would ask after her day, what she'd been doing. He'd answer her questions about what he'd done with Council. They'd talk about a million important and minor things, murmur things that could only be spoken in the dark. Finally, just as she sensed the dawn light cresting the waves that lapped up on the beach below their South American home, he'd whisper to her to sleep. "Dream of me, *habiba*, and how much I miss you. How I will touch you when I return, and make you cry out for me."

She returned to the present, finding her palm now had a light sheen of perspiration on it. She'd learned to be extraordinarily disciplined in her life, so it was amazing, how hard it was to resist the response his merest word could bring forth from her. As the bond had grown between them, his sensual ruthlessness had grown as well. It told her she was evolving, becoming more comfortable with the truth that he'd known from the beginning, that she was a natural submissive, a rare gem in his world. But it also told her he, too, was evolving. Back into the type of Master he'd always been, one that could help her explore that natural submission to the limits of her soul. If she could convince him that not only did she want him to do so, she'd reached the point she *needed* it.

God, she missed him. It wasn't so long ago she'd wished him straight to hell, had wanted nothing more than to be left alone by the whole world. She'd fought to survive, and believed surrender was weakness. He'd taught her it could also be strength. But in the process, he'd also made her fall so incredibly in love with him that the same strength turned against her in full force when he was away like this.

She gave herself a mental shake. Okay, time to stop thinking about how crazy he made her and instead focus on this, a way to prove that he didn't have to leave her behind.

At the beginning, she'd only made it to the door to this wing of the house before she turned back. Fled back, if she wanted to be honest. But it got easier, so then she pushed herself to move through that wing and get to the archway that led to this lower level. It had taken several weeks for her to have the courage to merely stare down that winding set of stairs that curved off into darkness, if she didn't turn on the wall sconce lights to guide her way.

Then, one day, she made it partway down the staircase, at least to where that first curve was, hiding what was beyond it. On his subsequent trips away from home, she'd come there just to sit on the stair. She'd bring a book to read or some of Mason's paperwork to do, having taken over most of the administrative needs for his myriad business interests. That spot became her plateau for quite a while. If she lifted her head and stared at that stone wall across from her, trying to coax her eyes to follow it down to the remaining stairs, their twisting descent, she'd feel a similar twisting descent in her feelings and thoughts, one that more often than not sent her scampering back to the safer parts of her world.

Which made her despise herself.

That was why she wasn't ready to share this with Mason, though she was willing to tell him so many other things. He patently disapproved of anything that made her think less of herself. He'd made it very clear there was nothing she needed to face behind that door in order to be the kind of servant he needed her to be.

She believed him. However, he'd agreed to serve on Council for the next twenty-five years, partially as a nod to the Council's clemency to her for her "crime" of killing the monster vampire who'd held her captive for five years. It required a lot of meetings, a lot of travel to Council headquarters and other Regions. Interactions with other vampires always meant sexual games with the servants, a gladiator arena for vampires to explore politics as well as pleasure. Because of that, and what she'd endured at Raithe's hands, Mason refused to take her with him.

With Raithe, vampire gatherings had always held a particular horror for her. But recently, when Lady Lyssa and Daniela had visited with Jacob and Dev, their servants, she'd seen more of what Amara had described, the way such gatherings were supposed to be. For a servant, it could be yet another way to prove loyalty, as well as experience pleasurable surrender to the vampire she called Master. A way to prove she'd step into the fires of her fears and trust that the flame wouldn't burn, as long as she wore his marks.

After that visit, she'd been sure she could soon take that step to the next level, to Council meetings or gatherings of vampires that weren't part of his inner circle. However, he could walk through her mind as easily as she walked through his extensive gardens, and he knew she wasn't there. Five years of brutal trauma didn't vanish overnight. When he made her face that she wasn't ready, even though it infuriated her, she couldn't deny the more-than-lingering signs of it.

Coddling her over it wasn't going to change that, though. She'd trained herself to fight. Why couldn't she train herself to overcome those nightmares and fears, separate them from her present reality? All she had to do was figure out the absolute difference between her past and her present, and believe in that truth utterly. So she'd begun to test herself like this, knowing somehow that room and what it contained would provide the test she most needed.

Finally, after several months of work, she'd made it to the door. Behind it was a personal dungeon that had been used—before Jessica's arrival—to serve Mason and his guests. It was equipped with every possible permutation of BDSM device and tool, things that could drive pain, pleasure, surrender and trust to their absolute limits. Amara had told her provocative stories that made Jessica's body warm as she imagined herself there with Mason. That was the other challenge she faced. *If* she summoned up enough courage to open that heavy oak door, she had to convince him to take his full pleasure of her there, to prove to him she could move on, that she could be more to him.

She liked the stories Amara told her. But what had kept her on the stairs all those weeks, sometimes trembling and caught in living nightmares of her past, was that those same types of implements had been used time and time again to torture her. Not for her pleasure or surrender, or to win her trust, but to win her screams. To break her, force her acceptance of a fate even a demon straight from the fires of hell might have considered heinous. It was a trauma she couldn't banish, no matter how much she fiercely wished she could. And the domineering male vampire she loved with all of her soul wouldn't budge on putting her in situations that he knew would take her back to that horror.

When he visited Council, he took Enrique, the laidback and hot-blooded French-Spaniard who was well suited to the vagaries of Council leisure pursuits. Though he and Amara were married, they'd been part of this life for decades. Amara missed him when he was gone, but she wasn't constantly pricked by visions of him in the midst of some creatively designed orgy for vampire entertainment. No, instead, she eagerly waited for him to come back to her and tell her about it with dramatic flair, more erotic tales to spur the intensity of their reunion lovemaking. Not that it needed spurring. Jessica wryly thought their private room should be designed to be flame retardant.

She slid down against the door, her back braced on that heavy wood, placing her sneakered feet where she expected

Mason's booted feet had often stood, right before he stepped over the threshold. He'd been alone for a long time, no servant, but even during that time he'd occasionally entertained guests. Probably watched or even participated in the things that happened here. Just like he was probably doing at Council dinners.

Though Amara took such things in stride, Jess couldn't. It was ridiculous. She knew Mason's heart. It wasn't that she doubted him, or thought she'd lose the way he felt for her. He hadn't wanted to serve on Council. Hell, the man had been a recluse for over three hundred years and had even scoffed at the idea of a governing body to "civilize vampires." But now he was right in the thick of it.

She knew that watching her, being with her, was what gave him the deepest physical and emotional pleasure. She knew that not because of any false sense of importance, but because she could *feel* it. He had his own demons, his own nightmares, and having her close helped him. Sometimes almost as much as it helped her. He insisted he didn't need her at those Council meetings with him, but she knew it would be far easier for him if she was.

In contrast, he was there for her, always. Even now, if her nightmares took an unexpected spike, or she fell into depression, Amara would call him, despite Jessica's protests. He'd be on the next plane back, the Council be damned.

So get up and open the freaking door. Closing her eyes, she beat her head in a slow tattoo against the wood, but stilled as she heard feet on the stairs. It was Amara. The woman always knew where to find her when Mason was gone. Either in his office, with the horses, on the beach, or sometimes, on the bad days, curled up in his bed, pathetically inhaling his scent. Jess spoke to the sound of those tapping slippers coming her way.

"If he doesn't come home soon, I'm going to put on his most expensive, most favorite shirt, and wear it to muck out the stalls. Then I'll put it back in his closet with all his other clothes and let the odor of horse manure hit him smack in the face when he opens it."

Amara chuckled, the musical resonance of her voice

soothing or stimulating, depending on how she used it. She came into view, wearing one of her translucent gypsy skirts, a deep purple color with tiny bells at the low waistline, and a snug dancer's top, telling Jessica she'd been practicing her intricate belly dancing moves. "And who do you think he'd make do all that laundry?" the woman asked with a gleam in her dark eyes. "Probably the old fashioned way, too, on a washboard over a steaming hot tub. Naked."

She sat down next to Jessica, her lovely backside sliding gracefully to the floor so the point of her hip pressed with affectionate intimacy against hers. "You made it to the door."

They hadn't asked her much about this battle of hers or stated their opinion of it one way or another. However, Amara and Enrique had almost psychic intuition. It was an attribute she'd come to appreciate, because it saved having to explain things. For the first time, though, Amara let that simple statement convey an encouragement that warmed Jessica. She understood what Jess was trying to do and, what's more, approved of it.

"I don't want him off without me, doing this kind of thing," Jess said. "It makes me crazy, imagining him watching other Council servants do whatever outrageous things the Council wants them to do, and him sitting there, all alone and removed from it. Or just as bad, I see two or three of them crawling across the floor to his legs, sliding their hands up his thighs, maybe one of them plopping her obscenely perfect ass in his lap..." She blew out a breath at Amara's amused look. "And it's not jealousy, not exactly. I just..."

"He's yours. Your Master to serve, not another servant's duty."

Jessica nodded, relieved to hear it voiced so accurately. "But you're his servant, and you don't get all that worked up about it."

"Because it's not the same for me and Enrique. Mason takes his pleasure with us, yes, uses us for blood, but our bond is affection, regard, service. It is far different with you. He is consumed by you, and you by him." Amara nudged her. "I would say love, but of course that's the most heinous of four-letter words to vampire kind. It's all right for him to whisper it to you in the night's darkness, but not to speak it aloud." She gave Jess a searching look, sobering. "Would you really want to be there, to see all of that going on?"

"At least I'd have the opportunity to be at the forefront of it. And I know him. He'd be watching them, sending me thoughts in that sexy mind-whisper of his. 'This is what I want to do to you later.' Or, if I'm in the thick of it"—she swallowed, refusing to let the cold fear take over at the thought, and instead focused on her imaginings—"he'd be saying 'pretend it's me, touching you like this, holding you.' Anything is better than being home where I'm going insane over it, over him being gone."

Despite Amara's teasing, Mason never concealed his feelings for her here. He'd told Jess he loved her, often and well, in various, immutable ways. She was just as bad about that. However, since she was a "lowly human," it was acceptable for her to be besotted. Sometimes it made her laugh at herself. She was like a lovesick teenager, wearing one of his shirts when he was gone. It made her think again of what she'd threatened to do with one of those garments, and Amara's idea about his punishment. She could see it, her muscles straining as she ran the shirt over the washboard, her breasts glistening with creamy rivulets of soap and perspiration. He'd come up behind her to slide his hands over those slick curves, pressing his body against hers. Whisper that she would continue scrubbing as he unfastened his snug riding breeches and plunged into her, working her body as she lost her rhythm, grasped the board for dear life and gasped her pleasure.

They were getting to the point she could actually believe he would mete out such a sensual punishment. And she would welcome it, enough to dare such a defiant act.

That was the key to turning that doorknob. How would it be any different, in this room behind her? *It wouldn't.* If he restrained her to a St. Andrew's cross in this room, or bent her over a spanking bench, it would be him doing it, the fascinating, powerful male vampire who loved her and protected her even from his own kind. Who she trusted not to be Raithe, to prove to her that all vampire gatherings were not like what she'd endured with him. She could do this, she was ready for it.

In her ruminations and Amara's words, she realized what bothered her the most of all. The real matter was trust. In order for him to believe he could take her with him, he had to believe she trusted him. That she could handle anything they threw at them, because she loved him and loved serving him. That anything that gave him pleasure would give her pleasure, and anything that didn't give him pleasure, she knew he wouldn't permit. In order to fully be her Master, he had to know she fully trusted him.

She took a deep breath, quietly amazed with what seemed so obvious now. It was a gift only she could give him, the male who seemed to have everything. But registering Amara's expectant look, she struggled to focus. "You came down to tell me something."

"Yes. Enrique will be home within the hour."

Jessica knew her face lit up like a Christmas tree, because Amara's reflected it. The woman was as excited as she was about the return of their men. "And Mason?" She seized Amara's hands, squeezed them so the bones creaked. The woman laughed, returning the favor. "Mason is on a slightly later flight, because he had to do some last minute shopping. Probably gifts for you, as well as some small token for me." Her gaze gleamed. "Which, given our different tastes, means a silver belt with cut gems for one of my dance costumes, and a set of rusty horseshoes from a junk store for you."

"Hey, not my fault that I'm the cheaper date."

Amara snorted, a delicate sound for her. It reminded Jess of Hasna, Mason's dainty white Arabian mare. "Well, if you're planning to invoke his wrath with your manure-scented shirt scheme, you only have a few hours to execute it. He'll be within range of your mind by full dark."

The thrill of that, of knowing he'd be home that soon, made Jess burn with impatience, a sensation that affected every part of her. Her skin heated at the idea of his hands on it, everywhere. Not just because of how he kept her stirred with his calls, but because the moment Mason came into the house, he always made it very clear that he'd missed her.

The first time, he'd cleared the kitchen with barely a look, the staff scrambling to make themselves absent as Mason lifted her without preamble and took her down on her back on the butcher block table. He'd possessed her with an animal hunger that could arouse her just in remembrance. Almost a rebranding of her soul, a reminder of what those three marks meant. Bound together, for all eternity.

Despite the blazing fire such imaginings brought her, she managed a smile for Amara. But then an idea struck her. She had to convince him that she could handle the type of punishments that existed behind this door, right? That not only did she trust him to take off the gloves, but that she *wanted* him to do so.

He kept a leash on his dominant male vampire nature around her, but she'd been feeling the strain on that tether, more and more. She wanted to snap it. However, as she imagined what provocation might accomplish that, it was far more than a manure-scented shirt. He was stubbornly protective of her, but more than that, he was possessive. And that, too, was a key to what she wanted. A key that might galvanize that vampire nature to full, terrifying dominance over her, no turning back. It gave her a shiver, one that she was absolutely, thrillingly convinced was not all fear.

"Amara, what's the one thing Mason expressly forbids me to do while he's gone? Other than endanger myself in any way, which in his mind includes even using butter knives?"

The woman laughed, but studied Jess as if she could tell she was up to some kind of mischief. Her eyes sparkled. "There are several things. You cannot make yourself climax. You and I cannot play with one another and instigate a climax, nor can Enrique, when he is here with us. It makes all of us quite eager to see him arrive, the scoundrel. And most importantly, he is quite adamant that no man touches you at all while he's gone. Not if that man wants to live."

"Hmm." Jessica shifted onto her knees to face the other woman. She continued to hold Amara's hands as she looked up at that door, the wood worn down by the placement of Mason's strong hand. Cocking her head, Jess considered her fellow third marked servant.

"Do you and Enrique feel like living dangerously?"

Part 2

One hour. One hour until Mason's mind would be in range of hers, if Amara's estimate was right. Jessica had had a despicable urge to wait until then, so she could use his presence in her head to give her additional courage to start this, let alone finish it, but she knew that was what she had to prove to him. That if she was at a Council meeting, and Lord Belizar said he wanted to see a threesome involving two males and one female servant, and she was the chosen female, she wouldn't disgrace Mason by bolting like a spotted fawn. That she could handle herself and he could rely on her to serve him as a Council-level servant should.

Still, she jumped, badly, when Amara touched her arm. Jess was at the top of the steps again, only this time she'd been waiting for them. Amara slid an arm around her waist. She was in one of her thin sheer robes, the peacock print of rich colors only accenting the glimpses of tempting curves. Her only other adornment was a collar of silver links that Jessica knew was a gift from Enrique.

"There's no reason to be afraid," Amara reminded her gently.

"Yes. That's my job," Enrique added. Jessica turned to him, trying to let his wry smile dissipate her trepidation. Despite him just returning from what was likely a grueling trip, he looked his normal self—sexy as sin, his features a devastating cross of the most appealing traits of his French and Spanish parentage. His closely cropped dark hair had a few loose unruly strands over his forehead, which only made the green eyes with their black eyebrows that much more direct and appealing. There was always a casual slouch to his leanly muscled body that suggested a lazy panther. He wore black slacks and a crisp dress shirt, simple, clean lines that sent a subtle message of power and authority, underscoring the role he would play tonight.

His mouth had that slight, sensual curve that implied all the sinful things he could do with it. And, if his wife was nearby, he often did. Though Jessica knew he was quite devoted to Amara, before she'd taken his heart, he'd accumulated a great deal of skill in bringing pleasure to women, a mutually beneficial education.

She could appreciate all those things about Enrique, even though tonight they sent a ripple of nervousness through her. She pushed it away, but she was already getting that cold ball in her stomach. An ominous sign, but she was determined to ignore it.

Not too long ago, before Enrique had left to join Mason on this trip, the three of them had watched *The Mummy Returns*. With Jess's mind on Mason's return, it wasn't surprising her mind now returned to one absorbing feature of the film. The Pharaoh's woman had been covered with intricate ink markings that would smear upon touch, so it would be clear if another had touched what was Pharaoh's. Over the past few months, Mason had branded Jess over and over again with mouth, lips, hands. He'd sunk deep inside of her, taken her in ways so gentle her heart almost broke. Or so rough and demanding she was sobbing with pleasure and exhaustion by the end, too drained to move.

Every inch of her was totally, completely his, such that she had zero desire for that design to be disrupted by the touch of another man, ever again.

But she was servant to a Council vampire, and those servants had learned that they could and would be touched by many others, merely as an extension of their Master or Mistress's desires for them. She had intimate knowledge of the dark side of such a world, violations of mind, body and soul that ignored any boundaries that compassion or simply viewing her as a living being might have imposed. But when Lady Lyssa and Lady Daniela had visited with Jacob and Dev, she'd had a brief glimpse how it could be.

Pleasurable caresses and laughter, demands that aroused desire, instead of destroying or subjugating it.

So while she was nervous with Enrique's presence, she was okay. She told herself that, took a few deep breaths and only stiffened a bit when he slid his arms around her waist from behind. He had strong, gentle hands. Warm, and they took their time, slowly molding the shape of her waist, thumbs sliding over her abdomen. He kept his palms still, so his fingers wouldn't exceed the reach of that location, but the sensation tingled uneasily above and below his knowledgeable caress. Moving in front of her, Amara gathered Jessica's hair up in both hands, then transferred it to one to bring it forward over her left shoulder.

"I love your hair long," the woman murmured. She combed it over the curve of Jess's breast as Enrique bent his head and dropped a light kiss, just a brush of lips, at the now bare juncture of shoulder and neck. A place that Mason liked to mark with his fangs regularly. It was something that Enrique had noticed, and now used, helping her recall her Master's touch and desires. How she could please him.

She had come such a long way, to be having such thoughts naturally. There was a time even thinking in such a way would have terrified her, horrified her. But with Mason she'd learned things could be different. That was the thought she needed to carry forward.

"I think we shall leave this up here." Amara tugged the sash of Jessica's robe loose. Hers was a pale blue satin, not nearly as see-through as Amara's, but one that Mason liked because of how the satin clung to Jess's curves, showing the tips of her breasts in profile when she turned toward him. The woman kept her gaze on Jess's face, gauging her reaction as she opened the garment. Underneath, Jess wore nothing at all, making her shiver from the draft coming up the stairs. Enrique slid it off her shoulders, and Amara produced something from the pocket of her robe that was unexpected. And startling.

She'd discussed what she wanted. Jess wanted to go to that dungeon room, and submit to them as a trusting slave would, so from this step forward, she was supposed to be theirs. She'd resisted the idea of choreographing every move, knowing that trying to control every step would defeat the purpose. Though now she wondered if she'd lost her mind. What was in Amara's hand was a slim silver collar and dainty tether.

"You will trust yourself to us, remember?" the olive-skinned woman said, her long-lashed, dark eyes on Jess's. "And see, this can be broken, so easily. It is practically a child's trinket. Vampires do not use safe words, Jessica, but with us, you merely need to say stop, and we will honor you still. All right?"

Jessica nodded, not sure she could speak.

Enrique put his hands back at her waist, making contact with bare flesh. With his next words, the quiet, firm tone, she was reminded that, as Amara's husband, he often served as her Master, though they both submitted to Mason.

"Ask Amara to collar you." His fingers played along her flesh, his knuckles stroking the curve of hip. His thumb teased her navel, the piercing that she'd recently gotten there. Amara had talked her into it, and Mason approved. It would hold against a third mark healing, as long as it wasn't removed. It had an amber center stone amid tiny diamond petals. Mason had bought it for her, an appropriate complement to the tattoo on her back, a tiger peering through bamboo, stalking his prey.

"Be sure and say please, as you would to a Mistress or Master."

"Please...I would like you to collar me." Her voice broke enough that she saw a flash of concern in Amara's eyes, but Jess tightened her chin and lifted it, giving the woman access. "I turn myself over to your pleasure...Mistress."

"Very good," Enrique murmured.

Amara's eyes glowed with similar approbation as she fastened the silver cuff around Jess's throat. The fit was not tight, lying on her collar bone. Jess wondered how they would react if she now blithely decided "yep, that's enough for one night," and hightailed it for the safety of her horses and her usual evening routine. The handful of staff who had quarters on site would be in the communal and workout areas provided for them. They'd be watching TV, playing pool and possibly talking the cook into making them snacks before they turned in for the night, if they didn't get embroiled in a marathon poker game. It was a safe hangout for her, a familiar haven.

Amara snapped the silver tether on the collar and gave it the tiniest of tugs, her fingers curling in Jessica's loose hair adding to that pull. "Come, darling," she said. "You're so beautiful. You can't imagine how we're looking forward to this."

Jess made that first step, then the second. She was going along just fine, if a bit hesitantly, until she reached that fateful curve in the stairs. Then she stumbled.

In an instant, Enrique's touch went from an easy caress at the small of her back to a full cinch around her waist, and Amara was pressed up against her, holding her steady so she didn't take a headlong tumble down the stone steps.

"I shouldn't be doing this," Jess said. "I shouldn't be asking you to do this."

"Yes, you should." Amara's voice was no longer seductive, teasing. The even tone revealed the core of steel that hid inside the otherwise perfectly submissive and beautiful dancer. She met Jess's gaze. "We believe you're doing the right thing, Jessica. He needs this side of you, and we think you're ready for it as well. We believe in you."

Jess glanced up to find Enrique's green eyes on his wife's face, but he turned his attention to Jessica and nodded, his handsome jaw set. "We will force you to do nothing, but we will not let you quit on yourself, either. This is too important, for both of you. We are here for you, Jessica."

Jessica remembered how often she'd let rage take over her terror, in order to get through horrible moments with Raithe. She'd used rage because she'd had nothing and no one else to help her get through it. Here she was, surrounded fore and aft by a man and woman who had given her friendship to the deepest level, enough that she thought of them as family. And the greatest threat she faced from Mason was his overprotective nature, the lengths he would go to keep her safe, happy and unafraid.

It made her feel foolish, even as it frustrated her. If she couldn't do this in such ideal circumstances, how would she ever do it at a Council event, where there would be unfamiliar faces, hands? Just that thought alone froze her feet into place. But they were ready for that as well.

"Enrique." Amara's voice had returned to that liquid purr. "I know how much you enjoy carrying a lovely naked woman in your arms. Will you do the honors?"

"My pleasure." He bent just enough to slide his arm under Jessica's legs, guiding her other arm around his neck as he lifted her. Though he had a third mark's strength, he also had a power of his own that made the way he carried her feel very capable, very secure. She knew Amara loved Enrique for his own unique traits, but he had much of Mason in him too, which she suspected enhanced their bond all the more.

"She's gained a bit of weight since she showed up here like a thin scarecrow," he observed, a teasing smile on his lips. "Now there are squeezable curves in all the right places."

Jess gave his hair, short though it was, a yank. He flashed her his devilish grin. "That will likely earn you your first punishment, not-so-little slave."

"You have to be in the practice room with me sometime," she pointed out, giving him a narrow look, though her lips quivered at the teasing. "And I'll put my not-so-little foot up your—"

"Tsk, tsk." Amara threw a look over her shoulder. "Don't make us start off the evening with a gag. Particularly when we were looking forward to hearing your cries of pleasure, dearest."

Just like that, the cold terror flooded her. Gags. Straps. Devices. They were approaching that door.

Suddenly, she was eight years old, going for her first operation. She was getting her tonsils out. Her mother had soothed her, just as Enrique and Amara were doing now, with their strategic teasing and artful touches, but when the moment had come, her mother had to withdraw and Jess had faced that operating room of sterile, sharp instruments, strangers in masks, bright lights. She'd felt terror deep in her gut, knowing she couldn't run, but sensing there were things that could go so terribly wrong in such a place.

"Jess." Enrique was trying not to tighten his hold against her struggles, trying not to add to her sense of being trapped, but not wanting to drop her either. "Look."

She saw the door had already been opened. The threshold and short series of stone steps just beyond it had been covered with petals. Soft white petals from the gardens outside. As she stilled enough for Enrique to take her over that threshold, Amara leading the way, she saw that all those devices, as well as the wall of paddles and whips, were covered with gauzy fabrics—blues, whites and lavenders, a few golds and reds with sequins, part of Amara's endless array of costumes and props for her private performances. The graceful draping transformed such objects into features in a sky, and she was just a cloud floating among them.

"You weren't supposed to do this. You weren't supposed to change things."

"Hush." Enrique spoke, his firm tone returning. "You ask too much of yourself, Jessica. We know this about you. You asked us to serve as your surrogate Master and Mistress tonight. What is the first role of a Master or Mistress? Not only to understand when a submissive is ready to stretch herself further, surrender more deeply, but also to know where her limits are. For tonight, this will be more than enough. Both to prove your serious intentions to my lord, and to yourself."

Amara nodded. "And if you'll notice, sweet, you've refused to look toward the one thing that *is* uncovered. Look toward it now."

Enrique let Jess down so she could stand on her own two feet, but Amara kept the tether taut and his hands were on her hips, both steadying her and reinforcing the command she'd given them over her person tonight. Swallowing, she forced her eyes toward the St. Andrew's cross. Tall and imposing, the heavy wood made it clear that anyone strapped to it would only be getting loose at the direction of their Master. There were no cuffs on it tonight, though. Just the metal handles for a slave to grasp, and the foot rests to support her if the cross was raised to a vertical position, as it was now.

Amara led her over to it, Enrique shepherding her from behind, male fingers teasing her flesh. It made her ache, thinking of Mason's return later tonight, how his strong hands would move over her, grip her hips to hold her still as he stretched her with his length. He'd make her stay completely still until he was fully to the hilt. Then he would slowly, slowly withdraw and surge forward, still keeping her motionless, repeating the torturous rhythm until the first climax would tremble over her like a shudder through the earth's plates. He'd devour her cries with his mouth.

But such a provocative imagining wasn't enough to banish other, far darker thoughts. When she was within ten feet of the cross, she had to stop again. Amara turned, looked into her face, and her own expression shadowed. "The horror in your eyes, love..." Threading her fingers into Jessica's hair, she brought her forward until her face was pressed into Amara's shoulder. "Those memories cannot have you here," the woman whispered. "We won't let them. Use that great courage of yours, sweet girl."

She needed Mason. She wasn't going to be able to do this without Mason. Yet Mason wouldn't allow her to do this. This room was the bridge between past and present, and she had to cross it. But he'd taught her she didn't have to do these things alone. He would be with her. Was she ignoring her own earlier revelation? By going ahead and doing this in this manner, was she not trusting him enough? Or was it because she needed to prove it to herself first?

"I can't look at it and do this," she whispered back. "I want to, but I can't."

"Then don't. Just hold onto me." Amara turned her, like they were practicing their dancing together. She started humming one of those haunting, exotic tunes, moving her feet forward and back, getting Jess to follow her lead, still holding her close. Adding some hip circles to it, Amara dropped her hands to Jess's hips, guiding her in the figure eights they'd practiced together and at which Jessica was now pretty good, enough that Mason would sometimes ask her to dance for him, just as he did Amara.

Jess was usually naked when he made the request, just as she was now. The idea gave her a tiny smile, and then her breath left her in a cold gasp as she was pressed against the hard wood. But Amara had her hands, was still dancing with her. She guided her arms around, up, then down, a graceful swan's wing move. Jess's eyes opened to find the woman's intent gaze on hers, as if to say, *Just dance with me, look at me. That is all this is. A dance.*

This time when she guided Jess's hands up, Enrique slid in between them and lifted Jess, putting her feet on the foot rests. Amara threaded her fingers under the silver handles, molding them over the cool steel so Jess was grasping them.

"Do not let them go." Enrique straightened. "Eyes down, and listen to me with all your senses. Your eyes do you no good here. They keep you from truly seeing."

"Don't blindfold me." It was a panicked request, and his voice gentled.

"No. Not this time. But keep your eyes down or closed unless we tell you otherwise. You are restrained by our command. You will not let go of those handles, no matter what." Then his attention turned to his wife. "Take off your robe."

It was an entirely different tone, similar to what Mason had started using with Jess in the intimacy of their bedroom. A commanding timbre that had told Jess her vampire` was becoming more confident in what level of Mastery she could handle, and which had helped to start her on this road.

Amara complied instantly, loosening her own sash and letting the silk pool at her feet. She had a clitoral hood piercing, the jewel there a trio of silver links, a tiny diamond threaded on the one that hung down over her labia. It complemented the silver links at her throat. Jess saw all that with a surreptitious look under her lashes. Now they were both naked, and her stomach was quaking as if a new enemy had been unveiled, rather than an ally.

She shouldn't be thinking of this in terms of enemy

positioning, should she? That in itself said she wasn't in the right mindset. Her palms were sweating, such that the metal handles were slick. She could do this. She could.

"Go to her," Enrique said to his wife. "You may seek your pleasure with her, arouse her as you will, but your hands must clasp hers, your feet on the outside of the footrests, your body covering her in a spread position, facing her. Your hair needs to be out of my way for what I wish to do next."

Amara knelt, a brief obeisance, and turned to Jessica. As Enrique moved away among the swathes of cloth, Jessica imagined that there was a secretive, anticipatory smile playing on the dancer's lips. Amara twisted up her long, black hair, knotting it deftly before she moved to obey Enrique's direction. She positioned her feet on the outside of Jess's, lithely balanced on the not-so-wide platforms, then clasped her hands over the silver handles. It stretched her lithe body in a matching X to Jess's, their bare breasts pressed together, those tiny rings at Amara's pussy brushing against Jessica's pubic mound, making her quiver.

She'd felt a tiny sensation when Enrique kissed her neck, but most of what she'd experienced so far had been warring with icy fear and tension. Now she was dealing with a woman who had superlative experience in arousing men and women, who knew that the idle, erratic friction of that pierced clit against Jess's, the grip of her hands, would help stir her blood.

"You are already thinking of what he will do to you tonight, aren't you?" Amara's mouth found the tender flesh under Jess's ear. Instead of Enrique's light brush of lips, this was a heated, wet nip and tease of the tongue, stroking with unerring accuracy along Jess's increasing pulse. "He will be wild for you, having been gone so long. Longer than he's ever been away from you. You already feel the quickening for him between your legs, I can smell it." With an impish smile that told Jess she was testing her own Master's command, Amara dropped one hand from the handle to stroke through the slickness between Jess's legs. Jess emitted a soft whimper, another shudder. "You miss his cock inside of you, his body holding you down, reminding you that you are his, helpless to his desire for you."

"Yes," Jessica whispered, arching her throat as Amara bit harder. Her fingers stayed between Jess's legs, spread and vulnerable to her touch. Though it felt so good, it made Jess imagine her legs actually bound, unable to close. "Amara, I'm afraid."

"There is nothing to fear. You belong to him. Anything you do to serve him only brings you pleasure."

Enrique returned then, and, though she wasn't supposed to look, Jessica saw he'd withdrawn a flogger from the wall. Multiple leather tails that would make a loud thwack when they landed. She knew from personal experience that style of flogger could also deliver a sharp, cutting sting when wielded hard enough. Over time, it would raise welts, then burst open the skin as the flogger was applied again and again and again.

Amara had both of her hands once more, so when she tried to pull her hands free, she couldn't get them to slip out from under the arch of the metal handles. "Let me go," Jess said sharply.

"No," Amara said, meeting her gaze. "These next few minutes, you are not going to be flogged, Jessica. I am. You will simply feel how my body reacts to it, how it can be when it's done correctly. Sssh...be still. Serve your Master, Jessica. Be still."

Jessica managed to stop yanking against Amara's hold. She hadn't gotten loose regardless, a reminder that, though they were both third marked, Amara had been third marked longer and had greater strength. She knew she was wide-eyed, and that spiral of tentative arousal Amara had started had evaporated in an instant of dry-mouthed panic at the site of the tool. But she'd said the right words. *Serve your Master. Serve Mason.* This was for Mason.

"Jessica, I want you to close your eyes."

"I...I can't."

"Try. I promise it will be worth it."

Jessica managed it after a few minutes of deep breathing, as well as some rapid-fire internal arguments, supplemented by Enrique and Amara's encouragement.

"I am coming close to you." Enrique's calm, relentless voice. "I'm not going to strike you or Amara with the flogger. It's going to touch your face."

She flinched anyway when the straps, deceptively softer like this, brushed her cheeks, her mouth.

"You cannot imagine how much pleasure Mason gets from using this. It's one of his favorites." This from Amara, in a soft, dreamy tone. "He can rouse all the nerves in your back and thighs, then make it lick against your cunt like a rough tongue, over and over. After awhile, he spreads out the strokes, making them harder, until you're feeling a faint sting, then a stronger one. But even as that happens, your clit is getting fuller, so swollen that you start crying out with pleasure at each strike. You can't really come, so over-sensitized, but you are so close. When you think you can bear no more, he comes and turns the cross over, so your pussy comes up to the level of his mouth. He buries his tongue deep inside, his mouth sealing over your clit. You explode like a ripe, juicy fruit, and that's what he likes best about the method. He has taught a different variation to Enrique, which he will show us now."

She could imagine what Amara painted vividly. Could see Mason's hand curved over the flogger's handle. The stern, sensual set of his mouth, the glow of the amber eyes as he used it.

She opened her eyes to see Enrique holding Amara's hand, the one that had been stroking Jessica. His eyes on his wife's face, Enrique suckled those two fingers, tasting Jessica and giving Amara a stern, reproving look. "You'll be punished for that."

"Whatever gives you pleasure, Master." Amara lowered her eyes, a slight smile on her face, and Enrique arched a brow, throwing Jessica a mildly exasperated look that eased some of the tension in her stomach. That is, until he replaced Amara's hand over Jessica's and gave the olive-skinned woman a meaningful tap with the flogger on one bare buttock. "Do not move it again," he warned.

Enrique's footsteps moved back and Amara's hands tightened over hers. "It's like the start of a roller coaster, love," the dancer whispered. "That sense of fear and trepidation about to be turned to exhilaration. Trust us to go over that hill. No, don't close your eyes again. Try to watch."

Jess lifted her lids to see Enrique standing at a proper distance behind his wife. Shaking out the flogger, he gave Jess a nod. "First, I will simply warm up her flesh."

She had to close her eyes again on that first strike, but she felt the way it struck Amara's back, the thud of it vibrating, quivering through her breasts. The woman's gasp against her cheek, the brush of her lips, the flick of a tongue as Amara moistened her own lips. Another strike, the sharp slap making it clear the flogger had a bite when Enrique chose to start using it. The moment he'd thrown the first overhand strike, Jess had started to shake, and now she was fully quivering against Amara, trying to hold her ground. It took ten strikes before she could open her eyes. The woman's nipples, pressed against Jess's chest, were hardening. Despite having her legs spread on the outside of Jess's, she was moving her hips, a slow, short rub against Jess's pubic bone with each stroke, a mewl of need. Jess expected that Enrique's view of his wife's sensually undulating hips, moving in circles over Jess's naked body, had to be arousing him.

Jess reached for her own building response desperately, knowing it was there, just out of her reach, that submissive's pleasure that came with surrendering. The flogger tails flashed out and Amara arched harder this time, making Jess gasp at the increased pressure against her sex, the building friction.

"Now underhanded, love," Amara managed. "Please."

Jess didn't fully comprehend until Enrique took a step in, changed his stance and swing. The straps slapped the inside of Amara's thighs...and Jess's. She jumped, the sensation tingling up between her legs, but Enrique had followed that strike with an immediate second one. It struck Jess's wet labia with a smack of sensation that had her pushing into Amara, increasing the stimulation to her clit by the other woman's. "Oh. *Oh.*"

"Our pretty little slave likes your technique," Amara said

when Enrique paused after five more strokes. Jess had let out a small moan on the last one, and Amara's voice was a bit strained as well.

Enrique arched a brow, idly swinging the flogger against his cocked hip. "I don't hear her asking for more."

"Ask for more," Amara suggested, catching Jess's ear in her teeth. "Please Goddess, ask for more for us."

"More," Jess managed, her voice quavering. She thought she might be about to split apart, divided between the way her body was reacting and the maelstrom of feelings this was stirring inside of her, a cyclone starting to turn faster and faster. So much pain and mental damage had been done to her like this, but Enrique was skillfully making it clear how much it *hadn't* had to be like that. But Raithe had been a sadistic bastard, a demon who was even now laughing at her somewhere, because that darkness was grasping at her with dry, sharp fingers, trying to pull the pleasure away from her.

She fought it. This was different, a wholly new world discovered in herself. But the dark was welling up on all sides, threatening it. She whimpered as Enrique resumed, because she was afraid of where her feelings were going, and what would happen when they got there. What would break loose with the physical explosion of a climax?

She cried out this time when the straps licked up between her legs. She didn't know if Enrique gave the order, but he must have, for Amara freed herself and backed away, kneeling nearby as her husband resumed the flogging, but now only on Jessica. Jess saw the flogger flash out, watched the straps hit between her legs, and moaned again.

"I can't..." No. She could, and that was the point, right? She could do this. She just hadn't expected this clawing spiral of irrefutable arousal to be so tangled with all the rest, as if the nightmares were coming to the surface with the orgasm. That tidal wave might overwhelm her, take her on a wild, thrilling ride, but when it got to shore, it would drown her, pummel her.

She lost time, her body bucking with the movement of the lash, getting heavier and needier by the moment, her ability to speak prohibited by the roar of that storm.

When Enrique paused again, a breather, she tried to marshal her thoughts, form words, but then Amara was there. The woman bent, cupping Jess's breasts in her capable, long-fingered hands, and began tonguing Jessica's nipples. Enrique took a seat on a stool to watch. When he braced a leg on one of the higher rungs, it outlined the prominent erection beneath his slacks. He twitched the flogger in his hand, a warning of more to come.

That, and the merest touch of Amara's hands and mouth, made Jessica cry out again. Everything was gathering, centering in her core. For days her body had been brought to a near-boil by Mason's nightly calls, held there by her anticipation and longing of his return. She hadn't had a single climax since he was gone. Now she was so perilously close to one, and it seemed they'd barely started.

A moment later she realized she was wrong about that. Apparently, it had been over an hour. Enrique had managed a commanding and masterful tone quite easily, but it was nothing compared to the silky and dangerous words that resonated through her mind now.

Habiba. That one word was enough to send shivers down her spine, make her heart leap into her throat. Her pussy tightened on its own emptiness, contracting on all the ready moisture there.

You will explain to me what you are doing. Right after you get down from there and put on some clothes. Now.

Part 3

Intro: During the time this vignette was written, a reader was offered the chance to win a "walk-on" part. The winner, Helen ("Shyness" on the JWH Connection fan forum), gave me a few basic facts about herself, and I interwove fact and fiction to create this section. We had quite a bit of fun with it. It's kind of a "step into her shoes" scenario, where each of us can imagine a chance encounter in which we not only get to meet a favored character, but help him out in some useful way (grin).

Because of the timing of it, this part featuring Helen was placed about an hour BEFORE Mason is within range of Jessica's mind. So he hasn't yet discovered what Jessica is doing, as noted at the end of the previous segment. After this part with Helen, we return to where we left off with Jess. Don't skip this segue, however! As noted above, Helen's participation provided a key revelation for Mason that is pertinent to the later sections. So here we go...

§

Helen Shyness slipped her feet out of her heeled sandals and buried her toes in the deep carpet, marveling at the lush feel of it, as well as the rest of her opulent surroundings. She still couldn't believe she was on her way to the American Geophysical Union to accept an award for the climate science paper she'd published. She hadn't expected publication to happen for years after her thesis, let alone receive an award. Hell, she'd been delighted to simply *finish* her PhD. The greatest prize she'd anticipated from that was no longer hearing, "How's it going? Are you done *yet?*" from her well-meaning family and friends.

However, this prize, as well as the full course treatment that AGU had arranged to go with it, was serious icing on the cake.

After making a landing from the long crossover flight from Australia, she'd been braced to wait for her connection in the crowded main terminal. Instead, she'd been escorted to a waiting area reserved for dignitaries and other parties traveling by private plane. Since it was late, at least in this time zone, she was the only one here, with the exception of an attractive, well-groomed concierge in a snugly fitted dark suit. The woman was standing behind a desk, ready to respond to Helen's every need. At first, the concierge had made her a bit uncomfortable, in that way that occurred when you were the only two people in a room. That awkward expectation of having to interact. Even in this, though, she was pleasantly surprised. The woman stayed discreetly busy at her desk, giving Helen a sense of privacy she appreciated.

She liked not having to talk to anyone as she looked at the comfortable reclining chairs and sectional sofa arrangements, accented with coffee and end tables that she'd have expected in a well appointed living room rather than an airport terminal. No chairs bolted to the floor in rows. No fluorescent lighting. There were lamps on the table that threw warm yellow light out for reading. There was even original artwork placed between the dim bronze wall sconces, and potted plants with a profusion of greenery and tropical flowers. She'd taken a closer look at a couple of spiral topiaries, digging in among the ivy to check out the forms, despite the concierge's sidelong look. She'd just finished creating a topiary of a sea monster in her own backyard, one that looked like it was about to dive into her manmade pond. On the flight over, she'd passed the time looking through a big book of forms, trying to decide what she'd do next. It was a solitary hobby—her favorite kind.

All that aside, the fancy surroundings and VIP treatment made her glad she'd dressed up a bit for the trip. While she normally preferred her long sleeved T-shirts and jeans, before she landed, she'd changed into a favorite pair of fitted trousers and a medieval style top in swirling blue-green color, the sleeves flaring just past the wrists. The ensemble was enhanced with silver and teal jewelry that brought out the blue in her eyes. She hadn't yet taken down her waist-length brown hair to brush it out and do a better job of re-pinning it, but as she took a seat on one end of a comfortable-enough-to-nap sofa, she found her brush in her bag and set it on the arm so she could do just that. She might still be a few hours from her destination, but she wanted to look damn good to reflect the way she felt inside. Deeply satisfied that all the hard work she'd put into earning her PhD, writing her thesis and pushing for publication had been worth it.

Because she had time, though, instead of doing her hair immediately, she decided to put on her ear phones and listen to her iPod. As the *Metamorphosis* track filled her head, her fingers played the notes out on her knee. She loved the music, which she'd heard on *Battlestar Galactica*, one of the plethora of sci-fi shows she preferred to watch above any other genre—she was a scientist, after all.

Heaven must be like this. A quiet room provided with every comfort. A panorama of windows, the darkness and jeweled lights of the airport coming through like a star-filled sky at eye level. It was so...satisfying, to be relaxing here, being treated like someone important, while at the same time not being so inundated with attention that she couldn't have this isolated moment of time to savor it without interruption.

Of course, everything was temporary. A surge of air told her someone had opened the door to the waiting area. She squelched the twinge of disappointment, trying not to resent the interruption of her fantasy, being queen of her airport domain. She hoped it was no one who would feel the need to be sociable with her. She cracked open an eye. Reflexively, both eyes came wide open.

Okay, she really was in a fantasy dream world. Because if this bloke was part of the amenities of this room, she was never leaving. Award? What award? She was keeping her ass right here.

He was well over six feet, which meant he'd be taller than her 5' 10"—six feet in her heeled sandals. That was a point for him already. His long hair was the color of a tiger's copper-gold markings, with the silken texture of a horse's well-brushed mane. Despite being pulled back and held by a silver buckle tie, a few strands of it had worked their way forward, gleaming across one broad shoulder. He wore belted gray slacks and a dark turtleneck that molded to his upper body and told her he was extremely fit. When his eyes briefly turned to her, it gave her a start. Those amber eyes were not made in nature. She thought he must wear contacts, but the idea didn't seem to suit him. Despite his awesome appearance, he didn't give off vain, pretentious vibes. It was almost like his appearance was an effortless afterthought. If he was a woman, she'd have hated him on principle. But in this case, Helen could only admire.

There was an impatient and very physical energy emanating off him as he nodded shortly to the concierge.

She'd asked if he wanted a drink.

"Whiskey, neat," he said. His voice was a tiger's purr. He moved like one, a flow of movement as he went to the window and studied the small plane she expected was his, pulled up to the refueling dock. Setting a briefcase down on a chair, he paced restlessly. Since he seemed oblivious to her after that cursory acknowledgment, she was more than happy to take advantage of her apparent insignificance to stare at him.

Then, abruptly, he turned around and looked straight at her. It took a concerted effort to hold her ground rather than shrink visibly back into the sofa, but she managed to look reasonably inquiring and mannerly as he cocked his head. He didn't speak at first, taking in her appearance from head to toe. The intensity of his gaze was riveting to say the least, and she wondered what kind of important personage or dignitary this guy was. If it wasn't for the aura of reserve and authority around him, she'd say he was a larger-than-life rock star. But she suspected he was some kind of Middle Eastern prince, despite the Western dress. She could almost imagine Bedouin robes on him, and she wasn't typically that fanciful. Well, okay, she did like watching all manner of sci-fi shows, from *Battlestar Galactica* to *Firefly*, so she supposed she was capable of a wide imaginative range.

"*Metamorphosis*," he said. Then nodded toward her hand, which had stilled. "You play the piano."

"I'm learning." She wondered how he'd heard the track, since she didn't have it on that loud, but as she spoke, a faint smile touched his firm mouth, distracting her.

"You're Australian."

Outside Oz, people often mistook her for British, because her dialect wasn't as pronounced as a lot of her fellow countrymen, but she expected this guy noticed a lot of details others didn't. "Yes."

"I have a friend whose servant is Australian. He's from Queensland, originally."

"Is the servant your friend as well? Or is he just a servant?"

She sucked at small talk, and had a terrible tendency to

latch onto an intriguing facet of the conversation rather than following the mundane flow like a normal person. As a result, she had to deal with the consequences. In this case, him lifting a brow, his gaze sharpening on her. She'd just made herself more interesting to him. Strewth, what had she been thinking? If she'd stayed as unremarkable as wallpaper, she could have just watched him to her heart's content and not had to worry about being in the spotlight like this. Even more harrowing, he moved over to the sofa and sat on the opposite end. Though there was still the space of one cushion between them, the way he sat sideways, putting an ankle on his knee so that he was fully attentive to her, made him feel unbelievably close. He smelled good, a masculine, clean scent flavored with something exotic, like sandalwood. "He is a friend as well. I owe him a debt, for he helped protect someone very precious to me."

"Your wife? Girlfriend?"

His eyes gleamed at the perception. "She is a servant, too. Which means something very much like wife or girlfriend, in my world."

"Oh." That was a pretty intriguing comment as well, but she wasn't sure if it meant what she thought it meant, so she figured she'd better not test those waters with her admittedly limited interpersonal skills. Realizing she must appear rude, she pulled the ear buds out of her ears. *Come on, Helen. Don't back away from this. What're the chances you'll ever be in this situation again? Even if you make a fool of yourself, you'll never see him again.* "Are you going to her now?"

"Yes. Not nearly fast enough." He shifted, stretching one long arm across the back of the sofa. God, did he realize how much he appeared like a sprawling tiger? She would almost believe the man could shape shift into such a beast right before her eyes, complete with lashing tail and a heavy ruff begging for hands to sink into the thick fur, feel the powerful muscles of the neck and shoulders. Those fangs so close, eyes so still and vibrant.

"What does servant actually mean in your world?"

That faint smile again. "If you are going to ask such

direct questions, I expect you should give me your name."

"I'm sorry." Helen felt color tinge her cheeks. "I'm just really bad at small talk, at stuff that doesn't seem to matter."

"I did not say I was offended. Your name?" He lifted a brow, and Helen felt a frisson of warmth go through her at that direct gaze, the hint of command in what should have been a polite request.

"Helen."

"Helen. Lovely. Were you going to brush your hair?" He nodded to the brush at her elbow.

"Oh, yeah. I thought about it, so that I'd look presentable when I land at the next place. People will be meeting me at the airport there, with a limo and everything." She flushed, wondering why she'd said something so ridiculous to a man who obviously rode everywhere in limos.

"I like to watch a woman brush her hair," he observed. "Do not let me interrupt you. It reminds me of home. Of my *habiba*. She is growing her hair out long now as well. Watching you brush yours would be calming."

Helen blinked. Was he really suggesting she should go ahead and brush her hair while he watched? And instead of recoiling from him, as she normally would from a intrusive stranger with a hair fetish, she was actually thinking she wouldn't mind doing that in front of him. "You kind of look in need of calm," she ventured, playing for time. "I guess you really miss her."

Instead of responding, he remained silent, studying her in that steady, intent way. She realized her palms were feeling a bit damp. Crikey, he was compelling her to brush her hair, just by that silence. Funny, but she was sort of okay with it, despite it being kind of a forward, intimate thing to do in front of a stranger. Now, instead of a tiger, she was imagining that Bedouin prince again. Inside a tent of silken walls, lounging back on cushions in a robe, the top loose enough to reveal a section of impressive musculature across his chest, the hint of shoulder architecture. His amber eyes were gleaming, watching his favored...servant, brush her hair. Those eyes and his regard would get more heated with every stroke, until that heat swept over his "habiba's" skin. As she brushed her hair forward, blinding herself with the thick fall of it, his lips would brush her bared nape. He'd take the brush away and comb his fingers through her hair instead, tightening his grip to tilt her head back, back, exposing the throat, until his mouth came down on hers as he stood over her.

What does servant mean in your world? He hadn't responded, but she had a feeling she knew exactly what it meant in his world. Yet she knew she was going to do what he wanted, as if nothing that happened in this dreamlike moment was wrong or misguided. So she unpinned her hair.

As it tumbled to her waist, it flustered her, how attentively he watched its track. If his servant did such a thing for him, she expected she was completely naked when she did it, her hair caressing bare skin. "I'm actually thinking of cutting it," Helen said, noting her voice was a bit thick. She cleared her throat. "Once I get back home, that is. Easier to care for and all that. You know, it's really unnerving, the way you're looking at me. Can't tell if it's making me nervous *because* you're looking at me like that, or because I'm doing this for you."

"My apologies." He straightened, looking genuinely chagrined, such that she felt reassured and guilty, all at the same time. "It was not my intent to distress you."

"Oh, I'm not distressed. It's just..." She gave a half laugh. "It's pretty ironic, that I hate small talk and would prefer to have real conversations like this with strangers, not that shallow façade. Yet now that it's actually happening, I'm freaked out. But in all fairness, you're about as intense as a final exam. Okay, I'm shutting up and brushing now. You sit there and just be...calmer."

The twinge of embarrassment eased as she closed her eyes and heard him chuckle. She adjusted herself in her seat and began to brush. She'd closed her eyes so that she could focus on the movement, instead of his regard, though ignoring that was like ignoring a summer wind caressing her face. Strangely, she didn't feel he was making a move on her, which added to the easing of her tension. He was like this with most women, she was sure of it. His passion, his...love, was all for that one woman, the woman that had had him pacing restlessly. But he was so confidently male, his way with women was instinctively easy, intimate.

"So, you can't call her on your cell? It sounds like you've been out of touch for awhile."

A pause, as if he was considering his words carefully. "I'm out of range right now. Once I get on the plane, I will be in range within minutes. It is part of why I'm impatient now. She wasn't happy when I had to leave her behind for this trip, and I want to be close enough to...make sure she is all right. Not through someone else's report, but through my own senses."

"You're really waltzing around something. But don't worry, I won't ask. Why wasn't she happy?"

"I travel a great deal on business, and it's not safe for her to come with me. She disagrees."

"'Not safe' as in life-threatening?"

"No, not exactly. She has had experiences that were very...traumatic. Where I travel would exploit those fears. I do not wish her to ever experience such fear again."

He shifted, she heard him, and the edge in his voice suggested she'd hit a nerve. She'd always been more of a listener than a talker, which was one of the reasons she hated small talk—it was just static. She'd honed her listening skills, such that she often picked up the true story from the nuances beneath the white noise.

"So you're afraid for her state of mind, not her life. And she disagrees with you, because she's as crazy about you as you are about her, and she doesn't want you to go places without her."

"Yes."

Helen opened her eyes then, putting down the brush so she could thread both hands beneath the now smooth fall of her hair and let it pour down her back, testing that it was all untangled. "Lovely," he said again, with a serious smile that made her toes curl into the carpet, for different reasons this time. "Would you like to see the gift I'm bringing her?"

Helen nodded. "Is this an "I'm sorry I totally pissed you

off" gift?"

The light in his eyes danced, a laughing tiger now, but he lifted a shoulder. "I suppose it is somewhat, but it's something I've wanted to give her for awhile."

Opening the briefcase, he withdrew a purple velvet box, the kind that was handed over a counter at Tiffany's or some other exorbitantly expensive jewelry shop. He lifted the lid and extended the box so she could see the necklace.

The slim choker was a one inch circlet, a melding of different metals into the pattern of a tiger's skin. Copper, bronze and gray, with threads of white glazing that made it an exceptional piece of metalwork. The closure looked like the talon of a tiger, and an amber pendant dangled below it. The choker could be locked, because she saw the key hole beneath the talon. Looking in the box, she saw a small silver key.

A servant...Which means something very much like wife or girlfriend, in my world. Yep, it had been what she thought. It was a collar, the kind that a Master purchased for a submissive, as binding as a wedding ring for two who shared such a relationship. Helen knew about such things, but to come face-to-face with it here, made her a little speechless. Then she found her voice. "She'll love it," she said. "But I think she'll say it just underscores her point."

His gaze cooled just a fraction, a hint of temper. "And what point would that be?"

"That she belongs at your side." Helen sighed, sat back. "Listen, I'm not trying to piss you off. I don't talk a lot, and I don't really know how to relate to people except to tell them the way I see things. And what I see is that it's really hard not to be with the person you love." She was pretty sure if she was this "habiba," she'd chain herself to this bloke's ankle to follow him wherever he went. "Have you explained to her why you can't take her with you?"

"Yes. But she is brave, to the point of foolishness. Courageous even when she's afraid, and I will not tolerate her ever being afraid again."

"And that's not foolish? I mean," Helen added hastily, realizing she might not want to piss off a tiger that was close enough to bite off her face, "No one can protect someone from everything, right? The only thing we can do is help them face their fears, get through them, and be all the stronger for them. It's like a baby. Parents want to protect them, but if you really did protect your child from every ugly, scary thing in the world, they'd never grow up, never get to be and do all the things you really want them to be, right? So in a way, if you protect them too much, you're only reinforcing the fear, rather than healing it. Even adults get past traumas the same way, if they really want to live life to the fullest."

"What do you do for a living, Helen?"

"Well, I have a PhD in atmospheric physics." It was the first time she'd actually said it aloud, and it felt good. Good enough for her to be giddy about it, and a little silly. "I'm brilliant," she mentioned with a grin, "for all that I'm socially inept and tick people off by saying things I shouldn't."

He smiled then, a true smile. For a blink, Helen thought she saw fangs, but certainly that was her imagination getting away from her, right? As devastating as he was without the smile, with it, he was irresistible. No matter how much his overprotective, overbearing arrogance routine infuriated his servant, the woman would forgive him anything. Helen was pretty sure of that.

"Look, you seem like the type of person who'd never let anything bad happen to her, and maybe she wants to show she trusts you to do that. And you just need to believe in that yourself."

"But as you said yourself, you can't protect someone from everything, particularly if they are in harm's way." The shadows that gathered in his eyes told her he knew that firsthand, and gave her another key.

"Well, we all lose people we love, don't we? But the only sure thing is that we never get enough time with them. Why would you deprive yourself of a minute of being with her, if you don't have to do so? If she's willing to overcome her fear to be with you as much as possible, she's offering you a gift. With both hands, and heart and everything. She sounds pretty amazing, and I think you should accept the gift. With as much enthusiasm as I'm sure she'll accept yours." She nodded to the velvet box.

A moment of silence descended between them, and she could tell he was considering her words, looking inside himself among a dark tangle of things. She kept silent, respecting that, until the concierge broke that pause.

"Lord Mason?" The efficient, trim young woman had left the desk and now stood several steps away. "Your plane is fueled and ready."

Lord Mason. So he was some kind of aristocracy or royalty, though she couldn't really place his accent. Maybe a trace of British or Arabic, but it was as elusive as a swirl of desert sand.

"Thank you." Putting the box back into his briefcase and snapping it closed, he rose, but then took a step closer to Helen. Before she could rise, he squatted on his heels. With his height, he was still fairly close to eye level as he reached out and smoothed a stray lock of her hair back over her ear. He had a large hand, but it was amazingly gentle, conveying strength and sensuality in the one touch. She wasn't a touch kind of person—didn't even particularly care for shaking hands, and this was far more intimate. Still, when he did it, it didn't feel intrusive in the least. He nodded, holding her gaze.

"You are a remarkable woman, Helen. If you do not yet have a man," that smile touched his lips, "the one to whom you finally give your heart will be very fortunate. And if you were mine, I'd forbid you to cut that beautiful hair."

His knuckles brushed her cheek before he straightened, offered another nod, and turned away. Laying a generous tip on the concierge's desk for her service, he spoke in a quiet tone to her, then gave Helen one more look before he left the room. As the door settled closed behind him on a whoosh of air, Helen leaned over the sofa arm to watch him stride back down the hallway toward the exit door. He looked as good going as he had coming, a sight worth watching in those trim, well-fitted slacks, the shirt creasing over his broad shoulders. She watched until he turned the corner. Glancing left, she caught the concierge craning her neck, doing the same thing. The break in the woman's professional mien made them grin at each other.

Yep, Helen thought. The icing on the cake.

Part 4

Habiba... You will explain to me what you are doing. Right after you get down from there and put on some clothes. Now.

He'd apparently shot that command out through all three of their minds, because Amara stepped back from her instantly, dropping to a kneeling position. Enrique captured the tails of the flogger in one hand and bowed his head in similar obeisance. They'd known he could react this way, though, so their expressions were quiet, accepting, making her feel guilty for what she had persuaded them to do.

It was my idea. It's not their fault.

His tone had made her bristle. She wasn't a child. She didn't deserve to be treated like a child.

Jessica.

How he could make his voice resonate in her head like approaching thunder, she didn't know, but her body reacted to it in instinctive self-preservation, despite her willful mind. She slid off the cross. Her knees were somewhat unsteady, her body still vibrating from the combination of Amara and Enrique's stimulation. Mason's awareness of it had somehow taken her arousal up a notch. That purring tiger's voice, with more than a hint of a growl, was capable of stirring her in ways that others might consider foolhardy, given how she was deliberately provoking his temper.

Enrique already had her robe in hand, but the man paused, an expression crossing his face that suggested he'd been given emphatic instruction. He passed the robe to Amara, such that it was her hands that brushed Jessica's skin as she helped her thread her arms into the robe, freed her hair from the back collar. When Amara kept the hair lifted, expecting Jessica to bring the robe all the way up, Jess gave her a slight head shake. The dancer smiled faintly, and fanned her hair out on her naked pale shoulders as Jess clasped the lapels of the robe barely above the line of her nipples. She looked at Amara and Enrique. "Can you leave me alone here, please?"

Actually, she wasn't sure if she was ready to be alone in this room, but fortunately, the other two knew her well enough to interpret what she needed. Amara touched her arm. "We'll be at the top of the stairs, within hearing distance. Call if you need us."

Enrique followed her, leaving Jess with another encouraging look. She guessed she should be glad Mason hadn't ordered them to take her out of the room with them, but she knew she was far from winning her point. She could feel his brooding presence in her mind like storm clouds in truth. It made her gather her resolve, steel herself as they disappeared out the door, though she found herself thankful they didn't close it. As they left, she sank to her knees, putting her buttocks on her heels, knowing exactly what kind of picture she made to her Master. Her hair spread over bare shoulders, the silken robe pooled on either side of her hips but open to expose slim thighs up to the point of her sex, the slope of abdomen and sparkle of her navel piercing. The robe so precariously held, he could see the areola of her nipples. She was looking down at herself, giving him not only her imaginings, but a clear vision of the reality.

You are deliberately testing me.

Yes.

I want you out of that room. I feel your fear of it.

It's my Master's job to come remove me from it. Or use what's here to punish me for my defiance.

There was a quaver in the thought. She couldn't hide her trepidation from him. But she was determined, and she wouldn't back down from it. *How would you punish me, my lord? I'll look at each thing here, and see what brings you the most pleasure. Find what is too irresistible for you to conceal your desires from me.*

This time the growl was unmistakable, incoherent enough to suggest he might actually be tempted to strangle her, if she'd been close enough. It sent a shiver through her, but he'd given her the confidence to be this reckless. She'd defied Raithe to the point of violence. She didn't fear that treatment from Mason, so she wouldn't allow those old memories to interfere with what she was going to prove to him now. She couldn't.

She made herself look around the room, at the things disguised in sheer cloths, muted by soft fabric and the scent of rose petals. Jessica knew all of those hidden items by shape because of her one brief time here, when terror had burned them into her brain.

You nearly took your own life.

I've grown since then. I trust you now. I want to be the kind of servant you crave me to be. Need me to be.

Habiba, you are already that and far more.

If that was true, you'd take me with you to Council meetings.

Stubbornly, before he could argue with her further, she focused on the gauze cloth that she knew concealed a spanking bench, a piece of equipment with padded, blue velvet upholstery. Black cuffs attached to the support structure for arms and legs. Gathering every ounce of bravery she could, she imagined Mason buckling her facedown on it, his strong hands circling each of her fragile wrists, tightening the cuffs so she couldn't escape, spreading her legs and securing them as well. His palm smoothing over her buttocks, teasing her cunt, already wet, aching for him, even as her body shook and tears came to her eyes, the past and present merging so painfully she needed to feel the burn of the lash to drive it away. Of his lash, no one else's.

Jessica...for the love of Allah...

She jerked her gaze to the next covered item as she swallowed on a dry throat. The crudely named fucking machine, where the slave was restrained on a table, level with the device. The dildo would be fitted to the pumping shaft and angled to plunge in and out of the appropriate orifice, at whatever rate and penetration a Master deemed fitting. Mason could sit back with his blood-laced drink, watch it fuck her. She'd be writhing and slick with perspiration, her breath coming fast, the climaxes crashing over her again and again as she begged for mercy he wouldn't give her. Not until she was exhausted and begging instead for him to take its place, to put himself inside of her, stretch her with his thick cock and never leave her, never break that connection.

It was how she would feel if she was at a Council meeting, given to the touch and penetration of other servants. Her mind would be locked with his, so everything to which she submitted would be his will, his desire. Every servant's touch would just be an extension of his, something she did for his pleasure, knowing that the more they touched her, the more aggressively he would take her later, burning away their claim on her flesh, erasing it so it would be as if it had never happened.

I would kill any other man who touched you. If I had been in the house when I discovered what you were doing, I would have broken Enrique with my rage. You risk much, habiba.

She trembled at that fierce thought. *If I went with you to Council, it wouldn't matter what was done to me. I am always all yours, my lord. It matters not who touches me.*

But I feel your terror at the thought. You cannot abide a touch other than mine. Even with Enrique, you had to use Amara as a buffer.

I was abused by female vampires as well as males. And I no longer fear Amara.

You are a natural submissive toward a Master. Your deepest betrayal was from a male, which is why your greatest fear is of them.

I only need you with me. To know you are there in my mind. Don't guard me from my fears. Help me overcome them with your love.

A pause, as if she'd touched a nerve. Or made him consider something that perhaps had recently been in his own thoughts. Encouraged, she forged on, considering what else lay before her. A colorful set of sheer sequined scarves was twined around a staff and fanned out around it like strips upon a Maypole. She knew that pole was anchored to the floor. It could be fitted with a phallus upon which the slave would be impaled vertically, the feet locked to the floor in steel boots. The servant had to stand upright, suffering and penetrated, like a mannequin on display as long as the master desired, possibly hours of torment. In the case of this dungeon, pleasurable torment. She made that correction, needing to believe that. Knowing rationally she could believe it, even if her irrational mind couldn't yet.

She grew bolder, imagining Mason there with other vampire guests, where the servants, including herself, were all arrayed on the various equipment. She was positioned on that pole, a thick dual-headed vibrator deep in her pussy and rectum. Her arms were pulled behind her back so her breasts were thrust forward. Her nipples would be clamped, chains running from them to attach to her navel piercing and an additional clitoral clamp. All of the stimulus would make her nipples hard and peaked and her clit flushed and prominent.

The vampires would speak casually, socializing as they wandered the room like they were visiting an art gallery. She saw a female hand caressing the taut buttock of a male slave strapped over the spanking bench, his ass already red with welts from his Mistress's earlier caning. Others watched a male slave grunting under the ministrations of the fucking machine. He was on his back, his knees bound and pulled up into a bent position with nylon cord that was tethered around his throat, such that he had to keep his knees up with his own straining muscles or choke himself as the fucking machine worked in and out of his ass. Sticky lines of semen from his previous climaxes dried over his taut abdomen and chest.

You seem to be imagining quite a few male slaves. No female servants visiting?

For the first time, there was a thread of amusement in his tense mind-voice, and she managed a nervous sliver of the same in her response. *Do you think I like seeing you touch other females, any more than you like the thought of me touching other males?*

You are fine with me touching Amara.

Not always. I'm fine with it, but...there are times I want you all for myself. To devour you with my eyes, my mouth, with all of me. I cannot get enough of you, my lord. It's an ache inside of me that never stops. That's why I can't bear you being where I'm not.

It was a remarkable admission, given how far she'd been from that when they met. She was making herself wetter, not only from Amara and Enrique's stimulation, but from her own imaginations now, despite her fear. She could feel the slickness on her calves, where her buttocks pressed near her heels. He was silent for a few moments, but she didn't censor herself, letting him feel the throbbing ache she had inside for all of him.

Sometimes there was no such thing as getting close enough. When he was away from her, she felt like a new amputee, no anesthetic, some vital part of her chopped off, raw and painful, horribly so, such that she might go mad from the pain. That feeling was far deeper and more vast than any fear she carried. In fact, the few times her terrors and depression had overcome her, she suspected it had as much to do with his absence as the ability of her memories to overcome her when he was not there to balance it.

I need to be with you, my lord. Always.

He stayed silent, but she felt his weighted attention in her mind, and took it for encouragement. He was listening, considering. So she pushed herself further, made herself look beyond the equipment to the wall behind it.

Paddles, gags, chastity belts with plugs for both orifices. She thought about the spreader bar that could be put over the shoulders, an unyielding yoke keeping the wrists at shoulder level. It was adjustable, so that the arms could be stretched out straight from the body and held that way. If he locked her in that, she would have to move carefully to serve him. She saw herself tipping gracefully at the bar to pick up his goblet in two fingers. But when she brought the blood, leaned down and twisted her naked upper body to give it to him, he would take the goblet, set it aside and put his hands on her waist. Gathering her in so her knee pressed beneath his spread thighs where he was sitting, he would lean her body into him, cup her breasts and sink his fangs into the left one just above the nipple. As she gasped, her eyes closing with the pain and ecstasy of it, he would hold her there with his strength as he suckled her blood from her breast.

Descending, his hands would cup her buttocks, play in

between them, tease the sensitive nerve endings there so she writhed and gasped against his stimulation. Then he would push her onto her knees, make her take his cock in his mouth. Grasping that bar on either side of her neck, he would use it to push her down on him harder, hold her there with his cock deep in her throat. As he came at last, jetting his seed into her, her cunt would weep, her hands closed into fists of need in their cuffs on the steel bar. Fluids would slide down her thighs as she came merely from the pleasure of serving him, pussy spasming around the emptiness she needed him to fill.

Habiba... His mind voice was hoarse, and she knew she'd made him impossibly hard. She wanted him to come for her now, wanted him to put his hand on himself and shoot that white, salty cream against his hard, ridged stomach and smooth pectorals, so she could lick it all off, tend to her Master. She would beg for it. She *was* begging for it.

More silence, but there was a rough edge to it in her mind, making her suspect he was getting himself under control, restraining himself from releasing as she desired. When he finally spoke, he had an ominous tone, a threat that only made her sex spasm, her breasts ache more intensely.

There is such a thing as topping from the bottom, Jessica. It usually earns a slave her Master's fiercest punishment.

I am yours to do with as you will, Master.

And you know when you call me Master, it only arouses and provokes me more. I should order you out of that room, make Amara and Enrique escort you if need be. I do not tolerate this type of defiance. You know this.

She held her breath, waiting, not sure of his mind now.

My plane will be landing soon.

Another long pause, and she bowed her head, her hair falling down over her shoulder, teasing the curve of her breast. During her imaginings, her grip had slipped, and she realized she now held the robe beneath her breasts, so that the robe covered very little. The stiff tips of her breasts were jutting with need, her thighs shifted slightly apart so she could smell her arousal. She knew he received those thoughts from her, those pictures, and though she hadn't deliberately intended to do that, she knew from the blast of heat she received from him that she had indeed pushed him beyond endurance. She just didn't know what that meant.

Please, my lord, don't...

Be still.

She tightened her jaw, curbing the desire to retort. Damn it, why was he so stubborn? But even she knew when she might have pushed it a little past where she should. Still, there was that unwise frisson of temptation, with him being so far away... Her fingers trembled on the robe, thinking she might drop it entirely. Her back still had that warm tingle from Enrique's lash, but she wanted it overlaid with Mason's punishment. God help her, she wanted to feel the sting of a whip wielded by his hand, feel a single tail strike the old scars on her back, overlay them and tease the tiger tattoo that had been interwoven through them.

You are a curse upon my very soul. The sound that followed made her wonder if vampires could grind their teeth. Then he spoke again.

Keep your robe where it is. I am telling Amara to turn up the temperature. I don't want you cold.

Despite the cosseting, his voice had become more stern and implacable, such that she despaired, wondering what else she had to do to convince him. She'd pushed herself to the limits of how far she could go without his help. Imagining had been hard enough, and her trepidation rose again, warring with the arousal, creating a tight barbed-wire coil in her lower belly.

You will stay where you are. You will wait there until I arrive and determine how to deal with your disobedience. Until then, you keep your legs open as they are now, your eyes down so I may gaze through your mind at what is mine. Your stiff nipples, your wet pussy, the blood pounding through your slim neck, every inch of your soft skin. You will sit there and imagine everything I will do to it with my hands, my mouth and my cock when I get there. Do you understand?

She trembled, tears biting at her throat, but they were mixed with hope. She managed to answer, speaking the words aloud as well as in her mind. "Yes, my lord."

Part 5

Though he'd said his plane would land soon, she knew his definition of soon and hers were different in this instance. It was a good thing the third mark gave a servant's body even more stamina, not just for exertion, but for stillness, because it took him several hours to get home. She'd actually expected it to take longer, so she'd gone into a near trance, keeping her eyes down, focused on her naked body as he commanded. But she wasn't idle in that trance.

While she waited, her mind rewrote the words he'd spoken. And each time she did, she crafted them into a new scenario where she would serve his pleasure. At first, she imagined just the two of them here, alone. He had her locked on a wheel rack, her body arched up toward him, muscles straining, and he was dripping candlewax over her breasts, tiny, artful patters of drops where she flinched and trembled at each burning touch. He would do it until the curves, the sensitive nipples, were fair molded beneath waxes flavored with vanilla, sandalwood, smoke. And then he'd smooth his fingers over those moldings, denying the skin beneath his touch, taunting her as he circled the tip of a hard, wax-coated nipple.

But she needed to be braver, and so she was. The next fantasy, she was here with him, but others were watching. He attached clamps to her nipples and clit, ran three silken ribbons from each of those attachments and gave the ends to nine in the audience. She had to dance for him as if they were alone, feeling the pressure of those ribbons tighten and slacken depending on which way she turned, how she undulated her hips, arched her back, lifted her foot and turned into the silken restraints. Eventually, he had all the ribbons again, and he bade her stand still as he increased the pressure on those tethers, pulling at the clamps on clit and nipples until the pain and pleasure were excruciating, until she begged him for mercy, to let her come to him.

When he gave her permission, he had her turn, wrap herself in the ribbons, so that when she reached him she was immobilized. Then he laid her on a table where they could watch her, reach out and...

She had to back away from that one, move onto another. She'd also kept those nine watchers in the shadows, their faces blurred. She had to do better than that.

There was an oak chair in this dungeon room, a large chair for a powerful man. The kind of chair that would have been placed at the head of the table in a great hall. It might be from a medieval time period, for it had artwork reminiscent of that era carved in the tall back. In her next scenario, he sat in the chair and lifted her onto his lap, guided her down onto his cock, holding her back against his body as he faced her outward. The hands came, those faceless guests cupping her breasts, stroking her hair, her face. Fingers teased her parted lips, invaded and explored her mouth, and Mason whispered to her to suck on them. Then they slid down her stomach, a wet trail, and painted that moisture on the stretched lips of her sex around his cock, enhancing the fullness inside her.

She realized she was imagining all those hands as his hands, as if she were in a room full of Masons, so every touch was his, no matter from which direction it came. She tried to imagine those hands as the hands of strangers, and found she had to accelerate it, like fast forward on the movie player. Then she had to take some time, breathe, get her nerves under control. She *had* to do better than this, damn it.

She kept going, thinking up scene after scene, even venturing into dark areas of pain and restraint that made things inside of her stomach flop uneasily, while other parts of her body responded in an altogether different way as she imagined *him* doing the restraining, inflicting the pain.

If she kept up at this rate, she was going to have a new version of *1001 Nights* laid out in her mind, just like Scheherazade. Only instead of trying to stave off her Fate at her lord's hands, she was welcoming it. However, if he didn't get here soon, she might just die from an explosion of bottled-up lust.

She was doing it to herself, of course. As she crafted her erotic stories, even with the jittering of nerves, arousal ebbed and flowed. Her nipples hardened into points under her gaze. What had dried in tracks on her smooth legs dampened anew as moisture gathered in her pussy, trickled along the pocket of her thigh, teased her knee cap. A few times during her more passionate imaginings, a shudder gripped her like a convulsion. If she tightened up enough, she might send herself over, just from her visions. But she refused herself. That was her Master's decision.

He was silent in her mind, but now that he was in range, she hoped he saw every lust-charged scenario. If he would talk to her, he might embellish them with ideas of his own. Not just to share as a story, but as a promised future reality where he would add the ruthless carnality of his vampire nature to the mix, taking each fantasy to an even deeper, more intense level. She was ready for it. She was sure of it.

She'd reached fifty-six detailed erotic vignettes and staved off several near misses in bringing herself to orgasm when she suddenly felt him. He was home.

His presence in the house was the difference between a gray shadow, half-dream state and full-bodied color and life, sweeping through her. She gave a soft prayer of thanks for his safe return, for him being a part of her life. It was something she did every time he came back to her and, though he didn't yet speak to her or give her leave to speak in his mind, he let her feel the reassuring touch of his presence, responding to that fervent thanks with a brief tenderness. No matter how she'd goaded his temper, he loved her. She knew that was what was most important, and she was willing to do whatever he wanted from her, but she couldn't retreat from this. Tightening her chin, she knew she'd fight him on that, if she had to do it.

As soon as she had the stray thought, the tenderness became something different, heat with a perilous promise. Despite his acknowledgment of her prayer, his feelings about what she'd done had not mellowed or abated. He was an extremely old vampire for his kind and, although he preferred distance from vampire society, in some ways he was more unyielding on matters of obedience and respect than even the other Council members. She also knew he had a way of considering things from all angles, exploring his options thoroughly before he decided exactly how he would handle a situation. And he'd had hours to decide how he would deal with her.

Though he didn't speak, he did open a visual channel into his mind for her. He went to his room first, rather than coming to her first thing. He blocked her from his thoughts, but she saw him leave the suitcase on the bed. Enrique would put his things away for him. She watched as Mason unbuttoned his shirt. Since she was looking through his eyes, she couldn't see him shrug it off his shoulders, revealing the tiger tattoo that had been marked with his blood to hold the design there, but she could well imagine it. Swallowing on a dry throat, she thought of how that tiger would ripple as he tossed the shirt over a chair. He unhooked his trousers, a simple, casual gesture that sent her pulse rabbiting. As they dropped low on his hips, he was moving with that catlike way of walking he had. The striated terrain of his abdomen would shift, tempting touch, as he moved into the bathroom and--for the love of fucking God--turned on the shower.

She'd stirred herself to near climax by imagining all the different ways she could serve him, be taken over by him. One of them had featured her on her knees in his shower, taking him in her mouth, the head of his cock pushing deep into her throat. Her eyes were shut from the spray of the water, everything focused on his scent, the steam, the clutch of his hand in her hair. Only she wasn't really there. She was here, looking through his viewpoint as he ran soap along his broad chest, then down, sliding his hand around the base of an enormously erect cock rising from between powerful thighs, a nest of heavy testicles. Her pussy contracted on itself, weeping anew, and her palms were sweating as she held them in tight fists.

She wouldn't speak, wouldn't cry out or plea. This might be Mason underscoring the control he held as her Master, which, in a torturous way, was an encouraging sign. This was part of her punishment. Still, the size of that erection said he'd most definitely been listening to the different stories she'd imagined. Fifty-six vignettes, filled with salacious details that, for as in depth as she'd thought they'd been, didn't come close to this mind-view of his body. She'd missed having him sheltering her at night as she slept, how often he touched her and allowed himself to be touched. And now here he was, so close it felt like she could reach down through his gaze and caress that hard organ, the line of hip and thigh. She wanted to be pressed up against him, nipping that chest, curling her hands in his wet long hair, the long copper strands gone to near black in the shower. She'd reach around to soap the muscular buttocks and his hands would close over her wrists as she tried to tease the seam between. His smile, the light in his eyes, could make her heart stutter. He loved it when she played with him like a mischievous child.

But now she experienced all that through this screen, this distance, that left her hands and her body empty. He was too far away, and she couldn't bear it another moment. She wanted to get up, run up those stairs, run to that shower. She didn't, but it was a near thing. She was breathing fast, a sob catching in her throat.

He didn't linger overlong there, thank all the gods. He pulled on jeans and a close-fitting long sleeved tee, pushing up the sleeves. He didn't bother with anything beneath the denim, and she knew just how good his lower body looked in it. As an Old World male, he wore dress clothes as easily as many men wore jeans, though he looked devastating in both. She preferred him in Bedouin robes most of all. When his arms closed around her, she could find his body through the wide sleeves or open front, if he only wore a tunic. But tonight, the jeans and knit shirt that delineated that mouthwatering physique worked for her.

He still didn't come to her. Ordering a glass of wine from the kitchen staff, he partook of it by himself in the dining room. He asked them to light the brace of candles on the table and spent some time studying the tapers while he sipped the wine. As he considered the way the ivory wax dripped down the sides and pooled in the silver catch tray, she wondered if he was imagining her first scenario, dripping hot wax on her flesh. When Melinda, one of the kitchen girls, brought him a small sampling of fruit and cheese, his gaze shifted and alighted on a peach half, the mauve-orange deep color. The fruit was so ripe it glistened with juices where it had been cut.

Oh, holy hell.

Jess swallowed as he picked it up, turned it over to the peel side to stroke that light fuzz that was like a woman's skin. When he returned to the fruit portion, he slid his finger along the valley where the pit had been cut away, leaving just a channel of slick flesh to taste. As he traced that area, he put pressure on it, making the juices swell around his fingertip. It made his knuckles start to glisten, the way they did when he slid his fingers inside of her, stroked the walls of her pussy and made her writhe under his clever touch.

When he brought the peach to his mouth, she couldn't see through his eyes, but she was tormented by other senses. As he nibbled at it, licked and sucked the juices away, she felt every stroke of his tongue, the prick of his teeth, and heard his enjoyment of the fruit. He loved watching her climax from his mouth, and he did it often, sometimes waking her from sleep with his lips between her legs, his tongue pushing into her pussy and swirling her into pleasurable waking.

"My lord..." She'd made the hushed plea before she could help herself, and the syllables echoed in the chamber.

He didn't respond, but he did put down the fruit and take another swallow of his wine. Then he rose and left the room. If he wandered off to his favored reading room to give *War and Peace* a leisurely perusal, she swore she was going to find something pointy and wooden and go after him with a vengeance.

The brief moment of desperate humor disappeared, though. He was headed for the dungeon. As he came in her direction, that silent, pensive intensity became something else. Studied, focused and deliberate, more than a hint of dangerous heat coming off of him. Mason was not a dramatic or overly vain man. She already knew the shower, the wine and fruit had not been idle teasing. He'd been making a point, driving up her need to an excruciating level simply because he could demand that from her. He could demand it from her eternally and endlessly. For the first time since she'd launched her goal to get Mason to remove the kid gloves, she realized he'd always known just how to dish out a Master's torment. In fact, she had a feeling he could make Raithe look like an amateur. Whereas Raithe had copped out, using terror and pain, Mason could destroy a woman utterly with mere sensual command of all her senses, taking over her mind and soul at once.

He didn't speak to Enrique or Amara when he reached them at the top of the stairs. That sent a trickle of nervousness through her, because she had wanted to hear the rumble of his voice, get some sense of his mood from it. His silence gave things a more ominous tone. Had he spoken in their minds, or sent them off with a look that told them they were dismissed and he would handle their part in this later? Regardless, she heard the sounds of their retreat, leaving her alone with him...and this dungeon room.

She started trembling in earnest the moment he started down the stairs. He was barefoot, but he wasn't less intimidating out of his shoes. She made herself stay as he'd bade her, eyes down, robe pooled about her naked form. As he'd ordered, Amara had turned up the temperature, so all during her wait she'd felt the warmth of the vented air at her back. Now, though, she wished the room had been cold. She wanted to give him that gift, rely on his body alone to drive the cold back, bring warmth back to her skin.

He'd stopped in the doorway, and she felt his gaze on her. She could hear her breath, the quick patter of her pulse. Oh, how she wanted to look at him, drink in every inch of him with her eyes. She could smell his scent, that unique musk, a male cologne and Mason mix that reminded her of desert sand and hot sun, jasmine blooms.

Having you shiver with cold would not please me, habiba. As your Master, I will not permit you a moment of distress.

She didn't want to do anything to keep him from touching her one second longer than necessary, but she reminded herself of the stakes here, what she had to win. "If that's the case," she said softly, "then I've failed you, my lord. Because every time you leave me, I feel nothing but distress. Until you return."

Silence. She closed her eyes, holding onto her resolve with everything she had, for in a minute she would abandon it just to feel his arms around her. Then he muttered an oath in Arabic, low and vicious. Before she could think of how to reply, or if a reply was even necessary, he was in front of her. As she opened her eyes, she had a glimpse of those bare feet, the columns of his thighs and what they cradled in denim between them. He kept her pressed down on her knees with a hand that coiled into her hair. She reveled in that single touch. Oh, how she wanted to lift up on her knees, catch her fingers in his belt loops and press her mouth against that line of taut skin just above the waistband, dipping beneath the hem of the shirt.

Lock your wrists behind you, habiba. You have no permission to touch me.

She obeyed, and those hands tangling in her hair pulled her back with enough strength she felt his ability to snap her neck. It conveyed his temper, even as it put her in a position to look into his face.

But she didn't. She made herself keep her eyes down. It would drive her completely crazy to sit here, to experience him through all her senses but sight. He could make her do this for hours until she might be weeping with the desire to look at him, but she still wouldn't lift her gaze until he commanded her to do so. She would prove her devotion, her commitment to him, how she could obey him without question or thought, no matter what she was asked to do. Anything to stay by his side.

Even in her mind, she knew that sounded too desperate, too raw, but she would hide nothing from him. He might pick up that note of distress, but everything she was thinking was true. The desire to submit, surrender to a Master, was a part of her soul Raithe had exploited and warped. His most heinous crime against her was making her believe it was wrong. Mason had healed that, had brought that part of her to a depth and intensity she kept wanting to take deeper and deeper, every day. Looking at it that way, it really was all his fault she had this limitless need to serve him, right?

Okay, she'd pushed it with that one. The next creative oath was fervent enough to tell her she was in serious trouble. She just wasn't sure what kind yet. It wouldn't matter. She wouldn't have done this if she couldn't handle the consequences. She was ready for that. But she wasn't ready for his next words.

He tightened his grip, pulling at her scalp, his thumb pressed just beneath her ear. "On the way here, I realized you were right about one thing. I haven't fully asserted myself as your Master. Otherwise, you would not have so utterly mistaken what I require from you."

The velvet growl of his voice was stern, unyielding. It was a note she'd heard him use before with Enrique and Amara, but never with her. Not yet. Now that it was turned full force in her direction, it gave her anticipatory shivers, but the words themselves stopped her in her tracks.

"M-my lord?"

Instead of answering, he jerked up her chin with two fingers, filled her gaze with fierce amber eyes and the planes of a ruthlessly handsome face. It was a flash impression, for a moment later, he clamped his hot and demanding mouth over hers.

Oh, God. *Bliss*. It didn't matter that the kiss was relentless, brutal. He wasn't just demanding complete submission from her. He was taking it, with the erotic thrust of his tongue and the strength of his hand, sliding from her chin to take a firm grip of her throat, holding her in place and controlling the kiss entirely.

This was an entirely different energy from him, something she'd only caught hints and promises of...until now. While she couldn't deny feeling a trickle of apprehension from it, it wasn't a shadow of Raithe. It was the sensual thrill of fear a submissive was *supposed* to feel from a Master like this. She couldn't stop the tremor through every muscle in her body, but she could open her mind to him fully, hope he was seeing how it was different with him.

Just his hand on her throat and their mouths touching, yet she fairly screwed her clasped hands into a knot at her back trying to keep them there. Her thighs were so slick she thought she'd never been so wet without a climax. She whimpered into his mouth, reveling in those strong fingers, the overwhelming mouth.

When he lifted his head, she could barely remember what he'd said, but at his stern, uncompromising stare, she forced herself to recall it, moistening her lips to speak, though it was little more than a whisper. "Wh-what have I mistaken, my lord?"

"The reason I do not take you with me to Council meetings has nothing to do with your past. For all that I cannot tolerate knowing that you still struggle with your nightmares—"

"But you make them better."

"Jessica." He pressed that clever mouth to her temple, his hand squeezing. His fingers were so long they could almost reach her nape. "If you speak without leave again I will gag you with the thickest phallus I can find on that wall, one long enough to press into the back of your throat, reminding you what it's like to take my cock there. I would get a particular pleasure at seeing those clever lips of yours stretched hard around it when you climax."

He knew her terror of sexual toys, but he called one forth now, gave her the vivid image of him making her open her mouth for it, take it all the way in and then remain still as he strapped it around her head. The fear she felt dissipated at the sensual imagining of his hands, the way his eyes would dwell, hot and desire-filled, on her face, lingering on her lips.

"Now," he continued, a predator's purr, "you will listen and hear your Master. The reason I do not take you with me is this. I will *not* tolerate another man's hands on you. Period."

Enough savagery was injected into his tone that instinct kept her still, though the astounding words themselves froze her in place, their meaning wrapping around her heart, a binding and confirmation at once.

"When Lyssa and Danny brought Jacob and Dev here,

certain things were different that night. But still, I warned you even then." He shifted, letting her see he was studying the room around them. "While all of this was not a wise course of action, it was goaded by what you correctly sensed. As you have grown more confident in your trust in me, my desire to be a more light-handed Master has steadily evaporated. And perhaps you are ready for that. We will see. But first, we will get one thing very clear."

He tilted up her face so she was so close to those eyes that amber flame was all she saw. "You are mine. As I told you from the plane, when I saw Enrique's hands on you"—now he changed his angle, bringing her head down so his breath whispered over her cheek—"I was ready to tear him to pieces."

She knew he was a lethal opponent, had seen that side of him in life-threatening situations. But even having seen that, the male holding her now was revealing the animal side of his nature more decidedly than she'd ever experienced. It was all directed at her, the full weight of it.

"I am not like other vampires, *habiba*. Have you forgotten? Three hundred some years ago, I *hand fasted* with a Bedouin girl. There was a reason who and what she was appealed to me. Though I don't agree with the brutality, the abuse of power that can come with restricting women's lives, I have a full understanding of the male need to protect what he considers his, on every level. It's part of who and what I am. Do you understand me?"

"Y-yes. I think so."

"Yes, what?" His tone sharpened, another delicious and new thrill.

"Yes, Master."

"I doubt you actually do. But by the time we are done in here, you will. You will be very, very clear on what kind of Master I am."

Part 6

On that thrilling and terrifying note, he released her, stepped back and took a seat in that oak chair on which she'd earlier imagined herself, riding his cock before voyeuristic eyes. "Come here."

Rising to her knees, she closed that distance naked, leaving the robe behind. On impulse, right before she would have been between his knees, she bent, her eyes on where the frayed cuff of his jeans brushed the ankle of that long, finely shaped male foot. She stopped above it, her hair falling down along the insole. It was an amazingly subservient desire, to kiss his foot, yet his words, the hint of total Mastery he might finally decide to exert over her, summoned it from that pool inside of her that seemed full of such surprising cravings.

As her mouth closed that distance and pressed against his flesh, he shifted, his hand touching her head. "Jessica." His voice, the rich timbre, had a hoarse note to it.

"I've missed you so much, my lord," she said softly. "I understand what you are saying, and I didn't mean to try and force your hand. But, if you love me, please stop leaving me behind. I can't bear it."

He sighed. "You are as stubborn as a mule. Come up here."

She straightened and put her hands on his knees. Sliding his hands under her arms, he effortlessly lifted her to his lap, one hand sliding over her thighs, the other cupping her breast. She automatically parted her legs, giving him access to what was between them, though he didn't touch her there yet. The mere touch of his hands in such intimate proximity was enough to have her body twitching, her nipple jutting into his palm. She could feel his arousal under her buttocks, and wanted so much to squirm against him, rub that hard cock.

"Be still." He anticipated her, a hint of steel in his voice. "You're in enough trouble already. You tease me, try to top now, and your punishment will be even more severe. Be still a moment and let me hold you. As I said earlier, you are a curse on my days. And the greatest blessing of my life."

Thinking of how he'd drawn out the wait, taking that shower, eating the fruit, she thought that curse and blessing went both ways. But she was still in his arms. Whatever else he did to her tonight, this moment, this was everything. His strong body surrounding her, his breath on her temple, those tempting lips so close.

"May I ask...how will you punish me, my lord?"

"However is necessary."

As he held her for several more moments, she stayed silent as he'd commanded, absorbing his touch, the way it felt to be held by him. Whenever he came home, she needed that surge of anticipation, being able to run into his arms, feel his embrace. To see the way his amber eyes lit with pleasure at her enthusiasm. It told her he needed it as much as she did. Just like his reassuring mind-touch when she'd said her prayer of thanks to have him home, this, too, was a reminder that, whatever transpired in this room tonight, he always thought of her first, what she needed. What they both needed.

"All right, then." He lifted her off his lap. "I want you to go to the cross and put yourself on it."

And just like that, the reassurance fled.

The St. Andrew's Cross, the item in the room that held the most nightmares for her. The blood he'd made so warm now froze in icy fear. She had as much power to control or stop her reaction as an infant trying to stop a car hurtling toward her. For all her imaginings while she waited for him, for all she was sure she'd bolstered herself enough, the first hint of actually doing it, and five years of memories slammed down around her like cage walls. That same despicable sense of helplessness paralyzed her limbs.

*No. Damn it, damn it, damn it...*The wail came from deep inside. She was better than this, better than this knee jerk reaction. He'd been right. He'd known. Hadn't she just acknowledged it? He always thought of her first, what she needed. Wanted.

He might be right, but he didn't understand how inadequate it made her feel. She'd fought to survive, but if she couldn't be the type of submissive she longed to be to him...it wasn't just that she wanted to be able to go with him to Council. She wanted to have no fear of anything he might demand of her. She wanted to finally be free of Raithe. Until she was free of her fear, it was as if she was still partially under Raithe's mastery, not wholly Mason's.

"Jessica." He'd risen from his chair and was towering over her. His hand curved around her nape as she stood there so rigid and cold, suffering. He pressed his mouth to the crown of her head, then he bent, scooped her up. He was going to take her back to his bed. He'd lock this door, she was sure, chain it so she could never come back in. No, knowing Mason, he'd have it destroyed, turn it into another billiards room or whatever other thing his huge estate didn't have, so it could never torment her again. Maybe an indoor swimming pool or a private movie theater. *Damn it.* She blinked back tears, her temple on his shoulder, her arms wrapped hard around him.

"I gave my slave a command, and she did not obey. At some point tonight, she'll be punished for that."

He wasn't moving toward the door. He was moving toward the cross. Her hands clutched his shoulders, despite herself, and he made a murmur in his throat. It was the sound he made when she slept in his bed during the day, if she woke from a nightmare, a calming sound she'd also heard him use with the horses. When he reached the cross, he closed his hand over one of hers, loosened her fingers. As he held her wrist, his fingers lapping over her knuckles, he took her hand to the dark teak wood and laid her palm on it, his own pressing down on hers so she felt the worn smoothness.

"So many servants have found mindless pleasure here, *habiba.* The servants of my guests, of Council members...Amara and Enrique have both spent time here, spread and restrained for my pleasure, their bodies gleaming with sweat—sometimes blood— quivering between pain and ecstasy, their eyes glazed and feverish, helpless to my desires. You're becoming more aroused, just thinking about it, and jealous, because you want to be the one serving me here. You despise yourself for your fears. You think you are cowardly and somehow fall short of how strong you should be for me."

He turned his gaze to her then, the amber eyes holding so much weight it squeezed down on her heart and lungs, making it hard to breathe. "You do not have any idea how deeply angry such thoughts make me."

He let her feet down then, continuing to hold her waist, her arm. "Step onto the foot rests, and put your heels, shoulders and hips against the cross. Face toward me."

Stepping back, he withdrew his touch. He was still close. If she reached out a hand, she could lay her palm on his broad chest, feel muscle and the heart that beat beneath it. He was here, beside her, and he was waiting. If she stepped toward him, she wasn't sure what he would do, but she sensed he would be one step closer to calling all this off. He'd gotten her here. She had to close the final step, in either direction.

As she warred with that decision, his attention shifted to the cross again.

"Amara has done far more time here. I do not know why it's the female slave who will goad the Master more, be more daring, as if begging to be restrained, whipped or caned, but Enrique never pushes me nearly as much as his wife does." His gaze returned to Jessica's face and his brow rose. "You have already eclipsed her."

Jess set her jaw. "Perhaps because I refuse to be less than the other part of your soul, my lord."

"And nothing challenges a man as much as the voice of his own soul. That is a blade with two edges, *habiba*. You are testing my patience. I gave you a command. It is the last time tonight I will repeat myself."

It was a leap of faith, and he was perhaps the only one in the whole world who understood how far a leap it was for her. Closing her eyes, she made that step. She had to take a breath, lay her palm against the smooth wood to steady herself. But she'd done it. There was less than a hand's span between her body and the cross.

"Now all the way on." A touch of gentleness beneath the steel. She put her bare foot on the right side rest and turned to face him. Closing her hands on the portion of the cross near her hips to balance, she positioned the other foot in the correct place. Now her legs were spread apart, past shoulder width. She knew there was an adjustable bolt underneath the small of her back where he could increase that span if he desired.

"Put your wrists in the channels above your head."

He could have guided them there, but she feared nothing when he touched her, and he knew that. He was making her face her fears. It was a beautifully made cross, with ornate scrollwork carved in the sides. Instead of being flat, the thick crossed pieces had shallow channels so the limbs and body were somewhat cupped inside the restraint system. When she laid her arms in the channels and fitted her wrists into the more narrow section which still had enough room for a man's wrists as well as a woman's, she nevertheless felt the threat of further restraint to come.

As she reached up to do his bidding, she was conscious of how he watched the stretch of her upper body, the arch of her ribs, the rise of her breasts as her breathing elevated.

Stepping forward now, he bent and secured the first ankle. Down here, play was with third mark servants, those who had the strength to break thin straps in moments of frenzied abandon, so chain was used. It pressed into her skin, held her fast, and tightened up as he secured it with a twisting latch. One limb only. All the others were free, but she began to tremble again, caught between fears from her past and something else, something responding to the touch of his hands on her ankle as he bound her.

He'd told her where to put her wrists, but he was here, so close. His long copper hair fell over his shoulder and brushed her thigh as he bent. She wanted to reach down, wanted to touch.

Did she twitch, or did he see her intent in her mind? Before her wrist could so much as shift, he was holding it, keeping it pushed in that channel, his body a bulwark against hers as his face bent close.

"You will be still."

The feel of his clothed body against her, over six feet of solid muscle and a Master's will, overwhelmed her. He kept her attention as he secured that wrist the same way. Then the other. The apprehension was spinning outward, cutting though her stomach lining, making her fingers curl. She could do this. She could.

Why do you feel you must do it alone, Jessica? He straightened from the other ankle, her limbs now secured at the four points. *Speak to me, from your heart. Do not think.*

"I need your help. Master." He was right. She didn't call him by that title much, except in not-so-subtle challenge, but it was different in this moment, and the flicker of his gaze registered it.

"Yes, you do. That is part of what you need to trust. You are frightened. But no matter how frightened you get, Jessica, I will make you serve my will tonight. Do you understand? You have no choice in this. As your Master, all choices are mine."

"Y-yes." She stared at him, reeling at such a stern declaration. No choices. She was his to do with as he would. Just like Raithe. But not. She had no choice but to trust him now.

"Very well." There were additional restraints on the cross and he employed them, putting straps over her thighs, her waist, above her breasts and then across her forehead, his hands lingering on her hair before he added an additional secure strap to her upper arms and elbows. She was completely immobilized, spread open, and there was no part of her that wasn't shaking.

He wasn't done yet. Turning, he moved to the armoire in the corner, one that held all manner of even more terrifying things. He opened two of the smaller drawers, and when he turned he was holding a set of small clips, a glittering silver chain attached to nipple clamps, and a pair of smaller metal pieces she couldn't readily identify.

Her body jerked in spasmodic reaction, a tiny note of panic caught in her throat. Giving her an even look, he moved to an intercom across the room, as if her trembling and such sounds were of no concern to him. When he pressed the button, Jessica was startled to hear the voice of Hector, the groundskeeper, responding to the call. "Yes, sir?"

"Hector, I need you to pick out two dozen white roses from the garden. Various sizes. I want the blooms half opened, and cut a foot of stem. Make sure they have thorns."

"Yes, sir. Where do you want them brought?"

She saw Hector every day. Would Mason have him come

here, see her like this?

"Give them to Amara. She will bring them to me."

The flood of relief was something she couldn't hide, and when his expression settled into those unrelenting lines, she cursed herself. She'd proven once again that she couldn't—

"I would strongly suggest you not finish that thought. You're not listening, Jessica. Hector will not bring the roses here, because no man will see you like this. None but me. Not now, not ever."

He was back in front of her. He'd moved swiftly, in that startling way vampires could, where even a third mark couldn't follow them. It made her jump, because she was already tense, but then he cupped her breast. His gaze was on it, his thumb passing idly over the nipple. While it immediately drew up into an aroused point under his familiar touch, she knew that wasn't his intent. His expression, his attitude, said he was touching her breast because he wanted to touch and fondle what was his alone to enjoy. And though she still quaked in the grip of her past fears, something else wound its way through that cold pool, something warm and serpentine, wicked and pleasurable at once.

He still held the nipple clamps. Like everything else Mason used in this room, they were handcrafted, the clamps fashioned as the jaws of two tiny silver tigers with glittering green eyes. They were like the tattoo on her back, the one that had transformed her scars into a declaration of her loyalty and devotion to him, the deepest reassurance possible. His and his alone. He meant that.

"You are learning, *habiba*." As his voice dropped to a husky murmur, he took her nipple between forefinger and thumb, squeezing slowly and with greater pressure as he lifted his attention to her face, watching her breath draw in as he increased the vise, restricted the blood flow.

"I haven't...seen those before."

"I had them made for you. I didn't anticipate using them so soon." When he withdrew his fingers, the sensation shot straight to her pussy, then contracted there, hard, when he replaced his touch with the tiger's jaws. Her breath sucked in. "Oh..."

"Yes, it hurts. But it is a pain I know you will embrace. More than once, you have climaxed when my fangs pierced that lovely pink circle around your nipple, when I licked your blood from it."

She couldn't find words, but cried out when he began that squeezing pressure on the other nipple, giving her the warmth of his fingers for that protracted moment before the second one went on. She writhed the tiny amount allowed against her multiple restraints, her throat arching as she pressed against the forehead strap.

"Ssshh...be still. Feel it spread out from your nipples. You are getting so wet. I can smell your cunt readying itself for me. You already want my cock there."

"Yes..."

"You will be waiting a long, long time for that. Your punishment and my pleasure."

There was a chain connecting the clamps, a y-chain whose silver tail ran down her belly and teased against her clit. Now he used one of those metal pieces he'd brought, attaching it to the end of the chain. The piece looked somewhat like a steel curtain pin. But she quickly understood its use when his fingers pressed down around her clit, pinching it up high so the narrow and long u-shape could slide along the base of that nerve-rich center on either side. When he got the metal piece positioned and then released the sides, it instantly compressed her clit inside its grip. She whimpered at the sensation, but he paid her no attention, because he wasn't done with this phase of her torment.

She moaned outright as he positioned the second metal piece. It was shaped like two crossed U's, forming a basket shape about the size of the broad head of a man's cock. There were four smooth and rounded prongs on the edges. He slid the basket portion inside her pussy, stretching it open, and those prongs, like the clit clamp, pinched down on her labia on the outside to hold it inside of her. With her pussy spread open that way, she felt warm air enter that space, caressing her. Blood was throbbing down there, her arousal heightened by all the restrictions and manipulations, and she knew she was all but panting. Her eyes coursed hungrily over Mason. He was hard and thick against his jeans, but he moved with utter calm and control, as if he had all the time in the world.

He returned to his chair, adjusting it so he could face her, peruse her at his leisure. Even at the sound of footsteps on the winding stairs, he didn't so much as flicker an eye lash in that direction. She kept staring at him, her body so needy for him that she knew her hips were twitching against their restraints, shamelessly wanting to emulate the rhythm they would experience if he was thrusting into her.

"Lower your eyes, Jessica. You don't have permission to look at me again until I command it."

God, the cruelty of it. But it was diabolical as well, because it meant all her focus was now on what was happening in her body, and knowing he was taking his pleasure of viewing her, his property, his slave, as long as he wished. Amara was probably going to bring him the *War and Peace* she'd thought about earlier, along with those roses.

"My lord." Amara's soft voice, and Jessica heard something being placed on the table next to him, the roses in a heavy crystal vase perhaps. A tinier clink followed. "I also brought you a glass of wine, as you requested."

"Thank you. That will be all."

Short, dismissive. He hadn't forgiven yet. Jessica had almost forgotten what events had led to this moment, and truth, she couldn't really lend any thoughts to it. It was the oddest feeling, those tiger teeth holding her with such incredible discomfort, but discomfort that had her nipples large as cherries, throbbing for the soothing touch of his mouth. Her pussy opened up and clamped down at once, as if she'd been widened for a cock, but since no cock was there, she was dripping her arousal on the floor between her spread feet, a small, viscous pool.

Mason rose. She heard the rustle of his clothes, and knew it was deliberate, since he could move without any noise if he wished. When he stopped before her, she saw he had three white roses in his hands. He took the middle one, a bloom almost as wide as her hand even half-opened, and touched it to that pool, collecting her moisture off the otherwise pristine floor. She wasn't supposed to lift her eyes, she knew, but she sensed him smelling it, could imagine those handsome nostrils flaring, taking in her scent, even perhaps touching his tongue to collect a drop off the silken petal, as he would if he put his mouth between her legs. A little cry came from her throat, incoherent need.

"Yes, you taste sweet, *habiba*. You and this rose together…it would win new prizes from an international rose competition. Smell yourself, and know that I find this the most prized of all scents in my garden."

Putting the bloom to her mouth, he teased with it, and she did smell her scent in the exotic fragrance. She wanted to kiss that taste on his lips. Wanted to put her mouth everywhere. Oh, God, she didn't know it was possible for pleasure to become agony.

"We are only getting started. You were right, what you thought earlier. Raithe didn't know that true torture lies in an intricate working of pleasure, denial and pain. But you will know this. You're already feeling the hint of it, aren't you?"

"Yes, Master." There was no challenge or manipulation now. Here in this place, under his command, there was no other acceptable way to address him. She embraced the title, embraced everything about him.

He lowered the rose and slid it between her legs. She cried out harshly, the mere feel of it sliding over her compressed clit, then teasing into that opening between her spread labia, almost unbearably exciting. He pressed the rose partially up into that open channel of her pussy, twirling it idly, so it felt like tiny, silken tongues lapping at those slippery walls. Her body shuddered, convulsed, and she couldn't keep track of all the noises coming from her throat, a symphony of involuntary responses to his stimulation.

"Lovely. I love to hear you sing."

When she thought her brain might just shut down from all the sensations he was inflicting upon her, he changed tactics. He drew a tiny knife from the pocket of his jeans, one with a slim, silver blade that flashed out at the touch of his finger, and cut the stem. Setting that on the table, he gathered the rose bloom in his palm, compressed it, and then began to insert it into her stretched pussy. The bud was so large that, once there and released, it spread out as much as the metal frame allowed. Her muscles twitched and contracted where the silken petals touched her inside. One petal, dislodged before he inserted the bud, fell on her foot, a tiny caress.

"That will stay there for now. Having it stroke you in response to your barest movement will make you wetter. You will saturate it and, when you climax upon it, I will take it and have it preserved, glazed and put under glass. It will go in my gallery, where I can gaze upon a very rare species of rose, Jessica's Pleasure, whenever I wish. But you need pain, too, don't you, my sweet slave?"

She couldn't nod with her head held the way it was, but she was all his. Her mind had no sensible thoughts. He wasn't bringing her toward climax. He was spinning an enchantment to keep her in such an intense state of arousal a climax might be torture when he was done, an overload of pleasure no one could survive.

"Oh, a third mark can, *habiba*. No worries on that. You are far more resilient than a mere human. But then, you always have been."

He'd brought the second rose up to her wrist and caressed her pulse around the chain. Then he made her close her fingers around the bloom, holding it as he cut the stem. She watched the silver blade move and imagined him drawing it along her flesh. The thought rippled across her nerves. But she didn't anticipate what he would do next. He pocketed the blade, and slid the stem beneath her forearm. She gasped when he used a pair of the small clips to turn it into a manacle there, cinching the thick stem tight enough the thorns bit into her flesh. And then he cinched it an extra half inch and she moaned as they pierced flesh, drawing blood. It was a hint of what his fangs felt like, sinking in, and her body responded accordingly, jerking against the pain and aching arousal at once.

Tears were gathering in her eyes. Not tears like Raithe pulled from her. This was destroying her, bit by bit. In some vague, hazy part of her mind, she realized she'd ceased worrying about Raithe from the first moment Mason had put the silver tigers upon her. Everything in her had centered upon him and what he was doing to her. Her Master was breaking her down, cell by cell, because when he was done, she would trust him utterly. Raithe would hold nothing in her mind but her contempt. Not even that. There was no room for that, for anything other than Mason.

"Look at me, Jessica."

When she brought her wild gaze up to him, she met eyes of pure red and gold fire, his mouth tight with male lust and determination that inundated her. A thin trickle of blood was working its way down her arm from where those thorns were biting into her. His gaze went to that tiny flow even as he spoke, his voice a tiger's growl.

"You thought, when I picked you up, that I was going to take you out of here. And I was."

She swallowed, tried to form words. "W-why didn't you?"

"It was your own thoughts, *habiba*. Your belief that a part of you would forever be Raithe's slave if you couldn't get past the fears. I told you at the beginning, I would tolerate no other male's claim on you. Particularly that male's. Who, if he's not rotting in Hell, when I get there, I will find him and drag him to the eternal fires myself."

She believed it, heard it in the deadly coldness beneath the heat.

"On my way home, you imagined me doing things to you...floggings, brandings. I could never take a whip to your soft flesh, or give you the searing torment of fire. But I can turn your yearning into the deepest suffering imaginable, an ache that goes on and on, binding your soul tighter and tighter, until you are pleading for mercy, yet not really wanting it, all at once."

The tears rolled down her face, but she didn't want him to stop. Maybe that was why she was crying. His hands cupped her face, thumbs spreading the moisture of those tears over her dry lips, and brought her eyes back to him again.

"There are twenty-one more roses behind me, *habiba*. You will feel the prick of all their thorns, the silk of their petals. You will bleed for me, come for me, beg for me. But in the end, I will bring you to utter stillness, because you will simply be mine. I will take your soul, chain it to me, and you will never fear anything again."

Part 7

I only fear losing you, my lord.

For wasn't that truly the fear that crept through her mind, spread out until it seemed the terror of it was coursing through her very blood? The fear that whenever he left this estate, she would never see him again? She'd lost so very much in her life, and he'd given her back passion, happiness, laughter...love. She wouldn't survive losing that again, and she wondered how he'd borne it for three hundred years, when he lost the first woman who had brought that to him.

"You brought it back to me, *habiba*. And the third mark binds us. You will never lose me. Wherever I go..."

"I follow." She stared up at him. But fate could play terrible tricks, couldn't it?

"Ssssh." He leaned in and pressed a kiss to her forehead, to her cheeks, then across her lips, teasing her when she tried to strain for him, for a deeper connection. Instead he played his tongue over hers, traced her mouth and gave her a tiny nip on the corner before drawing back and picking up another bloom.

"Something to take your mind from such nonsense." Putting that bloom in her opposite hand, he cut the stem and wound it over the other biceps, once again cinching it in for that delicate sip of her blood. God, she wanted the penetration of his fangs as much as she wanted the penetration of his cock. They meant the same thing. She was his, to give whatever he needed, however he needed.

Now he was trailing the next bloom over her breast, covering the nipple and teasing it with the thick cluster of petals, a contrast to the sharp tiger teeth. Leaning forward, he pinched that clamp, removed the one on the left side. As the blood rushed in and her breath sucked in hard at the pain, he soothed it with his mouth, suckling her, letting her feel the barest graze of his fangs before he replaced his mouth with the rose's sweet stroke.

During those few moments, as she drew in deep, shuddering breaths, she felt him sink to an even more intimate level of her soul, further than he'd ever gone before. She'd known of a vampire's power to do that to a third mark, reach so deep, into such dark places. On a mere whim, the vampire could tear apart the servant's mind, break her in a hundred different hellish ways. Feeling his power to do that was truly as terrifying as she'd heard. It was like having one's soul skewered by a steel spit, and the steel weapon was his implacable will. It made her mind and heart as helpless as her body was, restrained like this.

But it was Mason there, the implacable weight of his will. Her Master. She loosened her grip on the roses in her hand, realizing she'd crushed them. More petals drifted to the ground around her.

He removed the other clamp, nuzzled and cosseted that nipple the same way, but then he took two small tea rose buds, positioned them over her nipples and repositioned those tiger teeth. The pressure was far less, buffered by that floral cushion, but the teeth bit into the buds' thick layers, sending the sweet fragrance up to her nose.

Breaking off the heads of three more roses, he lifted them over her head. She raised her face as much as she was able, closed her eyes as the petals pattered down over her face, her bare shoulders. Several landed on her breasts. He wrapped the first stem around her throat, his hands collaring her there, a firm pressure for several delicious moments before it was replaced by the constriction of that stem. It was longer than the other two, but he wove the next two stems into it, creating a collar of intertwined pieces that pricked her in a random pattern.

She was licking her lips, needing him as he worked so close to her the fabric of his jeans leg brushed her knee. His amber gaze was intent, absorbed in what he was doing. It held captive any words she might have, because she was being treated as a true slave, expected to be still and compliant beneath his hands, his wishes, no matter what. She'd never felt so fulfilled, and yet needing-to-be-filled, all at once.

But as she watched him, she also could appreciate the creative artistry of the Master who'd claimed her. There was a small bundle of long wires that had been slipped into the vase, probably another of Mason's silent instructions to Amara. Using the wires and tiny clips to split, connect and tighten the hold of the stems, he was weaving her into a web of slim, sharp rose stalks. The next one attached to the collar went straight down her sternum. Two more branched out from that piece to curve under each breast. They passed under her arms and were reconnected to the collar in the back.

He had to move closer to position them. It brought him right up against her. As she made an incoherent moan in her throat, he pressed an absent kiss along her temple, then he tightened that connecting piece. The thorns bit into the tender flesh under her breasts, making her nipples tingle hard in their rose and silver constraints. The strands of thorns around her throat pulled against her windpipe, reminding her of that restraint. At the same moment, he slid one finger over her clit, a passing, unexpected caress that ricocheted through her like an electrical shock.

She bit into his flesh, the muscled pectoral beneath the stretch of his T-shirt, and heard his growl as she tried to puncture him through the heavy weight cotton. But he didn't draw back. He let her mouth him through the cloth, turn the bite into a random, erratic pull at the shirt with her teeth. She wanted it off, wanted to taste him. Instead, he hooked another stem to the binding he'd created in the back, down to her lower back. There he connected two more long green stems and brought them to the front, crossing over her hip bones, arrowing toward her pussy.

He stepped back. As she watched him with greedy eyes, he connected two stems to that connection point just above her mons, and threaded them along the crease between thigh and pussy, along the metal clamps on either side of her labia. She contracted on the rose bud he'd placed inside of her. As she did, he circled those stems around her upper thighs and reattached them at the labia with the help of those diabolical little clips. One more tightening, and here, too, he drew blood.

Stems now passed under her breasts, up and down her back, over her hips, through the juncture of her thighs and around the tops of her thighs. Around her biceps and throat. Though the cross held her fast, the delicate strength of the rose stems was what had her trembling the most.

Blood was trickling down her breast from the punctures at her throat. Two streams, one coming from the thorn at her shoulder, the other closer to the collar bone, on an intent, slow trek down her sternum. As she watched, the one from her shoulder made its way with sensual accuracy toward her nipple. Before gravity could slide it away from that goal, the tea rosebud clamped over it caught the flow, the blood staining the petals, outlining the ruffled tip.

Her eyes closed as her Master took care of the other stream, catching it with his mouth at the point right between her breasts, his hard jaw teasing the curves. He suckled the blood off her, licked his way back up to her throat, his tongue tracing around the puncture point and setting off fireworks in those sensitive nerves along her neck. Fighting her restraints to turn her head toward him, she caressed the side of his face, his hair, with her cheek. She sought any part of him she could reach with her lips, but he drew back again.

Two roses left. He put the stems around her ankles, above the restraints, and she was caught up in a storm of reaction when he knelt with his lithe grace to taste the blood there, working his way up to where the ones around her thighs were likewise producing small streams.

Bleed for me... She was bleeding for him. She would give him every last drop if he demanded it.

"If I ever asked such a terrible thing, I would expect you to do your best to stake me, *habiba.*" He glanced up at her, those amber eyes ablaze with passion. "For I would truly have lost my mind." Keeping his eyes on her, he followed the blood track with his mouth until he was high up on her thigh, his hands on her hips. So she was locked in his gaze when she saw his fangs, and let out an enraptured cry when he pierced the femoral, the fast rush of life-giving blood enough to send a squeezing, incredible surge of reaction into her pussy. Her clit spasmed and her mouth opened, sucking in air, trying for the words.

"Master...I can't..."

You won't come, habiba. Not yet. Those metal pieces won't let you.

And by all the fires of hell, he was right. It was the nearest thing to an almost climax she'd ever experienced, but the constriction, the tight hold that wouldn't allow any movement, prevented her from going there. But she was gasping and making the sounds of a climax, tiny, near screams, choking sobs as the sensation passed over her like a coquettish wave, just out of her reach. The feverish shudder through her limbs had her pleading.

"Please...my lord." She didn't know how many times she repeated it as he drew nourishment from her thigh, his other hand idly stroking the other leg. He was leaning into her, one knee bent on the outside of her knee, the other on the floor between her spread legs, so his groin was firmly pressed against her calf. He was always an impressive size, but perhaps it was her state of near hysterical lust that made him feel far bigger. His self-control was driving her mad, but as if she'd turned a key in the door, he yanked her into his mind.

What lay behind the self-control took her to a whole different level of madness. She was immersed in a raging storm of male lust, a flash of images and emotions, all the things he wanted to do to her, things that could strain her to the endurance of her mind and body. They battered her, sent her reeling. Then, after that brief immolation in the flames, he let her fall back from that door and closed it again, leaving her shaken.

He closed the punctures with the coagulants all vampires possessed and rose, his tumultuous gaze sweeping over her in a way that had her swallowing sound again.

"You'll stay with her."

Jessica blinked, realizing her whole world had narrowed to him. Amara was back, and she had no idea when the woman had arrived. She knelt beside his chair, her hands folded, head bowed.

"You will not communicate with her in any way. Your only job is to watch over her. You will tell me if she is in any discomfort that is unacceptable to me."

"Yes, my lord."

Mason's gaze slid over his other servant, then came back to Jessica. She stared at him. He couldn't possibly leave her, not like this. She was dying, her body consumed by desire so ravenous it was a dragon, about to swallow a virgin damsel in one bite. Perhaps it was the look in his eye that brought that comparison to her whirling mind.

"Good. I'm going for a ride on Coman. I'll be back in a while."

§

It wasn't until he disappeared around the corner of the stairwell that Jessica really believed it. It overcame her, such that she wanted to rage like a temperamental child, scream curses after him. He was leaving her alone in this state...and in this dungeon, tied to this cross. Amara was here, but...

No. He wasn't leaving her. The feverish euphoria of her denied and bound state refused to let panic take the upper hand. His mind would be with her every second. She knew him, knew he wouldn't let her suffer a moment of true fear. He wanted to see if she could trust him, trust her Master. He was punishing her, yes, but he was doing more than that.

It took a good few minutes to work all that out, however, since her mind was so consumed with lust, disbelief and trepidation, that thinking in any linear way took supreme effort. Amara kept her gaze down, only flicking it up every few seconds to check on Jessica's status, though she eschewed any direct eye contact, following Mason's command to the letter. Whatever he'd said to them, apparently Amara wasn't pushing any boundaries.

That was Jessica's job, and she'd accomplished it, hadn't she? Spread and bound, aroused and teased by rosebuds, thorns, nipple clamps, clit compression. Punctured with tiny floral fangs in six or seven key places, and the inside of her thigh still throbbing with the tantalizing impression of his mouth. She should have known, however, that he wasn't nearly done tormenting her – and that he didn't have to be in the room to make it worse. All those images in his head...the lingering impression of brutal lust and an all-encompassing need to take.

Jorge already had Coman's bridle on, but Mason apparently hadn't requested any other tack. He let her into his mind's eye as he swung up on the horse. Coman reflected his master's state of mind, because when Mason mounted, the horse was cutting a circle, his ears laid back, but the savagery of the two males were in accord. Coman was more than willing to be turned toward the beach. They took the dune at a canter, but when they hit the shore, Mason let him have his head.

As he crouched low over the horse's neck to steady him, they thundered across the sand. Every reverberation of the horse's hooves thrummed through Mason's thighs, his aching balls and hard cock. His mind was pummeled by visions of wanting to take Jessica off the cross, take her down to her knees and possess her utterly, the way Coman's instinct would take a mare in heat. Those teeth to the neck, the pressure of the male body pressing dominantly down on the female's. *Mine, mine, mine...*

Jessica closed her eyes, immersed in it, aching and short of breath. *My love...*

She didn't know what made her call him that, but whispered from her lips, she responded to the emotion under the fury. He was angry that she'd forced his hand in this. More than that, his own savage reaction, as her blood began to flow and she began to beg him, had driven him out here, to try and control a need for her that ran as thick and hot as hers did for him. His mind didn't tell her that, but the fire pumping through his blood, that she picked up from the glimpse of his mind, told her.

He slowed the horse at last, made the loop and came

cantering back. Coman shook his head, snorting, his sides lathered. Mason slid off him, tied the reins on his neck and sent him back toward the stables with a slap on his flanks and a mental signal to Jorge that the horse was coming for a rubdown.

Then he stripped. T-shirt, jeans, a mere two items that left him completely naked before the waves, feeling the cool evening breeze play off his skin, ripple over his thighs, his erect cock. He glanced down, giving her a full scale view of it. She'd been right. It was larger than even usual, the tip damp with fluid, his testicles smooth and tight. She wanted to touch him, close her hand over him, see if her fingers would reach around that impressive girth. Take him in her mouth, all the way to the back of her throat, let him punish her that way if he wished.

Instead, he walked into the tide line, laid himself down on the sand and let the foam laced waters wash over his thighs. She shivered, though the tropical waters were still warm from the day's sunlight. She let out a small, plaintive protest as he took himself in hand and began to stroke his cock with strong, clever fingers.

No, my lord. Please...let me.

He was imagining it as her hand, her mouth, her wet, sucking cunt. Her on top of him right now, his hands driving her down on his length. He'd watch her eyes grow wide and vulnerable, her throat straining out screams of pleasure and agony, the release powerful enough to destroy them both.

Part of your punishment, Jessica. You will get this later. When you know for certain what kind of Master I am, and submit fully to that knowledge.

No... She was protesting not his words, but the fisting of that cock. Her pussy clenched anew, unable to create any friction with that metal frame inside of her, just the taunting whisper of the damp rose petals. That excruciating near-orgasmic feeling once again swept over her, making her cry out, pull against her bonds, as he let her feel what he was feeling, the rolling power of the climax coming up through him. Whenever he came home from his travels, he spilled his seed inside of her first, nowhere else. Now he was going to give it instead to the sea, an offering to long-haired sea sirens who would taste the salt of him and wish that they could lure him out to them with their songs, where they'd forever make him their captive.

There is no song but yours I will ever hear, habiba. *Only you.*

Every part of her was taut, and she was having trouble breathing, straining against her bonds. He wasn't too far away from her to see. He could see everything through Amara's eyes if he wished.

Please, my lord. Let me... Come back to me here. I beg you. Take me however you wish, even deny me, but do not torment me like this. I can't bear it. I need you. You will tear my soul in half. Please, please don't.

His hand stilled. *What if I make you suck me to completion, but refuse you a climax, not just today, but for the next ten days, while I continue to torment you however I wish, keeping you aroused and wanting?*

I will want to stake you in your sleep, she admitted honestly, *but I will obey anything you desire, my lord.* However, though it took an effort so great it made tears roll down her cheeks anew, she managed to find her original resolve in the center of her besieged heart. The determination that had not dimmed throughout the past few interminable and ecstatic hours, but instead burned more brightly than ever.

Anything except being left behind. It's you who taught me what being a vampire's servant truly means. I'm here for you—for the protection of your heart and soul, even your body—and when you leave me, you deny me the right of being your full servant, of being all those things to you. I don't care what others may do to me – it will never be as unbearable as spending a moment without you.

Part 8

Perhaps it was because of how vulnerable she felt right now, how stripped down to the soul, but if he brought himself to completion, gave his essence to the waves and the sand, rather than to her body, it would be as sharp and devastating a rebuke to her heart as anything else he could do. She equated it with his choosing to leave her behind, not letting her share every part of his life. He was her Master, her life and will his to command, yet it wasn't that simple. She loved him; she had demands of her own, so many of them connected to her deep-seated need to serve him.

Those tears touched her lips, suppressed sobs fair choking her. He'd proven his point. He could break her down to this, to pure need and pain, no rational or sensible thoughts in her mind, only emotion. *Please don't...*

That feeling came again, that he was at the deepest level of her soul, a tender, quivering thing he held in his strong grasp. But this time that sense spread out through her, holding all of her, so strong an impression it felt like actual physical contact. She could smell him on her skin, even feel the pressure of his fingers on her flesh. This was what he could have done for Farida, if he hadn't been magically blocked from helping her during her tragic end. She could have avoided a single moment of true fear, and even more than that.

Jessica realized the sting of the thorns had disappeared, though they still dug into her flesh. She couldn't feel the hold of the manacles. It was as if she'd stepped inside of him, and nothing being done to her body could affect her...though the pleasure he gave her remained, a lovely, writhing coil that made her soul dance and undulate against his, a seductive dance. And she felt his ethereal response, a blast of male heat that twisted around her like a lazy tornado of glittering particles, making her part her lips and taste him on her tongue.

As a vampire, he'd always had this power, this sorcery, and now he let her experience it as the miraculous gift it was. It was a magic she'd never seen exercised by a vampire before, had never even heard about it.

Because it is only possible when the servant trusts the vampire so much that she completely surrenders to him, habiba, at every level of her existence. She fears nothing...no pain, no emotion, so long as he holds a claim on her.

He hadn't expected it either. She heard it in his tone, a thickness to it that suggested she might not be the only one awestruck and too choked up to give voice to it. They simply rode that feeling together. As she drifted in a haze that was nothing short of miraculous, she wondered if this was what they meant when they said a servant followed a vampire into the afterlife. Because this was more than him being inside of her. She was inside of him and they were melded together, as if once, long, long ago, before they'd first been created as two separate beings, they'd started this way, two souls entwined in the cradle of their creation.

"No..." She whispered it, because though she felt no pain or the abrasion of her restraints, she could still feel their hold, and the one at her waist was being removed. She didn't want Amara to take them off. *I'll wait for my Master to remove them. I'll wait as long as he wishes, if I have to stay this way for days and days...*

A fanciful and entirely foolish idea, habiba. *What kind of Master would do such a thing to your beautiful skin?*

It wasn't Amara. He was here. She opened her eyes, dislodging more tears clinging to her lashes, and he caught them on his fingertips. "Your devotion terrifies me," he said, his voice a low, unsteady rumble, his amber eyes so fierce and wild, as if he thought he might need to fight something off to protect her. It made her want to touch him, but the cross still held her. "All I want is to keep you safe," he continued in that same raw voice. "You're so fragile and delicate to me, a treasure so easy to destroy, and yet your love makes you determined to throw yourself against every rock, including my will. If anything shatters you, *habiba*, it will shatter me. Do you not understand that? Can you not find the mercy to see why I *can't* take you where I can't keep you safe?"

Still so deep inside of him, she could feel it, that deep darkness Lyssa had warned her about, a darkness capable of destroying far more than himself if it was stirred up again. The vampire tiger with the soul of a desert djinn.

"I don't know how to resolve it, my lord," she said, just as softly, as those tears kept falling. He continued to collect each one on his fingers as she struggled for the words. "I feel it, I do, and it tears me to pieces to cause you such pain. But...perhaps..." *Just as there is a wisdom that vampires have about what their servants need, things we ourselves don't understand... As your servant, I know for certain, with everything I am, that my place, my destiny, whatever it is, is to be by your side, always, for everything you face.* Then she spoke aloud again, staring up at him. "Whatever each of us faces was meant to be faced together. And to deny either of us that is to deny what is meant to be."

He cupped her cheek with that large hand that could almost cover the side of her face, and she pressed her lips to his palm, her wet lashes marking him. "Stay here," he said. "Don't worry. I'm not leaving this room."

She saw Amara was gone. He moved to the doorway and, with one switch, he cut the torchlight in the room. Then the stairwell light was gone as he shut the heavy oak door, plunging them both into total darkness.

A third mark could see in the dark, as long as there was some component of light, however dim, but with no windows, there was none. This is what Raithe had done to her, shut her in a dungeon with no lights, marked her with blood and let rats and roaches crawl over her. Whereas before tonight she might have cringed, struggled against the terror, now she drew on that certainty of Mason being inside her. With a savagery that could match his own, she used it like a scythe, severing herself from even a hint of such fear. She wasn't alone in the darkness. She never would be, not ever again.

His touch on her ankle brought a soft sigh to her lips. "Afraid that I might see you weeping, my lord?" she asked, a tremor in her voice. "I feel your emotions inside of me."

In answer, his mouth touched her leg, just above her ankle bone. To do that, he had to not only be kneeling, but bent forward, a position of total homage. When he lingered there, his mouth grazing her insole, her emotions matched the strength of his. She was the one bound at his behest, helpless to his will, yet he was giving her this, an act of servile devotion, a message so clear that it didn't need to be said.

As much as she was his slave, so, too, was he hers.

He made his way up her calf, but he took a very long time at it, teasing his way down to her foot and back up again, caressing the back of her knee with his tongue in a way that shot her focus back to her unabated desire in full force. It was like he'd pulled her out of warm water in an underground spring into the cold, brilliant shock of ocean waters under the bright sun. She realized then that he'd unlatched the manacles around her ankles, and freed the rose stems there.

As he worked his way up her thighs, he did the same to the stalks he'd wound around her upper thighs, used his fangs to slice the ones that he'd drawn along the crease of hip and thigh from her waist. His lips came so close to her mound, her aroused clit, she let out a moan, chased by a full cry as he didn't deny either of them. Sliding over to give her a slow, wet lick there, he sealed his mouth over her clit to gently suckle it. He teased her labia and the opening below with the tip of his tongue, sliding into her for a languid exploration. With his mouth, he drew the soaked rose bloom from her, and she sensed from his shifting he'd carefully set it aside. She knew he'd do what he'd promised. Preserve it, and ever after when she saw it in his gallery, she'd remember this and remember every feeling, every fervent desire.

The basket clamp was removed, withdrawn from inside of her and replaced with his tongue, punctuated by her shuddering sigh. She was in such a chaotic haze of the physical, emotional and spiritual, she didn't move, not even to strain toward him. Her nerves were compact and dense with sensation, her muscles holding her utterly still so she could feel everything he did to her.

He moved away at last to lick the places the thorns had dug into her, soothing her skin. Then his hands were at her waist and he straightened, his body pressed against her as he cut the stems at her back, and sternum, so that everything fell away except the collar of thorns he'd worked around her throat. Now she did move. Tightening her stomach muscles, she used them and the brace of the cuffs holding her arms to lift her legs, twine them around him.

He wore only a towel, wrapped low around his hips. The salt water on his bare skin brushed her breasts, the pressure of his chest rocking the clamps and tiny rose buds up in a way that had her strangling another agonized sound of pleasure. As he cupped her face with both hands, he kissed her mouth with unutterable tenderness. Slow, his tongue moving in deep, coiling around hers, no rush, nothing but the two of them in that mind to mind, heart to heart, soul to soul, perfect merging.

When he lifted his head, he removed the stems around her biceps, then her forearms. Only the wrists and forehead were left. That and the clamps.

Deep breath, my love.

She drew it, and he removed the clamps at the same time. Even with the rose buds buffering them, their bite had been cruel, and she sucked in deeper at the rush of pain, but his hand dropped, massaging her clit, balancing it. *When you join me in my bed for my dawn sleep, I will suckle and soothe them, massage healing balm into them with my own hands.*

She would be content if he fell asleep with his mouth on them instead, her arm around his wide shoulders, her other hand stroking his hair. Her Master, her terrifying, ferocious, yet incredibly tender and loving Master, held in her arms like a sleeping babe, so she might bring him comfort for every fear he had.

Ah, habiba. The thought won her another kiss, and he removed the binding across her forehead. At last, he slid his fingers over her wrist and flicked the binding free there, and then from the other. His arms stretched out to meet hers, body leaning into her, holding her still pilloried, only now with the restraint of his hands, his fingers tangled with hers. She tightened her legs over his hips, holding him even closer, and rubbed herself against his hard, blessedly unrelieved length beneath the Egyptian cotton.

Temptress.

I need you, my lord. She spoke against his lips, wanting the sound of the whisper in the darkness. "Please. I need you inside of me. I'm begging you."

I cannot resist your pleas, but first...

He slid his arm around her waist, and she clasped his shoulders, giving an ecstatic mewl as she was able to hold him at last, his chest tight against her sore breasts, his ribcage brushing her abdomen, her thighs locked around his hips. He carried her through that darkness as easily as he would carry a child. When he sat her down on one of the stools at the bar, she heard him opening something like a briefcase. She hadn't remembered there being a case there, but she hadn't been entirely cognizant of anything but him for quite some time now.

She blinked as he lit a taper candle on the wet bar, creating a dim flicker of light. The first thing she wanted to see was him, and she immediately lifted her fingers to his face, traced the strong bones of his jaw, his brow, his lips. He allowed it, watching her every movement, the slight, tremulous smile that lifted her own mouth.

"I love you so much, my lord."

Those amber eyes darkened, and he took hold of her wrist, pressing his mouth hard against her palm, so hard he gave her a tiny nick with his fang. He was always so in control, that unintentional blood draw told her how moved he was. Then she saw what he'd brought her and she was overwhelmed.

"You proved to me beyond doubt tonight that you don't need this," he said, lifting the collar before her wide eyes. "But if you will accept it, then perhaps it will always remind me of your devotion, your trust and faith in me." He paused, so much in his eyes it almost burned her skin. "Maybe that will give me the strength to yield to your will, this once, and believe that Allah will help me protect what surely must be one of his greatest treasures. I know you are mine."

She gave up the attempt to hold back any more tears. The one-inch circlet, with the metals patterned to look like a tiger's skin, was perfect. As he unhooked the closure, which looked like a tiger's talon, she noted the amber pendant dangling below it. She reached out, cupping it in her hand, and looked at the unusual swirling pattern inside of it, two intertwined crimson spirals.

"My blood and yours, *habiba*. The clear amber was

infused with it by a very special jeweler, one who also blessed it with a great many protection spells. The collar will lock on your neck, and only I have the key to remove it."

"I'll never ask you to do so," she promised. She raised shining eyes to him. "Please, Master. I accept it with all my heart. Please put it on me."

When they'd lifted her onto the cross, Enrique and Amara had removed the temporary slim silver collar. As much of an impression as that accessory had made on her, it was nothing next to the weight and significance of this one. If he was placing a ring on her finger in front of an assembly of the entire disapproving vampire world, including the Vampire Council, it couldn't mean more.

It fit her neck closely, holding it as lovingly and irrevocably as his hands might. After he latched it, he picked up the key strung on a silver chain. He was going to thread it over his head one-handed, but when she reached for it, he let her do it, dipping his head so she could guide it down, using both her hands to free his long hair from it and take the chain to his nape. The key slid down the provocative track of collarbone and sternum, resting at last between the flat planes of his pectorals. Leaning forward, she kissed the key, and the heated skin beneath.

Sliding his hands beneath her arms, he lifted her off the bar. Holding her only with the strength of his arms, he backed them up, until he'd reached the heavy oak chair again. Lowering her to her feet, he gently but firmly set her from him. When she lifted her gaze, she saw the stern, steady gaze of her Master.

Her eyes automatically lowered and her knees bent, taking her to a kneeling position before him. She didn't even have to consciously send her mind the command. As he took a seat in the chair, the towel parted high on his thigh, giving her only a shadowed view of what it concealed.

"Come take me in your mouth as you desired to do, my sweet slave. Prove your devotion to your Master. Prove to me how intent and uninterrupted your focus would be, if I commanded you to your knees to do this before the whole

Vampire Council."

It could be the whole Council or the whole world. As far as she was concerned, from this moment forward, with that collar on her throat and all it symbolized—whether it was just the two of them in a blissful moment like this, or in the middle of the Vampire Gathering—there was only him.

Part 9

Jessica put her hands on his knees, sliding over the bone to the firm joining point of the muscles that layered his thighs. All her senses were open to the nth degree, such that the nerve endings in her fingers registered each element of the terrain. Smooth, slim bands from the knees, tributaries to those wide muscles leading up his inner thighs. She hooked the opening in the towel, tugging enough to have it loosen at his waist, then slid her hand under. She enjoyed the pleasure of first finding him by touch, caressing his testicles, then the pulsing life of his cock. As she closed her grip over the thick base, she rested the side of her hand on the heavy sac beneath it. With the other hand she pushed the towel back, revealing the impressive length and breadth of him. She felt a surge of quaking delight at the viscous fluid collected at the top, waiting for her parted lips.

Can you imagine it, habiba? They are all watching, the most powerful vampires in the world. Their servants stand still behind their chairs, yet every eye is on you, every mind wondering if you will serve me well.

There is only you, Master. She repeated the thought, letting him feel the resolve in her, the simple truth of it. She nuzzled the top of his cock, touching the tip of her tongue to the wet slit, her grip tightening and sliding upward, letting him feel the friction. She spoke, so she could breathe on him. "Nothing but your approval will matter to me."

His fingers twitched on the chair arm, and it made her lips curve, even as her heart tightened with such love she thought it could crack from the pressure. "It will be only you, even if...even if one of them orders his female servant to kneel behind me, turn on her back so she is laying between my knees, which she pushes open wider to accommodate her, so her mouth has access to my cunt." Male interest in a female's mouth on another female's flesh was eternal, and she used it to ease into the other idea. "And another Council member gives an order to her male servant..."

A thread of tension ran up his thighs, but she slid her hand over one of them, her knuckles stroking, then dipping to cup his testicles in her hand again. As she caressed them, she tilted her head to trace the flare of the broad head with her tongue, a slow circle.

She'll tell him to kneel and spread the legs of that female servant, and drive into her. But as he does, he slides his arm around her back, lifts her up. She curls her arms over my hips to steady herself as she uses the angle to put her mouth on my pussy and start eating it for their viewing pleasure...and yours. When he fucks her slow, deep, building her response as she is driving mine, you'll be able to feel it. Not only in my mind, but in the way I suck on you, how hard it is for me to concentrate as she nibbles on my clit, sinks her delicate tongue into me, that place that craves the far more substantial thrust of your cock.

"Jessica." His voice was a growl. "Suck me."

She took him in, stretching her lips to get over his substantial girth, a noise of pleasure in the back of her throat as she slid down his length as far as she could go at this angle, her hips off her calves. She'd given him the image, but now there was only him to her, no ability to maintain any other focus. She sucked him deep, hard, then came up slow, the way she knew he liked it. Mason was as good at using denial to prolong his own response as he was at administering it. He knew the power and pleasure of making her work for his release. She hungered to feel it, to feel that powerful hand convulse on her hair, pulling hard and painful at her scalp as he drove up into her mouth, pumping his seed into her. Some sense of her punishment lingered in this, such that she knew she couldn't hope to have his cock sinking into her cunt this first time, joining them together the way she needed so desperately.

Work for it, my sweet slave. Earn it. The Council is watching.

It's only your approval that matters to me, Master.

His fingers grazed her nape, tugging on her hair, a gentle affection, but with a hint of strength to it. She savored the taste of his thick shaft in her mouth, going down then back up again, sliding her tongue all over it, random erratic patterns, then settling into a rhythmic pump, vividly imagining it shoving into her wet heat, the muscles of her pussy sucking on him in a torturous drag every time he withdrew, then came back in. The intimate tissues between her legs contracted at the thought. Sometimes, when he didn't have her hands pinned or bound, she could let her fingers slide over his buttocks, feel those muscle groups tightening and releasing, increasing the drive of his thrusts.

She should have known the danger of planting a seed in Mason's head. With only a brief mind touch for warning, Amara's hands settled on Jess's hips, gripping to lift her up, changing her angle so she was tilted further forward. Levering Mason's cock to a more horizontal drive into her mouth, Jess braced one hand on his leg with the other still gripping him firmly. She was determined not to break her rhythm, even though she knew what was coming. Mason of course had to do his best to scatter her concentration, sending her the image so she saw Enrique come behind Amara, slide her robe off her shoulders. As he did, he bent to press an open mouth to her throat, his hand tangling in her hair roughly. Her hands, returning to Jess's hips after the robe was removed, tightened there, responding to the provocation. Enrique slid an arm around Amara's waist, another over her firm, high breasts, and turned her in a flexible, graceful movement. When he lowered her to her back between Jess's spread thighs, his smooth, lean and tan muscles flexed.

Enrique wore only a pair of cotton trousers and he shed them, kicking them to the side and leaving himself as naked as his wife. His dark eyes were hot on the curves of her body, the way she instinctively spread her legs, bending them at the knee, an open invitation to the man who claimed her as husband, through whose eyes the vampire who claimed her could see all that she was offering. It made Jessica shiver, all the layers of possession and meaning in the relationships between them.

Having trouble focusing, habiba?

Not at all, my lord. She renewed her efforts, nipping the velvet stretched skin, stimulating that taut vein that ran up the base of his shaft.

Then we shall have to try harder.

Jess's moan vibrated against his cock as he showed her Enrique's view when he knelt between Amara's legs. The servant seated his erect cock against her damp flesh and pushed inward, the slick lips of the labia giving way, the channel pulling him in so he slid in to the hilt. Putting his hands beneath Amara's back, he lifted her like an offering, bending to lick one nipple as her mouth found Jess's pussy. Her slim but strong hands curved over Jess's hips, her thumbs pressing into her buttocks.

Amara was well-versed in lovemaking skills of all kinds, a trained consort as well as dancer. Plus she was a woman, who well knew what made a woman respond. She also had the ability to merge into Jess's mind through Mason's, particularly if he was facilitating it, like now, allowing her to pick up the current of Jessica's arousal—when Jess needed the oral stimulation to be rough or gentle, a consistent or erratic stimulation.

Jess's hand constricted on Mason's thigh and she gave a hard, uncontrolled pull on his cock as Amara's tongue circled her clit, pulling it into the cavern of her mouth. Jess quivered at Amara's breath of hot, teasing air, her response to Enrique pushing even harder into his wife's body, a long, demanding thrust that bumped her nose against Jessica's labia. Mason's hand moved to Jess's hair now, tangling his fingers in it and tightening there, pushing her down deeper on him, bringing his own demand into play.

Jess couldn't close her eyes on the images, but neither could Mason. All three of his servants, two on their knees and one on her back, arranged to serve and please his senses. Enrique pumping into Amara's pussy, so wet they could hear the sound of it as he reached his hilt and withdrew again. Amara's upper body flushed and breasts full and quivering, the nipples hard and needy, still marked with his mouth. Her back and throat arched both to receive him in her body and to give her a better angle to tease and lick Jessica's cunt. She used those relentless third mark and dancer's muscles to hold herself, as well as the strength of her husband's hands.

Mason showed Jessica herself, kneeling between his legs, her mouth working his cock, the thick breadth of it glistening with the moisture of her mouth as she slid up and down, sometimes going all the way to the tip, then sucking the head in again, teasing the edge of it with her tongue. Her slim shoulders were bowed forward, the line of her spine curved up as she serviced him, too tempting for him not to trail his fingers along the bumps of vertebrae, caressing the pale skin. Her hand on his thigh moved upward with her effort, bracing herself against his ridged abdomen, fingers curling in, thumb caressing the smooth pubic area right above his turgid length.

He was huge now, and she wanted him inside of her so badly, but she had to prove it, had to give him this. *Earn it, sweet slave.* The words drove her, inspired her, held her in thrall. She treasured the rasp of his breath, the tightening of all those splendid muscles as he used them to drive his cock into her mouth more forcefully. She was having to concentrate to keep pace, and concentration was getting very difficult.

God, Amara was too damn good at this, and the little hitches and breaks caused by what Enrique was doing to her, pushing her toward the edge of control, just added to it, a mix of chaos with skill, a devastating combination that was having a domino effect on all of them.

It's not enough. The thought hit her mind like a desert sand storm, and then Mason had her under the arms, lifting her away from Amara, the vibration of the woman's mouth still rippling through Jessica's cunt as he put her upon that large cock and drove her down, with ruthless passion.

The feeling was indescribable, the mix of the two

sensations enough to have Jessica grabbing onto his shoulders for support. But those amber eyes, like fire upon all her exposed flesh, demanded, wanted more.

I will direct your movements, habiba. Put your hands on your breasts. Cup them, tease the nipples, display yourself for me.

She obeyed, and immediately cried out as he took over the movements of her body, lifting and then shoving her back down on him, as if she were no more than a doll he could direct at will. A climax was spiraling up, irresistible, from that joining point. The moment she squeezed her nipples, she imagined his mouth upon them, the pressure of his suckling hold, the unexpected score of his fangs. She couldn't help the thought, but her mind as well as her body wasn't her own now. She was all his, a creature purely of his pleasure, and she gave herself to it. The rub of his cock against her clit, how he filled her inside, the idea of his mouth on her nipples...

More than anything, she wanted to wrap her arms around his broad, sheltering shoulders, bury her face against all the thick, copper-silk of his hair, and let the feelings and sensations take her. Let him take her, wherever he would.

Do it, habiba. Let me feel the beat of your heart against mine, and trust me to take us home.

She immediately complied, letting out a soft cry of joy and arousal both at that meeting, for he banded his arms around her as well, wrapping them together, her upper torso flush to his, bone, muscle, sinew, and the life sustaining organs beneath, all moving and reacting in sync. Her fingers slipped over the scarred lines of the tiger tattooed high on the back of his shoulder, even as his fingers spread out over the one on her back. A tiger gazing through a bamboo forest of scars, a reminder that the tiger was always there, watching over her, making sure those scars had no hold upon her.

As she closed her eyes and put her face into his hair, she slid her fingers into it, gripped his neck and inhaled everything about his beloved, familiar scent, the danger and sex, the love and safety of him. All hers. Her vampire.

Sweet slave. My beloved. Though she'd expected him to keep the same pace, she wasn't surprised that, bonded this way, he slowed them down. He showed her Amara and Enrique were gone, having taken their finale elsewhere. As aroused as they both were, she expected that wasn't much further than the room at the top of the stairs. The lights were dimmed, all the things in here in shadows, so it was just candles and stone walls. Fire and earth, and her and Mason.

He held her banded in his arms that way and moved inside her. Slow, slow pushes deep, to the hilt, then equally slow withdrawals, controlling everything. She made tiny cries, letting him know how excruciating it was, how close she was, as sensation rippled along her cunt from his advance and retreat, a rolling rhythm like the gradual movement of waves far out from shore. As he kept doing it, his cock convulsed inside of her, his expression tightening as she lifted her face, stared into his. They held gazes, each feeling the sensations of the other as Mason opened his mind to her, let them feed on one another. He was very close to release, as was she, but he was prolonging it, a quiver in all those fine limbs, wanting her begging.

She could hold out a little longer, knowing he would want to test her limits, because that was his nature. But not much longer. His eyes glinted, knowing it, as he brought her down, driving in deep again. "Oh..." She gasped, hands clutching his shoulders, nails digging in.

"Drink from me, *habiba*." The demand was hoarse, feral. "I want to feel you nourish yourself from me. I want my blood on your tongue when you come."

She'd gotten better at it, learning how to use her canines so it wasn't as difficult to break through the skin, but she knew any pain she caused him was outweighed by what it offered to them both. She put her mouth to his throat, her breath clogging as it changed the angle, drove him deeper, and then she bit.

Rich, metallic, life giving. The visceral bond between vampire and servant, the stuff that could restore her energy even if she was grievously wounded. She knew. He'd given her his heart's blood once before, and it had nearly killed them both, but he would do anything for her.

Anything but live without her.

At last, she understood, because she could truly feel him all the way to her soul, as open to her as she was to him. He *would* do anything for her, but if she loved him as much, she had to do the same.

When she licked the blood from the wound, swallowing, she made herself say it, though she had to do it in her mind, too difficult to say aloud. *I will abide by your will, my lord. Whatever it is. I want...to be with you, but if your heart cannot bear the fear of it, the fear of seeing me exposed to others...I will serve your heart and soul, as much as I serve your body. I love you and will learn to take joy in every command you give me, as an expression of your love for me.*

His arms confined her further, and he turned his head to take her mouth in a kiss, tasting that blood as he'd desired, one hand coming up to cup the back of her head. As he did, he moved her down, then up, then increased the pace, holding the kiss as they rose and fell, as fire moved up her thighs and centered in her loins.

"Mason..." She gasped it against his lips. "I can't—"

"Come for me, *habiba*. Prove your devotion and obey."

She was already going over, but she clamped down on him with her inner muscles, wanting and needing to bring him with her. *Please, my lord, don't let me go alone.*

She arched back, a scream breaking from her lips as the sensation took over, gripping her relentlessly, all the denied pleasure, all the stimulation, coming together so her pussy rippled and spasmed upon him, her hands now claws, digging into his skin. He abandoned finesse, hands vising on her hips once more, bruising, punishing, and as she writhed upon him, scream going to shriek, he began to release. The hot jets of seed drove her up and over again, before the first wave had even finished.

There was nothing so primal, so basic and clear as this, being taken by her Master. His amber gaze lifted to fasten on her face, taking in her every expression as she took in his, the fierce pleasure, the uncontrolled flood of desire that not only came from his cock, but from the heat emanating off of him, washing over her, making her buck, writhe and rock, undulate and grind herself on him with total physical and emotional abandon. When his hands stilled her enough to take one of her breasts in his mouth, sucking on her powerfully as he was still coming, her shrieks went into mindless wails. The climax kept thundering through her, incredible, building waves. She trusted him to hold onto her on the tossing storm waves, even as she gloried in knowing he was in that storm right along with her, his muscles shuddering, his cock still hard and pumping.

As they were finally driven to shore, her arms fell limply around his shoulders again, her face against the side of his. He wrapped his arms around her once more, holding her so close they were a tangled pillar of flesh, one of those intricate sculptures inspired by the Kama Sutra, its celebration of the joining of two hearts at all levels of existence. She never wanted to move.

"It is a closed circle, *habiba*," he said at last. She noticed his voice was thick, both with residual passion and something more. "You will stay here, because you love me too much to see me worried and fearful for you. I will take you, because I cannot bear your loneliness and fear for me when I am away."

His hand traced her face, lifting it, and he drew her back so her bottom was pressed deeper against his thighs. She made a small whimper at the feel of him shifting inside of her. Pressing her mouth to his palm, she bit him gently, but brought her gaze to his. Putting her trembling fingers on his mouth, she teased a fang, following his jaw, trailing along his brow.

"When it comes down to it," he rumbled, "I cannot deny my servant's wisdom, or the eight hundred years of my own." Those amber eyes held hers. "There are always things to fear. As you said earlier, there is never enough time to love, and so to let fear steal one single moment of loving you...that is something I would be a fool to permit."

"And you are not a foolish man." She whispered it, but her lips curved, inspiring a quirk from his own tempting mouth.

"Perhaps not. But it's also my experience that fools love the best and deepest of any of us. So maybe I will strive to be a fool, and give up my wisdom to love you with everything I am."

She was overcome, but she knew her Master well, that hint of a smile. Cocking her head, she gave him a dubious look, though she knew it couldn't diminish the telltale adoration in her eyes. "Give up your arrogance? Your know-it-all attitude? I don't know, my lord. That might even be beyond your significant capabilities."

"You think so?" He settled back, lifting a brow, his knuckles sliding along one of her breasts, stroking. "Perhaps the same could be said for a woman giving up her stubbornness, her belief that she always knows best."

"But we do, my lord." She blinked at him innocently. If her limbs had had an ounce of coordination right now, she would have hopped up, instigated one of their playful cat-and-mouse games that he could easily win but he always indulged, letting her play until he was aroused enough that the play became something else. As if he expected her to try regardless—and he might have been right—he surged up from the chair with her held securely in his arms.

"None of that right now."

"I think you far overestimate my stamina, my lord."

"Not at all." He hitched her in his arms, a quick bounce that made her grab onto his neck, hold him closer. "But I might test your weakened state by taking you to the beach. We can discuss who's right. While I hold you underwater."

"You know third marked servants can't drown."

"I know that full well, *habiba*." He gave her a wicked look. "Perhaps you can occupy yourself with something down there until I decide to let you up."

Jessica let the bubble of laughter take her, content to be held as he carried her toward whatever he next had planned for them. Maybe he would forgive Amara and Enrique fully and let them join them on the beach. They'd eat dinner out there, the cook would make cookies for desert, and Mason would taste the sugar and chocolate on her lips as they all lay out under the stars, naked and wet. Amara would tell stories of desert djinns and treasures hidden in the sand, and Jess would lay with her head on Mason's chest, feeling his heart beat and knowing there was no greater treasure than her desert tiger.

He was right. No fear should steal away the precious time they had, and she was determined to honor that, with every moment she was given with him. She would give him her faith, and they would banish fear forever.

Dark and Light

A vignette featuring David and Mina of A Witch's Beauty *from the* Daughters of Arianne Series.

Originally posted January 2011 in serial format.

Background: *In* Mermaid's Ransom, *the third book of the* Daughters of Arianne *series, it is revealed to David, an angel in the Prime Legion, that his mate Mina, the powerful sea witch, is pregnant. As he was unaware of this, in this vignette he is swiftly winging home to confront and handle Mina's volatile feelings about this unexpected change in their lives.*

Part 1

David banked sharply and swept beneath the belly of a Stealth fighter, cutting through the jet wash with the precision of a knife. He was torn between an ebullience that made him want to ride the chaotic air currents like a kid on a sled in Christmas snow, and an urgency that told him he needed to get home to his mate as soon as he could. Mina was pregnant. Not only was she pregnant, she knew she was pregnant, and she hadn't told him. He'd had to learn it from the accidental slip of a clairvoyant human, Alexis's friend Clara.

"Congratulations. You must be really excited. I didn't know angels . . . well, I guess they can, because Alexis has never said she couldn't have babies... Oh, crap. She hasn't told you yet. I think she was getting ready to tell you pretty soon. If your wife or girlfriend is scary, don't tell

her I was the one who told you."

No, his sea witch wasn't scary. Not to David. Yes, she could twist the universe like a pretzel, turn it inside out or pulverize it like a piñata, but from the moment he'd met her, he'd only seen her compelling complexity. Courage beyond anything he'd ever met, an odd code of unbreakable integrity. Irascible as a badger but fiercely loyal. She'd been horribly scarred then, but he'd met her bi-colored gaze, and seen the beauty of her soul. A soul that had stood fast in the fires of hell, and not just because half of her blood came from those fires. He'd seen the tenuous balance between light and dark within her, her stubborn resolve that *she* would determine who and what she was, not her Dark One sire or sea witch mother, or anyone's dire expectations of her.

In that blink of time, he'd known the very reason for his existence was to help her to do that. Not for the good of the world, not because it was some cosmic task he'd been charged to fulfill by the Legion. No. Instead, it was because he couldn't tolerate her bearing such a burden alone. He wouldn't allow her to feel another second of loneliness. Being with her might save the universe, and that was all well and good, but the main thing he cared about was being with her, because she'd ended his loneliness as well. She was *his* balance.

Over the twenty-two years they'd spent together, she'd finally started believing that. At least a little bit. And she trusted him more than she trusted anyone, but that didn't change the fact she had to fight an internal enemy with every breath. Because he was her mate, her champion and protector, he'd dedicated himself to helping her shoulder as much of that burden as possible.

He'd become adept at detecting the slightest shifts in Mina's moods, because with her, they could be warnings of significant swings—something akin to the shifting of tectonic plates under the earth's crust that would bring about major quakes. However, the Prime Legion Commander's daughter being kidnapped and yanked into a Dark One world had thrown everyone off. Since Mina and he had been as much a part of the effort to retrieve her as anyone, he hadn't been able to follow up on the clues she'd left him earlier in the week. Clues that should have been obvious.

§

The most significant one was when she'd told him she wanted to go spend time at their old desert home. They'd explored plenty of other worlds, dimensions and isolated places, but the desert was the first home they'd shared together. When Mina wanted to come back there, it was almost always because she needed to center and ground herself. To return to basics.

They'd been at a monastery, deep in the mountains of China, but it hadn't taken long to get back to the desert, not with the winged speed David could summon when needed. Mina had simply shut her eyes and hung on. She didn't like heights, but she coiled in his sure grasp, her fingers clutched at his nape, legs hooked over his thighs, and he relished the way she felt there. When she completely depended on his care and strength like that, he often had the desire to lazily spin and float, as if he were rocking her in a cradle of air and sky and the reassuring heat of his body. Sometimes she was okay with that, but this time, he felt her vibrating need to return to the desert, so he didn't indulge the whim.

Sam always kept the house ready for them, so after they were settled, Mina unwound from their trip by going to the front porch steps, taking a seat on the top one, and gazing out over the terrain. When he joined her, David sat on the step just below her, his back against the rail, his leg stretched out. She curled her bare feet on his thigh, toes dug in like an exotic dark bird perched there. He trailed his fingers idly along the tender pocket behind her knee, the line of thigh accessible under her skirt. Her little shiver stirred his blood, but then he felt the energy unfurl from her.

As he caressed her with a slow, easy touch, she rearranged the landscaping of natural scrub and sand into a large rock garden like they'd seen in their Asian travels.

She sculpted serpentine lines in the sand, carefully placed red and blue stones in balanced stacks, and used other rocks and sand tracks to make oblong circles around the low-lying, hardy shrubs.

And she accomplished all of it sitting on the front porch steps. Still, quiet, only her bi-colored eyes flickering and her lips pressing together as she manipulated the elements. It was like watching a small child drawing, holding the pencil so carefully, the mouth just so. A great deal of magic was effortless for her, but when she was creating something for her personal desires, she was like an artist who wasn't sure what the canvas would reflect when she was done. So she was far more meticulous in every detail.

She had one crimson-colored eye and one blue, both outlined with sooty, thick lashes that only enhanced a breathtakingly beautiful face. However, he'd noted an intensity to her gaze that suggested she was deeper in her head than usual, driven by something unsettling. Between that and her desire to come here, he knew the time was right to probe and see what was disturbing her.

"Mina, what is it?"

Those eyes turned to him. The flash of desperation was so unexpected that he immediately straightened. Closing one hand on her leg, he reached up toward her delicate face with the other.

Before he could say anything further, he'd received the rapid fire mental communication, alerting him, Mina and the entire Legion to Alexis's kidnapping.

§

Returning to the present, he knew that wasn't a good enough excuse. Though he was experiencing his own reaction to the news of Mina's pregnancy, he punished himself by shoving it down. He couldn't rejoice, not until he made sure she was okay. He wanted to celebrate it together, when he could convince her it was something to celebrate. Because he knew that desperate look she'd given him before they had to attend to Alexis. His courageous sea witch was terrified. And fear fed that venomous Dark One blood within her like candy.

The desert, with its raw beauty and utter desolation, was good for her, a reflection of the balance. He hadn't questioned her wanting to come back to it after her part in Alexis's retrieval was done, because she couldn't be around the Legion for too long. Any elements of pure good upset that precarious seesaw inside her. He didn't, for they shared a blood link and other history which had apparently offset that aversion to angelic energy, thank the Goddess.

Good thing you don't have the same kind of feather dander as the other winged testosterone carriers. Else I'd be allergic to you, too.

He remembered her saying that years ago, his typically irreverent mate. She still came up with deprecating names for Jonah, Marcellus and the other angels. The Avian Testosterone Team was one of her latest. At this point they took her deprecations as endearments. Perhaps they were, in her charmingly backhanded way.

He could feel the beat of her heart like his own. But there was a beat he'd missed. Something so earthshattering, Marcellus had given him permission to come and see her right away. Every angel in the Legion understood that when Mina needed him, a delay could quite easily become a serious matter for the whole universe.

Learning to manage energy flows like powerful ocean currents inside her fragile frame had not been an overnight thing. Over two decades, she'd learned to wield powers far beyond anyone's expectations, even with her Dark One blood, that poison that could tip her toward much darker forces when excesses occurred.

While the years had made some things pleasurably predictable, with quiet intimacies and familiar moments he cherished, the Dark One blood could stab through her defenses, trying to take over unguarded moments. Like this one. Learning she was pregnant would knock her off her axis on so many levels. He hated that she couldn't simply embrace joy, that she always had to stay conscious of that venom in her system, else she might upset the carefully guided boat in which she followed the winding river of her life. Their life.

But he could help her embrace joy. He would help her embrace this. A child. A child they created. He pushed that sense of elation down again. Not yet. Not until they could share it. Not until he was certain that her reaction wouldn't result in a rift through the desert that would rival the Grand Canyon as a tourist attraction.

Despite his grim humor, his heart told him that it wasn't the universe in danger, but her peace of mind. He cursed himself again for not attending more closely to her. She would have wanted his focus to be on helping Jonah find his daughter and wouldn't have wanted to be a distraction. But when she was overwhelmed, she turned inward, his prickly sea witch. And that was when the lava threatened to overflow, incinerating everything in the vicinity.

§

As he landed in the sculpted garden in front, he reached out for her with his senses. It wasn't difficult to find her. He followed the scent and sound of the ocean.

He'd gotten a brief glimpse of it, which was why he'd landed in the front. In the backyard, she'd created a sea. Small waves rushed up to kiss the base of the porch, then ebbed back from the sandy strip of beach she'd made. She could create illusions, but this was the real thing, the smell of salt water filling his nostrils, the spray spattering up along the porch boards. He saw small fish swimming in the current and, when the water receded, crabs and crawdads tunneled back into the wet sand. The sea stretched out a good half mile in three directions, fading into the shimmering illusion that was the horizon where the sun's heat met the sand. A trio of dolphins surfaced a hundred feet away from the porch, cavorting then submerging, telling him she'd created the ocean's depth as well.

A few weeks ago, one of the things she'd done with that agile mind of hers was to create a very large and wide pit, simply depressing the earth with her mind like a large thumb pressing down into the sand and rock. She'd pushed the displaced earth up to form the lip and reformed the terrain of an area the size of a football field. She'd shifted plants, bugs and animal life of all kinds, because restoring what she disrupted was part of her many exercises in controlling her power. She could create and destroy. And some days, the urge toward one was far stronger than the other. That was where he came in. He helped her pull back from that darkness when the balance was disrupted, when things became too difficult.

Because of that, when he saw her, he knew he had been right to come home.

She was sitting on a rock protruding from the center of that sea, and she'd shifted to her merform. She didn't have the typical tail, the whimsical rainbow of scales that many mermaids did. *Sea Barbies*, she called them, in her caustic tone that had a sultry rasp to it. To him, her voice was like fingers trailing up his spine. He knew the pleasure of that feeling. More than once, when he'd left their bed because his sleep had been restive, she'd come to find him. He might be sitting naked in a window sill, looking out over whatever place they were visiting, and those slim fingers would trail up the line of his back, to his nape. Her lips would press against his skin, arms circling him in comfort and invitation in the darkness. She showed him affection and love in a way he alone experienced from her.

When she was in merform, her legs were replaced by two long, powerful tentacles, complete with rows of suckers on the bottom to anchor her. Those tiny cups contained a venom which stung like hell. She'd unfurled the tentacles over the rock to hold her to it as the water washed over the stone surface. Before she transformed, she'd been wearing a simple blue dress that fell to her calves. So now the thin cotton clung to her hips, hiding the blue and black gleaming scales he knew marked the transition from the tentacles to the curve of hip. The wet dress, the blue color now a dark blue, molded to her breasts, the tight nipples. Her ebony hair was wet and slicked back on her skull, beads of moisture still clinging to her thick lashes. Her hair obscured the blue eye, revealing the crimson one only.

She was watching the movement of the water, a brooding Goddess. Crabs had crawled up onto the rock with her. One, balanced on the broadest part of the fabric-covered portion of the tentacle close to her hip, cracked some form of shellfish and shoved it into his tiny mouth with pincers.

Her gaze lifted and met his across the sea she'd created as her fortress. Her expression was pale, strained.

To most people, guarded was her natural state. However, when she was that way with him, it was a trigger. It was a signal to prepare for battle, only the steady, dangerous calm with which he responded went to a far deeper level. He took a stance on the bedrock of his own soul, because it was from there he could best anticipate where she would need defense and reinforcements. Inside Mina dwelled a difficult female who had deep passions, great curiosity and a heart far larger than anyone realized. But the blood of her Dark One sire always wanted to destroy all that. It wanted to make Mina what every Dark Spawn before her had become—a creature of dark evil, with no redemption.

That wasn't going to happen. Not as long as she had David to fight for her. Using his wings to take him aloft, he skimmed over the water and came to her rock. His bare feet gripped with sure purchase as he landed just behind and to the right of her. When her head turned, he could see the blue eye through the strands of her hair. It studied him in a more intimate way, roving over his mostly bare body in the belted half-tunic, the harness over his chest that held his daggers. She knew every inch of his skin, had explored him with a child's delight and a woman's endless craving. Seeing that in her look, he could tell she'd missed him. It eased his gut, but he remained cautious, careful. Particularly when her gaze flickered up to his face and what she saw there tightened her own expression.

"You know."

He knew Clara had told him the truth, but hearing it verified from Mina's lips made it real. He wanted to reach out and pull her to him. But she'd recoil, so he quelled the compulsion with effort and merely nodded. "You should have told me."

She shifted, a bitter curl to her lip. "It shouldn't have

happened. You promised not to..."

"You asked, Mina. Remember?" He could be careful and tender, but he wouldn't allow her to deny what he was to her. Because of that, he closed his hand on hers, his fingers wrapping around her wrist so she couldn't withdraw. "Actually, you begged," he murmured, his voice filled with husky memory, and a hint of demand that brought her attention more fully upon him.

§

While angels climaxed like most males, they could choose when to release fertile seed. Not long after they'd met, he'd done it to her; an attempt to ensure she didn't give up on her own life if he lost his. But he'd made that decision without her knowledge or consent. Perhaps because of that, or because Fate was not yet ready for a child of their making, it hadn't taken. He'd promised her he wouldn't do that again, not unless she asked. Since then, she'd asked only a handful of times, and only in moments when it had to do with a need to overcome the antithesis of creation that roiled through her blood.

A month or so ago, she'd had an awful day. The magic that rolled through her so powerfully could twist her muscles into knots—and her mind. That night, when she slept, the nightmares came for her. She woke, trembling and sweating in his arms. He started by kissing her, turning her over to knead her shoulders, her back. Sensing an even more complicated knot inside her heart, he drew her up onto all fours, spreading kisses along her spine, teasing that shallow valley at the top of her buttocks. It made her quiver, even as his strength and will held her motionless.

When he nuzzled the top of her thigh, then moved over, finding her sweet cunt with his mouth, her thighs parted automatically, opening to him. *David, I need you. Help...*

He teased and tormented her, got her gasping and himself aroused to the point of painful hardness with her taste on his tongue. He needed to be inside her. Turning her over again, he laid down upon her as her eyes drifted over the spread of his wings. One white and one black, a physical mirror of what was within her. Recognizing it, she spread her arms out to clutch a thick handful of feathers in each hand, stroking that texture. As the wings quivered, flexing to help increase the strength of his thrusts within her, her lips parted, a soft sound of need. He pressed his mouth to her throat, her sternum.

Surrender everything to me, Mina. Let the darkness recede. I'm here.

Give me life, David...let your seed go tonight and fall where it will. I need to feel life, not death. I need your life.

She clasped her arms over his shoulders, buried her face into his neck and kept whispering it to him, until the climax crashed over them, stealing away all words.

§

Because of the morass of Mina's dark soul, he wasn't always privy to everything happening with her, so he'd assumed, as had been the case those handful of other times, that she hadn't conceived. Raphael had long ago said it was a distinct possibility they couldn't create children, given the physical trauma she'd endured as a child. And since over two decades had passed, David had accepted that. It was a dream he would have cherished, but he knew with Mina there was no certainty to anything, and his focus was her. It was enough.

But she had conceived. She was carrying their child right now. This close to her, he was nearly overcome with the desire to lean forward, lay his palm over her abdomen, feel life and creation, the proof of their love. Proof that it did overcome death and evil. But she was a spinning top right now, not sure how to land, no point of reference for dealing with this.

Because she'd said nothing else to him yet, he released her and eased back. Gesturing around them, he noted, "I'm guessing there are some lizards, scorpions and other desert creatures not so happy with you right now."

She made a dismissive noise, jerking her head toward the opposite side of the house. For the first time, he noticed an intriguing orb made up of a slowly oscillating parade of the displaced animals, plants and crawling insects. They were in a trancelike state, the orb glowing with a green mist, indicating the earth-based energy holding them there. It floated around the side yard like a large, sphere-shaped balloon. "They're relaxed, asleep in a way," she said.

Such multi-faceted tasks were nearly effortless for her now. Though Sam, the nearby shaman who worked with her, was a stoic soul who didn't show much emotion, David knew he found her powers to be awe-inspiring. While David never underestimated her abilities, there were other things about her he found awe-inspiring. The way she looked when she slept in his arms, her mouth soft and hands curled against his chest. Those rare times she smiled. Her clever mind and sharp tongue.

"I miss the ocean." She stared down at it.

David touched her shoulder. When her lashes flickered up, he saw the desperation in her glance. "I can take you there," he said quietly, letting a knuckle drift up her cheek. "I have wings, super speed and everything."

Her lips twisted. "But we have to fly. You know how I feel about heights. That warp-speed flight from China was bad enough."

"I told you we could have taken a more leisurely pace. You wanted it to be over fast."

When she made a face at him, he smiled. He moved his touch down her arm and found her fingers. The hungry crab scuttled away. "Shift, Mina, and I'll take you to the ocean."

When she didn't move, he leaned in and brought his mouth to hers. She nipped at him, but he simply cupped the back of her skull, keeping his movements steady but inexorable. He gave her the heat of his mouth, his desire and demand. Her fingers curled into the harness that held his weapons, nails scraping his skin. As she tightened her grip, the straps cut into his shoulders. The emotions unfurled, and he brought her further into him, pulling her loose from the rock so she was coiled in his lap, her tentacles briefly sliding over his back, his hip. Energy shimmered over her and they became a woman's legs again, locked around his hips, her straddling his lap. As he framed her petite face in his hands, threading his fingers through her hair to hold her, her eyes were tormented.

She pulled back, enough to whisper. "I can't do it, David. I can't. I see how you feel about it, and I can't share that."

"Sshhh." He cupped her face, brushed his lips over her mouth. "You will be a wonderful mother. I know it."

"No." She shook her head. "I can't...David, what if—the Dark One blood...a child is delicate, fragile..." Surging up abruptly, she pushed away from him. "You'll have to take it away from me. Keep it elsewhere. And it will need a parent, it will need you, so I'll lose you. I'll lose everything. We can't let this happen. I won't let this happen."

There it was, that hated, roiling darkness, feeding off her terror, making it worse. As she did a rapid-shift of form again, he ducked the swipe of a tentacle that would have bruised the hell out of his thigh and left a trail of welts. Propelling himself vertically to avoid injury, he swept over the lashing appendage and caught her shoulders and waist to bring her against him, his wings curving on either side of her. "It has happened, Mina. It's done."

"It's a mistake."

"Nothing that ever happens between you and me is a mistake." When he interjected calm authority in the tone, he felt her tremble. He sensed the shift once more, as if she were the pendulum of a manic clock. The height difference between them increased as she stood on human feet again, the top of her head barely at his chin. To draw her attention, he closed his fingers on her wrist, bringing her hand up so he could match it, palm to palm. "Look. Look at this. Look at me."

As she did, her bi-colored gaze flashing, he directed her gaze to the connection, his larger, broader palm pressed to her smaller, slimmer one. "It will be as easy and wondrous as that. You remember how many times we've done this, lying together at night? You're half asleep, dozing, and yet you find my hand, lift it from where it's cupped around you, around a breast, or your waist or shoulder, and you hold it up to your palm in the dusky, predawn light. It's a touchstone for you, a way to remember we're together."

Her mouth tightened, but he wouldn't let her move the palm away, though she tried. He just tightened his grip. "Now, imagine a tiny hand between ours, held there between us. There's nothing we can't hold together, right? We've proven that for a while now. Fate knows we're ready. It's time for the next daughter of Arianne to have her own sea witch, just as the legend promises."

"No. It wasn't meant to be." That darkness was in her eyes, and it spawned a chill in his vitals, recognizing its desires and intentions. He had to take a moment, steady himself and determine how to respond. He knew the true danger wasn't his volatile mate destroying the universe; the problem was the war she fought with her soul. So the moment was entirely, extremely personal. For both of them.

"Would you kill our child, Mina? My child?" His fingers flexed upon her, bringing her closer, so their bodies were flush, every curve of hers against every hard muscle of his. Her head was tilted up because his fingers had wound into the strands, tugging back so she had to stare up into his eyes. "Don't you let that sire's blood of yours answer the question. I want it from your lips, your heart. The heart you know belongs to me."

Part 2

Yes.

The Dark One blood within her hissed it. David had some ability to read her mind, an ability Mina knew he didn't need to use. He could command the truth from her with a simple, intent look, like now.

And though the blood's answer was the truth, looking into his brown eyes, at the strands of hair that fell carelessly over his fine brow, the taut, stern lines of his handsome face, he'd commanded the answer from a different part of her. A part that responded to everything he demanded from her and begged for more.

Mina closed her eyes, her fingers sliding into the openings of his, lacing them together even as everything else in her body went rigid, afraid. "I can't be a parent, David."

"Answer me, Mina."

"No. And yes. Two answers from the same person, the same twisted creature that no one but you trusts. I can't be a parent."

"Anna trusts you. And I'll bet you can be a great mother."

"I have no experience, no point of reference."

"My mother made me jump off of a building, and your mother never showed you an ounce of affection. So there's two things we know *not* to do. How could we do any worse than them?"

The unexpected and absurd comment was a stick jammed in that dangerously spinning wheel of her mind. He gave her his slight smile, a half curve of his mouth, as he retrieved her other hand, laying it on his chest. "We can do this, Mina."

His heart was beating faster than usual. Her own accelerated, because he'd deliberately placed her touch on the imprint of her hand that had been burned into his flesh so long ago. He'd allowed her to mark him, connecting her to him irrevocably. Of course, he'd really accomplished that the first time she'd ever met him. *Call me if you come to any harm...* Those were the words he'd left her with on that first fateful meeting, and he'd never backed away from them since.

When he is away with the Legion, the babe will cry, but you will be afraid to touch her. The Dark One blood was an insidious whisper, a serpent coiling through the maze of her mind, impossible to track or silence. *You will run away in the desert, leaving her alone. She will learn that no one comes, so there's no point to crying. The lesson your own mother taught you. But one day, you will be unable to resist, and you will come into her nursery, a malevolent spirit among all the pink and pretty things that David has given or made for her, for his daughter. You will crush her tiny skull with a mere thought, and you will smile at the feeling, laugh as her life vanishes like a blown out candle... And then your angel will leave you.*

What is it they say? Sons marry their mothers. His murdered him, so it all comes full circle. It is fate.

She clawed at her eyes. She was going to stab her fingers through the soft tissue and gouge out her mind's eye, wherever it was lurking, so she wouldn't have to see the images unfolding there. But it was like a recurring dream where she was sliding over a cliff and there was no purchase, no way to stop herself from falling into the abyss below. The baby was screaming, but she cut the scream short. The head would give like a ripe melon, so easy. She wouldn't have to do it with magic. She could do it with her bare hands.

David had a firm grip on her wrists and was pulling her nails away from her eyes. He anticipated her so well, she hadn't had a chance to make the first puncture. Unfortunately, he didn't anticipate the percussion of energy that exploded from her, probably because she didn't see it coming herself. It simply detonated, like a timer hidden in her mind. He was flung away from her, the blast somersaulting him over the sea she'd created, the waters heaving in agitation. Above, the sky was dark and ominous, storm clouds gathering over their part of the world.

Earlier, she'd shifted from human back to merform in rapid succession, as if trying to shed a skin, but she was still Mina in all of them. The only purpose to it was movement, a way of keeping ahead of the pain, like walking out an agonizing cramp that would never end. Now she let the volatile energy propel her into the air and she twisted there, screaming out her rage and frustration as she morphed into her dragon form. Her scales flashed as lightning forked from the sky and struck the sea in several places, electrifying it. She shot upward, toward that boiling sky, the violence of it, locked in full pitch battle with the Dark One blood.

It was a monster, a red demon with a gaping, fang-filled, saliva-dripping maw. It stared back at her mind's eye with a burning gaze. She could meet it, hate for hate, fury for fury. *You won't touch my child. You won't. I will give her to David. I will let him go, for her. You will never take from me what I'm not willing to give.*

She'd go through the storm clouds, far into the universe until she couldn't breathe, until she choked off air for both sides of herself. It wouldn't kill her, but it would bring blessed oblivion for awhile.

She already knew she wouldn't survive without David. A miraculous, terrible truth. Perhaps, in some twisted way, the Daughters of Arianne curse wasn't gone. Only now, it was the sea witch, not the mermaid, whose life would be forfeit to ensure the survival of the next generation. She'd never kill herself, but without David she couldn't contain the darkness within her. And if she couldn't contain the darkness, she couldn't be allowed to live. He'd made her an oath, all those years ago. If ever it had to be done, it would be him. He'd promised. But she hadn't expected to care about him so much, and now she wasn't sure if she could do that to him. She'd ask Jonah to do it. She wouldn't inflict that upon David's daughter, the knowledge he'd been the one to take her mother's life, no matter how necessary an act it would be.

David had recovered as fast as the lightning streaking through the sky, but she'd expected that. Feeling him coming up behind her, she spun and shot out a stream of flame that illuminated the boiling clouds. He evaded the strike, deftly missing being singed. The power and grace in his warrior's move reminded her that there was a reason he was one of the youngest lieutenants in the Dark Legion. And he was hers. For now. But not forever.

Her heart folded in on itself, a pain so great her roar changed, became shrill and piercing, a keening cry of loss and grief. She couldn't bear it. She went higher and deeper into the cloud cover. The lightning and thunder electrified and reverberated, both reactions shaking her to the core. She wanted closer to it, wanted to feel their shattering touch, those powerful, indifferent elements. They wouldn't hurt her, or the barely just conceived life growing within her. She could let her daughter feel what it was to be in the body of an infant Goddess, exultant and dreadful at once.

Feathers brushed her back. She twisted with a snarl, but he'd already whipped beneath her, coming up between her lethal front talons. She swiped, but again, he was already gone, though she was close enough a spray of feathers swirled through the air over her claws. Behind her again. Under, over. She was disoriented, flipping over and back to try and see him, the dragon part of her mind responding with mindless bloodlust to the taunt of prey. She was okay with that. She didn't want to think, didn't want to be Mina again, because then she'd see that delicate baby, her baby. She'd be painted with blood and death in hundreds of different ways. Mina would go mad long before it became more than a tiny heartbeat deep in her womb.

David landed on her back, his strong arms sliding around her dragon's neck, his thighs pressed into her shoulders. As her wings pumped, trying to dislodge him, his own were providing a counter force, pulling her back out of the heart of the electrical disturbance, but since she was creating it, it would follow her wherever she wished, so the clouds continued to swirl around them like a black tornado, the static and heat from the lightning crackling through the air.

She was braced for him to attempt all sorts of brutal methods to bring her back to reason, to get her to shift and dissipate the storm. Instead, he began to sing.

David had a particular gift for music magic. In battle, she'd seen him charge his daggers with specific tones to increase their deadly potency. When he'd first come to

Heaven, his aptitude with it had suggested he might become part of the Choral Legion, instead of the Dark Legion, but he'd had too many demons to purge from his own soul, so he'd brought both skills to bear when fighting Dark Ones.

But this was another face of his talent, one he used only on her. It was a song she didn't know, and try as she might, a part of her embattled mind couldn't help but lock onto it, trying to figure it out. Her wings beat hard, one more furious spasm, then she was hovering, breathing fast, smoke coming from her nostrils. Thunder vibrated through her body and his legs tightened on her sides. The hands gripping her neck constricted over her windpipe, hampering her breathing. He did that sometimes during their rougher lovemaking, gripping her throat, inflaming her need that much more, making her get even wetter for him. He understood that about her, her need for pain and discomfort, his aggressive possession to balance the softer emotions. Somehow David always managed to bring both into any moment, even a very difficult one like this.

They'd been together twenty years, and still, when things went this far, she was always taken by surprise by the miracle of it, that he pulled it off every time. That he could bring her back.

Trust me, Mina. Shift. Shift to human form.

She made one more half-hearted attempt to dislodge him, to reach his unprotected bare thigh with her back set of claws, but that was the dragon more than herself. He made a disapproving noise of warning and tightened his hold again, but he added a provocative caress of his fingers along her flesh.

"Obey me, sea witch." His voice was an implacable command that shivered over her nerves, giving her warmth and the tingle of response he could compel from her with it.

She growled. Another block of energy would not only knock him from her back—maybe—but also turn the funnel of clouds around them into a full hurricane system. Sam had recently replaced the windows of his trailer. It would really annoy him if she shattered them with an unexpected weather front. That in itself was a temptation.

There's my sea witch. Shift, Mina.

You'll let me fall.

I might, just a little. You raked my other leg pretty good on that last spin. It hurts.

Big baby.

Her flanks heaved with a tired sigh, and then her body was melting, shrinking, the angles and curves of dragon becoming the angles and curves of a small woman. It didn't really matter, did it? As he'd said, it was done. She was pregnant, and that couldn't be undone. Wouldn't be undone. Not by her.

He was holding her in his arms, and he didn't let her fall. Instead, he leaned back, folding his wings beneath them like the overlapped sides of a boat's hull, carrying them on the air currents like a river. She was coiled up against him the way she sometimes did on their roomy couch at the desert house. He'd lie on his back while reading to her, or sometimes they'd watch TV. She'd be curved half way over his body, feeling quite secure nested in between the sofa back and his strong body. His wing would be tucked around her like a blanket, like now, feathers whispering along her bare flesh, because he liked to be the only thing that kept her warm on such nights. She liked it, too.

Her gaze fell to his leg, the raw stripe of bloody flesh where she had scored him with her talons. She hadn't even been aware of it. She wanted to touch it, but she couldn't. Contact with wounds she'd made in the heat of a Dark One fit could call back that madness too easily. Even now, she had to tear her eyes away from it, swallow back the roiling stir of dark energy. But not being able to ease his pain brought the despair back anew.

Children got scrapes. Mothers were supposed to kiss the shallow wound and put a colorful Band-Aid on it to make it better. She couldn't even touch and offer comfort to the male who meant more to her than anything ever had.

"Mina." He held her closer but she shut her eyes. She didn't want to be told things she knew weren't true. She just had to accept it, what she'd always known. That he wasn't hers to keep.

"What was the song?" she asked before he could say anything more. She could hear the desperation in her voice, the strain.

"Mina." His fingers stroked over her hair, that strong, sure touch that so often made her believe he could figure out anything, fix all of it. He couldn't fix this.

"Please, tell me."

He'd hummed it before, but now he gave her the words. He didn't have a cultured, smooth singing voice, but there was something very appealing to it, the way he could linger over the notes, infuse each with meaning and feeling. He told her he'd never wanted anyone the way he wanted her. That every breath took him deeper and, when he was with her, time stopped.

"Madonna. 'Crazy for You,'" he murmured. "When I was in high school, I thought it was the best song to slow dance with a girl. One of these days, I'm going to take you to a high school dance and slow dance with you."

She kept her eyes closed, even as he began to stroke her face, fingertips threading into her hair, slight tugs and releases. The storm was still near, still dense and unsettled, but it was lessening. She knew they were floating down below the cloud cover, dropping back toward earth, for gentle rain pattered against her skin. Dropping her head back, she opened her mouth and took in the rain drops, letting him stroke the hair away from her face.

"Mina, I won't let you hurt the baby. Open your eyes. Look at me."

"I don't want to."

"Tough."

With a sigh, she opened them and met his warm brown gaze. There were a lot of things in it. A lingering fierceness from their battle in the air, an implacable resolve, and that tender, painful knowledge of her soul that was capable of unraveling her.

"I'm not going to leave you," he said. "Not now, not ever. I don't believe it's going to happen, but if the babe isn't safe with you, we'll ask Jonah and Anna to raise her. We can visit her. We'll do whatever we have to do to be her parents, which means making sure she's safe and loved. Even if it can't be by us, not directly."

She stared at him. "But... you'd need to be her father. You couldn't bear that. It would break your heart."

"Yes, it would. The same way it would break yours. But we'd heal together, handle it together. The way we do everything."

She'd torn her clothing when she'd shifted so quickly to the dragon form, so now she was entirely naked in his arms, just like on the couch. But she felt naked for more reasons than that with that quiet declaration. He was in her heart and mind, but she was in his as well, and what she felt there overwhelmed her. His hand slid down her shoulder, palm curving around her breast, feeling the weight. His thumb made a gentle brush over the nipple, a familiar touch, before sliding down her rib cage. She trembled. Seeing it, his eyes darkened.

He curved his fingers inward, so his knuckles followed that trail. Her breath caught and held as he moved in slow inches until he reached her abdomen. His hand unfolded there, rested on it. She kept her eyes locked on his face, saw the sudden surge of strong emotion in his eyes that made her want to cry, but he wouldn't leave her out in the cold. With a ripple of muscle, he shifted her so she was lying upon him, her head on his chest, hip turned into the cradle of his thighs. One of his legs was firmly locked over her as they stayed twined together in air. Closing his hand over her wrist, he guided her palm until it settled over the one he had on her stomach, both pressed over that new life, swimming somewhere beneath their touch.

When she dreamed, she dreamed of the Dark One world, so sleep was rarely easy. It was better when David slept with her. Then the Dark One world could become white noise, like static on the TV when the reception went out. And sometimes when that happened, other dreams could happen.

"The other night..." She paused, pressing her lips together. Her fingers dug into his. She was missing the tip of one finger, a reminder of what she'd been, as well as what he'd become to her. How much she trusted him, needed him, enough to take all the steps she'd taken to come to this moment. "I had a dream about her. I was in my tentacle form, but I was swimming inside...me. Inside my womb. I found her, this tiny curlicue thing. She was floating so aimlessly, so carelessly. I wrapped my tentacles around her, held her still so she wouldn't bump into the walls or end up in cracks and crevices where she might get stuck."

"And did you start to constrict your tentacles, to choke her, squeeze the life out of her?"

"No. I just...held her. That was all. It was still, quiet. Like this."

When he nodded against the top of her head, she clutched the knowledge he'd just pointed out to her, the seed of hope. "I'm so scared, David."

"Me too. But I think that makes us pretty much the same as every new parent since the beginning of time." He moved his free hand to her hip and stroked her upper thigh. "Spread your legs for me, Mina."

He'd had her do that before, often enough she obeyed on instinct, a known ritual that pleased and oddly soothed her, the submission to his desires and her own. She shifted, sliding her knees over his thighs, parting herself to him and the open air. His fingers trailed along her skin, close to the soft petals of her sex.

"The very fact some part of you wanted my fertile seed, asked for it, says you know this is meant to be."

"Maybe," she said, then bit her lip as he touched her labia, gave it an idle stroke with his thumb. "But that doesn't mean it will turn out the way we want it to. Lots of things are fated. Good and evil."

"You have to have faith. You're so much more now than you ever thought you could be."

"Which is why we need to be even more careful, more wary."

"Even after twenty years, you're waiting for the other shoe to drop."

"Yes, because it can. And you know I'm right, because you're in my head." She felt that frisson of panic start up again, but it was arrested by his fingers, sliding over her pussy. He pinched her clitoris, the kiss of pain making her dampen against him, as he knew it would. "David..."

He sealed in that sensation with his whole hand pressed against her mound. She quivered against him. "I like touching you. And wanting you. Tormenting and pleasuring you. You need both, and I like giving you both." His fingers stopped moving, his breath against her temple. "I do understand what you fear, Mina. But I understand something else. The baby is about three weeks along, right?"

She managed to nod, gasped as he did something wonderful. She could feel him, hard and ready against the small of her back, and she wanted to defuse all the energy still crackling in the air, give it a channel, a focus, by straddling him here in the air. But he held her fast, the pressure of his fingers, as well as the steady, deliberate way he spoke, helping her pay attention.

"You've been carrying a pure innocent inside of you for three weeks. It's upset you, worried you, because of what you might do to her. You reacted violently to me now because you bottled that up, and it's all come spewing out. But you haven't become unbalanced *specifically* because she's inside you. I'm willing to bet my life that the Dark One blood inside of you could roar like a banshee, and you wouldn't harm one hair on her head."

She hadn't even considered it. He was right. She'd been so caught up in what it could mean, having the baby, she hadn't really thought about the significance of the child already being in residence. Raphael, the healing angel, thought Mina was able to tolerate David's pure light proximity because they'd shared blood, years ago. Whether or not that was true or there was more to it, she and that fetus shared blood in a much more direct way. And while she'd felt the stirrings of life within her, she hadn't felt the stirring of anything else connected to it, that itchy feeling that could start in her lower back when she had too much exposure to beings of pure light, which would expand into a crazed madness over time.

Her mind whirled over that revelation. Her gaze flitted up, desperate and seeking his. David tightened his arms around her. "Let me take you to the ocean for a little while. We'll talk about this—without storm clouds and dragons." His fingers dipped, pushing into her with unexpected firmness and ruthless demand. She arched, a whimper catching in her throat. "After that, we'll talk about what you can do to make my leg feel better. Actions have consequences, sweet witch. When you misbehave, reparations are required."

Part 3

He didn't take her to a sand bar in the middle of the ocean, as she expected. Instead, he took her somewhere she'd never been before. He saw her dare a glimpse as they came in for a landing. The unique blue color of the water would tell her that the small, uninhabited island was in the

Caribbean. When he glided in over the thick tree cover, he dropped down into it to bring her to the narrow beach of a secluded lagoon. The water was flanked by caves and, as he took her hand, guiding her into the mouth of one, her face brightened at the discovery of a chain of pools that formed when the current receded. That left the sea life washed in on the high tide trapped until the next cycle. Right now, that included a small school of darting, bright-colored fish and a languidly gliding barracuda shark, unconcerned about his circumstances, probably because of the darting fish. The pools also included a scattering of crabs that might have scuttled up from the beach, preferring to dine on what the ocean left in the tidal pools.

David watched his witch dip a toe in, a pleased look flitting across her normally wary expression as she found it comfortably warm. He knew how much she disliked the cold. He also knew she liked to explore new surroundings before she settled into anything else. So unstrapping his daggers and setting them aside, he squatted in a casual perch on a rock, his bare toes making sure purchase on the wet surface as he watched her circle the smaller tidal pools to see what was in them. When she returned to the largest one, the one containing the shark, she stood on the opposite bank, studying the sand-dusted rock below the water's surface. He was reminded of a sharp-eyed bird, particularly when she dove abruptly into the water. Her hand brushed the barracuda's back as she moved to the center of the pool and descended to the bottom. She came back up with what looked like a cheap bangle bracelet, the rhinestones glittering from the shards of sunlight coming in through the cave opening. Making a satisfied noise, she put it on her arm.

"My mate loves a sparkly," he observed with a faint smile.

"There's another one," she said, and dove again. David chuckled. He made a casual leap from the rock to a lower point, using his wings for balance. In reaction to his avian-like shadow, the troop of fish darted away, then back. A couple narrowly missed the snap of the barracuda's jaws as they swarmed around him, careless of the danger he posed in their attempt to escape the threat of what David was sure they thought was a swooping pelican.

"Whoops, sorry about that guys." Folding the wings along his back, he eyed the barracuda, back to lazily swimming. "You're more irritable than hungry. I have a feeling there were a lot more fish in here earlier."

Mina emerged again, this time with three more bracelets, in different colors, same style. "It's always amazing, how they'll stay together like this," she observed. "They may have floated together for miles."

She had three on one arm, one on the other. While dark and light had to stay perfectly balanced inside her, David had noticed she had a penchant for wanting other things to be out of balance. If they were staying in a human abode, and it was furnished with two end tables for the couch, she would move one to an unexpected place, like the kitchen. Or into the bathroom, so she could sit on it while propping her feet on the commode and trying different cheap toenail polishes. Usually different colors for different toes. Candles were always arranged in prime numbers. His contrary witch, always full of surprises.

His beautiful witch. She was completely oblivious to how she looked at the moment. Her elbows were propped on the bank of the tidal pool, her legs idly scissoring in the water. She was turned at an angle away from him, not a stitch on her, such that he was watching the shift of her buttocks with her movements, the sweet profile of her breasts wavering beneath the water. The slope to her abdomen, which before long would be swelling with their child. He couldn't wait to see her fully round and pregnant. In a perverse way, it aroused him, though he wasn't sure why.

"Because it's proof that you're virile." Mina's voice deepened, emulating a caveman. "See my mate—look like fat-bottomed potato, walk like duck. I am male. I can reproduce." Her voice returned to its usual sardonic tone. "Just like a Xerox copier."

"Reading my mind?"

"You were thinking it at me. You wanted me to know you feel that way." She slanted a glance at him, then her lashes lowered again, considering her bracelets. "You knew how it would make me feel."

"And how's that?" Stripping off his tunic, belt, weapons, and the beaten silver gauntlets that protected his forearms from enemy blades, he slid into the water. Stroking across it, he kept his gaze fixed on that enticing pale female bottom. Her legs scissored at a more indolent pace.

"You know."

"I want to hear you say it."

Her nose wrinkled, her eyes flashing with irritation. "I don't want to feel that way yet. You want me to feel good about this. Maybe she's just not big enough yet for the pure light thing to affect me. Or she could be a being of pure evil." Her fingers tightened on the bangles, her chin dropping to her chest as her jaw set. "She'll be part Dark One, David. And that means she'll have to fight it, the way I have to fight it."

"You're just confirming that you're going to be a good parent. Already worrying about the challenges she's going to face, wanting her to have a better life than you've had." He dipped down so he could catch her ankles below the water and slide his hands up her legs. He indulged himself with a thorough caress of her buttocks. As she let herself be pulled away from the ledge, she turned to twine her legs around his hips, but her crimson and blue gaze was troubled.

"Mina, she'll also be part you. Strong, stubborn sea witch. And me; all-powerful and wise angel."

She arched a brow, and he saw her fighting one of her tiny smiles. "All-powerful and wise? Did you get Inflated Ego Re-Certification with the Legion this week and forget to tell me?"

"Cute." He acted as if he was going to dunk them both beneath the water, and she slipped away, treading across the pool. She stayed in human form, though, drawing his eyes to the sinuous movement of her body as she twisted in a spiral and did a lazy flip beneath the water, as lithely as if she were in merform. Her dark hair twined around her body like silk. He moved in a steady stalk, dropping down so he was gliding after her like a crocodile. "We have a more important consideration, though," he said as her head broke the surface again.

"What's that?" Mina considered her escape options, as well as how much effort she wanted to put into evading him, how hard she wanted him to work for her capture. Those factors also depended on how long her mate was willing to play the game. At a certain point, his hunting instinct would kick in and he'd prove—short of cheating and using her considerable magic on him—that she wouldn't escape him.

"Discipline. Considering our daughter will have your genes, I'm thinking I better practice spanking now. Now, *who* can I practice on...?"

"You did plenty of practicing way before you even knew I was pregnant." She gave him a challenging look, but she couldn't help remembering those times, her body stirred by the memories.

"Well, you give me plenty of cause. It's either spank or strangle you, and spanking seems to work out better for us both."

He made a mock lunge, letting her sweep beneath him and get away. She emerged on the other side of the tidal pool, treading over the ripples they'd created. She saw him note appreciatively the way they lapped at the upper curves of her breasts. It made her nipples tighten, her skin tingle for his touch. Good. She didn't want to think about the darker things that had brought them here. Maybe if she just ignored it, it would all go away.

"You're not fooling me a bit," Mina retorted. "You won't even be able to raise your voice to her. I saw Jonah with Alexis. Anna had to do all the disciplining when she was young. And send him off with the other angels so he wouldn't try to sneak behind Anna's back to comfort her with hugs and toys."

"I remember that. Anna didn't have to discipline her much, though. All she had to do was threaten to send her to live with scary Aunt Mina, who might or might not chop her up as ingredients for her foul-smelling brews."

Mina's gaze narrowed to slits. Before she could retort, though, David had moved, faster than she could follow. But it wasn't to grab her. He was positioned in front of her, with a dagger gripped in either hand. Even in the water, his stance was tense and battle ready as he faced the cave entrance. He'd moved so fast, the pool had barely rippled when he'd retrieved the daggers from the rock and returned to her. It couldn't help but thrill her in low, swirly places, so Mina was already annoyed by whatever force was daring to intrude. She might turn the offender into ingredients for one of her potions in truth.

"David?"

He relaxed. Mina let her fingers do an itsy-bitsy spider crawl up the line of his spine as she hummed a short segment of the nursery song. "I'm going to tell him you let him creep up on you," she whispered. "He'll put you on the training field with his drill sergeants for a week."

"You are mean," he murmured back, and shot her a warning glance. "Do it, and you'll get a spanking that will keep you sore for that whole week I'm gone."

"I'm here," David called, though Jonah already knew that. His commander was giving David fair warning as a courtesy, since Mina was with him. Truth, it had been a somewhat unsettling couple of hours, but it was unusual for David to be unaware of another angel's approach. While it was inexcusable, there was male pride to consider. Before his commander came into the cave, David shot back over to the rock and replaced his daggers, returning to his position with Mina in a blink and flash of feathers. When Jonah made his appearance, he was ostensibly in a relaxed stance, though firmly in front of his mate, who he was pretty certain snickered at him. He really should have brought some clothes for her.

Mina was not in the least bit modest, but David had some old-fashioned ideas about not letting other males see her naked. Since she knew that, he wouldn't put it past her to tease him by swimming around like a sensual water nymph doing a Playboy centerfold shoot while Jonah told him whatever he'd come to say. Something that apparently couldn't be communicated telepathically, in the way that all angels could communicate. David pushed down the prick of annoyance at the interruption, feeling guilty about his reaction, particularly when he saw Jonah's concerned expression.

Jonah entered the cave on foot, his magnificent silver-white wings folded along his back like a centurion's cape. From two other shadows outside the cave, David realized he wasn't alone. Jonah had been intuitive enough to have them wait out of view. Hell, if he'd missed three angels approaching, maybe he *should* be on the practice field for a week.

"Problem?" David asked. When Mina moved, her breast brushing his arm, he reached back, caught her wrist and kept her in place behind him with an admonishing squeeze. A tentacle slithered around his hips, revealing that she'd shifted. It coiled low on his hips and around his waist as she slid her arms over his shoulders, holding onto him piggy-back and looking at Jonah over his shoulder, her wet hair covering all but the crimson eye. David was pretty sure she looked like a much prettier Tolkien's Gollum, peering out in a sinister manner from the shadows. Jonah's lifted brow and wary glance confirmed it.

"We sensed...a disturbance. Your mind was closed, so I couldn't contact you. I thought we better check on you, since Marcellus said you left his company rather abruptly."

"A disturbance in the force, Luke," Mina intoned in his ear, then pushed her hair back, taking a better grip on David's shoulders to haul herself up where Jonah could see her full face. "I am pregnant," she announced. "He was trying to convince me that's a good thing."

"I see." After the initial flash of startled reaction, Jonah seemed to take that in stride. "How is he doing on that?"

"I still think it's a bad idea, but apparently what's done is done. No way to send her little soul back to the manufacturer. What do you think?"

David cheerfully thought of all the ways he was going to strangle her in truth. However, as he held his commander's gaze, he saw a lot of things in the male's expression, and wondered at Jonah's response himself. After a long pause, the second-in-command for all the Goddess's angelic legions inclined his head.

"You have known what it is to grow up without love,

Mina, so I think she will be the best-loved child that has ever graced the Goddess's vast universe. And I think you will be an extraordinary mother." His gaze shifted to David. "Just as I know you will be everything a father should be. As long as you start paying better attention, even when domestic crises are occupying your mind."

Jonah pivoted, heading back out of the cave. "Spend some time on the training field with Cassius this week," he called over his shoulder. "He'll beat that lesson into you, so next time I don't have to drop everything to find out why your mate is causing a hurricane with storm surge in the middle of a landlocked desert. Sam says you owe him north-facing windows, Mina."

David stared at the cave entrance, listened to the rush of wings as Jonah and the other two angels took off. *I know you will be everything a father should be.* Jonah had known what those words meant to him. And as for his sea witch...

He turned, but she refused to relinquish her hold on his back. He slid both his hands over the sleek tentacle on his waist. "You all right?"

"Everyone but me seems to think this is going to be okay. They think a baby's mere appearance means world peace and chocolate rainbows. There are places where a baby just means one more for a mother to watch starve to death."

"Mina." He forcibly loosened the tentacle, slid her around and under his arm so they were face to face. The suction cups on her tentacles slid along his leg, the faint sting a brief kiss of pain before she had legs again and he was holding her against him, arms around her hips and back. "Our child won't starve to death. Come here."

He moved her over to the tidal pool's edge, bringing them up to the rocky ground with a brief pump of his wings. Carrying her out of the cave into the afternoon sunlight, he laid her down on the sand, where she could look up and see the breeze moving through the trees. "Don't think; just feel."

He bent and kissed her, the narrow line between her breasts. As he did, he stretched out one wing fully, touching the tip of it to the top of her foot, drawing it up along her ankle, the inside of her calf. She squirmed at the sensual tickle, then stilled as he went higher, over her knee, folding the wing forward so it was sliding along her thigh. He registered how it felt in her mind, that soft, furlike brush of contact, a part of him. He adjusted so the wing tip glided over her mound. Gripping her thigh with his hand, he moved it at a deliberate pace so he slowly widened the spread of her legs, his gaze falling on the intimate folds revealed there. She pressed her lips together, her hands curling into the sand.

As he straightened, his gaze moved up her body, over her breasts, her mouth. Threading his fingers through her damp hair, he shifted his body, kneeling between her legs. When he bent to her breasts again, the tender skin inside her knees was pressed against his thighs. He folded his wings along his back so the crossed tips were caressing her ankles, the soles of her small feet.

Closing his hands over her breasts, he increased the pressure of his hands so the constriction was a delicious stimulation. When he put his mouth over one nipple, nudging and nuzzling, then doing a slow, teasing suckle, her hands had moved to clutch his hips.

Imagine a child here, suckling your breasts, nourished by your milk.

He gave her his voice in her mind, and she closed her eyes, intensifying the intimacy of it. Moving down to her abdomen, he laid another heated kiss on her belly, his tongue teasing at her navel. He smelled her arousal. Through the palm of his hand, low on her stomach, he felt the subtle shift of her pussy muscles contracting. She loved his mouth on her there, though he could never get her admit to that. She wouldn't admit to anything. His stubborn witch.

Think of the way it will feel, the skin stretching, becoming fuller here, a tangible weight as the child grows.

He moved down even further, his tongue taking a brief taste of her clit. She shuddered.

Imagine my cock inside of you, the two of us together, making her, a creation of our love. For some it's mere biology, but not for us. She will be special and amazing, and you will love her with a loyalty and passion as fierce as the love I know you bear for me.

Her breath was shortening, and she was not alone in her aroused reaction. David slid his hands to her hips, cradling her as he stretched out on the sand, bracing his elbows for the best angle to bring her to his mouth. *I want you wet and quivering, sweet witch. I'm going to get you begging, and then I'm going to turn you over in the sand, put that tempting bottom of yours in the air and beat it raw for getting me in trouble. For worrying about things that don't need to be worried about. I will always take care of you, love you, protect you. And our child.*

He smiled against her flesh at the thought of all of it, his cock getting harder at her reaction, a delectable mixture of apprehension and desire. He was close enough not only to inhale that irresistible aroma, but catch those tiny drops of cream on his tongue, swirl them over her clit, making her glisten from that and the stimulation of his mouth.

He would do everything he promised, because he knew she needed it, because it would give them both pleasure and help her push away her fears. Before he was done, he was determined she would feel at least one tendril of joy for the new life she carried. The life he was certain would show her once and for all that the Dark One blood would never rule her.

A miracle baby, in more ways than one.

Part 4

Angels, at least those of the Dark Legion, were far more carnal than the religious texts suggested. He was never so glad for that than in a moment like this, when he had his witch at his mercy, his mouth hovering so close to her cunt he could inhale her musk with every breath. It was so easy, such an intimate, incomparable pleasure, to take a long, dragging lick from the perineum to the clit. He slid his tongue over that tight furl of flesh, feeling it quiver and change under his stimulation. Then the deep thrust in, bringing his mouth right up to the labia, sealing over her pussy and breathing into her, breathing her in, as he licked and swirled along the velvet slickness inside of her channel.

Mina made a guttural, animal sound, twisting beneath his hands, her fingers reaching for him, clawing and sliding off his shoulders as he slowly fucked her with his tongue, taking his time, watching her eyes open wide in dazed pleasure, then close, lashes fanning her cheeks. Her stomach muscles were rigid with need as she moved against his mouth in shameless want. As she lifted up to his mouth, he captured her soft buttocks in both hands, kneading and working her so her clit was pushed up against his mouth even more insistently. He knew her body so well, it was second nature to find his way to the cleft between those cheeks and stroke the sensitive rim there.

It resulted in another short gush of cream on his tongue, and she cried out. She was fighting her climax, he could sense it. He'd brought her so close, so fast, and she refused to be a pushover, his stubborn witch. He smiled against her, traced his tongue around her clit, then sucked on it, biting. As he did, he slid three fingers into her, rubbing the sweet place that could make her come to pieces. His other finger dipped into her rectum, just the tip, enough to make her feel the penetration.

There she was, so close, teetering over... he waited one more beat, then pulled free, administering a sharp slap right onto the outer labia, possible because of the wide spread of her legs. She jumped at the unexpected blow and gave a short, resentful mewl. "Not until I tell you that you can go, sweet witch," he reminded her.

Giving him a calculated look, she let her hands slither around her breasts, cupping them and teasing the nipples in a way that riveted his attention. She arched her back. "Maybe I'll just entertain myself."

"Stop." The stern command had her freezing in that position as his hot eyes covered her. "Arch your back more. Offer them to me."

She did, her fingers tightening over breasts and nipples. "Now hold that position," he murmured. "Your legs spread, your breasts cupped and offered in your hands, waiting for me to take you, waiting for me to let you climax. Don't move an inch."

Leaning forward, he made his way down to the left breast. When he tongued the nipple, a tiny brush of contact, she shuddered. Putting his other hand over her cunt, he slid two fingers in, a gentle scissor of movement. As he continued to touch her nipple with those light presses of his tongue, not a lick or a suckle, the moan became an incoherent plea, and more thick honey dampened his hand. He moved around the nipple now, licking her fingers, pressed so hard into her flesh there were white circles around the pads.

"That's it, baby. Squeeze your beautiful tits for me. Your cunt is just weeping, begging for my cock. You want to be bad, but you don't know how to be anything but my sweet slave, do you?"

Sometimes he wasn't quite sure where the thoughts and feelings came from, this desire to completely subjugate her with pleasure, the way humans did it with leather and whips and fetish magazines, but it was definitely in his blood. He hadn't had much time with other women before he met her, but even with them it had never come forth as strongly as it did with her. As a warrior, he thought it was like having a dormant weapon, one that hadn't made itself fully known to him until the foe for whom it was specifically intended stepped forward.

Mina was his to protect, not to fight, but the analogy wasn't entirely inaccurate. Her craving to be dominated was directed toward him and him alone, a vital craving that helped her manage so much of the dangerous darkness within her.

She was wriggling against his touch, unable to help herself, and she was going to make herself come. "Uh-uh." He caught her wrists and pulled her arms out to either side of her as he shifted his body upward, pinning her arms beneath his calves. In that position he gripped his cock, temptingly close to her mouth and avid gaze. "Take me deep," he ordered. "You keep your focus on me, my desires. What I command."

She opened, and he could push himself practically down her throat, she was so good at trusting him for this. He had to suppress a groan, realizing he'd given her a chance for payback as she sucked on him like a vacuum, her tongue stroking the underside of his cock. Her eyes lifted again, gazing up at him as he stretched her mouth, made her serve him, and she knew just how crazy that drove him. Mother Goddess, but she was beautiful. And amazing. All his...

She was bringing him too close. With regret, he pulled out of her, but in one swift movement, he turned her over and put her on her hands and knees. He'd take her this way, after he lived up to his promise.

He found himself filled with a different inclination first, though. Standing on his knees behind her, he cupped her breasts, more gently now. They were small, but attuned to every detail of her body as he was, he could already tell there was a little more fullness to them. Merwomen had monthly courses like human women, though Mina's had always been wildly irregular, possibly contributing to how long conception had taken between them.

But everything happened in its own time, at its own pace. Like now. Though his own body was raging with need, his cock so hard it was painful as hell, he didn't want to rush this. There was far more involved here than simple lust. His palms slipped down over her abdomen, cupping that curve, then over her hips, slow, stroking.

"My love."

She looked back at him, her hair falling over her shoulder, her expression uncertain at the tenderness suffusing his voice. "You've never called me that."

"I've thought it. I know how you are about sentiment, but that's what you are to me, Mina. My love, my mate. The center of my universe. You're everything I could ever want."

"You just feel that way because I'm carrying a baby."

"No." He shook his head. "It's a turning point for us. This is an expression of your love for me, of our love for each other. The faith we have in it. The faith you have in yourself, and in me, in us. It chokes me, the way you don't realize how you've sent a message even after you've sent it, sweet witch. I'm saying thank you."

She stared at him, so many thoughts going on behind her eyes. Some he could see; others were too jumbled to make out, but they were all powerful. Hard for her to handle. "I want to come," she said plaintively.

He grinned then, though the pain in his cock was matched by an ache in his chest, the pressure of loving her so much his ribs creaked. "Put your elbows on the sand, your forehead into the cup of your hands. Spread your knees."

She accommodated him, and David drew in a steadying breath at the sight she made, the pink mouth of her sex, the tracks of fluid her arousal had made down her thighs. The tight points of her breasts, brushing the sand. The small puckered rear entrance. All of it offered to him, so blatantly sexual and needy.

He struck her with the flat of his hand across her buttocks, a practiced blow that made the pretty cheeks wobble, an effect he made sure she'd feel deep inside her pussy. He saw her flesh contract in confirmation, heard her suck in a gasp. "Better brace those elbows," he advised.

He spanked her on alternating cheeks, then between them, giving her exposed cunt some artful slaps that quickly brought her close to climax again. Then he moved back to her ass. He kept going until both cheeks were reddened, and her arousal was dripping into the sand, forming a pattern of tiny dark droplets. He bent, licked along the inside of her thighs, caught the fluid glistening on the edges of those flushed lips. Playing around the clit without touching it, he teased her rim with his nose, then brushed his mouth over those abraded buttocks.

"David..." She was nearly in tears. "I want you. Now."

"You know the rules. Beg me, sweet witch. And say you're sorry."

"I'm sorry...for getting you in trouble with Jonah...for being difficult. For being afraid..."

He swallowed as her voice broke. He always knew this game was not a game at all, but he hadn't expected to bring it boiling up in her so abruptly this time. It told him just how close to the surface it had been.

He moved back over her, his arms on either side of her

body, blanketing her with his own as he slid an arm around her waist, cupped her breast and laid his head next to hers. "You are the most courageous woman I've ever met, Mina. There's none braver in the whole universe. You never have to apologize for being afraid. Only for not trusting me to take care of you."

She sniffed, pressing her face into his braced arm. "You have an entirely male, entirely unrealistic view of your abilities. As considerable as they are."

"And you have an unparalleled gift for backhanded compliments." He shifted to bring the head of his cock to the mouth of her pussy, sliding in just enough to stretch the lips, holding there. She could have pushed back against him, but she waited, quivering, making it more intense for both of them.

"Pull your hair over your right shoulder," he commanded, low. She shifted on her elbows, making a sexy little noise at the way it rubbed them together, but she managed it, gathering all those thick raven locks in both hands and bringing them into a tumble over her shoulder, exposing the pale line of her neck to him. He touched his lips there, tracing her pulse. Her elbows were still planted in the sand, hands clutching her hair as her knuckles rested against the inside of his braced arm. When she unconsciously tilted into his touch, he deepened the contact, suckling her throat, marking her with that force as well as his teeth, then lightening the touch again, caressing and stroking. Her neck was extraordinarily sensitive, and her slippery flesh quivered against the head of his cock, her arousal becoming more concentrated.

"You're going to come for me like this. Holding still, my cock barely in you, my mouth on your pulse." The flutter of those tissues told him he was right, but hell, it was going to be torture to feel it. He didn't mind. He was going to drive his witch crazy, drive out the fear and anguish moving through her. Those emotions and the despised forces behind them were doing their best to extinguish the stuttering spark of hope he wanted to fan into a steady candle flame.

She set her fangs to his forearm, biting hard enough to

punch through flesh and find his blood. He couldn't help but bare his teeth in a grim smile at the frustrated gesture, even as it made things tighten low in his gut. Giving her breast an admonishing squeeze, he won a small yelp as he pinched the nipple, a little rough. "Easy there, witch," he reproved. Then he put his mouth on her neck. Traced the pulsing vein once again, bit her as well, more gently. In fact, he made all of it gentle. Teasing, caressing strokes of his tongue, tiny nips and nuzzles, then to her nape where he suckled the point of bone there, his warm breath tickling the aroused nerve endings further.

She whimpered, making more of those incoherent noises. Her tissues contracted on him as her cunt tried to draw him in. The ripple of that heated flesh along his cock head was enough to have him shuddering and biting back a groan, the shaft flexing in reaction. It gave her an extra stroke of contact at the joining point of their bodies. She'd released her hair, her fingers opening and closing spasmodically, digging into the sand. He felt the rough grains sticking to her damp palm as it moved over his braced hand and she clutched his fingers. Her mouth pressed in mindless need against the top of his hand. Her thighs were trembling, her whole body starting to quiver as it reached for that release.

"Do you want to obey me?"

She nodded, a quick jerk. "Want to...come for you."

He brought his body down on hers even further, dropping her lower into the sand, canting her ass back into his so his cock slid in another inch. Pushing his jaw beneath hers, he levered up her chin and clamped his mouth hard on her jugular, catching her breath in her throat. Holding her fast, he spoke in her mind, one short command.

Then do it.

She let out a strangled cry, her weight all on her knees as she lost the ability to hold herself up. He had her, though, one arm firm around her waist, the hand squeezing her breast, giving the nipple another ruthless tweak as he launched her straight over the edge, no chance to grab on or resist. She screamed, the vibration against his lips, her pussy frantically trying to milk that one part of his cock he was letting her have. It was too much temptation for him. He shoved into her in one hard thrust, and that scream reached breaking point. But hell, he was right there with her.

He pistoned into her, holding onto her throat, relishing every cry, every quiver of her body. Both her hands eventually found the arm around her body, latching onto him there. It was as if she was depending on him for gravity, for everything, afraid of nothing, at least in this moment. Yet even in the midst of all that, she wanted more.

"Come for me, too," she begged. "I need to feel you."

I'll give you whatever you want. Always. My mate. My love. He let go of her throat as the climax overcame him, but he kept his temple pressed close to hers, holding her tight as he drove into her, drew out her climax and brought forth his own. His wings had unfolded to brace him and add thrust to the movement, and she reached, wanting. He saw what she desired in her mind, and managed to bring them forward enough she could grab the curved edges and bring them down so his wings flanked his shoulders and curved around in front of her, her face pressed into them.

She cried out again as he released fully, and he kept them going through those delightful, almost unbearable waves, their bodies moving together. It was like a never-ending tide, going higher and higher, but then, at last, came the ebb. Still, he took his time, slowing the pace but keeping it going as long as she was making those delicious little aftershock quivers, clutching him inside. When at last he eased to a halt, he dropped his head so his face was pressed into the center of her back. He liked the resting spot, brushing languid, wet kisses on the line of her spine as he slowed his pounding heart.

She took a deep, shuddering breath. When he moved them into a spooned position, propping himself on his side, she kept hold of his wings so one was beneath them. She overlapped them in front of her, the one dark wing and one white wing, tangling the two sets of feathers together. As she sandwiched them, white, black, white, black, then white, white, black, he pressed his lips against a smile and stroked her hair, her shoulder.

"This makes me want Oreos," she said. "Double-stuffed."

He laughed, he couldn't help it. When he put both arms around her to squeeze her in a hard, far-too-strong hug, she squirmed in half-hearted protest, but then subsided. "I'm imagining all the cravings a pregnant sea witch might have," he said. "And the different parts of the universe I'll have to visit to satisfy them. 'I'm sorry, Jonah, I know we're facing an invading force of XYZ right now, but Mina really needs watermelon. And chula berries from the Zorgon galaxy.'"

"You made that up."

"Yes, I did. You're so smart."

"You're an ass." She pinched his arm, then laid her head on it, still playing with his feathers. Her gaze was outward, though, toward the lagoon, or so he thought. Following her gaze, he saw the sand shifting, turning. Feeling the frissons of energy moving along her flesh like a warm breeze suddenly called from over the tropical water, he propped himself up further on his elbow to see what it was she was creating.

"Once, when walking down the beach," she said, "I found a sculpture someone had made in the sand, of a mermaid. It was complex, beautiful. So much time and effort for something the tide and wind take away in a few days. It's so short. Everything is so short. What if she hates me?"

"If she's a normal kid, sometimes she'll think she does. That's the way it works with kids and parents. Sometimes in other relationships, too. Like you and me. Sometimes you hate me, but you always love me."

"I do not."

"Which one? You don't hate me? Or you don't love me?"

She sniffed, refusing to answer, and he smiled again, watching the sand turn, settle, shift.

"Do you ever hate me?" she asked in a low voice, not taking her eyes off what she was doing.

He wouldn't disrupt her magic, but he did close the

small distance between their bodies again, tightening his hand around her waist, putting his lips to her temple.

"No. I have thoughts of spanking you or dunking you in cold water, or sometimes tying your hair in knots when you sleep, just because you make me crazy, but I've never hated you, Mina. And I never will. I feel so much for you, sometimes I think I'll burst the seams of the universe with it."

She swallowed. When she spoke, it was barely louder than the wind, but he heard it, just the same, thanks to his angel hearing. "I feel the same way about you."

She so rarely said it, it was always a gift, but he knew better than to make a big production out of it. He just held her and wished he could give her everything, heal every wound, destroy every fear before it had a chance to enter her mind, a guardian at the gate. He couldn't do that. But he could get her Oreos. Double-stuffed.

"I was wondering why you were still here. You should have been back with a tubful of them by now."

"Eavesdropper. I wanted to see what you're making."

"You'll see when you get back." Her hand closed over his, fingers twining in a rare moment of intimacy she initiated. "I want to surprise you. Please."

"Okay. I'll stretch it out. How long do you need?"

"Five minutes. Maybe fifteen."

"Fifteen's too long. How about ten?"

"You just like to have the last word."

"I like having you." His hand slipped down, caressing her between her legs, enjoying the wetness still there from their coupling. Her thighs loosened automatically at his touch, which never failed to stir his arousal again.

"Oreos," she said, with a touch of annoyance. Though her hips moved against him, telling him her body was responding, despite her supposed irritation.

He was laughing as he took to the sky, wondering what she'd concoct by the time he came back.

Part 5

Sometimes he liked watching her when she wasn't aware

he was there. It wasn't to eavesdrop or abuse her trust. He just enjoyed seeing what she did when she was all by herself, because there was no part of her he didn't want to know or experience.

In the beginning, watching her without her knowledge hadn't been easy. She'd lived her first twenty years in a constant state of vigilance, beset by a variety of enemies. As such, he pretty much had to employ all the stealth abilities he had, because her senses, both mundane and magical, were as fine-tuned as a bat's radar. As time progressed, however, he'd been secretly pleased to notice a minute change. Her subconscious recognized his presence before the rest of her did. Even before she saw he was there, she'd start relaxing, the tension going out of her shoulders, her focus increasing on what she was doing, rather than startling at every noise, looking around like a watchful animal.

Then there'd been the day he realized she was starting to be comfortable in the places he left her when he had to be with the Legion. Her faith in the connection between their minds, the one that could put him at her side in a matter of seconds, had grown. At that turning point, it became far easier to observe her for a few precious moments unannounced, because she trusted he would be there if she needed him, to ward off any threat.

That was the case now as he silently made his landing on the lagoon beach. She was sitting on her hip, her legs folded beneath her, her head bent in an attentive manner to something she was holding. It was the timeless maternal posture of shelter, of nurturing. As he moved toward her, his heart skipped a beat, his breath catching in his throat.

She'd created a child out of the sand, an infant. A little golem with the glitter of sand crystals in the rough-textured skin, but a babe nevertheless. She was holding it as a mother would, against her bare breast, rocking and singing to it. Tiny fists waved, and dark eyes blinked up at her, a small mouth opening and closing against her flesh as if seeking nourishment.

As he watched, Mina shifted from human to merform, coiling one tentacle around the babe. The venom in the suckers couldn't affect the sandy form, so she lifted the creation above her head, making gentle dips and lifts, as if she was showing her how to fly through the air without the benefit of wings. The infant cooed and chuckled, even when Mina turned her upside down and rocked her that way. The sea witch turned her head sideways as if trying to look upside down as well, and a small smile played on her beautiful mouth.

"Yes, that's the best way to see the world sometimes," she informed the babe. "Completely topsy-turvy." Then she stilled and glanced over her shoulder. "You like sneaking up on me."

"Sometimes. I get to see some remarkable things." He found his body was a little loathe to move, caught in the spell of watching her, but he made himself do it, not wanting to spook Mina by reacting too strongly.

He needn't have worried. She sniffed at his comment, but her focus was on other things. "My cookies?"

He grinned. He'd gotten a whole package. Unlike many of the angelic legion, because he spent time with Mina in the desert and other human-inhabited areas, he carried a small amount of currency. He'd whisked through the store unseen, but left the money tucked into the cash register. It wouldn't show up in inventory, but at least he wasn't a thief.

"You and the Legion have saved the planet about a billion times. I don't think a store owner would begrudge an angel a box of Oreos. Unless he's completely heartless and needs to spend time in Hell with Lucifer."

"You're eavesdropping again."

"Tit for tat." She opened the cookies, bringing the golem back down to her lap, holding it there in a coil of tentacles. Disturbingly, the position seemed part yoga lotus position and part sunning snake, holding its prey.

Biting into one of the cookies, Mina closed her eyes, an act of involuntary bliss that amused him. "When I figured out that humans didn't really belong here," she said, "I thought it wouldn't matter if they got obliterated. Didn't really understand why you expended so much effort for them. But this..." She picked up another Oreo, inhaled it deeply. "This justifies their existence. Are you going to sit with me?"

Though he knew the sand baby was illusion, it awed him enough that he eased down next to her with a funny sense of reverence. Looking at his face, she stopped chewing, her eyes getting a similar stillness as she considered his expression. She swallowed. "I just thought...I thought we might want to see what it would feel like."

As his gaze shifted to her, she lifted a shoulder, giving in to full honesty, because he never let her get away with less. "*I* wanted to see what it would feel like."

He nodded. "So what do you think?"

She looked back down at the babe. When she reached down, it captured one of her fingers in its own. Grains of sand scattered over her knuckles. "It was unexpected. I felt...shaky, when I held her for the first time. Which is entirely ridiculous."

"No, it's not. Because you're preparing for the reality." Tentatively, he reached out toward the golem's other hand and had his own finger seized. It tightened his throat, seeing tiny fingers around his one large one. Sand sprinkled his battle-callused knuckles. Glancing at Mina, he suppressed a sudden soft smile, leaned in and kissed the corner of her mouth, taking away a few Oreo crumbs. Then he shifted for the full taste of her, teasing her tongue with his own, tasting chocolate, cream icing and Mina. He felt a small ripple of energy right before he did it, and knew his sweet witch had made sure he could taste the cookie, since without that magical effort, everything but manna tasted like sawdust to him. It was something she never forgot to do for him, a small, precious gift that said so much to him about what and who she was.

"Are you glad she'll be a girl?" Mina studied him with serious eyes as he lifted his head at last. He braced his other arm behind her so she could lean up against the shelter of his shoulder. When she put her head down on his chest to study their practice baby, he buried his nose in her hair, enjoying the way the raven strands felt drifting across his face with the lagoon's light breeze.

"I'm glad she'll be ours. I don't care what the baby is.

She's part of us. That's all that matters."

"I just wondered. Sometimes men like sons. You know, to carry on their bloodline, or teach them how to play baseball. In the books I've read, that's what humans feel."

"I'm not human."

"But you were. A lot of you still is."

"Mina, when you gave me your heart, you gave me everything I could ever want. Having a child with you...it's like finding out Heaven has a whole other level I didn't know about, but it's still Heaven. You understand?"

Lifting her head, she gave him her trademark suspicious look. "You are a very strange man," she decided. "It will arrive completely helpless, unable to feed or clothe itself, with no regular sleep patterns. No proper hygiene habits for the first several years of its life, so you have to do all sorts of unmentionable things to manage its waste. That's what you're calling a different version of Heaven. A different version of Hell is far more likely."

He laughed out loud. "Though I refuse to tell you where I learned this very important lesson," he said, attempting to look solemn, "I have discovered the things I love most in this life are quite capable of representing both Heaven *and* Hell." He snuck a cookie from the tray and held it up. "Dark and light often taste best together."

She narrowed her gaze at him, but then shrugged and looked back down at the infant. It had grabbed her hair. She touched its stomach, spoke softly. As they watched, it twisted, moved around to all fours, and then managed to make it to its feet. The sand child precariously swayed, then toddled a few steps. Bending to capture two more handfuls of sand, it tossed them out with jerky movements and a delighted laugh. David automatically shifted, curving his wing to shield Mina's face as the sand blew back over them in a playful sweep.

Mina dug into the Oreos again and lifted one to David's mouth. Taking a bite and chewing, he gazed down into her lovely face. "You're feeling generous."

"It happens." Feathering her fingers through the hair on his brow, she stroked the side of his face, her expression becoming pensive. Her thumb passed over his lips, collecting the crumbs then placing them on his tongue. Her body was pressed to his, and he could feel a need in her, a mixture of the physical and more. Brow creasing, he slid his arm around her, palming her buttock and hip to hold her near.

"Mina?"

"I want to take you somewhere. I checked with Jonah. He said it wasn't technically okay, but since, quote 'You pretty much do whatever you damn well please anyway', he said he wasn't going to stop me. Which I think was his way of saying it was all right. It's only breaking a few rules that are stupid, anyhow. And no, you're not taking me there. I'm taking you. I've been practicing my transporting through the folding of space and time, and it's going pretty well. I felt a lot less squashed the last time I did it. And I ended up in the dimension I expected. Your feathers shouldn't be too matted when we come out the other side."

"Oh, good. I feel reassured." But he was truly less concerned about that than the odd confusion of emotions he felt going through her now. He knew when she didn't want him to pry and read things ahead of time, and he definitely got that vibe now, so he curbed it, since it seemed important to her. "Mina, are you sure...whatever it is you're about to do, is it something *you* want to do?"

"You're a liar," she said bluntly, startling him. "There are things that are important to you, beyond me. Things you wish and hope for. You always make it about me. This is something I'm giving to you." Lifting the Oreos, she gave him a querulous look. "These were about me. So the next few minutes get to be about you."

"All right." But as she shifted back to human legs and rose, dusting herself off, he still did his own check, reaching out briefly to Jonah's mind. Fortunately, with angels, intent and feeling were sufficient, no need for specifics. His commander's response was reassuring, a confirmation of Mina's position, in less acerbic terms. Whatever she was planning, Jonah was on board with it, though David caught the same sense of apprehensive expectation. As if they weren't sure how *he'd* react. Curious.

"We need to go now," Mina said. It took David a

moment to tune in and realize she wasn't talking to him. The sand child turned and toddled back to her. Mina bent over it, her hand on its head. When she extended her other hand to David, he took it, letting her draw him closer. He put his other palm on top of hers, so they were both touching the babe. It looked up at them with laughing eyes, eyes that swirled away in a cloud of sand as it dissipated, becoming part of the beach again. In the same moment, David felt the reality around them start to shift. Mina's hand tightened on his, a small direction to remain motionless as her focus went inward.

As an angel, he'd raced a shooting star across the sky, following it into Earth's atmosphere. His intent was to slow its descent, give the meteor a safe landing, but those few moments before he'd had to do his duty, he'd reveled in the speed, twisting in the chaotic storm of its wake, riding the tail that appeared like a streak of fire from the ground. The couple of times he'd transported with Mina had reminded him of that, and this time was no exception. He trusted her, so there was no fear, just pleasure in the wild sense of movement, of disorientation. Then a sudden, somewhat jarring stillness, like a carnival ride braking to a halt.

It had been afternoon at the lagoon, but now it was night. He smelled marsh and salt in the air, evidence of a body of water nearby. He could hear the water lapping along a bulkhead. The scent and sound were familiar enough to make him realize why Jonah had felt some apprehension about allowing this, and why Mina had her own reservations, despite her obvious determination about it.

He'd occasionally visited here, always unseen. Well, except once, but that had been long ago. Only it wasn't long ago. Not tonight. Mina had gotten rather adept at folding time, though she was still learning the rules about that. Learning them at the knee of the Lady Herself, one of the few places he was not allowed to accompany her, though she gave him awe-inspiring visions of what she saw and did in the Lady's company. Enough to simultaneously amaze and assure him she was well-protected under that Great Mother's wing.

Based on what the garden looked like, the relative newness of the winged statue he saw placed amid an array of Japanese maples and other delicate-looking plants, this was over twenty years ago. Mina had conjured herself clothing, a simple dress, so she was no longer naked. Now she moved to the statue. Her knees pressed against the bench next to it as she looked up into the sculpted face. "It's a good likeness of you."

"Mina, what are we doing here?" His voice sounded strange, thick, and she heard it, coming back to him to take his hand in a rare gesture of reassurance.

"You're going to tell your sister you found the love and happiness she wanted you to have." When she looked up at him, her own voice quivered a bit. "As hard as I continue to find that to believe, I know it's the truth." She couldn't hold onto sentiment long, his witch, and sure enough, her expression shifted, becoming vaguely irritated. "Jonah said I should do this while she was sleeping, so she wouldn't be sure if it was real or she dreamed it, but I saw no reason not to do it while she was fully awake. I don't think the universe is going to explode because of one teeny-tiny space-time continuum infraction. He quoted some ridiculous story about a time travel tour group during Prehistoric times and a smashed butterfly that ruined the future, blah blah blah. Really, you'd think an angel who's lived over a thousand years would be less dramatic about things. I don't even think butterflies existed during Prehistoric times."

"Mina." He closed both hands on hers, stilling her. "I don't know if this is such a good idea. If—"

Her gaze shifted, at the same moment he realized they were no longer alone. "Too late," his witch murmured.

§

"David."

The voice was a bare whisper behind him, but it captured his words in his throat. He couldn't move. Mina's blue and crimson eyes locked with his, her fingers sliding from his palms over his forearms. "Just because you have feathers doesn't mean you're a chicken," she said, low. "And they're flightless, besides. You're not."

He gave her a look between apprehension and exasperation, but she reached up, stepping on his feet to kiss his mouth. She held herself there a moment before she went back to her own soles and moved away. She was giving him the wing range to turn toward that voice, but she didn't go far. She went to the bench, sinking down on it.

David slowly pivoted. His sister wasn't alone, of course. Whatever had compelled her to come visit her garden in the dead of night had brought her husband with her. A good man, a protective one. He stood at her back instead of in front of her only because Tyler Winterman had seen David once before, a long time ago. It was how he'd known how to commission that statue, his one-year anniversary gift for Marguerite.

Well, correction—he'd seen David a long time ago, based on the time from which they'd come. Here, in this moment, it had been no more than a year or so ago.

Marguerite had lived in painful loneliness and emotional isolation for most her life, caught by the horror of her past, the losses she'd sustained, while David was dead and gone, helpless to do anything to make that better. Rationally, angels learned to understand why things unfolded the way they did, but the heart remained a child's domain, only knowing that it wanted to give, to comfort, to make better.

Though he'd been an angel for nearly sixteen years at the time it happened, it wasn't until he'd been able to see his sister accept the unconditional love she'd deserved for so long, feel Marguerite's true happiness in the arms of a man who refused to let her run from him, that Heaven had meant something real to David, a gift he could finally give himself.

Mina was offering him the chance to give his sister the same kind of gift. If he didn't blow it. Things like this were discouraged because they could go really badly. However, he and Marguerite were twins. Mina had known the connection was deeper, that his sister likely suffered the same pain over his unresolved fate, only Marguerite hadn't been able to see into David's world the way he had hers.

Taking a step forward, he studied Marguerite's face. She was a beautiful woman, pale moonlit hair and blue eyes, a slender, elegant body. Tall. Not quite as tall as Tyler, but she was all statuesque strength. And at the moment, so unutterably fragile he didn't blame Tyler a bit for having his hand on her hip, a reassuring touch.

There were no words, he realized. At least not at first. Hell, Mina had made it so the rules didn't count, not in this moment, and so he was going to do what he'd wanted to do for so long. He didn't want to scare her, but he wasn't sure if he slowed his speed. All he knew was one moment he was staring at his twin sister, and the next moment he'd closed the distance between them and was holding her as tight as he dared without crushing her. Tyler had smoothly moved back in time, so maybe that meant he hadn't moved at angel light speed after all. Or that the man had just anticipated him that well. David wrapped his arms around her narrow back, his wings enclosing her so tightly they brushed his own shoulders again. Her pale hair was almost the color of his white feathers, he saw, looking down at the mix.

The other half of his soul. That was what they sometimes said twins were, one soul split at birth. Holding her, both of their bodies shaking, feeling her tears wetting his shoulder and knowing they were rolling down his face as well, he understood why they said it. It was as if they were two halves of a heart, brought back together. He loved Mina with all he was, loved being an angel, was connected to the Lord and Lady, but this...Mina had been right. This was an important missing piece.

He might have held her for days, he didn't know. All he knew was her grip didn't slacken for a long time, and neither did his. When he finally lifted his head, he kept her that close, so that their faces were inches apart. He smiled at her then, even as more tears spilled for them.

"Hey, sis."

She put her hands up to frame his face as she stared at him, tracing every bone with her gaze. "Tyler told me. Told me what he saw that day. It didn't surprise me at all. Not a bit. You were always my angel, even before we had to part."

Her voice was of course a woman's voice, cultured and soft, but he heard the girl beneath it. "I don't think we have a lot of time," he said softly. "This may be the only time...until you know...you get old and gray and decide to come live on my side of the world. But I wanted to tell you. You're going to be an aunt."

Her eyes widened. He loosened his grip enough to step back, though he held onto her hands, and she clung to his. He nodded toward the bench. "This is my mate, Mina. She's carrying a little girl." Looking back toward Marguerite, he met her eyes, brimming with emotion. "I'm happy. I love her very much. And everything that happened...I would do anything to change it for you, to have made it better, but what happened to me...it led to this. So I wouldn't change that for me. Don't suffer a moment of pain or worry about that, not ever again. All right?"

Marguerite gazed at him, then over her shoulder at Tyler. His amber eyes tracked every emotion on her face, and David could tell he was ready to be or do whatever she needed. She returned her attention to her brother.

"Only if you promise to accept the same is true for me. I couldn't have been here, in this place, without all that. And he is worth absolutely everything I went through."

The nature of moments like this was they became a gift to everyone involved. He saw the impact of the amazing statement register with Tyler and tighten the expression on his face, such that he mouthed her name, a voiceless caress.

David understood completely. He squeezed her hands, then brought each up to his mouth, pressing his lips there, hard. She freed one to stroke it through his hair and put her forehead to his. "I love you always," she murmured. "My brother, my heart. Thank you."

He stepped back after another long moment, reluctant, but knowing he really couldn't prolong this. Jonah expected him to know the difference between bending and shattering the rules. It was okay. He knew what and who he was, though Mina had given him the chance to be something else for a precious blink of time. His witch came back to his side now, looked up at him, spoke in his mind.

We should call her Marie.

His sister's birth name. He nodded, and spoke it aloud. "We plan to call her Marie."

New tears spilled out of Marguerite's eyes. Tyler put his arms around her, his own eyes suspiciously wet. In contrast, Mina gave them her stern look, pointedly directing it at Tyler. "This isn't a dream," she said. "Be sure she doesn't think it is."

"It *is* a dream," Tyler replied, a quirk at his firm mouth. "A dream come true. The best kind. Thank you."

Mina, apparently satisfied with the response, touched David on the arm. It was a gentle touch, very uncharacteristic of her, but he knew her heart. There were times when she was all tenderness. *You really* will *be a wonderful mother, sweet witch.*

In answer, she simply rolled her eyes, took his hand, and let that energy swirl start to build again. David kept his eyes locked on Marguerite's as long as possible, until the folding of space and time swept the image away. But he knew he'd hold it in his heart forever. Just like he'd hold onto the realization that happiness was a limitless state of being. Particularly when he was loved by a witch who thought she didn't know the first thing about love, but demonstrated daily that she understood it better than most.

§

They were back at the desert house. For a while, they walked along a familiar path under an early evening sky, Mina examining lizards and rocks, him holding her hand when she wasn't bending to do that. He'd stayed quiet for some time, and she'd given him that, but he could tell by her sidelong looks she was hoping he'd say something to reassure her it had turned out the best way possible.

It had. Better. But he gave her an arched brow now, a speculative smile. "Jonah is a pretty big stickler on the rules, particularly the one about contact with humans.

What did you promise him?"

"You're suggesting the Prime Legion Commander, Mr. Perpetual-Stick-Up-His-Ass, bartered to gain an advantage from a rule infraction?"

"Before he had exposure to you, I would have said he'd never consider such a thing. But we all know you're a bad influence."

Mina gave him a shove, then tried to evade him. Catching her elbows, he cinched her about the waist, pulling her off her feet when she tried to wiggle free. He thought he caught the rare music of a breathless chuckle, then he left the ground, earning a yelp of protest. As well as the pleasure of that squirming body pressing close, her limbs clamping around him.

"I hate it when you do that."

"Tell me what you promised him, or I'll go higher."

"You are a very mean angel. I don't think I like you at all." She tossed her hair out of her eyes, but settled her arms around his shoulders, giving him an exasperated look as he nudged her chin up and put his lips there, teasing her pulse, which tripped up in an intriguing way under the attention.

"He said it's a wild card."

"A wild card? So you promised him an open-ended favor for this?"

"I did. I had a moment of insanity, valuing you far more than you are worth."

"No doubt." He tangled his fingers in her hair, tightening his grip so the angle of her throat reflected the demand and restraint. Her thigh muscles flexed against his hips, registering her reaction to that, and his cock stirred against her. "I love you, Mina. I love you so much you're never going to be rid of me. I'm going to make you happy every single day, whether you want me to or not."

Her mouth softened at the words. If he said things like that too often, it made her suspicious, uncomfortable. But at the right moment, he knew it brought warmth to those dark parts of her that always feared abandonment, betrayal, the places the Dark One blood infested. He'd never let it get the upper hand. Never.

She hesitated. Then she raised her face to his, letting him see her eyes, the tentative emotion there that was so rare for her, but which she gave him now. "I want her," she said, low. "I want to hold our child. I want to love her. I want to be her mother and you to be her father."

"All right then," he said.

A quiet exchange of words for something so momentous, something that rocked the foundation anew of everything she thought she could or couldn't be. He knew what she needed to steady her in such a moment, and in truth, he kind of needed it as well. His hands cupped her backside, slid with sensual intent beneath, stroked her so a tremor went through her, her breath drawing in.

He found her beneath the dress. With the bare covering of his tunic it was a simple matter to push the cloth out of the way. This wasn't about foreplay and teasing, but about need and connection. So, with a light stroke to verify her wetness, that she was ready and he wouldn't hurt her, he slid his cock into that heated channel. Her breath left her in a sound that was mixed between a quiet sob and a gasp, and he held her even closer. *I'm here, Mina. I'll always be here. We can do this. Together.*

He'd flown higher, so now they were spiraling above the desert where they could see the rock formations against the deep rose of the setting sun. The stars were getting brighter in the darkening sky above. She clung to his shoulders, buried her face in his neck as he slid deeper into her. He wanted to be as close as possible, in all ways, and so did she.

"I won't share my Oreos, though," she muttered, though he heard her breathlessness, knew a smile was playing in her heart, even if it wasn't on her face. "Kids need to learn boundaries."

"Yes, they do." He pressed his lips against her ear. "Just like sea witches. If they don't have rules, and discipline, they just get into all sorts of trouble."

A deeper thrust this time, a little more demanding, and she gave him a satisfying noise of desire in response, her nails digging into his shoulders. "Rules are made to be broken," she managed.

Loving her, every dark shadow and spark of light that made her who she was, David let the pleasure build in them both. He'd draw it out until she was begging for release. Not from his hold upon her, but to let the pleasure of their eternal connection explode in a shower of magical energy that could rival all the power in the universe.

Even that of one irascible sea witch.

Retribution

A vignette featuring Ben and Celeste from the Knights of the Board Room Series.

Originally posted January, 2012 in serial format.

Background: *This vignette is a prequel to Ben and Celeste's individual books. Ben's story is Book V, Hostile Takeover, and Celeste's is Book VII, Soul Rest. In this vignette, Celeste, who gave the K&A executives the derisively-intended name, Knights of the Board Room, learns far more about who these five Doms really are, thanks to the skills of one of their number, Ben O'Callahan.*

Part 1

Celeste stirred her drink and flicked her lashes toward the opposite side of the club, up to the VIP section. Of course they'd be there. Like kings or gods, they could see the entire club floor from that level. Knights of the Board Room. She'd given them the name in derision, but the rest of the world acted as if she'd merely gilded the lily. Her editor thought the five-man executive team of Kensington & Associates walked on water. The case of Scotch that Matt Kensington sent him every year for Christmas probably contributed to his worshipful feeling. Fucking boys' club.

Since the men were sitting at a round table, she'd say they were mocking her—if they knew she was here. The mask she was wearing protected her identity. She'd chosen a bracelet that indicated she wasn't here to play—hell no to that—and to keep everyone at a distance. It didn't make her conspicuous. Lots of people wore decorative masks and the same type of bracelet. Voyeurism and discretion appeared to be a popular *modus operandi* in a club where public displays of sadomasochism were happening pretty much everywhere around them.

On her first visit, she'd studiously tried not to be a voyeur, then reasoned she'd be more noticeable if she was trying not to look. Plus, she was a journalist. She wasn't supposed to flinch from gathering data. But even on this, her third visit, it was difficult to look at the guy sitting two stools down from her. While he was talking to another man, a completely naked woman knelt on the floor next to him, wearing a dog collar and leash, for God's sake. The physical details were appalling enough, but it was the woman's body language and expression Celeste couldn't stomach. Her fingers were touching his ankle, something he'd permitted, and occasionally the woman would press her mouth against his calf in pleading, yearning need. If she got too carried away with it, he would reprimand her with the light touch of a crop he carried, but sometimes he would reach down and feather his fingers through her hair, indulging the affection.

She'd rather see someone decapitated in a public square than look at something like that. At least an execution was honestly horrific. No shades of gray. This was twisted, rationalized perversity that confused her mind, her senses. In college, she'd done a thesis on the sexual subjugation of women in modern day society, and included a sampling of fetish clubs in her research. She hadn't liked what she'd seen then, either, though she'd been far more obvious about her distaste, the mistake of a novice journalist. She'd made it crystal clear she was there to do a research project, to observe them like animals in the zoo.

In return, they'd treated her as an outsider, but not unkindly. They acted as if they pitied her, like she didn't understand, like she didn't have the secret password. It had haunted her for a long time, such that when she'd caught hints that Surreal, Baton Rouge's premier fetish club, was a major hangout for K&A's executive management, she'd been determined to drive up from her New Orleans' home base and observe them there, no matter her motives for doing so.

Her lip curled. *"Do a follow up story on Kensington's charitable works,"* her editor had said. *"We can dovetail it into the opening of the new domestic violence center K&A has funded."* What would her editor and Matthew Lord Kensington—Jesus—think if she submitted a story about Matt and his boys being regulars at Surreal, where women were tied up and beaten? Well, women and men, sometimes in very elaborate, artistic displays, but brutal perversion couldn't be masked by a classy setting.

If she could catch just one of Matt's boys tying up a woman and spanking her within an inch of her life, screaming in pain... Okay, in a lot of cases, the woman was acting like it was orgasmic ecstasy, but if Celeste could capture it on camera it would look like agony. Damn Surreal's strict policies. She'd tried to smuggle in her phone, and had to pass it off as forgetfulness when it was immediately detected. No electronic devices of any kind allowed, and their scanners were tuned to pick up even the smallest micro camera. Thank goodness she hadn't tried that, because at least she could explain the phone. A micro camera would have gotten her tossed out on her ass. Even for the temporary membership she'd purchased with her own money, she'd had to sign an ironclad privacy agreement, which said if she in any way abused the privileges of her presence here, she could be sued within an inch of her life and then some.

Her name and social were run through a computer, so they knew she was a journalist. It earned her a steady look from the host when she signed the agreement, an unspoken message that they'd be paying extra special attention to her, even though the temporary guest pass allowed her only three visits.

So here she was on visit three, and she'd gotten nowhere. She could sit in the parking lot and shoot pics of them coming out of the club, which meant nothing. She'd learned Matt and his team didn't play publicly, except once in a blue moon. And she couldn't afford anything more than the temporary membership. Game over tonight.

A flogging was in process on center stage. The woman in the stocks curled her fingers in reaction, her cries undeniably pleasure-driven as her ass, thighs and back became redder. Her Dom strolled around her, a massive bald man, tattooed and stripped down to tight leather pants and thigh-high boots. He looked like he should be mugging someone in an alley, or straddling a Harley, but it was difficult not to notice the sizeable erection under the pants, the muscular curves of his ass. As he stroked his victim's back, his fingers glided down to give her an additional pinch, a quick slap that made her buttocks wobble. She flinched, but then she begged for more.

Watching such things made Celeste quiver oddly. It was a little warm in the club tonight. They probably kept the temperatures up because there were so many mostly naked people here. She told herself her reaction was normal. Humans were fascinated with the macabre. It was why public executions and brutal gladiator games were popular throughout history, and that fascination cut across all classes. Hell, the Roman emperor himself attended them. Hence, Matt Kensington and his wunderkind, sitting in the very center of it. But it seemed so wrong, in the age of Starbuck's and hybrid cars, that such barbaric behavior had persisted.

Unlike her, Ben O'Callahan, the K&A man clearest to her line of sight, didn't have any problem looking at the flogging display. His eyes were laser steady on the sheen of sweat on the woman's back; Celeste could almost see him tracking a single drop rolling down the valley between her butt cheeks. The woman was obviously close to orgasm. Incomprehensible.

The most bizarre piece of the puzzle was Matt's wife, Savannah Tennyson of Tennyson Industries. A Fortune 500 CEO, a role model for independent women everywhere, and yet she'd fallen head over heels for Matt. Married him in a small, private ceremony at his Texas estate before anyone even knew they were dating. As the business social news columnist, Celeste had requested a photo at the time the community got wind of the marriage. When she'd received it from K&A's public relations office, it had been an undeniably touching shot of Matt and Savannah standing on the balcony of his house, overlooking the Gulf. Their eyes were full of one another as the four men of his team toasted them and smiled. They were apparently the only attendants, beyond the minister himself.

Savannah wasn't here tonight, but Celeste had seen her on her first visit. The subtle interactions between her and Matt had told Celeste the shocking truth. Savannah was one of those women who liked to be...her gaze went back to the naked woman on her knees and she shuddered.

Celeste wasn't unsophisticated. She had read the academic articles about BDSM; how surrender, loss of control, could be an avenue to trust, to unlock repressed passion, blah blah blah. Crap was all it was. Women wanting to give up the power that countless feminist activists had sacrificed to obtain for them, looking for a psychological justification for it. Yet Savannah continued to run her company with incredible aggression and ability, no indication that it had become another pawn in the K&A empire. She and Matt still occasionally locked horns on business matters, and he didn't always win.

Celeste sighed. Maybe she was here because she couldn't solve the puzzle and, no matter how her family belittled her job because she was stuck with business social news, she did consider herself a journalist. Yeah, yeah, K&A was extremely generous to worthy local causes. They even rolled up their pristine shirt sleeves and took time out from their corporate raiding to volunteer. But that wasn't why she'd stuck the Knights of the Board Room name on them. As she'd gathered data, she'd found out the appalling fact that most companies wouldn't send women to do business with them. Apparently, the five-man team had the ability to turn the smartest and most independent woman's mind to mush with their outdated sexist attitudes. Opening doors, pulling out chairs, refusing to split a check or let a woman pay her way were the least offensive manifestations of it. Hell, they looked like an Absolut Vodka commercial even now. No women allowed. Unless she was there to sexually service them, of course.

There. That put everything back in its proper perspective. And yet...she could also be here because they were a personal dilemma to her. Leave it to Valerie, her current roommate and an aspiring romance author, to point that one out. *You've got a personal beef with them, girl. The funny thing is, I don't think you really know what it is. Or maybe you do, and you just don't want to look too closely at it. Why is it journalists always look outside of themselves for answers? Fiction writers know you look inside first. I think you should be a bit more of a fiction writer when you think about these guys.* Then she'd cut the psycho-BS with a mischievous grin. *I know I much prefer fiction and fantasy when I think about them.*

Celeste had been obligated to call her roommate a slut, and was affectionately called a beeyatch in return.

Be a bit more of a fiction writer. Yeah, right. Crap. There was nothing to be learned here. She had no clue why she was hanging around. She'd write the editor's fluff piece, eat a quart of ice cream, and say to hell with it. "I'll take my check," she told the bartender. He shook his head.

"Already been paid, ma'am."

"I've been running an open tab."

"Yep. Covered. Compliments of..." When his gaze shifted, his mouth firmed in a smile. He offered the new arrival a significant nod and returned to his other patrons. Celeste turned her head.

Oh, hell.

Up close, Ben O'Callahan was a green-eyed, dark-haired, smolderingly sinful-looking lawyer, and he was leaning against the bar right next to her. A foot between them, yet she could feel his heat impinging on her personal space. He was over six feet tall, broad shouldered and, like all the Kensington men, had a personal presence that could drown a woman in charisma. "Picking up the tab is the least we can do for the lady who bestowed such an undeserving title on us," he said, the sexy timbre of his voice clearly useful for delivering compelling arguments.

Fuck. He knew who she was. She'd like to bestow a muzzle on him. And some restraints. In here, that led to some seriously disturbing thoughts.

"White zinfandel?" He glanced at her glass. "Such a mundane choice. One would think our worldly journalist has never left Louisiana."

She hadn't. Not for lack of desire, but lack of funds. That tended to happen when your father split on your mother, and you had to live at home to help raise the other kids while attending community college. She had no doubt Ben knew such personal details. It just confirmed her opinion of him, that he took such a cruel shot. But when he ordered a beer, he slanted her a relaxed smile. "Of course, I've never found much outside Louisiana better than what I have right here. Why pretend to like caviar when we all know an Acme po'boy tastes a hell of a lot better?"

Uncertain, Celeste stiffened as his fingers brushed the small of her back, an incidental gesture as he took a seat on the stool next to hers. However, he braced that hand on the back of her seat, creating an intimate space between them. "Another for the lady," he said to the bartender.

"No, thanks. I buy my own drinks. Even if it does offend your sexist code."

"Celeste, your fawning adoration for us has really got to stop. It's embarrassing." He nodded toward the center stage. "What do you think of the show?"

The bald man had opened his tight pants to reveal an enormous cock which he fed between the woman's eager lips, painting them with pre-cum. Celeste felt an annoying flush rise in her cheeks under Ben's amused regard. They were all here to look at sex stuff, right? She shouldn't be acting like a teenager caught with a skin mag.

"I think she's an embarrassment to the entire feminist movement."

"Really? How so?"

She gave him an incredulous look. "She's allowed herself to be conditioned to restraint and pain solely for male pleasure."

Ben's lips curved. "It looks to me like the pleasure is mutual. Look closer, Celeste. At what's going on, and how you described it. Allowed. I'm sure you've done your research and you know all the protocols of the BDSM world. Nothing happens up there that she doesn't want, and she can call it off at any time."

"Yeah. Every cult tells you that the members can leave whenever they want, totally ignoring the psychological domination that turns them into drooling lemmings." She took a bracing swallow of her wine. "Let me guess how you knew it was me. You pay the staff to tell you if anyone comes in here who's a threat to Matt specifically."

"We're not the mob, darling. Though sometimes I long for their more direct methods when dealing with the snarled fishing line otherwise known as our legal system. I knew it was you. I don't forget women."

"You met me once. At a dinner party."

"Yes, where you were gathering data for your gossip column."

"It's business social news," she gritted out. Then immediately regretted letting him get to her.

He shrugged. "Us southern folk tend to call that a gossip column. Doesn't make it any less entertaining or informative. I liked your piece on Lewis. Most wouldn't have dug deep enough to find out that he takes care of a brother with Down's syndrome, or that he backpacked across Europe when he was a kid and ended up on a short ride with Prince Harry. Most writers usually stick to surface crap, what they're fed by the company or government press offices."

"That's not journalism."

"No, it isn't. But most reporters these days think it is."

She looked for a trace of sarcasm, of derision, and found none. That gave him one up on her mother, who called it "Celeste's little column." She cleared her throat. "You can cut the charm. What do you want?"

She'd been out of college long enough to cultivate her cynicism. She was twenty-nine, after all. She could sound direct, dismissive, even if the man smelled wonderful. His clothes were obviously custom-tailored, making the most of the broad-shouldered body. His dark hair fell in strands over his forehead, accentuating the vivid green eyes. That strong jaw and direct gaze probably made female judges swoon.

He flicked the feathers on her mask. "An odd choice for

a self-proclaimed feminist. Colorful peacock feathers are male plumage. Used to intimidate enemies or impress the females."

She gave him a stare that should have dropped a ten-point deer, and instead he just smiled. The bartender put down a drink for him, and another glass of wine for her. Just ignore what the woman wants. She was tempted to sweep it off the polished surface. "Again, are you bothering me for a purpose?"

"You don't want me here, just say so. Surreal's rules are very clear. If I don't move on when you tell me, they'll throw me out. But you're not here looking for a playmate." His gaze flicked to the bracelet. "At least that wasn't your original intent. You're looking to nail Matt's ass to the wall. But I think you're better than that, Celeste."

"I wouldn't trust your opinion of better." Though she disliked the uneasy feeling, she took it for the warning it was. She was getting out of her depth, and was experienced enough to know when it was time for her to go. However, she couldn't seem to move. He still had his hand braced on the back of her seat, his body canted toward her. His polished dress shoe was braced on the bottom of her stool, right below her dangling foot. Her shoe had come off her heel, exposing the silken nylon beneath. When his gaze slid down and over it, she almost felt naked. Why did they make these stools so tall?

"I came over to offer you a chance to find the answers you're seeking." He nodded to the flogging session. "You've formed a derogatory opinion of the motives, decided that any positive spin is just that, mass rationalizations by deranged minds in an overly indulgent, morally decaying society. But underneath, you know there's some key piece you're missing and, to figure it out, you have to get closer. But there's no safe way to do that. Or is there?"

She blinked at him. "Is this the sales pitch before you give me my beads and the flower wreath to wear at the airport?"

He grinned, and she had to school herself not to draw in a breath at how attractive it made him. "I'm giving you a chance to dig deeper, what every good reporter wants."

"And every curious cat."

"How about this?" He shifted, so she could still see the scene over his shoulder, but his knee flanked hers on the stool. The Master had tucked himself back in and was now sliding a vibrating dildo into the woman's sex. She was convulsing against her bonds, crying out. He'd told her she couldn't come until he allowed it, and it was obvious how hard she was fighting to obey. She was going to lose, and the Master's expression was fierce, triumphant...tender.

A touch on her face jerked her gaze back to Ben. The movement nearly toppled her wine, but he had his fingers around the bowl, steadying it. "What if you had the chance to see it from the inside, go through a session yourself?" His gaze slid over her. "You can wear a club robe and keep the mask on, so your identity is concealed."

"I'm not stupid. There's a trick here. You have enough money to make this go however you want it."

"True. And I don't expect you to trust me. But then, trust is the issue, isn't it? You see it happening around you, in a hundred different undeniable manifestations, yet you can't figure out the why, the drug of choice for the true journalist. It's making you uncertain, confused and angry. But you're curious, Celeste. And I can offer you something else." Those green eyes sharpened. "I'll request that the session be taped, which is permissible as long as we both sign an agreement for it. That tape can then be purchased and taken home as a keepsake. I will give it to you, to do with as you will. I won't be masked, my identity clear as high-def. You can take proof to your editor that not only do all the K&A executives have memberships to Surreal, not very damning itself, but that at least one of the charmed five 'knights' indulges in the sins that occur there. You can expose our contributions to the domestic violence shelter as the guilt money, or mockery, you believe them to be."

"I don't..." Put that way, it sounded wrong. Bad. "That's not..."

He shook his head. "It doesn't matter. Do whatever you want with the information. But as far as my end of things, whatever happens between us will go no further than that room, if you don't want it to do so. You have my personal word on that."

She met his gaze, now entirely serious. There was a set to his mouth, a firm intentness, that unsettled her, inexplicably. Everyone in the business world knew when Matt or one of his guys gave his word, he never broke it. She'd looked for evidence to the contrary and never found it. Another piece of the puzzle.

Look inside for the answers. This is personal for you, Celly. Valerie's irritating voice, goading her. Celeste squelched it. "Is this a pickup line you use on a lot of women, O'Callahan?"

"Do you think I need lines to pick up women?"

"I'm not attracted to you." Yeah, like any woman with a pulse could say that with a straight face.

"Then it will be all the easier for you to stay objective. I find you very attractive. Even more so if you'd get rid of the ugly, rectangular I'm-too-smart-to-be-pretty glasses. May I?"

She had 20-20 vision, but she'd gotten them...exactly for the reason he'd said. It was kind of dumb to be wearing them over the mask, but she was so used to having them as part of her arsenal, she'd almost felt naked without them. She should tell him to get the hell away from her. Instead, she sat still as he slid the glasses from her face and brushed a tendril of her short hair back over her ear. "Beautiful hazel eyes," he murmured. "Thick lashes that are all yours. Christ, no wonder you hide them. A man couldn't look at them and not want you. So what do you say, Celeste? Going to be brave, or cautious?"

She knew she was average pretty when she took the time to show it. She also had a decent figure. Compliments didn't usually affect her. They were far more likely to put her on the defensive. But Ben wasn't insulting her with flirtation. He seemed like he was evaluating her. The flirtation would be preferable, because she knew how to handle that. But hell, this was how they did it, right? Turning an independent woman's mind to mush with this singular, concentrated appraisal. She wanted to detect artifice, practiced charm, but of course if they were this good at it, she wouldn't find it. Just because it felt sincere, didn't mean it was.

When she drew back, stiffening, he nodded. "You come off as a total bitch caught in a steel-leghold trap of bitter. But you're good at what you do. Determined. You act like you want dirt, but I think what you truly want are answers. Forget the whole news angle for a minute. Would you really like to get to the bottom of it, Celeste?"

He left that hanging, a blank for her to fill in. Get to the bottom of what the D/s scene was all about? Or why she was so fixated on them? Or why she was sitting here instead of telling him to fuck off, paying her own tab and leaving?

She could have that tape. She could get what she wanted, if she kept her focus on exactly what that was. Her jaw tightened. "Where's that agreement?" she asked.

Ben shook his head. "We'll sign it, but you'll do something else first." A calm authority entered his tone. "Do you have a good friend, someone you trust? Don't tell me who it is," he said, before she could speak Valerie's name.

Ben signaled the bartender. "Jerome's going to let you use the bar phone. I want you to call her and tell her whatever you're comfortable telling her, but you tell her where you are and who you're with. Additional insurance."

She wanted to bristle at the white knight routine, but how could she bristle at what made good sense? It just pissed her off that he'd thought of it before she had.

"Fine," she said, ungraciously. "If my body turns up somewhere tomorrow, I'll have the satisfaction of knowing you go down for it."

Ben gave her that dangerous grin again. It made her feel like she was facing a great white shark, swimming slowly around her, knowing he could devour her at his leisure. But for some reason, the idea of being eaten wasn't as horrible as it should be. Disturbingly enough, she was a little impatient for him to get on with it.

This was a big mistake. No. It was going to be his mistake. She would go through with it, with all the safety precautions, and he'd be the vulnerable one. She'd have the tape when all was said and done. Right?

Part 2

Agreement signed, clothes and jewelry removed and locked up in the Surreal changing room. She'd donned the silk black robe with the Surreal monogram. It went down to her knees, keeping her tastefully covered, though the silk clung to her body and made her feel more sensuous than she should have for what was essentially a work assignment.

She'd kept on her panties and bra. She wasn't planning on getting totally naked, and only Valerie could identify her by her underwear. She hadn't had a date get that close in quite a while. Not since she'd been a little tipsy on a past birthday and let a one-time friend-with-benefits spend the night. He was off with the Peace Corps, thankfully. By the time he returned, the memory should be less painfully embarrassing, more of a laugh-it-off recollection. Here again, gone tomorrow, no muss, no fuss.

Before stepping into the private room Ben had arranged, she noted the security guard at the head of the hallway. Video cameras in each room were monitored exclusively by DMs—dungeon masters—throughout. She'd done her research, so she knew he'd also have to ask her about boundaries, limits. Right? All the correct trappings in place. So this was safe.

No, of course it wasn't.

Okay, at least on the surface, he'd done everything to assure her she was going to be safe. She hadn't expected his insistence on her calling Valerie. When she reached the apartment answering machine, he told her to call Val's cell. He'd been pretty clear that, if she didn't make actual contact with her roommate, they wouldn't be going through with their deal tonight. But Valerie had answered her cell. Celeste wasn't sure if she was thankful for that or not.

During her very short conversation with her roommate, Ben had stepped away, giving her enough privacy to vet Val's mixed reactions of concern, WTF, and titillated amusement. "I want video," Val had threatened. Since her roommate didn't know the details of the devil's bargain

Celeste had made, Celeste imagined showing up with the tape and her roommate's eyes popping out. The thought made her smile, something she was surprised to find she needed. Her nerves were like tight springs punching through worn upholstery.

She didn't have to do this. But it was like a dare. If you didn't take the dare, you had to face a truth instead, usually a pretty uncomfortable one.

All in all, it was a little...unsettling, how determined he'd been about ensuring her safety. He was practically a stranger, about to engage in a very sexual, yet still impersonal situation with her, but he'd been as a protective as... She was *so* not going there.

Third private playroom on the left, he'd said. She moved up the hallway, glad she was alone. Hearing voices and heels approaching from the public level, she quickened her step, not wanting to see anyone. Taking a deep breath, she turned the latch and stepped inside.

She wasn't sure what she'd expected. Him wearing leather studded chaps and nothing else, schlong hanging out, a sinister-looking whip in his hand? The picture almost made her giggle, a little hysterically. Probably because the way he actually looked made her way more nervous, which was ludicrous, since he looked exactly like he had at the bar.

Well, that wasn't entirely true. Clothing-wise, he did. Still in his custom-tailored suit, though he'd removed the jacket, hung it up, rolled up his sleeves and loosened his tie. However, something had changed about him. The attitude, the focus, something... Or maybe she was just imagining things, and it was merely the change of environment, the two of them alone in this small room increasing the intimacy, intensity...danger. Nowhere to run or hide.

Yes, that could be contributing to it, but she wasn't mistaken. Her increased nervousness had to do with an indefinable something emanating from *him*. In here, he seemed even more formidable, despite him slouching with deceptive casualness against the wall. Arms crossed, toe of his dress shoe hooked around the opposite ankle. Because of the position of his arms, his shirt pulled across his broad shoulders, the slacks following the long lines of thigh. The candlelight praised his jaw in a powerful, controlled line. When his green eyes lifted to hers, they were calm, cool. Direct. And remote, in a way that made butterflies jump in her lower belly.

As she paused in the open doorway, taking in her surroundings, she suspected she looked like Bambi, hesitating on the edge of the meadow, making sure it was safe. No cruel torture devices on the walls, no chains hanging from the ceiling. There was a large walnut cabinet, a curtained area beside it. Beyond those nefarious possibilities, the room was like a turn-of-the-century parlor. Oriental carpet on a polished wooden floor, a scattering of small pieces of art on the walls. Candle sconces gave the room a dim ambiance. Along the wall beside Ben were several wooden straight-backed chairs. No bed.

She stepped into the room in her robe and her heels, which she'd chosen to wear instead of the club disposable slippers. He seemed to like the look, gaze coursing over her bare legs. Since she had a weird desire to simply stand there until he told her to do something, she decided it was way past time to take control of the situation. Spreading her arms, she executed a mocking twirl. "So, what do we do first? Give me a good spanking? Make me call you Daddy?"

When he said nothing, she crossed her arms over herself, tried a hip cock and a look of indifferent amusement. "What are you doing?"

"At the moment, just looking at you. What do you want from this, Celeste? I know you want the tape, but what's your true motive? Don't answer me."

She frowned. "You're asking me a question, but you don't want an answer?"

"Women don't think about what they want. They feel it. I want you to stop thinking and feel. You don't have to talk at all. If you keep talking for the wrong reasons, I'll gag you, so you can focus on what's happening in your head instead of fencing words with me."

"I don't want you to do that." The very thought panicked

her. Her sharp tongue was her best weapon.

"Then stop talking. Feel it. What do you want?"

Answers. Relief from this anger. This frustration. She was surprised when those thoughts leapt to the forefront of her mind. He didn't say anything, though his gaze flickered as if he knew her response. Even more strange and unsettling.

"When I look at you, I see two people. The reporter and the woman. The reporter is sharp, intelligent, overqualified for the work she's doing. From what I know of you, that won't always be the case. You'll get what you want, because you don't blame anyone for failure except yourself, and failure isn't acceptable."

"Do I strike you as the kind of woman who needs her ego stroked?" She arched a brow.

"You don't have an ego, Celeste. There's no room for it with that big to-do list in your head. The reporter part is obvious."

Apparently not so much, because he was the only man who'd ever voiced it.

"Who and what we are, that's what intrigues the woman *and* the reporter," he said. "You want to know more. You want to experience what we do to women, but you're worried it will be just as debasing as you claim it is. Another part of you is terrified it isn't, that it will unlock something inside of you that you don't necessarily want unlocked."

He uncrossed his arms, showing he was holding something in the hand that had been tucked under the distracting biceps. It took a moment to make sense of the shapes, but she'd seen enough items like them at Surreal to know he was holding a satin eye mask and a ball gag. He also held his folded white handkerchief. Did he iron and wash those himself, the way she had to painstakingly clean her silks and wools, since she couldn't afford to have them professionally dry-cleaned? Not likely. The man drove a half a million dollar sports car, after all.

Her attempt to distance herself from him with the reminder of his wealth, his sense of entitlement, fell short as he continued.

"You've seen Masters and Mistresses use these. You assume they're to take away free will. A woman's ability to run her mouth." When amusement wreathed his expression, she tightened her lips, refusing to rise to that bait. "As far as the free will, you aren't completely wrong, but these objects deal with the illusion of free will, not the reality of it. We use our eyes and our mouths as defense mechanisms, things that keep us from noticing what's important, from listening to and feeling not only external sensory input, but internal input as well. There's a reason monks take vows of silence. There are powerful things in silence. In darkness."

She wasn't entirely sure how to grasp a corner of his logic and unravel it. She just wanted him to get on with it. As soon as he spanked her, she could end the session, take her tape and go. He hadn't set any stipulations on it, any time limits. She was in control here. That quivering low in her stomach wasn't fear. But he was holding a ball gag. A blindfold. And now he wasn't saying anything, just watching her.

She got the whole silence/darkness Zen thing, but if he didn't start talking again, she was going to bolt. Which meant she was relying on him for control, stability. Fuck, no way was that happening.

As she opened her mouth to retort, to get this thing rolling her way, he shifted. She jumped before she could stop herself. Giving her a considering look, he closed his hand around the top of one of the chairs, bringing it to the center of the room. "Come sit here."

A reasonable enough request. Though his tone didn't suggest a request at all, which should have raised her hackles and inspired her to say something sarcastic. But she'd said she wanted to experience this. She was a journalist. She should at least try to get into the mindset of a...submissive. Meek, compliant.

Not. She was holding her jaw so rigidly it was starting to hurt. Ben's gaze moved over it. "Do you want me to come over there and get you?" he asked softly.

Why an obvious threat should make her stomach do a triple somersault and send an aching twinge between her legs, she didn't know, but it startled her enough to get her moving.

She walked stiffly over to the chair, slowing as she drew close enough to be within touching distance. When she swallowed, she saw he was cataloging every reaction.

"It's all right," he said quietly. "Nothing will happen here that you don't want."

"I don't want to be here. You could just give me a tape of you beating up some other girl, and we could call it a night."

Something flickered through the green eyes, his mouth tightening. "I can assure you, I don't beat up women. Not the way you mean. And that tape is the excuse for you being here, not the reason. If you think I'm wrong, the door's behind you."

Okay, so he'd turned on the charm at the bar, but it was definitely in the off position in this room. He stood in front of her, unrelenting, mouth stern, eyes serious, not a trace of persuasion. She almost felt like she needed to apologize. It *had* been kind of a crappy remark, after all.

What the hell? He *did* smack women around. No, she hadn't seen it, but he played private, and she was sure that was what went on. What he was doing to her now was no different from indoctrination into a cult. Emotional abuse, even. A clever manipulation to make a woman feel subservient and apologetic for having an opinion.

"Sit down." He nodded to the chair.

She tightened her chin. She'd do it because she'd see it through. A research project. If she could keep the academic analysis going in her mind, she'd stay in charge. Detached.

Yet she couldn't quite seem to make her legs bend. Not until he closed his hand on her shoulder, a startling heat, and applied simple pressure. She was sitting, without remembering when her knees had decided to give. He guided her hands so they were curled over the sides of the seat, by her thighs. Laying his palm on her abdomen, just beneath her breasts, he made her stiffen, straighten.

"There you go. Back against the chair. Shoes flat on the floor, hands holding the chair sides. Just like that. Hold that position."

Picking up another chair, he brought it over and took a seat facing her, putting a few feet between them. As he laid his ankle on his opposite knee, he stretched out the bottom leg so his dress shoe rested alongside her neatly aligned feet. Hooking his arm around the chair back, he regarded her in silence. "Focus on the picture directly over my left shoulder."

She'd noticed there were pictures, but not the details of them. She'd assumed they'd be some erotic acrobatics to stir the libidos of the room participants. Though she prided herself on her observation skills, her survival instincts had kept her focused on the more mysterious and sinister aspects of the room. Like him. Now she was surprised to find the picture over his shoulder was a close-up of a single white rose, hit by a touch of morning sun.

"Keep your eyes on it."

"What will you be doing?"

"Looking at you."

Her gaze flicked to him. He made a noise, a single syllable, unintelligible, but her gaze shifted back to the picture. Had she just responded to a command? No, he hadn't said anything. But he'd made it clear with body language what he wanted her to do. And she was doing it. Because she'd agreed to it, made a choice. *Not* because she was obeying Ben O'Callahan.

The rose looked the way it did right after the sun dried the dew off it. Something about seeing flowers in the morning always made her feel better. She and Valerie shared the expenses of a New Orleans Garden District two-bedroom apartment, with a little narrow outside balcony, on which she kept a small garden of potted roses. Her favorite thing was sliding out there early in the morning with her coffee to watch the sun come up and kiss them good morning with its beams of light. She would sit and inhale the flowers' fragrance, stroke the petals. In that moment, she wasn't a reporter, Valerie's roommate, her mother's daughter or anything else. She was just flowers and sunshine.

She'd closed her eyes. There was a warmth, a heat here. Not the room itself, though the temperature was comfortable. It was coming from his regard, her reaction to it. Oddly, in this stillness, it was like her reaction to the morning sun on her flowers. Noise from the public floor of the club was muted. She could hear his breath, a quiet sound. He didn't move, but she remembered how close his foot was. She thought about when they were at the bar, when he'd been even closer, so close she was almost inside the span of his thighs.

"What are you looking at?" she asked. She chose not to open her eyes. It felt right not to do so.

"Your face. The small movements of your lips. They tighten as you get nervous and think too much. Then they relax, get softer as you give yourself to sensory input. You have a very responsive mouth. Most of the time, the corners are turned down, even when you smile. There's a current of unhappiness, discontent, inside of you. Restlessness. Your skin creases on your forehead and around your eyes as you think, wonder, worry. Imagine."

Her mother had often said that. *Don't frown so much, Celly. You'll look old before your time. For heaven's sake, smile when you smile. You look like you're grimacing.*

Her fingers tightened on the chair seat, but he was continuing. "Now I'm looking at your throat. The way you swallow as I talk to you. Your pulse is jumping. That stiff blouse you were wearing, it was professional, intended to be businesslike, straightforward, but it also showed you have a toned upper body and nice breasts. They're soft and full beneath the robe, just like the line of your hip. You take care of yourself, Celeste, but you let yourself indulge enough to keep the curves. It's sexy."

Sexy. No one had ever said that to her, straight out. Opening her eyes, she found herself staring directly into his. "Dark and endless," he murmured. "You can see straight to your soul through your eyes, Celeste."

She shut them again. Not sure why, just obeying instinct, but what kind of instinct, she didn't know. Self-preservation? He didn't tell her not to do it, apparently content to continue looking at her. At least she assumed that was what he was doing. Her body was tingling, her nipples tightening as she thought about him touching her breasts. He had large hands. He'd cup them firmly, squeeze, enjoy them with pure masculine pleasure. Possessive pleasure, because in this room at least, the moment belonged to him.

She tightened her jaw. *Stop it.* This was textbook mind manipulation. He'd told her she could leave. She could leave at any moment. She didn't need his damn permission. But she was here for the tape.

When he rose, her breath caught, a quick show of anxiety. She kept her eyes shut. To show him he couldn't rattle her? To close him out? She could barely hear him move on the carpet, but if he went toward that curtained area and touched any scary metal implements or chains, she'd know. She was closer to the door than he was. "Aren't we supposed to be talking about limits...safe words?"

"What word would make you feel safe, Celeste?"

She jumped. He was right behind her. His fingertips slid over her collar bone, teasing the edge of the robe. "Tell me the first word that came to mind."

Not likely. Not when it brought an ache to her throat, an automatic denial. "I can pay a therapist to do this."

He chuckled, a warm, sensuous sound. "But it wouldn't be as much fun. Tilt your head to the right."

When she did, she drew in a breath as his mouth settled on her pulse, tasting her, the tip of his tongue teasing along the erratic beat. Then the press of teeth. The great white shark again.

"Most people thought I was paying you a compliment, calling you the Knights of the Board Room."

"We knew better. You hate us."

"No." She felt like she had when he'd implied she wanted to undermine their donations to the domestic violence center. She struggled for a more rational response, summoning her usual cynicism. "Corporate raiders, doing charity to detract from the—"

"Blah, blah, blah." It was a bedroom whisper. Curling his fingers in her hair, he tugged her scalp while keeping her head in place. The contradiction made her belly flipflop. "Page 101 of the media handbook. All corporations are evil, so said while you drink your Starbucks and buy clothes at The Gap. It's far easier to objectify us, lump us in with general rhetoric, than to admit what it is about us that really bothers you personally."

Her lashes flickered at the touch of satin, her shoulders stiffening. "Just the eye mask for now," he said. "You're already showing your preference for keeping your eyes closed. This will help you feel everything more intensely, notice the details."

"But I won't be able to see what you're doing when I want to."

"You'll feel it. Every single thing I do."

"Okay then." She struggled to clear her throat, since her voice sounded thick. It was an odd relief, to not have the choice of seeing. His fingertips were a firm pressure as the mask was secured, but then they were running lightly beneath the sensitive skin of her earlobes. Wetting her lips, she tried for a reasonably scathing response. "You sell a bill of goods. That's what bothers me. It's all an image."

"Hmm. Closer to the truth, but still not the bull's eye. Maybe it's not an image, and you can't afford for it to be true. You can't afford for there to be men who stand fast, who protect, who love with all they are. Who don't leave. Who take honor, commitment, and responsibility seriously. You can't afford to trust your fate to the hands of another, not even for a moment."

"You treat women like porcelain dolls," she said desperately.

His chuckle was dangerous. "If that were true, by the end of tonight you'd be shattered in a million pieces. I know the strength of a woman's soul, Celeste. I've held dozens of them in my hands. Fragile as an egg, yes. Perfect, smooth, beautiful. But they contain all the violent power of creation, so when I crack one open, handle it right, I get to see a magic most men never see."

"How do you get there?"

"Through pleasure...and pain. Because the beauty of a mature woman's soul is created from both."

Underscoring it, he dug his fingers into her scalp again and pulled her head back so she felt the strain. Instead of feeling violated, she felt...hungry.

She couldn't stand it anymore. He was turning her into something she wasn't. He wanted her to keep her hands clasped over the sides of the chair, and she was clenching them in a death grip. Now she jerked her right hand free. He could fire off some boorish observation about her cowardice, but she wasn't going to let him play this game with her.

Instead, his fingers closed around her wrist and held it fast, even when she struggled. Not rough, just strong, unshakable.

"I gave it sixty seconds before you'd get into trouble. You made it to fifty-nine."

"Let me go."

"Is that what you want? Again, feel it. Don't think. I'm not hurting you, Celeste. I'm merely holding your arm. Don't let your panic rule you. You're far braver than you know."

He waited a bated moment, then took her hand back to the chair. "I'm going to put a mitten on your hand, to hold your fingers together. This cuff will buckle around your wrist, holding it in place. Just the one hand."

The mitten he worked over her fingers was a strong nylon, like pantyhose, where she could feel the touch of air, but her fingers were unable to move without strenuous effort. He was comfortable dressing a woman, no hesitation or awkwardness, and that swirl in her stomach intensified, a small dust-devil. She imagined him sliding actual stockings on her legs, working the silky garment upward toward her thigh, teasing quivering skin as he connected it to a garter.

Okay, she was going into pure fantasy-stuff. She'd never worn a garter in her life. Then she felt the touch of the cuff. The plush liner was comfortable, but the outer wrap was stiff, heavy. With the curl of her restrained fingers, she felt the links on the side of it, which he used to attach it in some manner to the outside of the chair seat. As he locked it down, it held her arm straight and immobile.

He'd told her what he was doing. Quiet, factual information, but it was still a surreal feeling, imagining herself sitting here, allowing this to happen. *Allowing.* Just like he'd said about the woman on the public platform.

He would eventually do the same to other hand, she was sure of it. The thought alone caused a surge of panic, one that tightened her thighs and demanded she jump up, drag the chair to the door with her and scream to get out. It made her start when his hand closed over her other wrist.

"Sssh. Easy. Only my hand as a restraint right now." He was exploring her palm with his lips, that clever tongue. His moist, heated touch between her fingers was erotically obscene, like he'd put his tongue into her sex. Her fingers went into a half curl, and she was touching his face. That quivering in her lower belly became a volcanic tremor.

She opened her mouth to be derisive, mocking, something...instead her mouth was dry. Then Ben O'Callahan knelt in front of her, because her knee brushed what she was pretty sure was the inside of his long thigh. Keeping his grasp on her wrist, he used the other hand to slip the tie of her robe, letting the light silk fall open and bare her to him. Once again it was a confident, easy move, the move of a man used to exploring every crevice of a woman's body.

She tried to be casual about it as well, but instead she strangled on her reaction as he slid his fingers down her abdomen, into her Victoria's Secrets panties, and right into the narrow triangle of space between her closed thighs. It wasn't a swift, jump-out-of-a-closet kind of move. It was deliberate, authoritative, like he had every right to do it, such that she didn't think to move until he was where he intended to be. Right over her clit and against her shockingly not-dry-at-all labia. She was *wet*. Oh God.

It shocked her even more than her delayed reaction to his invasive touch. Hell with this. She clenched her thigh muscles, squirming, trying to expel him, trying to force her mind to obey logic. He withdrew, but his voice, silky and warm, didn't sound offended.

"That's right, darling. Close your legs tight. Hold them just that way."

Now he was at her ankles. "What are you doing?" She sounded shrill, even to her own ears.

"It's a rope wrap. Just breathe." He was winding what

felt like a thick nylon rope around her ankles and working his way up, binding her legs all the way to her knees. It didn't cut off circulation, but it was snug enough to keep her from parting her thighs, emphasizing the fact he was making her more physically helpless. Her breath was catching in her throat enough she couldn't deny she was one step away from gasping. He kept making those soothing, unintelligible noises, a deep rumble in his throat.

He hated her as much as she hated them, right? He shouldn't be like this, careful and almost tender. It was a trick. But there were cameras. A safe word, if she could bring herself to say it. She'd rather die first. Or endure whatever he did to her, a worse fate. Except she couldn't figure out if she thought that was worse because of what he was planning to do or how she feared she'd react to it.

He took his time with the wrap, testing the binding, her level of movement. She was perspiring, but not from heat. As he restrained her, things were happening to her. A dense stillness in her head, her chest. "Wha—at...why am I feeling this way?" She knew she didn't have to explain it to him.

"The more you give up physical freedom, your dependence on your eyes, your voice, the more your mind cuts free and takes you to a different plain. Think of it as astral projection, but instead of floating off somewhere, you're in the very real here and now, in a way you normally aren't. There's only this moment."

"I thought...Jon was the philosopher." She referred to the quiet and slimmest of the K&A team, the one the business columns called Kensington's Archangel, for several reasons. His appearance—silky black hair to his shoulders, jewel-toned blue eyes and the voice of a late night DJ; his genius level skills at most aspects of their business—operations, finances, mechanical wizardry; and his rumored pursuit of spiritual enlightenment through yoga and other related pursuits.

"Well, he's infected all of us to a certain extent."

The warmth in his voice was undeniable. The Kensington men were as closely knit as a wolf pack. Whereas that usually made her lip curl in derision, for some perverse reason, the evidence of affection reassured her a little.

She made a noise she refused to call a whimper as he tied off the wrap, adding a loop over her thighs and giving it an extra cinch that compressed her clit and labia with the pressure. The rope was both silk and hemp against her skin. "On occasion, I'm going to remind you to wiggle your toes, and I'll keep an eye on your color. But if you think you're having any circulation issues, let me know."

She wondered if he counted light headedness, but she had a worrisome feeling that was a psychological reaction, not a physical one. "I'd think most guys would want the legs spread."

"Depends on the Master. I don't have any trouble fucking ass or pussy in this position, and the sensation is different, tighter, more precarious. A woman has to trust me more."

"We haven't talked about fucking. I don't want that. I haven't agreed to it." She'd just said that on the tape, so there. If he didn't want to be brought up on rape charges, he'd ease the hell back with the tone and the touching and...all of it. "I don't trust you at all."

"You will. You've already started. Part of the breakdown process, if you want to jot that down in that little notebook you're keeping in your head."

When she tried to shift, it only reminded her how her legs and arm were bound. Only her left hand was free at this point. Which meant she could do the Miss America wave, but that was about the only effective use she had for it. Unless she counted the desire to flail frantically.

"What's the point of all this prep, if all you want is to spank bare ass?" She could be crude, too. He wasn't going to intimidate her by throwing graphic words around. Though the way he said pussy should be illegal. His tone was as honey-warm as the mentioned area itself.

"Not a damn thing, if my only intent was to give you a beating. You wanted to know what this is about and, because I think you're a good reporter, I'm giving you that. The woman...I have something for her as well. She's going to find out what it's like to be tormented to mindless submission, where she'll beg me for everything she wants."

"No." She shook her head, hard.

"To get free, to make it stop, all you have to do is use that safe word, the one you won't admit to me. As far as fucking goes, nice as your pussy is, that's not the part of you I'm after. Though I plan to enjoy that fully."

She understood why the chair had a plain wooden seat. She was wet enough to dampen the silk robe caught under her hips. Though she wore the eye mask, it was like she could vividly see what he was seeing. Her mostly naked body, the quiver of her breasts in the lacy bra, the jut of her nipples through the thin fabric. The vee of her damp sex, delineated by the panties. She had a crazy desire to spread her legs, let him see how soaked she was getting. What the hell was that? Thank God he'd tied her so she couldn't do something so absurd and shameless.

Focus, Celeste. There's a reason these women get so lost in this sick crap. Don't let your mind succumb to it. Recite the periodic table or something.

"Okay, this arm here." He'd bent over her and drawn her left arm around his neck. In the same movement, he unsnapped the cuff of her right arm from the side of the chair. She gripped his broad shoulder with her left hand.

"What are you doing?"

"We're just going to lift you up and put a cushion on the chair. Then I'm turning you around and putting your knees on the front edge of the seat. There we go."

He did all the work, turning her with effortless strength, guiding her so she was kneeling on the chair edge, her cuffed hand braced on the wooden back. He re-attached the cuff to the slats, curling her fingers over the top edge. "All right. Now a mitten and cuff for the other hand."

She swallowed. "I...no. Not sure."

"Then use the word, Celeste."

"Not fair. It's not all or nothing. There's always negotiation...limits..."

"Sometimes. It depends on the Master and the sub. In this room, the terms you've set, what you want, it *is* all or nothing. You follow my direction or you call an end to it. With that one little word that's not so little at all, is it?"

"Shut up." She closed her eyes tighter beneath the eye mask. "Don't. Don't make that part of this."

"It's all a part of it, Celeste. You'll understand that before we're done, and it won't make you afraid."

"Stop it."

He went silent and stroked her hair. "All right. Give me your hand. Lift it out toward me."

She did it, and realized her arm was shaking. He steadied her elbow with one strong hand, directing her to rest her hand on his forearm while he positioned the mitten. With his sleeves rolled up, she felt heated skin and the soft layer of hair she knew was dark, like those artful strands across his forehead. Then he reclaimed her hand and worked the mitten on. When the cuff was wrapped over it, her pussy contracted at the feel of it, getting even more disconcertingly responsive when that cuff was attached to the back of the chair, next to her other hand.

He'd moved away and was circling her. A brush of air and silk and she realized he'd tucked the tail of the robe into the tie at her waist. "You look like a pretty mermaid, with your legs wrapped like that. I much prefer those pretty panties hiked up on your cheeks than scales, though."

Exposed. She was on display for him and, instead of sardonic outrage, she was feeling something else entirely. A shudder went through her thighs. This could become an uncomfortable position after a while, but he'd thought of that, and not just with the addition of the cushion.

"I want you under a certain amount of physical strain, but let's give your legs some help."

A strap was run behind her bent knees and then buckled beneath the chair seat, so her knees were held on the edge of the chair. "Now we get rid of this."

The cool edge of something trailed over her arms and down her spine. A heart-stopping moment after it was used, she realized it was a knife blade. The robe fell away. She was kneeling backwards on a chair, her legs wrapped, in only panties and bra, blindfolded.

"I'm scared." It was out before she could stop herself, and her cheeks flushed. Her voice quavered.

"You should be. You're supposed to be. But in a good

way, not the way you feel when you're walking in a bad area of town at night. It's more like when you're about to do something that you're not sure where it will go, what will change. Right? Feel it."

She knew he was right, but she wanted to run, to panic, to fly. His knuckles whispered down the line of her spine. "Beautiful," he murmured. "Celeste, would you like to know why you gave us the name Knights of the Board Room? Why you taunt us through your columns, why you goaded us by showing up at this club three times, looking for something to pin on Matt?"

She went still. His voice had changed. Still calm, but there was something...ruthless to it, an edge that made everything female inside her go on alert. Waiting. Anticipating. Knowing she should run but somehow not wanting to run at all.

"There's a term for it. It's called bratting, actively seeking retribution. Asking for something you don't truly understand, but something inside you craves. You'll get the inside scoop on that tonight, though it won't be something you can ever print in your paper. Whether you learn the lesson and benefit from it depends on whether you're as brave as you pretend to be."

"No. I don't want...I don't think I can do this."

"I know you can. As a Master, I tailor my response to the women who submit to me. However, my specialty...my craving, is women who need to challenge a Master full on. I'll tear open your soul before it's over, I promise. But I also promise to take very good care of it, and send you out of here no worse than you came in."

Wow. As a pickup line, it was overwhelming, probably because it wasn't one. He meant every terrifying word, which meant she should run shrieking. But she couldn't. She was tied up. Even without using a gag, he'd paralyzed her vocal cords.

He leaned in, so close his breath was pure heat against her neck again. She felt his teeth, moaned, and clutched the edge of the chair. No. He wasn't doing this to her. He wasn't.

"Surrender is the most powerful gift a woman can give a

man. But I want something deeper, the surrender you've given no one, the deepest, darkest wells of your free will. When I take that from you, Celeste, that's when you'll get all your answers. That's when you'll find out what freedom truly is."

"What do you get out of it?" she whispered.

She could almost imagine him baring his teeth in a feral smile. "I'm going to blister your ass until you cry. Just the way I've wanted to do, ever since you wrote the first word about us. While you're crying, you'll beg for my cock." His tongue teased the bite. "That's a promise."

Part 3

Okay, yes she'd had sex before. Nice, vanilla sex. Every once in a while she'd played with the idea of what it would be like to spice it up in some nebulous, amorphous way, but she hadn't broached it with the males in question. In truth, she never let them hang around that long. And when she fantasized...well, she just didn't. It made her uncomfortable. Usually, if hormones overcame her and she masturbated in the dark of night, she didn't let herself think of anything much other than the friction of her fingers, and how it felt good.

Well...maybe she thought about how it might feel if there was a strong, warm body curved behind her, his fingers over hers, taking over, doing it for her, letting her clutch his forearm under her head, dig her nails into his warm flesh, press her face into firm biceps. Press the tears there when the climax came.

Hell. There was no way she could pretend to be as sophisticated as this. But there was no other choice, was there? Unless she told Ben she wanted to quit. Which meant she'd be telling those cameras and the DM watching through them that she couldn't do this. All she had to do was say she'd had enough.

"This isn't about pride, Celeste. Competition." He slid his knuckles along her cheek. "Your muscles are all locked up, like you're getting ready for an ice bath, but you're hell bound and determined to get hypothermia before you admit you're cold."

"Is this how you do it? Alternate all the mesmerizing sexual charisma with kindness, make them think they can trust you? Then they melt like butter and you can have everything you want from them, because so many women are desperately looking for a man they can trust?"

"Yes." He answered her frankly, with no apparent affront. "You've boiled it down to the simplest form, but yeah. Except for one correction. They *can* trust me. In this room, you can trust me completely, Celeste. Anything you give me won't be abused. It won't be destroyed, unless it's something you want destroyed."

The knuckles stopped on her jaw, and then it was his whole hand, holding her face, his thumb sliding along her throat. "Most women are desperately looking for a man they can trust. It pisses me off that so many of my gender have let you down, have abused the gifts you could give them, looking only for pussy. They've overlooked how much more erotic, how much more of an experience it is-- for both of us--when your heart and soul are included in the conquering."

"Conquering." She fought the emotions swelling inside her, making her ribs hurt. He was a lawyer, a damn good lawyer. He knew how to use words as weapons, and he was trying to break her open with them, as well as with that unsettling firm touch on her throat, the heat of his body against her hip and leg. "You slipped with that one. Pretty un-PC, the idea of conquering a woman."

"That's because our shallow PC world has made you forget what it truly means. Take her over, overwhelm her, possess her...and then, in the possessing, give her an oath to care for her, protect her, cherish all that he's won."

"I think someone should gag you." She tried for a scornful laugh that came out nervous, shaky. "You're confusing what's really happening with a bunch of words. You're setting women's rights back about a century. You did hear there was a women's rights movement?"

His fingertips slid along her sternum, down, down, following the curve of her breast over her bra, then back up, just as slow. Her arms shook, fingers clenching the top of the chair through the constricting mittens. He'd said she was tense, and she was, such that his movement made her tighten up further, anticipating him making a dip into the cup to tease her nipple, but he didn't. Just a caress of the curve, then he cupped his palm to hold her breast. A firm pressure, thumb so close to the nipple, but not touching. Her pussy contracted, and she had to suppress the desire to shift to prolong the feeling. She wanted the bra off, wanted the contact between her bare flesh and his palm.

"There you are," he said. "We'll get there, Celeste. You want to be aroused, you want to give yourself to this. But there's a lot of crap to get out of the way."

"You haven't answered the question, counselor." She was proud of herself for having the breath to speak, especially in her exposed, highly sexual position. "Susan B. Anthony? Elizabeth Stanton? Suffrage?"

"I don't think the intent of giving women rights—the right to vote, to not be abused, to have the chance to pursue a career—meant they had to give up their right to have someone in their life who can love and protect them, shelter them from the storm, hold them when they cry and open a fucking door for them. Giving women rights wasn't a license to abandon our responsibilities as men."

"Maybe a woman can take care of herself." His words made her angry. She didn't want to feel angry.

"How do you take care of yourself, Celeste? Let me take a stab at it. At night, in the dark, you put your fingers between your legs and give yourself a release that only makes you cry. Your pussy gets relief, but nothing else. Women need far more from an orgasm than the orgasm itself."

How had he crawled in her head like that? "Don't mock me."

She snapped it, and immediately despised herself. When anger took over, you showed your throat to the enemy. Sarcasm was the properly controlled tool for anger, but in this case, she'd simply lashed out.

He'd moved behind her, because now his hands followed the line of her shoulders, dropping to her elbows, to her back. Things in her belly quivered as he unhooked her bra, releasing the slim ribbons of the shoulder straps. The garment fell away, gently pulled free of her body by his hands.

Hands that molded to her sides, following the slope of her rib cage to the flare of her hips. His thumbs teased under the elastic of her panties, then ran back up along either side of her spine. He had big hands. "You're going to get tired in this position. We have too much to do. I'm going to change this...here."

His arm slid around her waist, strong, supportive, functional. "I won't let you fall. Take your hands off the top of the chair. I've unlaced the cuffs."

When she complied, she found he held her weight easily, with no sense of tension. He slid her forward, so her knees were more squarely on the velvet cushion. It brought his whole body up against her. His broad chest against her shoulder blades was distracting enough, but her breath sucked in when something very hard and noticeably large pressed against her ass, gone so quickly she couldn't get freaked out by it. Much. It left a definite impression.

She'd heard a lot of BDSM sessions didn't involve sex, but he'd said she'd beg for that part of him. Would he try to make her service him with her mouth—yeah, right. Or...did he think he'd fuck her tonight? No chance of that. No way. He probably wouldn't go that far. This was all to prove a point, right? But her pussy was so wet, as if it was already begging.

It was just an arousing situation, that was all. She might be sexually inexperienced, but she was a sophisticated, rational woman. Everything her body was doing was rational. It didn't mean she couldn't stay in control.

He'd changed her position so that her breasts were resting on the top of the chair, but the carved wooded edge had been covered by a cushiony foam of some type so that it didn't hurt. He passed another one of those nylon silky-rough ropes over the top of her breasts, through the chair slats and under her arms, securing it at her back in a series of smooth crisscrosses that didn't irritate the bumps of her spine. The constriction on her breasts made her nipples ache. The overwhelming physical stimuli had to be part of how they made women surrender to them, their minds overcome by all of it.

So you'll have a great excuse if it happens to you, right? She pushed away the traitorous thought. Celeste didn't surrender to any man. She usually took fierce pride in the thought, in outwitting her male counterparts, proving herself better and stronger than them, more in control. But right now, the thought was hollow. And merely an irritating whisper behind other internal responses she was experiencing.

The touch of the ropes gave her a provocative idea of what she looked like, restrained in this elaborate rope bondage. Now she found her weight distributed more evenly as he adjusted the rope around the back of her knees so they were firmly held in the center of the chair seat. Her muscles still took a certain amount of strain from the position, but it was a stimulating stress, oddly enough. She heard a metal snap, close to the floor, and Ben's hand was on her back again.

"The chair's been locked down. No matter how you squirm or rock, it won't fall."

She gasped as he bent over her again, this time pressing his hips deliberately against her ass, executing a good rotation against her that made it very clear the cock beneath those custom-tailored slacks was hard as steel...and the size of Florida. Her hips jerked, but she couldn't have said if it was to get away or to try and rub against him. His hands cupped her breasts fully, covering the nipples so they pressed into his palms. This time, there was no doubt her attempted arch was to reach for more of his touch. He put his mouth against the back of her neck, going completely still for a number of silent seconds. Listening to her breath rasp in her throat, she felt her body quiver. He was simply letting her shudder, react, worry...wonder.

"I don't mock women, Celeste," he said at last. "You haven't been touched much, or not touched well, which is why you tense when a man puts his hands on you. So let's work on that. What's that safe word?"

"Red," she said defiantly. That's what all the books said

to use, after all.

"The color your ass will be when I'm done with it. And when I finally get your real safe word."

She didn't want to be hit. But it was a spanking, right? With his hand. She could handle that. But her muscles were staying rigid, tense, prepared.

He moved away from her, hands trailing down her back, over her buttocks, stroking. With that rope wrap from ankles to thighs, her ass would be a front and center display, especially at the canted angle, poked out like it was begging for attention. Jesus, had she lost her mind? Why had she agreed to do this? Why was she so nervous about a little spanking?

He'd shifted, or...knelt, because now his hands were squarely on her ass. He worked her panties down so they rested on the rope wrap and exposed her to the air. Gripping her buttocks, he parted the cheeks with his thumbs, a smooth economy of motion. What was he...

"Aahhh..." She cried out, partly in protest, partly something else entirely as his heated breath caressed that opening, and his tongue touched, licked. Began to explore her rim in a way she'd never been explored. It should have revolted her and caused her to stiffen up even more, but sensation exploded in her lower belly, making her nipples tingle like crazy, her whole body trying to squirm and wiggle and move in its confinement. Being so restrained as he was doing it made it even more intense and, when his hand dropped and stroked her labia, compressed by her legs being bound together, she let out another cry. Alarm, a plea...something unintelligible and primal. She was soaked, the fluid so slick that two of his fingers slid slow and easy into her, giving her a teasing finger fuck in the tight area as he continued to have oral sex with her rear entry.

"Ohh..." Thinking was not an option at all. Just pure, mindless stimulation. Apparently her lack of sexual experience wasn't a problem, because he was doing it all, controlling it all. He was going to take her where he wanted her to go. All this was going on a tape...a tape where her identity was concealed...but...

His mouth and fingers withdrew and, in the next

second, her cry became a yelp as his hand clapped on her ass, a blow that made her right buttock wobble. The combination of it with the other stimulation made her wriggle harder. Her nipples stimulated by air were stiff and large, needing actual touch, wanting touch. But he didn't give it to them. He spanked the other buttock, then returned to the first one to dish out some more. The feeling reverberated in her pussy.

"I thought you might need a vibrator to relax you, but that's not what you want, is it, darling? You're so hungry for human touch."

"Help..." She didn't know what she was saying. What did it mean? But it was there, on her lips, in her head. *Help me...* A plea for more, for saving, for what? What was he doing to her?

A whistle of air and suddenly a searing stripe of actual pain, running from her upper thigh to the roundest part of her buttock. With the yelp this time came a surge of alarm. Ouch, holy hell, that *hurt*. It burned... She tensed for another, but instead he hit her with his hand, prolonging the sting but adding another element to it, confusing her. In its aftermath, the burn became a warmth. And she wanted him to do it again, even knowing how much it hurt.

"Stop that. That hurt. Don't do that again." She was breathing hard, making her sentences choppy.

"Then use the safe word." He waited. Why wasn't she saying it?

"What are you...doing to me?" she asked instead.

He didn't answer, just hit the other thigh and buttock with the switch-like thing, following it up with the same firm spank from his hand. A flurry of blows followed, quick switches and spanks, all rolled together, so the pain became intense, overwhelming, and she was screaming. "Stop...stop...stop."

He did, but she knew it wasn't because she'd demanded it. She panted, her hands curling against themselves where they were cuffed to the sides of the chair back, below her breasts, on display on that cushioned foam. She should tell him to let her go, but that wasn't where her mind was. It was just reeling, stumbling, rolling, her ass on fire, her

Joey W. Hill

breath caught in her throat. "I can't..."

His fingers glided down her spine, slow, easy. Back up. "Take your time and get your breath, girl. Fuck, your ass is beautiful. It has my handprint, and the marks of the switch. And we're just getting started. Tell me you want more."

"I'm afraid."

"I know. Tell me anyway."

She squeezed her eyes shut, mortified to find she was close to tears, and she had utterly no idea why she wanted to cry. "I want more."

Okay, time for her rational mind to step in. She'd sat in this club three separate times, watched men and women come unraveled emotionally from this experience. She understood it, in an academic way, and now she was experiencing it directly. It didn't make it right, normal or good. But it did help her understand it. She was still doing research. And she was still getting that tape.

She could stop right now, tell him it was over, get her tape, and be done with it. That's what she should do. But she'd been sucked into it. Endorphin release, whatever you wanted to call it. She could see it through to the end. Or at least until she reached a line she couldn't cross.

She had a sudden terrifying thought that, at the hands of Ben O'Callahan, no woman reached such a line. He had a way of blinding her to everything but what he wanted. If all the K&A men were like this, it was no wonder women had a difficult time standing toe to toe with them. They were sex gods, sent down from another planet, and that explained women's lack of will against them.

Okay, she was punchy, giddy, and babbling internal nonsense.

"Your tits are so swollen. They want attention, particularly these nipples." When his fingertip brushed over one, she made that shameful whimper. "Here we go. This is something Jon invented. I particularly like using it."

It felt like the sensual touch of paraffin wax being brushed on, but it was obviously some kind of warming oil, except it did more than warm. In a matter of seconds, her nipples started tingling, and sensation shot along the nerve endings around them, stimulating them further. She pulled against her bonds restlessly, gasping in reaction.

"Oh, yeah. That's a beautiful sight. You feel your pussy gushing in reaction? I can smell it, see it dripping down your thighs, dampening your panties, wetting the rope."

"Arghh. It's...too much..." She was fighting the restraints. Her nipples were throbbing, needy, her pussy clenching on too much nothingness. "Touch...them."

"Ask, Celeste. 'Please touch them, sir.' In this room, I'm in charge. You control nothing. Everything is according to what I want, what I'll allow."

"Please..." She threw her head up and cried out as a particularly strong wave of arousal passed through her whole body, originating from those two jutting points. "Please..." There was no mind to this, simply desire. "Please...touch them...sir. Please!"

An agonizing moment later, his hands closed over them, and she screamed at the pleasure of that mere contact. She strained, pressing her nipples into his palms, seeking relief, and the pleasure spiraled deeper into her womb, making it even more intense. When his hands backed off, the tips of her nipples brushed the calluses of his palms. The rough friction was an almost unbearable sensation.

"Work those pretty tits against me, Celeste. Show me how shameless you are."

She already was, jerking against him, but at the command she was writhing, bouncing her breasts against his touch, trying to grasp every bit of sensation she could get from that light contact, and it just kept getting more and more intense. Her pussy rippled, her thighs rubbing together. She was going to orgasm from just this. Ben O'Callahan was going to make her climax from spanking and switching her ass, torturing her breasts, from tying her up...from making her into exactly what she'd sneered at. She was one of those women on the public floor, begging for more.

She hated herself for it, but she couldn't fight past his will. He was too bloody in control, and she couldn't do anything about it. It tore something in half inside of her, and the strangled plea that broke from her lips came from both heart and pussy. "Help me..."

"Okay, getting too close. Not going to be that easy. Ssshh...ssshhh."

The bastard called this easy, when he was ripping her apart? He was actually soothing her, his hands closing over her breasts again, her nipples stabbing into the fleshy part of his palm. The pressure made her whimper in relief, though the shudders of near-climax kept rolling through her.

"Let's get that off of you for now." A warm, wet cloth removed the oil. Though she bleated and jerked through all of it, arousal running down her thighs, the intensity did lessen, pulling her back from that brink. Until he got down and put his mouth over one nipple, sucking it into his mouth.

Oh God... She bit down on her lip, her fingers sweating in hard knots inside the stretched fabric of the mittens. He suckled her, teasing the crinkled areola, flicking the nipple with expert precision, before he moved to do the other one. She'd never been so aroused in her entire life, and he was holding the orgasm out of reach like the Holy Grail.

Fuck, she did *not* just use a medieval reference. Did she? Yes, she had. Knights of the Board Room. She'd given them the title in derision. *Remember?* Sexist...assholes. Thought they could take care of women, take away their...choices... Like they were medieval lords.

Please touch me sir... In that moment, she'd meant it with every fiber of her being, treating him like a Master and lord in truth. "I've got to stop this. You need to let me go."

"Then say the word, Celeste. Red...or the other word. 'No' doesn't work here, because your mind says it even when you mean something else." Catching her chin roughly, he tilted it up so she knew he was staring down into her face. His body was so close, that aroused body, the thick cock probably within inches of her. He could take it out, rub it between her breasts...

"I just...I need a moment."

"Then you know how to ask for it."

She gritted her teeth. "I'm not your fucking slave, asshole. I need a moment."

He chuckled, a dark, sensuous sound. "There she is. The

brat asking for punishment. Inside this room, you are my slave, Celeste. So you either ask properly, or say the word that will end all of this."

Red, red, red. She couldn't get it past her teeth, though. Teeth that were chattering. "Please...I need a moment. Sir."

"Not the most gracious request I've ever received. You don't need a break yet. You need something else more."

Her hands were released from the mittens, the rope around her back and knees loosening. She was surprised how shaky her body was, how much support the chair and the ropes together had been providing, but when she sagged, she was turned and scooped up in his arms, lifted. Her hands were limp against her thighs, in the cradle formed by her hips, but he had her.

The man knelt while holding her, without a sign of strain to his body. He was that powerful, and it couldn't help but make those butterflies in her stomach start up again. Still, at the rock of the descent, she automatically slid her arm around his neck, though it was an effort, since the limb was shaking.

Then something extremely peculiar and horrifying happened. She found herself tightening that arm, pulling herself closer to him, putting her face into his shoulder and throat...holding onto him. Not so he wouldn't drop her, but for a different kind of support. Something different entirely. And her mouth opened against his throat, speaking quivering words she was sure she hadn't told her brain to say.

"Please, sir. I just need...I need a minute."

"All right then." His voice became very different. Still stern, but with an underlying, devastating note to it. Tenderness. Taking a seat on the floor, he cradled her in his arms, rocking her. "A little training exercise first, though."

He shifted her, forearm sliding along the backs of her knees, such that she realized he was holding something. Something warm and slick pressed against her ass and, before she could tighten up, he'd slid it through that tight ring of muscles, letting it sink deep. "There you go. Just a slim probe, but it will keep you stimulated there. Get you used to the feel of it when I decide to stretch you a bit more."

She'd never had anything there. After the initial clutch of alarm, it felt unsettling. The reaction to it that rolled through her was like desire, but it had an even deeper level. An emotional one.

"Breathe, girl. Just breathe. This is going to get a lot rougher."

She let out a half laugh, a desperate noise. What did it say about her that something in her breast leapt at what was undeniably a threat? "You...you destroy a woman's mind. That's why I'm acting like this."

"I destroy her shields. I'm not there with you yet, Celeste. But I will be."

Part 4

But I will be. He made it sound so inevitable. He'd take what he wanted, because she'd let herself be that vulnerable and let him have that power over her. She thought herself so independent, armed against this kind of patriarchal domineering bullshit, this don't-you-worry-your-pretty-head-I'll-take-care-of-you sand trap, yet here she was up to her ass in the grit, and sinking fast.

"No. *No.* I'm done. That's it." Shoving out of his hold, she rolled, not caring how awkward or stupid she looked as she staggered to her feet and ripped off the blindfold. Damn probe in her ass should have come loose on its own, but she'd tightened up all over, clamping down on it. She spun, groping for the flared base. She'd rip the thing out of her and—crap, she was lightheaded, had gotten up too fast. Didn't matter, she was *so* out of here.

As fast as she thought she'd moved, he was faster. Before she could get herself oriented, blinking from the infusion of light and images, he'd maneuvered her back against the wall. Snaking his hand around her, he pinned her wrist against her ass, preventing her from pulling on the probe further.

"I told you I'm done, asshole. Red, red, *red*. That means stop and get the hell away from me."

She could hear the rage in her voice, the trembling that betrayed fear. What if he didn't stop? But that wasn't what scared the shit out of her, was it? She needed to get out of this room, out of this place, out of this situation. It was full-blown panic and, though a rational part of her was standing to the side, exhorting her to get a grip, she couldn't. Only that word gave her control. "Red."

"You're too tight. I'm not going to let you hurt yourself. You pull it out without waiting for the muscles to release, and you'll make yourself bleed. Let me help. The session is over. You used your safe word. All I'm doing now is helping you come out of the session safely. Easy, *cher*."

He wasn't agitated. His voice, which had taken a surprising—and incredibly sexy—Cajun turn, was as smooth as it had been from the beginning. He was as in control as she was the exact opposite. She hated him for it, but not as much as she hated herself for gravitating toward it, the authoritative calm that settled her down and made her focus on what he was telling her. Lifting her face, she looked into his green eyes. "It's over." She'd intended it to sound like a hostile declaration, not a questioning squeak, but either way, she'd said it.

"That's the way it works. You used your safe word. It's done. Let me get this out of you. All right?"

Instead of having her move her hand out of his way, he adjusted his grip to close his fingers over hers. "Now, take a couple breaths. You have your tape and, in less than a half-hour, you'll walk out of here fully dressed, all your armor in place. Same as you walked in."

The same. An hour ago, that would have been a source of pride. In control. Hating everything the Kensington & Associates team stood for. Old boys' club, power, subjugation of women...

Closing her eyes, she put her head back against the wall. His fingers were stroking over hers. The angle of her arm, folded behind her like this, was somewhat uncomfortable, but it pushed her breasts into the solid wall of his chest, where he was leaned into her, keeping her body pinned, but not oppressively so. His shirt, the silk of his tie, teased her skin. He smelled like spicy aftershave, a trace of whiskey.

His face was so close, she could feel the heat of his skin caressing hers.

"Okay, keep breathing. This isn't supposed to hurt. You never shove or yank when it comes to this area. You feel your way." He'd tightened his grip over hers, and together they were bringing the probe out. There was a hitch as they got started, because the muscles were still constricted, but he made that quiet rumble in his throat, somewhere between command and reassurance, and she took another deep breath. It started to move, helped along by the lubricant and his steady pressure. The head of the probe came free with another pause, and he had it in his hand.

Ben gave her a searching look with those emerald eyes, then nudged her toward the closest chair along the wall. "Take a seat. Get your legs beneath you again."

After he made sure she obeyed, pressing his other hand into her shoulder to reinforce the need to stay where he'd put her, he turned away. Moving toward the curtained area, he pushed the cloth back enough to pass through. As he did, he tossed the probe into what sounded like a metal basin, probably for discarded toys. She closed her eyes again, but heard water running. So there was a sink back there, allowing him to wash his hands of her.

She frowned at herself, integrating the metaphorical with the actual, like it meant a damn one way or another. She'd done it. She had the tape. That was all that mattered. Opening her eyes, she looked toward the exit. Another robe, she assumed to replace the one he'd cut off of her, was hanging on a hook, but she had no idea when that had arrived. If she could make her shaky knees work, she could walk over there, put it on and head to the locker room. Session was done. He was done with her. Was that it? Would he say nothing else?

She didn't rise. Instead, she turned to look back at the curtained area. The fabric had shifted back a few inches when he passed through it, so now she could see a slice of him. He stood at the sink, drying his hands and forearms, revealed by the rolled-up sleeves of the dress shirt. His dark hair fell over his brow. He didn't look like a man who'd lost a bet, who was about to be ruined by her possession of that tape. He didn't even look concerned that he'd be reamed by his boss for taking such a reckless risk. When he turned toward her, still drying his hands, he met her gaze through that curtained opening. She was sitting here naked, yet he met her eyes. Didn't let them wander.

"All right?" His tone was firm, no-nonsense, but compassionate as well. Not detached. There was some kind of...energy behind that gaze, in every line of his powerful body. It suggested the sexual potency, just ready and waiting. He'd reined it back, but it was definitely still there.

She stopped the spinning top of her mind long enough to realize he'd asked her a question about her overall well-being, probably because her knees were still visibly quivering. His gaze slid over them, then lifted back to her face. This time he did take his time, but in a way that kept things in her stomach jumping. He no longer had a right to touch her, but that wasn't how he looked at her. Or how her body responded to him.

"You're going to get cold," he said. "I'll get you the robe."

As he moved across the room, she watched the lines of his shirt crease over his shoulders, across the chest and back. And the fit of the slacks over his ass and other...extended areas. "Jesus, you're not even embarrassed about your—the way you're worked up." *C'mon, Celeste, you're a grown woman. You can say 'erection'. Erection, erection, erection.*

He stopped, hand on the robe, and glanced back at her. Now those green eyes contained an additional element, one that made the word stay firmly behind her teeth. "I make sure my cock is never an embarrassment to me," he said.

She blinked, not sure whether she wanted to laugh at what she was pretty sure was dry humor, or bolt at the sensual threat.

"You don't think I'll use it, do you?" she demanded. At his raised brow, she gritted her teeth. "The tape."

"I don't think that's the reason you came into this room, Celeste. I think it was the excuse you used."

She should bristle, tell him to fuck off, but there was no accusation in his voice. Slipping the robe off the hook, he brought it to her. As he stood before her, he opened the silken fabric and gave her an expectant look. He wanted her to rise, turn, so he could help her put it on. She thought about that, him sliding it over her shoulders, turning her around to belt it, the constriction around her waist as he twined the sash around his fingers, tugged her closer with the tether. Rubbed that heavy cock against her pubic mound...

She shuddered and looked away. Focused on the ground to the right of his feet, past that fall of cloth. She noticed her hands had become hard balls on her thighs. "I will use the tape."

"That's your choice." He let the silence draw out between them before he spoke again. "But that's not what's happening right now. Speak to me, Celeste."

"I don't..." She shook her head and was startled when the robe dropped over her thighs. He tapped her jaw, making her lift her attention to his unsmiling, stern face.

"Say it. Or leave."

How did he do that? He could have exuded the charm, coaxed, but the sharp order was so much more effective, spearing her very vitals, holding her into place. "I didn't mean to...say the word." She was whispering, halting after each syllable as if the words had to be cut out of the tense coil under her rib cage.

"You didn't mean to use your safe word?"

"Well, I did, yes, but..." Oh, screw it. Clutching the robe, she began to rise, an ache in her throat. "Whatever."

He put his hand on her shoulder, keeping her seated. When his thumb pressed against the base of her throat, her eyes locked with his again.

"You used your safe word when you didn't mean to use it. You cried wolf, Celeste, with no wolf?"

With him this close, she wouldn't say there was no wolf present, but he was right. The choice was in front of her, on all of it. A choice that, as he said, had absolutely nothing to do with her shallow need to strike back at Matt Kensington and his ilk.

"Yes." She didn't know what gave her the bravery to say it, because those emerald eyes went to fire, that sexual potency going to full out flame. He stroked his knuckles down her sternum, spreading gooseflesh over her breasts and tightening the nipples once again.

"If you want to continue, you'll need to ask me for that permission. Properly." His touch moved over her breast, fingers toying idly with a nipple as she bit her lip. "Now."

"I...I want to continue. Please."

He pinched her, hard, and the address came out on a yelp. "Sir!"

"Stay still." She froze as he put his fingers over her nipple again. This time it was more of a vise than a pinch, a gradual tightening that grew more excruciating as the seconds passed. Her shoulder dipped, her fingers digging into her thighs once more as she somehow tried to both lean into the pain and convey an anxious need to move away from it. She gasped, "Hurts...please..."

When he eased the pressure, she felt the tingle of the expanded blood flow on a direct line to her pussy. She glanced up at him, startled. "I'm going to do it to the other one, now," he said.

No. Yes. Please. God. "Yes, sir."

"Good. You're learning." He moved to that one, and fuck, he had strong fingers. Just when she'd passed the point she couldn't take another second, he released her again, massaging the nipple as she tried so hard not to squirm. She was smearing her cream along the polished wooden seat.

"Don't make me tell you to stay still again. Feel, Celeste. Don't think. That's the way to learn what this is about. It's like sniffing out a story lead. You trust your gut more than your mind. Let the rest go."

He'd chosen the right way to get her attention, the intuitive bastard. She found the best angles on her stories, fluff pieces though they were, by listening for cues with something more than just her ears. She couldn't explain it, but then he just had, hadn't he? Okay—*ow, fuck, that one hurt...oh, oh*—the rubbing afterward felt freakishly good, making her want the pain to get the pleasure. That, as much as his words, made her take the leap.

It was crazy, but she went as motionless as possible and tried to push away the thoughts, the rationalizations, the defenses. It took some time, but he wasn't in any hurry. He continued to play with her breasts, pinch and tug on the nipples, with varying levels of pain or arousing stimulation. It kept her mind jumping like a frog as she fought to stay still and not give in to the arousal that was getting as intense as an orgasm. The fact he was standing in front of her, that tempting, ready-to-fuck cock so obvious beneath tailored slacks, made staying mindless pretty damn easy.

And then, suddenly, it was there. A glimpse...for just a brief second, she understood what was required. Nothing but stillness, waiting on his word as to what would happen next. Relinquishing control to him in the safe confines of this room, where it didn't threaten who she was outside of it. In here, she could be anything. *Anything.* Immerse herself fully in the experience. Let him pleasure them both.

The idea was intoxicating, terrifying, irresistible. And letting herself do that... Her gaze flashed up to his, a tingling flush swirling over her skin. It was only possible if she trusted him utterly, even it was only for this one moment. By telling him she'd cried wolf, she'd made a conscious decision to trust him. Which was why they were both still here.

"Will you...what will you do if I say 'red' again?"

"Ignore it." Brushing her sternum with his knuckles, he dropped his hand to trail his fingers down her thigh, a casually possessive gesture. "Red was too easy from the beginning."

Kneeling in front of her, he spanned her rib cage with his large hands, thumbs beneath her breasts. Despite the position, it didn't feel at all like he was kneeling to her. She was hemmed in by his heat and strength, overwhelmed by being almost eye to eye, which she realized was his intent, to emphasize his next words. "Your new safe word is the one you keep avoiding. You really want me to stop, meaning you're not faking it or panicking over a breach of shields, that's the one you use."

"That sucks."

A light smile touched his lips. "You can be such a charming girl when you try."

Her teeth had chattered a bit over her words, such that

she bit back her reply now. Her hands were so cold. His covered them, squeezed, but then he rose, stepped back.

"See that circular mat over there? I want you on it, on your hands and knees, head and ass up."

She was left staring at him as he went behind the curtain again. With only a slice of him visible, she couldn't piece together what he was withdrawing from what sounded like wooden drawers. There must be a supply cabinet back there.

She shifted her gaze to the circle he'd indicated. Harmless enough. Like a yoga mat, except there were openings in the mat for metal handles bolted to the floor, perhaps for gripping. Or binding.

"If you're still in that chair when I come out, I'll put a leash and collar on you and make you walk to that circle *on* your hands and knees."

"Yeah, right." But she muttered it, and rose. Fortunately, her knees could hold her now. Though she felt more uncertain and self-conscious about it once she reached the mat, she dropped to one knee, then the other. Just like a yoga class. Getting ready for strenuous exercise. That was what this was. She closed her eyes, remembering his scent, that spicy aftershave, the heat of his powerful body. It wasn't often she'd had that experience, a male pressed up against her with such sexual confidence and certainty. Maybe if she'd let herself get laid more often this past year, she wouldn't have come unhinged so fast.

Shut up, Celeste. Remember how it felt a moment ago. Just letting go. Seeing what would happen. She knew the safe word. She could bring it to a halt, if there was anything in the universe more unsettling than the word she hadn't allowed herself to say for years.

"*Hands* and knees. Now."

She tipped forward, giving a little head toss and a hint of a sneer. "Yes, O Lord and Master. Want me to kiss your shoes? Or will your ass do?"

Celeste sucked in a gasp as a capable hand closed over the back of her neck, another pulling her right arm out from under her. It happened so swiftly, her face was plunging toward the mat before she could stop herself. But he controlled her descent, so she stopped just short of a face plow, her nape still in his grip, her wrist pinned behind her back.

"You think you deserve to kiss your Master anywhere, with that kind of behavior? Your hand, here." He guided it to grip the handle to her left, then did the same to the right. The span between the handles had her hands spread slightly wider apart than shoulder width. He ran a set of straps through the handles and over her wrists and knuckles, binding her there. As he squatted before her, he was holding something that looked alarmingly like a harness. He fitted it over her shoulders, down her sternum and cinched it snug beneath her breasts, like a short halter top that framed her breasts rather than covered them.

"Keep your eyes down. Your focus is on how I'm making you feel, not what wiseass comment you can make." As he circled behind her, she bit her lip when he gave her a hard smack on the left buttock to emphasize the point.

An adjustment between her shoulder blades and the strap around her rib cage pulled her shoulders back. He was straddling her body to do that, and the intimate position made her quiver again. When he stepped back to her left, she saw he held a remote. The mat vibrated beneath her, making her realize it was a dais, a dais that was rising out of the floor, taking her up about a foot higher. He'd shifted directly in front of her, and didn't stop the lift until she was looking directly at the distended front of his slacks.

When she moistened her lips—she couldn't help it—he let out a sound somewhere between a snort and a growl. "You haven't earned that yet. I'll need to hear screaming and begging before I'm hard enough to fuck that smart mouth of yours."

He moved behind her again. Celeste's heart accelerated as his hands settled on her ass. There was a whirring noise, but when she tried to twist her head around to look, he smacked her again, this time directly between her legs, a sting against her labia that startled her enough to make her snap her gaze back to the front.

"Eyes straight ahead unless I tell you otherwise." His

fingers probed her anus, and she bit back a whimper as that weird spiral of sensations spread out from the area. He'd lubed up his hand, because two fingers slid into her to caress and thrust, such that she gasped, lifting up to him.

"Nice. Just the position I want. Keep your ass up." He cupped her pussy, putting pressure on it to make sure she obeyed. As his fingers came out, she made a nervous noise as something else went in, then expanded unexpectedly.

"That's a balloon plug. It will keep getting bigger as I use the remote to expand it, stretch you out. In the meantime..."

A more alarming pressure as something far more rigid was pushed in behind the balloon, something she thought might be fastened to it. She felt the brush of cool metal between her buttocks. Ben stepped up on the dais, straddling her again to tighten a strap between her shoulder blades and that metal thing in her ass. She let out another gasp, panicked as the pressure increased inside at the same time her shoulders and ass were drawn up so she was in a straining convex shape.

"Very pretty. An anal hook and harness look good on you."

"Ben..."

"First, a punishment for crying wolf. Then we deal with the rest." Leaving her there, he moved back toward the curtain with purposeful strides, though he stopped when he got there and looked back her. A slow, heated smile crossed his face. "Yeah. Very pretty. You look totally fuckable, Celeste." As he made the comment, he idly rubbed his hand over his cock, cupping his balls. The involuntary noise that broke from her lips startled her. Her pussy and ass convulsed in reaction to his obvious lust for her.

"Yeah, you're getting as hot as I am. Can't wait to hear you screaming."

As he disappeared behind the curtain, she heard water start running again. The position was uncomfortable, in the most stimulating way. She could never have imagined it. Celeste whimpered as arousal trickled down her thighs. Her back was arched to display her breasts, ass and pussy like a female in heat, wanting to be fucked. Instead of being appalled, she wanted his cock wherever he wanted to stuff it, just that crudely. She was slick and ready for him. A terrifying thought, but she might actually beg, just as he said.

No thinking, just feeling, just feeling...

When he emerged, she was braced to see all sorts of terrifying things, but he carried a basin of steaming water and two thin towels. Rolling a small table up to the dais, he put the basin and towels on it and began to soak one of the towels in the hot water.

"Wh-what are you doing?"

He glanced at her. "I don't have to explain myself to you, Celeste. You simply submit, feel and serve."

Gooseflesh rippled over her arms and breasts. She saw his eyes track it. "I'm scared again."

"Some fear is good. It helps."

"I'm not sure I want you to do...whatever it is you're going to do."

"I'm pretty sure you don't. But unless that safe word crosses those fuckable lips of yours, you're going to have to take your punishment."

It scared her further to hear it. But as she contracted on that bulb inside of her ass, her pussy was still weeping. He wrung the towel out with hands she was pretty sure could break bones, if the pressure he'd put on her nipples was any indication. As he held the cloth twisted in both hands, he lifted his gaze to her. "No more talking. Close your eyes, or I'll blindfold you again."

She shut them, actually sort of grateful for it. Her breath was coming shorter and shorter. What was he going to do? She groaned as one of the things he obviously did was increase the size of the balloon, stretching her to a less comfortable, just-this-side-of-painful and yet stimulating feeling.

"Your pussy is slick and wet, Celeste. You want a cock ramming into you there. But you won't get that. Not from me."

There was a noise, like a ceiling fan or curtains swishing from the passage of air, or...

She yelped as the wet towel end popped high on her ass

with a sharp explosion of pain. Just like her younger brothers used to do to one another. Only this had a far more sexual application. Another pop, on the opposite cheek. She jumped, tried to twitch away, but he was already landing another sting high on her thigh, then direct on her pussy. With her butt lifted this way, she couldn't get away from that stinging kiss, and could only imagine the red marks he was leaving. All her twitching was shifting that plug inside of her, the hook, making things feel even more out of control.

"Ow...stop. *Stop.*"

"Not even started yet, Celeste."

Her eyes sprang open, she couldn't help it, as one of those potent stings landed on the side of her breast. She tried to flinch away and couldn't. The negative stimuli was building, making her gasp, even as she couldn't believe how she was still imagining the image he'd planted, of him ramming into her. She looked up at him, still idly twirling that towel, suggesting he had more in store for her. He did, but not with the towel. Tossing it back on the table, he picked up something she'd missed. A black flexible paddle, one that had raised silver lettering he showed her now, with a glint in his eyes.

Bad girl.

"No." She shook her head. "Don't."

"Told you not to look. But I think we're going to leave the blindfold off, because it's too damn hot to watch all those mixed emotions in your eyes. Fear. Arousal. Need." Threading his fingers into her hair, he tightened his grip painfully on her scalp to hold her still. "You're going to scream for me. Beg me to stop. Beg me to let you come."

Was he insane? Or was she? She was smarting as if bee-stung in seven places. "No."

He moved alongside her, letting his fingers slide along her spine. He did something to that hook, pushing the balloon in deeper, and she let out a moan, her hips twitching up. "You're such a bad girl, Celeste. You're wet and wanting, but still you fight. You won't let yourself give in until you've been punished enough. Until you can let it go and say you're sorry. To Matt, to all of us."

"Fuck you," she rasped, fighting panic.

She cried out as his fingers slid down from the hook and burrowed deep into her cunt, probing in ways that had her wiggling and gasping against him. The pads of his fingers were rubbing in such knowledgeable ways, such that when his thumb idly flicked over her clit, she nearly bit through her tongue.

He'd disappeared from her view and she wasn't brave enough to risk the punishment that would happen if she looked behind her. She strangled on a cry as his mouth went where his fingers had just been, tongue plunging into her pussy to taste, teeth nipping. Then he moved up from there. His mouth sucking and tongue lashing around her stretched rear opening was mind-boggling. Things spiraled out of control again. She was making animal noises.

"I've had about as much of your mouth as I'm going to tolerate, Celeste. The next thing out of it better be an apology. A sweet one."

"You can shove—"

The first blow from the paddle felt like a hundred bee stings against her ass. She screamed, and then screamed again in a different way, as his mouth came back, teasing her rim, making her writhe. Then he pulled back, and landed another blow on the opposite cheek. "Stop, please."

Fingers deep in her pussy, thrusting, stroking, and her hips were pumping, short little jerks against him, pulling against the shoulder harness, working that balloon in tiny little shifts, like a cock in truth. Then he withdrew and struck again, this time against her upper thigh.

He didn't have to tell her not to think now. She couldn't wrap her mind around any words, expletives or otherwise. He did it so seamlessly, blending the pain with the near orgasmic pleasure. He cupped her clit, massaging her with his fingers while the rough heel of his palm worked her labia. Then he knocked her knees out wider with his own knee, and landed another slap of that paddle on the inside of her thigh.

"Spread them out as wide as they'll go, Celeste."

He was going to hit her full on between the legs with the paddle. No, she couldn't do that, she couldn't.

"Do it."

She was doing it, and things were dissolving low in her belly, in her chest, which was as tight as a heart attack victim's. She trembled, wondering why she was obeying such an insane command. He was going to hurt her, really hurt her, and she was going to let him do it, leaving her open to a wealth of different kind of hurt, a worse kind. She'd told herself she'd never let a man have that power over her. But it didn't matter, did it? Because the alternative was this anger and hate, this festering poison that the pain seemed to be driving out of her, leaving this pitiful shell, what was truly beneath all of it.

"No, please don't." Her voice was broken. "Please."

Instead of the flat end of the paddle, the opposite end of it, a thick phallic shape, slid into her, heated, vibrating, and apparently hooked at the end to come in full contact with her clit. At the same moment, the balloon apparently expanded to its maximum size, because she was stretched beyond pain. Pain and pleasure together, just as he'd promised, breaking her mind wide open.

"No...no, no, no..." Now the word meant something entirely different, as she was propelled up a rocky slope toward a tearing, ripping-the-body-wide-open-to-bleed orgasm. He had her rushing up that slope, and then suddenly it was pulled back. The paddle vibrator was gone, but the balloon still there, holding her open. He'd used the pleasure to make the pain bearable, but pulled it away at the last moment to now make the pain push back the pleasure, to hold that climax out of reach. He really was Satan.

Before she could get her mind wrapped around that, he was in front of her, opening his slacks, gripping her hair again to bring her attention to the massive organ that stretched out from the dark boxer briefs beneath. He had the timing of Satan himself, because she'd never wanted to suck a cock so much in her life. She took him in, as much as she could, sucking, licking, because she needed to service him in a way that went down deep into her gut. A need to serve a master, to give pleasure, to be cherished for such devotion, for such mindless submission...

She didn't think at all, just worked him as hard as she could. She hadn't given head much in her life, and could barely get her mouth around more than several inches of his considerable girth and length, but he helped her, directed her, and the rest was driven by pure emotional need. Her ass was on fire, inside and out, her pussy was drenched, her response dripping down her thighs. She was tied up, on her hands and knees, so vulnerable and exposed, and it didn't matter. All that mattered was this. Though he'd rolled on a condom, she still smelled the male musk of pre-cum. She pressed her lips against the steel of the aroused organ, nipping the flared ridge of the head.

He didn't let her finish him, even though she whimpered when he pulled away, stripped the condom and tucked himself back in. She couldn't lower her head much, but she wanted to hide her face. Tears were running down her cheeks, both from the stress of taking him and from other things. When he returned to her ass, where she couldn't see him, she felt the paddle against her thigh.

"Ask for punishment, Celeste. Whatever words come to mind."

"Please punish me. Make me feel better about...everything."

He slid the paddle over her buttock, his hand following it, teasing at her pussy, making her tremble. He stroked her clit with his fingertips, so light, so very light. "Hold still," he murmured. "Don't move a single muscle. It's all concentrated, right here."

It was like a nuclear explosion. He stroked, stroked, just those light touches, circles, taps, then more strokes. His thumb began to tease her rim in the same way, little pushes against the hook, caresses of the opening. Her back arched, her mouth opened, throat constricting, thighs shuddering.

"Ask me for permission, Celeste. Beg for it."

"Let me come. Please let me come. Oh...God, please let me come!"

He made her ask three times more, and then he gave her the answer she needed more than breath. "Come for me, Celeste. Squeeze down on that balloon while you do it. Squeeze, now."

She tried, she really tried, and she understood why he told her to do that as an incredible orgasm became an indescribable one, her pussy and anal muscles contracting at once, her body jumping in short jerks in its restricted position, skin glowing with the marks he'd put on it. The room was spinning, just spinning away, her hands holding those handles in a death grip. She was screaming her lungs out, probably shaking the building on the foundation. Everything was vibrating, as if the electrons in the atoms of all matter around her had been energized into tiny frenzied circles.

She didn't want him to stop, but with the release came a sudden, glorious rage. She spat at him, cursed when he started using that paddle again, hitting her with greater and greater strength, rocketing pain and something harder through her as he alternated the punishment with the relentless pleasure of his mouth, his fingers. The waves kept crashing over her as she let it all loose and told him exactly what she thought of him. Sexist, fucking asshole, fucking sadist, liar...

The connector between the shoulders and anal hook was released, the hook tossed to the side, leaving the balloon in place. Before she could react to that, he had her face pushed firmly to the mat between the handles, his hand on the back of her neck as he whipped her as thoroughly as any father had ever let his kid have it behind the woodshed.

The orgasm had reached its peak, was headed for the downward rush, but the punishment kept the aftershocks going, especially when he hit her labia at unexpected moments, making her jump and squeal as if she'd been hit with a cattle prod. He pulled his strength for those more sensitive area blows, but her nerves were all in screaming agony and pleasure, such that she wasn't sure he wasn't rewiring her brain, making it all the same. A mind-altering orgasm in reality.

He didn't stop until she was crying out from more pain than pleasure, flinching away from the blows and making tiny, bleating protests. But she couldn't bring herself to want him to stop. He was a sadist, yet he'd pulled her into a desire to serve his sadistic tendencies with every fiber of her being. When he at last put the paddle aside, she was almost sorry.

He rubbed his hand over the marks and bruising, giving her idle pinches to keep her flinching, but mixing it up with those pleasurable caresses. She was hoarse. Worn out in every sense of the word. He'd taken his hand off her neck, but she stayed in that triangular position, content to rest on her shoulder and cheek, her ass and pussy presented to him to do with as he would.

As he had.

"A liar, hmm? What did I lie about, Celeste?"

Nothing. He'd lied about nothing. She squeezed her eyes shut. That was what was so painful.

"What's the word, Celeste?" His tone was unbelievably gentle now, though he kept that firmness. He was still in charge, as if he knew she needed that to answer the question.

"I didn't use it."

"But you need to say it."

She swallowed. "I know you know it. That's enough. It's a stupid, fucking cliché. I'm better than that. I'm more than that."

"Yeah, you are. You're a whole hell of a lot more."

"Please...please don't come up here yet." His hand had left her buttock, and she was afraid he was going to come to the front of the dais, make her sit back on her heels and look at him. She couldn't do that yet.

His fingertips slid along her spine, her neck, and she closed her eyes. When he touched her chin, her cheek, following tear tracks, she quivered. "Don't."

"You don't give the orders in here, Celeste. Look at me." Quiet, inexorable. Tender.

When she lifted her lashes, she was gazing right into his face, because he was kneeling, his head cocked. She'd seen a lot of things in his countenance tonight. Ruthless determination, charm, humor, occasional flashes of disarming gentleness. Disarming because she now knew he craved a woman's pain, and he didn't find that at all inconsistent with his chivalrous protection of her wellbeing. Given that she'd just had the orgasm of her life, she wasn't sure she could disagree, no matter how illogical it sounded.

But there was something else in this moment. Staring straight into his eyes when she was at her most vulnerable, she thought she glimpsed what lay deep inside his own darkness. Something that connected and understood her pain all too well. With that gut feeling that took her deeper into a story, that helped her know what the true point of telling it was, she saw something in Ben O'Callahan's eyes that she was pretty sure he didn't want her to see or know.

"There you are," he said quietly, touching her lashes with a light finger. "You're too brave to hide. What's the word, Celeste?"

He knew it. He understood it. Probably understood why she couldn't say it, because now he said it for her.

"Daddy. You strike me as the type of little girl who would have called him that. And cried for him in your sleep after he left. He disappeared from your life, leaving one big, terrible message. That men can't be trusted. That men don't take care of you. That men will hurt you, leave you. That they make you feel worthless and unloved. So any men who behave differently from that have to be an act. A lie. Because if they're not..."

"It means he just left. And there's nothing more to it than that."

"No. It means he was a cowardly bastard who managed to have a kid who was far braver and smarter than he was." When he touched her nose, that glimpse she'd gotten, of a man who understood abandonment, who understood the rage and fear, what it took to make something of oneself even after he'd been discarded like garbage, was gone. Now she simply saw compassion and care. As well as a lot of simmering lust. She'd had her orgasm, but he hadn't...

He rose and moved back around her. Same soothing noises, relaxing her as he deflated and removed the balloon, unbuckled the harness and freed her from all her restraints. She could just imagine the marks she was going to have on her body. She already anticipated the delicious, inexplicable pleasure of looking at them.

But it said he was done. He was going to help her clean

up and put on her robe. This was the end of it. He helped her sit back on her heels, moving her slow, as if he knew she was sore, muscles rigid from her anger, from fighting all of it, but she didn't...it couldn't end with this. Not like this.

As she came back on her heels, she reached out and touched his face. He caught her the second she made contact, as if he would have preferred her not to touch him so intimately, but he didn't take her hand away. Just held her there as she grazed his cheek bone.

"I want..." God, what if he rejected her? Laughed at her. No, he wouldn't. He'd just proved that, hadn't he? She'd expected his scorn, and for him to treat this as a big fucking I-told-you-so. She'd seen so many negative outcomes in life. But to be treated this way, to have this gorgeous man with green eyes, his expression stern and unyielding, beside her... He was so attentive to her needs. He'd known what she'd needed, a gift far greater than what she'd thought she'd wanted.

"I'm still going to use that tape."

"Sure you are." He stroked her cheek. "What do you want, Celeste?"

"I want...please...I want you to...be where the balloon was." She knew that was what he wanted. She could give him that and, though she was a little uncertain about her physical ability to take him, she trusted him to get her there. "Will you, please?"

He studied her for a long moment. "You haven't been very good."

"No."

His teeth flashed. "That's all right. I prefer bad girls."

Part 5

It would have made her smile, if she wasn't all of a sudden so nervous. "I haven't ever...there. What you just did, that was it. And you're pretty large."

"Getting cold feet now?" But he wasn't teasing her in a mean way. He gave her short hair an affectionate tug. "Don't worry. You're not my first virgin. If you can keep trusting me, Celeste, I'll take care of you. All right?"

When she nodded, he rose. "Stay on your knees."

God, he was good at that commanding tone. She tried to control the little quivers from knees to shoulders as he went back to the curtained area. Was she crazy? Did she really want to do this? When he was that close, it seemed obvious, but all he had to do was move a few feet away and she doubted her sanity. Then he re-emerged, and she was sure she'd lost her mind.

He was carrying another dildo. No, it wasn't a dildo. It was a freaking baseball bat, masquerading as a sex toy. About two feet long and as thick as a caveman's club. All it needed was the saber tooth spikes.

"Oh, no way in hell." She was scrambling to her feet, headed for the door, when he caught her around the waist. She shrieked as he swung her around, holding her back against him. Flailing, she smacked at that impossibly oversized weapon, and was in the middle of giving him a scathing piece of her mind when she realized he was laughing.

He tossed it to the side and enfolded her in both arms. Since he was still holding her against him, his cock, scary and impressive enough for any woman, was pressed against her bare ass with only that thin barrier of his clothes between them. Though he was still chuckling, he was also pressing his lips against her temple, her jaw, nudging her head to the side to reach her neck.

"Christ, your expression was worth it. Forgive me, darlin'. Had to loosen you up there."

Irish. He'd switched to Irish. The man was a damn chameleon, and utterly irresistible. She caught her lip in her teeth as he suckled her skin, dragging moist, heated lips and tongue along her pounding pulse.

"You are such a bastard."

"Yes. Yes, I am. And this bastard is going to fuck your ass. But before I do, you're going to give me a pretty apology for calling me such a disrespectful name. Ah, there, keep squirming against me that way. Makes me even harder. Be shameless, Celeste. Reach for the pleasure of it."

She wouldn't have thought she could do such a thing, be

that wanton, but those large, capable hands slid up her bare abdomen to take possession of her breasts, his long fingers pinching and plucking at her nipples again. She moaned, arching into his touch. She'd just had an orgasm that rocked her world, but she rotated her hips against him, learning the shape and feel of him, bucking as he pushed back against her and brought her to the wall.

"Forehead and palms against it, love, like I'm a cop telling you to spread 'em. A cop whose patience is at an end because you've opened that smart mouth and told me every one of your constitutional rights, how I should have something better to do than harangue honest citizens, and that you're a reporter who's going to do a story on the uselessness of local law enforcement."

"I have a lot of respect for...police officers. I've done stories on their work with community... groups." The last word became three syllables, because he'd let one hand slide back down to her thighs and curved it between her legs. He put two fingers inside her at the same moment he knocked her legs out wider and pulled her lower body further away from the wall. It drove her pussy down deeper on those thick digits. "God..."

"Palms stay on the wall," he said sharply. "I'll have that apology."

He slid out, then in, pumping her like a cock, and her still slick pussy couldn't help the spasm as she imagined just that. But she knew he wouldn't take her there. It didn't matter. He could make the ass-fucking good, she had no doubt. Well, her body had no doubt. *She* was starting to feel a little anxious, reminded of how ruthless he could be. But it didn't matter. She remembered how she'd craved more of it, even through the pain.

"If a cop stopped you on the way home tonight and decided you needed a spanking to teach you manners, he'd take your panties down and see that *bad girl* imprint all over your ass. He'd know you like punishment, and maybe he'd give you a little more with that wood baton of his."

"What...if it's a female police officer?"

He huffed a laugh against her spine, making her shiver. "Teasing me, are we? I'd like to see that, the two of you getting it on. Maybe on my bed. Nothing prettier than two women going down on each other, twined together like flowers. But I think you need a Master's hand first, teaching you to behave a little better."

It was role playing, just a visualization, and one that should have her snorting in derision. Instead she could imagine Ben in one of those police uniforms, the shiny shoes and hat, the direct gaze, the Irish accent, and his sure grip on that thick baton... Okay, her mind was no longer her own. He was taking it wherever he wanted. And she wanted him to do it.

"I'm sorry for calling you a bastard. Sir." She pressed her lips together against a sudden smile. "I promise I'll be a very good girl from this moment on. Forever."

He sighed with exaggerated patience. "A liar. Can't say I'm surprised to hear that, now."

Withdrawing his fingers, he smacked her ass with a firm hand. The soreness from the paddling and towel snapping had her jumping as he hit the right set of nerve endings. "You hold that ass up for me, girl, or I'll make it that much worse."

It was amazing how exposing herself to him further, subjecting more of her tender skin to his sensual abuse, made her even hotter. He swatted her several more times, firm claps that had her making small noises of confused protest and arousal.

"Down on your knees."

She slid down the wall, keeping her palms flat on it, and felt his hands at her waist, steadying her as she folded into the proscribed position. "I want you to walk back to that mat on your hands and knees. You keep your ass and head up the whole way, and your eyes on the platform, not on me. You'll get the rest of your punishment there. As well as on the way."

This was a little different, but she was starting to understand how it worked. Each level of submission took her to the possibility of an even deeper level, a place she'd never imagined herself to be prior to those other experiences. The women and men she'd seen on the upper level, in impossible positions of subjugation, extreme bondage and flogging, were starting to make more sense. She wondered again if anyone could hit bottom with Ben O'Callahan, or if a woman would let herself descend all the way to Hell for the pleasure he could offer her. Her comparison to Satan might not be as far off as she'd imagined.

"You hesitate, I'll use that collar and leash."

She turned, tentatively going to her hands and knees. It wasn't that far to the mat, perhaps twenty feet. But she wasn't anticipating his hand settling on her shoulder, bringing her to a halt. "I think you need some help getting there."

Oh, no. It was that same hot wax feeling, being painted over her clit. Unlike when he'd used it on her nipples, where there was a gradual arousal that rippled outward, the effect this time was immediate, perhaps because her clit was already swollen from her climax and from what he was building within her again. She began to gasp and shudder as he strapped a pair of Velcro cuffs snugly around her thighs, just above her knees, and linked them with a short chain. Briefly kneeling before her, he did the same to her wrists, a short length of chain between them. His expression was intent on his task, almost detached from her, as if she were an object in truth, and that managed to be arousing as well. It was insane.

"Close your eyes." When she obeyed, she bit back a protest as the blindfold was slipped back over her eyes. "You'll rely on me to get you there. I'll tell you if you get off course."

She was completely off the beaten path emotionally and physically, such that she was already relying on him to guide her, but this made it literal.

"Walk. Very small steps." She yelped, startled as some kind of switch lashed across her ass. She started forward, and the hobbles on wrists and knees limited her to barely six inches of movement. Those twenty feet had just become a much longer journey.

"What would you have done to me...if I hadn't...apologized?" Her attempt at humor was lost in another groan as even her small movement increased the sensation to her clit from that topical oil.

"Walk, Celeste."

Another lash from that switch. *Oh, God.* He was going to hit her with each step, stripes of fire across her ass, her pussy throbbing.

"You're not holding your ass up. I want to see that pretty ass begging for my cock. Teasing me with the sway of your hips, the flash of your wet pussy lips, begging to be fucked."

She tried, but the stimulation was almost too much. He had an answer for that, though. What felt like the anal hook pressed back between her buttocks, but now it had a short, thick plug on it, not the balloon.

"Push against me, Celeste. That will let it in. Take it deep."

The lubricated muscles gave much easier this time than she'd expected, but there was still pressure, discomfort. Yet as it sank in, she clenched around it, imagining his cock there. She had to get to the dais. If he didn't kill her with pleasure first.

It was more than surreal. She, who'd barely done anything more than vanilla sex, was in the middle of the kinkiest, most outlandish sexual journey, one far beyond her experience or imaginings. It had happened in less than a couple hours, at the hands of a beyond-imagining experienced sexual Dominant. There was a story there, how he'd become this way, how...

She cried out as the switch hit her flanks again. Using the plug and hook combination, he propelled her forward. "Keep moving."

She'd been grasping at a sense of control, trying to keep her thoughts on her own path. How the hell had he recognized that from her body language and taken that control away from her again? It didn't matter, because the hobbles on her legs and arms, the stimulation to her clit, the way he was easing the plug forward and back, as if she was being ass-fucked as she walked, the brush of his pants leg against her flank, telling her he was right beside her, escorting her where he wanted to go, took everything else over.

It happened too fast. She came to an abrupt stop,

shuddering hard. "I can't...I'm going to come...help..."

The hook and plug were removed, and she was lifted, right onto the dais. She'd reached it, and hadn't even realized it. His hand was on her neck, pushing her down to her elbows like before. She wanted to spread her legs for him, make it clear she'd give him anything she wanted, no matter how crazy that would have sounded a few hours ago. But he left the hobbles on. Her elbows were folded beneath her like a bird, such that she needed his hands on her hips to steady her. The press of something much bigger than that plug reined her back—just slightly—from that precipitous edge.

"The condom is lubed up thick, Celeste. Push against me, and I'll take care of the rest. It'll hurt, but it will be the kind of pain you'll love. Trust me. You've got it in you. You want the bad girl punished, so you can let the rest go."

She pushed against him, gasping, afraid, needy, her body shaking with all of it. Incredible arousal, nerves, pleasure, fear of pain, fear of the emotions he'd unlocked in her, but it didn't matter. It was a tornado of response, and she could only ride it. There was no control anymore.

Now she understood what she'd glimpsed earlier. He'd given her the key with his words. It wasn't about him controlling her. It was about finding someone to trust enough to let this part of her go, experience pleasure, pain, joy and sorrow as they were meant to be felt...

She pushed against him, hard, and he slid in, at least partly. Holy fuck. Maybe he *was* the size of that baseball bat dildo he'd had. At least that was how it felt. That heated oil was still doing its thing, however, making her impossibly willing to lift her hips with the pressure of his strong hands, adjust back and forth, back and forth, taking him a little deeper, a little deeper...

She pressed her head hard to the mat, her mouth open on a long, drawn out cry, gasping for air. He dropped over top of her then, and she knew he was as far as he was going to go for the moment. She couldn't take all of him, but what she had she'd serve well. She clenched around him, knowing he liked that, and was rewarded by a warm breath on her shoulder, his hand closing over hers on the mat as the other stayed in a hard grip on her hip.

"Good girl. You just hang on for the ride."

That brief, intimate touch, and then he'd straightened behind her, both hands back on the wheel, so to speak. Easy slide out, then back in, and she lifted up to him, strangling on another sound of guttural pleasure.

"Beautiful. You're so good and tight. I'll bet that pussy of yours is just dripping." His fingers left her hip to explore and she jerked, taking him another inch deeper. "There we go. You're a fighter, Celeste. Let that passion out. Take what you want. Don't be afraid to open up because of what some asshole took from you long ago."

Her breath shuddered out, her throat closing up tight, but something else exploded in her heart, a painful jailbreak from her hard-edged façade, shields that were just a way to keep herself from what she really wanted, really desired.

She would have shoved herself to the hilt against him right then, pushing against the mat, but his hands gripped her hips tight and held her. His dark chuckle made her pussy cream. She wiggled, wanting to get close enough to rub herself on him, mark him.

"There she is, the fighter. But I won't let you hurt yourself. We do it together."

Putting his fingers back on her wet pussy, he began to flex those capable digits, smearing the cream and the heated oil together, swirling, dipping into her cunt, teasing and making her jerk, lift, adjust, adjust, and then he was there, pelvis flush against her ass, so she could rub her wet pussy against his balls. He had the slacks down to his thighs, and she wished she could see him, though she knew that wasn't going to happen. This wasn't about the baring of his soul, but of hers. He was leaving her no choice but to accept those terms.

"Now, then." He dropped down over her again, arms on either side of hers, holding her under his body, his thighs firm against the inside of hers. "I fuck you the way I want. If you ask me nicely. Can you ask me nicely, Celeste?"

She squeezed her eyes shut. His hands were too widely spaced for her hobbled hands to reach one and close around his wrist the way she wanted, but she could turn her head toward his biceps and press her lips there, giving him the edge of her teeth through the dress shirt. "Yes, sir. Fuck me the way you want. Please."

"You bet your ass I will." He lifted his hips, just a slight amount, then went back in, making her shudder.

"God..." she breathed, as he did it again. And again.

In no time, the strokes started to get longer, deeper, more powerful. It hurt, holy hell it hurt, but it seemed to catch that oil on fire. She was begging to come, and he just kept on going, pummeling her ass, somehow holding it out of reach by only touching her now and again to keep her hot and bothered, to keep the pleasure balancing the pain. She'd dug her fingers into the mat and was biting his arm. Tears were rolling down her face, and her mind centered on only one thing. *Fuck me... Fuck me into oblivion...yes...*

His upper body rippled against her, all that fine muscle tensing. "Yes...please, sir. Come."

He did, working himself even harder against her, his arm banding around her waist to hold her fast. With his strength, she was sure he would have broken her bones otherwise. She reveled in his harsh grunts against her ear, the sound of him taking his pleasure with her ass, in her subjugation to him. In this moment, she knew she'd given him pleasure and was all his.

It was a startling, darkly pleasurable revelation. The desire to be possessed by another like this, the willingness to give her soul as well as her body to him. An elixir from the Heavens that would be worth it to find, not only from a man willing to give his body to her as Ben just had, but his heart as well.

"Your turn, bad girl." His fingers returned to her clit and started to manipulate. What he'd held out of reach from her came rushing back like a freight train. He stayed still inside her, still hard and pulsing, and gave her the ruthless command. "Squeeze down on me, like before. Your pussy, too. Clench it like my cock is there. Keep doing it."

She came in a matter of seconds, screaming in a high, thin pitch she'd never heard from herself, having never reached that height before. It was even more intense this second time, more dense somehow. She didn't care if it unbalanced her, she reached out with both hobbled hands to grab one of his thick wrists and hold on for dear life. She was screaming "No" and "help" and "please", all the while never wanting it to end, as much a contradiction as the sensations of pain and pleasure together.

When at last the universe stopped spinning, she was still gasping, like she'd finished a marathon and stopped too soon. She was dizzy, aching, disoriented. She was holding onto his wrist like she might fall off a cliff if she let go, her body contorted, shoulder pressed to the mat.

"Here, there. Easy, girl." He was pulling out of her, and she whimpered. "Just like the probe. A little at a time. It will come out on its own. The muscles are still spasming. Jesus, it feels good. I could fuck you all night."

"I wouldn't survive it. You'd be faced with a murder charge. Valerie does know where I am." Her words were slurred like she was drunk. "Help. Feels...weird."

"It will. Just give everything time to return to normal."

Her fingers clenched over his wrist. "Don't want that."

He stilled, then he was around her again, his hand sliding under her cheek against the mat. He used it and his other arm to turn her into a more ergonomic position, bringing her back up onto hands and knees, though he kept his one hand on her face so she could continue to rest her cheek in his palm. Like a bird. So trusting, so safe.

Even more remarkably, he leaned in and pressed his lips to the corner of her mouth, brushing her cheek. "That's your choice, Celeste. To walk out of here different from how you walked in. Only you can take that choice away from yourself."

It loosened things low in her belly. When he removed the blindfold with a quiet, "Keep your eyes forward for now," he went back to working himself carefully out of her backside. She tried to hold onto him with those muscles, her pussy rippling, more warm fluid from her climax trickling down her inner thighs.

"Still a bad girl." He gave a soft snort. All the way out now, he moved his hands down to her sides, her thighs, holding her still as he backed off enough to give her even more pleasure. She made a soft noise as he licked the come away, his tongue teasing slick flesh. "You should let a lover enjoy your cunt more often. It's hungry for a man to fill it."

A comment that would have earned a scathing retort from her a few hours earlier, but now she understood what was behind it. He wasn't mocking her.

As he took off the hobbles, bending over her, the door opened. She saw a female club attendant with towels, lotions and other things she was sure were intended to help her put herself back together. When Ben knelt beside Celeste, a balancing arm still around her waist, her gaze lifted to his face for the first time since he'd walked her across the room to this epic finale.

The green eyes showed the simmering remains of the lust he'd expended, his expression attentive. In one sweeping glance, she knew he'd evaluated her condition and would give the attendant instructions to make sure she was cared for properly. He didn't leave unfinished details. But he wouldn't be doing the aftercare himself, and not because he was lazy.

She wanted to touch his face, but remembered how he'd reacted to that earlier. Despite the intimate pose, she could feel more emotional distance between them now that it was over. Even though the knowledge of what she'd revealed about herself was in his expression, and she felt that was safe with him, she realized he hadn't offered her more. This wasn't part of that.

"She'll be really, really lucky." *If she has way more reckless courage than I have. Than most women have.*

"Who?" He raised a brow.

"Whoever you finally trust to give your heart."

"I can say the same for the Master who convinces you to belong to him."

"Oh...well." She was going to say this was a unique experience, that it was Ben's particular skill that had taken her down this path, that she really wasn't into any of it...that she might be just as distrustful and suspicious of men tomorrow, no matter how fervently she wished she could hold onto the magic of this room. Instead, she decided she was going to have to think long and hard about all of this before she figured it out. "About the tape. I think..."

"That's yours to do with as you wish. We'll talk in a bit. Let Lainie put you back together. She'll make things hurt less. You follow her direction the way you'd follow mine. No lip. Or I'll be back."

He gave her a direct look, a warning pinch of thumb and forefinger on her chin, and she couldn't help the tears that filled her eyes, an odd contrast to the smile that trembled across her lips, the sassy tilt to her brow. "Yes, O Lord and Master."

He smiled back, a gesture that didn't quite reach his eyes, but was still an obvious appreciation of her spirit. "I'll give a thousand dollars to your favorite charity if you call me that in front of Matt and the others."

"One time?"

He pursed his lips. "Too much to hope you'd do it all the time. Yeah. One time."

"Deal."

§

He was right about Lainie's skills. She used all sorts of lotions, oils and soft towels to bring Celeste back to a semblance of reality, a pleasurable grounding that included a brief hot tub experience, a full massage by a male staff member with hands straight from the gods, and then two other female attendants helped her dress, do her hair, and make her look better than she had when she'd come in. She had to hand it to Ben—he didn't overlook a single thing. Torture a girl, give her a couple mindboggling orgasms, then the spa experience of her life. If all five men were like this, no wonder women couldn't keep a brain cell intact around them. It wasn't their fault. Who could resist sorcery like this?

Her body was relaxed, her mind spinning in slow, thoughtful circles. He'd given her every chance to re-don her armor. Clothes, hair, makeup all in place. He could have taken the tape from her at a weak moment, but he'd dismissed that option, making it clear it was entirely up to her, out of his hands. When Lainie brought Celeste her purse from the locker area, the tape case was on top of it. "Thank you for visiting the club, ma'am."

Nodding, Celeste made her way back to the main club level. She wouldn't have been surprised to find Ben gone—wasn't sure if she hoped for that, given her uncertain state of mind—but there they all were. Still sitting at the VIP table. Her lower belly quaked. She had come a hundred eighty degrees from the beginning of the night, and she had a lot to digest to decide how it changed things. Not just in her attitude toward them, which was really the least of it. Ben had changed her attitude about herself, what she wanted.

She could just leave, but in some way, she realized that would be running from what she'd learned about herself in that room. Clinging to what she'd been before, and she'd told Ben she didn't want that. That she wanted to be different. She was a kickass reporter, and she didn't run from the truth. Particularly the truth about herself. Just as Valerie had said.

A fighter. But that fight doesn't have to be with myself. At least not tonight. She had no illusions that her doubts, fears and insecurities from her less-than-ideal childhood would vanish from one night of over-the-top sex. But Ben had opened a door she didn't think could be unlocked, and shown her a path she hadn't known was there. It would take time to determine if she wanted to step over the threshold. It was her choice. Always her choice.

Straightening her back, she walked to the VIP section. She was prepared to say whatever was necessary to gain entrance, but the attendant merely nodded to her, removed the velvet rope barricade and gestured up the steps. "Mr. O'Callahan said he'd be pleased if you'd join them for a drink." The man's lips twitched. "He said he will require the proper password when you get there."

Celeste suppressed a snort. Yeah, trust him not to forget that little detail. She made her way up the stairs. It had gotten late, so except for a couple of tables, the K&A men pretty much had the upstairs to themselves. With every step she felt like bolting. Yes, she was an accomplished reporter. She was also a woman who'd just had the most earth-shattering carnal episode of her life, and was approaching the man—and men—who were behind it.

It startled her, but also made her smile, when they all rose as she approached the table. That gentlemanly courtesy she'd sneered at earlier now gave her butterflies...the good kind. It helped settle things a little, as did the mischief in Ben's eyes as he met hers. The smug bastard. She almost meant it affectionately. She cleared her throat.

"Thanks for the full spa treatment... O Lord and Master."

He grinned, that devastating expression that made him utterly irresistible. "You haven't smuggled in a gun, have you? Peter's pretty sure that's how I'll meet my end, by a woman shooting me."

"How very insightful of him." She glanced over to see Peter flash a smile. The K&A operations manager was also a National Guard captain who'd done a couple tours in the Middle East. He looked like a military man, with his bulging biceps, steady gray eyes and short cropped hair. But what she noticed even more than that was that his smile wasn't smug. None of the men looked that way. Their expressions weren't supercilious or I-told-you-so at all. She detected something far more unbalancing. Simple kindness, even somewhat protective, as if they'd expected her to feel a bit off balance and wanted to make her feel at ease. It didn't feel wrong, like they were undermining her own strength—just ready to supplement it if needed.

"You can keep using that title if you like," Ben suggested. "It sounds good on your lips." His gaze lingered there, bringing her the immediate recollection of her kneeling, her mouth stretched by his cock.

"Once was the deal. Ask again, and I *will* find a gun." Clearing her throat, she pivoted toward Matt Kensington. The CEO was giving her that same attentive look as the others, but there was always a different quality to it with him, something that made it clear he was the leader of the group. "You took a pretty big risk."

"Public opinion is a false god, Ms. De Mille. The only

thing that matters is honoring the truth. I've seen that quality in your writing. I hope your editor has the good sense to let you nurture it." He nodded to the tape in her hand. "That is yours to do with as you will, with no influence by me or mine. And you may be assured that what's on it is something that won't be discussed outside this circle. Not now, not ever. We don't impugn a woman's reputation, though I think I speak for all of us in saying whatever's on that tape is something any man of worth would admire and want to have for his own."

"You guys really are medieval." It took her a moment to find the words, but when she did, she noted the creasing around his eyes, a near smile, showing he wasn't offended. Of course, she'd expected him to take it as a compliment. The surprise was that she meant it as one. She extended a hand. "In the future, if I use the name I gave you...I'll mean it differently. Or, if you prefer, I won't use it again."

Matt took her hand, closing strong fingers over it. He had dark brown eyes and dark hair, the beauty of his Italian mother mixed with the powerful ruggedness of his Texan oil rancher father. When he shook his head, his brown eyes glinted with a tender humor. "My wife is quite fond of it. As well as the other women of our family. They enjoy teasing us with it."

"Though my girl Dana actually prefers 'Outdated Neanderthals,'" Peter offered. "If you want to switch it up sometime."

She chuckled. "Someday I'm going to ask for an interview with your wives."

"That's it. I knew I should have made her sign a confidentiality agreement," Ben said.

She made a face, but couldn't help indulging a longer look at him. The expression that was easy and charming now could so easily disappear to reveal a darker, more dangerous and even more irresistible side. Realizing it was safer not to linger over that territory, she turned her attention back to Matt. He was still holding her hand, which made it easier for her to say what she wanted to say.

"I know my editor has been very impressed with your contribution to the New Orleans community, particularly your generous sponsorship of the domestic violence center. The article I write will reflect that." Tightening her fingers on his, she met his gaze without flinching. She was more than a fighter. She wasn't a coward, and she did believe in telling the truth. "New Orleans...or anywhere, needs men like you watching out for their women and children. It will be my honor to state that publicly."

She couldn't eat crow any better than that. It was time to get the hell out of here and go home to a night of deep reflection, supplemented by a lot of chocolate. Giving Matt a nod, she withdrew her hand, but before she could make her graceful retreat, Ben's hand closed on her elbow. Looking up, she found him right behind her, all his heat and strength.

"Unless you have someplace to be, we'd be happy to have you join us for a drink. Matt has some inside info about a reporter leaving your paper, from the crime beat. He thinks that slot could be yours if you move on it fast enough. Care to hear more?"

She blinked. "You bet I would. If it's not a bribe."

Lucas chuckled. The Kensington CFO had a leaner build than Matt or Peter, but that was because all his appealing muscle was sculpted by his leisure time passion—competing as an amateur cyclist. It was rumored he biked almost everywhere that he didn't have the K&A limo take him, including to and from work. He raised his glass to her now, his brow lifting under a fall of silky hair streaked blond by exposure to sunlight. "She's smart, Ben. And ethical."

"Yeah. I'm trying not to hold that against her. No bribe," Ben said, lifting a hand in the Scout's honor pose. "Just ask Matt, if you don't trust me."

When she automatically looked toward Matt, she was rewarded with amusement from the rest of the men and Ben's mock pained expression.

"It's true." Matt gestured to the seat next to Ben, across from him, and motioned to the bartender. "What drink can we buy you, Celeste? Jon is finishing up with another lady in one of the playrooms, but he'll be joining us soon. He'd love to see you."

"I think water with lemon, to keep my head clear." But when Ben put his hand on her lower back to usher her toward the chair, she hesitated. As she rose on her toes, he obligingly dipped his head, his breath caressing her cheek as she managed a dignified whisper in his ear. "Um...if you don't mind... I need a pillow to sit on."

Ben gave her a look that qualified as pure sin. "You can sit on my lap if you like, darlin'."

She doubted his lap would be as soft as she needed, but the offer was tempting. In fact, everything about the Knights of the Board Room was tempting. K&A was putting its fitting touches on their post-Katrina renovated New Orleans' offices and would be moving back to their home base from Baton Rouge soon. That, plus tonight's events, said that the crime beat was going to be decidedly safer in the future for her than the business social news. Not to mention, there were definite advantages to hanging around cops, firemen, EMTs...

The world was full of possibilities.

Christmas at the Mall

A vignette featuring Jacob and Lyssa of Vampire Queen's Servant, Mark of the Vampire Queen and Bound by the Vampire Queen from the Vampire Queen Series

Originally Posted 12/13/2011

Background: *In thinking about what a Christmas mall trip would be like with Lyssa, my thousand-year-old vampire queen, and her servant, Jacob, I decided to tag along on an actual trip and see if I could hear a few snippets of conversation. They of course decided to bring their son Kane with them, because what could be more fun than shopping with a vampire toddler?*

While this story is barely more than a few pages, much shorter than what has become my normal length for vignettes, it kicked off two follow-up Christmas vignettes. The very next year, I wrote one where Lyssa hosted a Christmas party for a variety of the Vampire Queen Series characters (You're All Invited). And a few years later, an incident that occurred in this very short vignette inspired another Christmas novella about Lyssa's son as a grown-up (A Season of Giving). As a result, I felt it deserved a spot in the compilation.

§

"We don't have too many left on the list, when all's said and done." Jacob pulled the folded paper from his back pocket and examined it. "Gideon? Get him a 5-pack of

357

black Hanes t-shirts, slap a bow on them, and he's good to go. He'd consider it a treat, getting them new. I've seen him pull them out of dumpsters. Most of the time he gets them from the Salvation Army for 50 cents apiece."

"Speaking of which..." Lyssa nodded at a volunteer dressed as Santa, ringing the bell next to the red donation bucket. Before Jacob could reach for his wallet, she stopped him, her long-nailed fingers moving into the space provided by his bent arm to reach into his back pocket herself, caressing the muscular terrain beneath the denim. He gave her a wry smile, sliding his arm around her waist as she opened the wallet, pulled out one of her hundreds and handed it to him.

"You know, most women carry a purse. You just haul me around."

"Far more convenient. With the added benefit of finding things much better in your pockets than lint and gum." As he stepped away to give the money to the volunteer and re-pocket his wallet, she plucked the list from him. Kane was belted into his stroller, but his eyes were darting everywhere. Jacob obligingly brought him close enough to an animatronic display of Rudolph that he could pet the deer's felt-covered leg.

"How about custom-made boots for Gideon?" Lyssa suggested. "With a pocket sole for an extra blade? Your brother would like that."

"It's a little close to the holiday to order custom-made boots."

"Not if I ordered them three months ago. I just need you to pick out the knife."

He was pleased, but on principle he rolled his eyes. "I think you're way too fond of my brother. I bet I won't get a Christmas gift half as nice."

"You won't if you keep acting like that." Giving him her sultry smile, she nodded toward the tobacco shop which offered high end knives for sale. As he rolled the stroller up to the display case, Lyssa reached down to keep Kane's candy cane sticky hands off the glass.

"Oh, what a beautiful boy." The sales girl crooned it, leaning over the counter in her low cut Santa elf suit. She was besotted as everyone was by Kane's long lashes and jade-colored eyes, even if his focus seemed a little intense for a toddler. It became even more intense as her position exposed more of those plump breasts. Even though Kane was nursed on his mother's blood, Lyssa preferred to feed him that vital nourishment from a vein at her breast. Most vampire females honored with the rare privilege of birthing a born vampire did.

"Yes, honey, you're a little too young for knives," the buxom elf told Kane as Lyssa kept his hands off the glass. "You could nick yourself."

Jacob thought the more likely danger was Kane nicking the sales girl. They'd have to peel him off her like a leech. Lyssa registered his thought, a frisson of amusement passing from her mind to his.

For the pocket heel, Jacob chose a blade that could spring open with the touch of a finger. He also picked out a wicked eight incher to go on the inside of the boot, his personal gift to his brother. Gideon didn't feel dressed if he wasn't carrying three or four blades. And a nine millimeter.

As they moved from the tobacco shop toward the toy store, he tucked the bag in the back of the stroller. "I could buy you one of those elf suits for our Christmas dinner," he told Lyssa. "All the male guests would find it very festive."

"And how fortunate, it's the color of blood." Lyssa sniffed. Jacob brushed his lips over her ear.

"I wouldn't be able to keep my hands off you. You'd probably have to punish me, a lot."

"Stop trying to distract me," she told him, but he saw the curve to her lips, the glint in her green eyes.

On their way into the toy store, Kane snagged a plastic handgun from the wall display. It came with soft rubber projectiles and targets. Lyssa pried it out of his fingers. "No, we have no use for that."

"Oh, good for you," a matronly woman gushed, leaning down to chuck Kane on the chin. Jacob put a hand on his son's small shoulder, a strict "no biting" warning. "Definitely good to teach them that lesson young."

"Yes," Lyssa said. "He can disembowel someone far faster than he can shoot them."

The woman's eyes snapped up. Meeting a mature vampire's gaze was unsettling on the best of days, and when it was the gaze of an irritated vampire queen, it was downright disturbing. The woman edged around them and disappeared.

"My lady," Jacob said reprovingly. "You know he's not old enough to disembowel anyone yet. Plus, aren't we trying to blend?"

"I'm blending. She was annoying."

Jacob had to hide a smile. He'd been nonplused that Lyssa wanted to go mall shopping, but once here, the reason for her decision was clear. This mall had a variety of animatronic Christmas displays: elves hard at work in their workshop, feeding the reindeer in their stable, or hitching them up to the sleigh, getting ready for the big night. She'd wanted Kane to enjoy all of those, as well as the center atrium, where faux snow was falling on a giant Christmas tree made of sparkling wrapped presents. Carolers strolled through the mall in Dickens period clothing, and all the mall employees were dressed as their favorite Christmas characters. The entire setup was intended to be a pleasure for children and adults alike.

His lady was proving, no matter the age of the parent, seeing Christmas through the eyes of your child was hard to resist. Jacob had no objection. Since the things they usually faced were life-and-death decisions or the volatile world of vampire politics, he was all for a Christmas outing with his lady and their son. It gave him a twist of poignant memory he put away as Kane started making excited noises. The toddler was bouncing in his stroller. Fortunately, when he laughed and made such noises, his kitten-sized fangs weren't all that noticeable.

Following his insistently pointing fingers, Jacob saw a toy train coming out from under an archway of stacked puzzles. It was a vehicle large enough to seat children Kane's size. The track apparently ran throughout the store.

"You know, we could put that in the sunroom, run it out to the garden and let it circle through the garage. He'd love it."

"Yes, he would." Lyssa took Kane by the wrist, shaking

his hand playfully as she made a face that delighted him, as well as Jacob. He loved to see her act silly, girlish. Relaxed. "I think he wants to test drive it first, however."

"What gave it away?" Jacob snorted. Unbuckling Kane from the stroller, he lifted him out and put his son on his feet. The child made a dash for the train, which Jacob interrupted with a neat snag that swung him up in his arms, masking the fact Kane was far speedier than most toddlers. Actually, more than most teenagers. When they reached the train, Jacob set him down and Kane dashed again, this time for the first car. Another child was already climbing in. Kane wrinkled up his face, bared his teeth and hissed.

"Hey, hey, none of that. Jesus. Just like your mother." Jacob pulled him back with a stern, quelling look and motioned to the other child to board the train. But that one was already running white-faced back to his harried mother.

Lyssa came to his side. "I heard that."

"Nothing I wouldn't tell you to your beautiful face, my lady. You do like to have your way." Hooking an arm around her hip, he nudged her hair off her shoulder and kissed her throat. "Last time we were in a mall," he murmured, "you had me carry you behind the center fountain so you could second mark me. And do other things."

"Behave." But her jade eyes glowed at him, her hand slipping into his back pocket again for a more intimate caress.

Giving her a smile, he turned back to their son, still firmly in his grasp, but who looked perilously close to tears because the train had taken off without him. "No sir. You wait until the next round, because you were rude. You going to behave this time?"

Kane nodded, pointing insistently at the train. Vampire children didn't verbalize as early as human children, because of the interference of their fangs, but his face was as expressive as a book. Jacob had no trouble reading it. "Yeah, I know you want to ride the train. But we're going to do it with manners. All right?"

Watching them, Lyssa couldn't deny the strong mix of emotions she felt. Possessiveness, love, pure pleasure. Before the arrival of their son, she would have said it was impossible for Jacob to be any more irresistible than he already was. But a handsome, powerful man who obviously adored his child could attract the eye of every female within a hundred mile radius. As such, when he looked around for a sales clerk, one trotted up to him instantly. She was a pleasant-faced, dark-haired girl in a much more child-appropriate version of an elf costume. Nodding to the train, Jacob put his hands over Kane's ears, to Lyssa and the girl's amusement. "We want one of these, please. I assume you can deliver?"

"Yes. Oh wonderful. We only have two more in stock and we were hoping to sell them both by Christmas. Credit or cash?"

The train came back around, slowing for new passengers. Kane started pulling Jacob toward the front. Glancing back at Lyssa, Jacob tugged out his wallet and tossed it to her. "Ask her," he called. "I'm just a kept man."

The sales clerk watched him lift Kane into the train car, his T-shirt pulling across the broad shoulders, denim snug on his long thighs. Though the girl whispered it under her breath, Lyssa's enhanced hearing picked it up clearly enough.

"Baby, I'd be happy to keep you anytime." Then she pivoted to face Lyssa. "Cash or credit, ma'am?"

"Credit." Lyssa said, hiding her amusement. *But he's not yours to keep, love. He's all mine.*

After she handled the transaction, she went to find her boys. Kane was still circling in the train, where she expected he'd be happy to stay until the mall closed. After circling with him a couple times, Jacob had found a perch on a stock ladder where he could see most of the train's circuit. He wasn't aware of her perusal yet, so she indulged the private pleasure of watching him, a rugged thirty-something who could handle himself exceptionally well, whether it was in a fight or in a woman's bed.

Now, she allowed herself a quiet dip into his mind, to see where his thoughts were going. While keeping watch over their son, he was letting his gaze was wander over the store, looking at all the Christmas decorations and sparkling trees. Since their parents' deaths, he and Gideon had not celebrated a traditional Christmas. This Christmas would be the first time in some years the two of them had been together on the holiday. His emotions about that were a tangle of old regrets, sadness over his parents, and yet a quiet, eager anticipation of the coming holiday. Which in turn made her want to make sure it was his best Christmas ever.

She commandeered another sales clerk. "I want the five decorated trees as well," she told her. "And that Christmas village display over there, plus the toys that sing Christmas carols…"

When she at last came back to Jacob, he was still on the ladder, though he turned his head toward her as she came, telling her, not surprisingly, that he'd been keeping an eye on her whereabouts as well. Climbing up the two steps, she leaned against him as he cinched an arm around her waist, holding her. "You know," he chided, "between us and our guests, we're going to have so many gifts for him, we'll need to add another wing to the estate."

"I wasn't buying more gifts for him. Not technically. Are we done with our list?"

"I don't have anything for you yet." He cupped her cheek, caressing her mouth with a thumb. She nipped him with a discreet fang, tasting a drop of his blood, enough to whet her appetite for more.

You are my gift, Jacob. Lifting up on her toes, she pressed her lips to the corner of his mouth. He smiled against her skin as she added, "But you know I always appreciate your taste in jewelry."

Her jewelry collection could compete with the Queen of England's, but she still prized the simple ring he'd bought her at a Renaissance Faire, so much so she wore it even now. He lifted her hand to his lips, touching his mouth to it. It always touched him that she wore it, which she realized was why she did it. She was a thousand-year-old vampire queen, yet she was quite simply in love with him, this heroic man who'd been a vampire hunter, a Faire player, and now her bound servant.

"Whoops, hold on. Trouble." He stepped down off the ladder, keeping his arm around her and supporting her weight to set her on her feet. "They're shutting down the train for a few minutes. If the conductor tries to pluck him off, he'll go after him like a rabid dog."

"Oh, that reminds me. We need gifts for Bran and his siblings."

"Already handled. I have an order out to the butcher shop. Plus squeaky balls for Maggie, new collars for everyone, etc etc etc."

"You are proving quite useful. I might keep you around a century or two."

He tossed her another grin as he went to retrieve Kane, fortunately before the conductor reached him.

Several stores later, they were approaching the midnight closing time. A tired Kane was tucked into his stroller, as well as several more packages. Jacob had reviewed the folded receipts, amazed at all the additional Christmas items his lady had bought. He was going to be doing a lot of decorating at the Atlanta estate. He'd love every minute of it. Gideon was getting there a few days early with his two vampires, Daegan and Anwyn. He could help Jacob, Kane and John, their majordomo's grandson, decorate some trees. Maybe Lyssa and the vampires would help as well. Christmas miracles did happen, after all.

Lyssa had wandered into one of the dress shops, a place she finally wouldn't expect him to be in close attendance. Throughout their trip through the mall, he'd been carefully scoping out the jewelry, filtering it among the other pieces of information in his mind so as not to catch his lady's attention. Now he returned to a kiosk where a girl was sitting on a stool, bending different weight silver wire into jewelry. He touched the body of a green-eyed silver fairy, her wings an elaborate interweaving of Celtic knots, and sent it swaying on its delicate chain.

"What do you think, Kane? Will Mama like this?" Kane gurgled at him tiredly, but with a sweet smile. "I agree." Jacob fished out his own money from his other pocket. It was a much smaller largesse, but it was important to him that he had those separate funds for moments like these.

When she emerged from the shop, he was back where she'd left him. She tilted her head toward the checkout counter so he could pick up her purchases, which included two new pairs of shoes to wear with her holiday outfits. His lady, a mass of contradictions. She eschewed carrying her own packages, but while he retrieved them, she had no problem finding a towelette in the stroller pack and wiping drool off Kane's chin. Of course, picking up the bags revealed she'd bought more than shoes. There were some tiny, transparent bits of silk and lace in there that he definitely classified as Christmas gifts to him.

"Men are so easy," she said, reading his mind and face.

"Yeah, God love us." He took over stroller navigation as she slid her hand into the crook of his elbow. "I see they gave you a stuffed animal."

"Yes, the polar bear came with a purchase over a certain amount." Kane held the white stuffed bear, and Jacob had a feeling in a few minutes he would be using it as a pillow.

There was a large box by the exit, intended for toys for the local homeless shelter children. When they'd entered the mall, Lyssa had directed Jacob to drop a sizeable cash donation in their jar, just like she had for the Salvation Army Santa. However, a group of adults and children from the shelter were now there, performing Christmas carols to add to the festive mall environment and draw more attention. They were using silver bells to punctuate their tunes. Kane started making noise, pointing at the shiny objects, so in mutual accord, Jacob and Lyssa drew closer to listen for a few minutes.

It was then Jacob saw two children sitting behind the box. Since Kane was continuing to wave his arms and fuss, he realized it wasn't the bells, but the box and children that were intriguing him. Like most toddlers, Kane loved a large box, so Jacob rolled him right up to it. "No, you can't get into it. There are toys in it."

The two children sitting behind the box were now studying Kane. While those that were singing were smiling and having a good time, Jacob could see these two were less socialized. They were wary, their lives filled with too much uncertainty to be comfortable with all this.

When he gave them a warm smile and a calming nod, the little girl spoke up. "He...he has strange eyes."

She turned beet red, as if she hadn't meant to speak aloud. Jacob looked down to see Kane staring back at her, just as intently. "He seems to think you're just as fascinating."

Kane made some unintelligible noises that raised her brow. When he made a face, it nearly made her smile. She put her hand up to her mouth, hiding it. Then Kane extended his bear, shaking it at her over the mouth of the box. Thrusting it at her with unmistakable intent.

"Charmer," Jacob murmured. He glanced at Lyssa. Kane might be unaware of the significance of his gesture, but it had moved both his parents. The little girl got up, came around the large box and took it from his hands, giving Jacob and Lyssa an uncertain look.

"Yours," Kane said. "Yours."

While he had few words yet, Kane knew "yours" and "mine". In fact, Jacob was pretty sure "mine" had been his first word. The little girl nodded. "Thank you."

She retreated back to her brother, who put an arm around her and stared at them suspiciously. Kane looked up at Jacob, and Jacob tousled his dark hair. "That's a very good boy," he said. Not for the first time, he realized how fiercely he loved his son. As well as the woman who'd given him birth.

Lyssa's hand covered his, drawing his eyes to her. "Go back to the toy store," she said. "Have the other train delivered to the shelter. Make sure you buy enough track for it."

"Yes, my lady." As always, he was reluctant to leave them, even knowing the mall was one of the safest places they could be. When he reached the center atrium, before heading toward the toy store, he stopped amid the faux snowfall and looked back. His lady, beautiful and remote, the type of being that even the mass of intent shoppers gave an unconscious berth, had lifted Kane out of the stroller. She was holding him on her hip, the two of them swaying together, her holding Kane's fist as if they were dancing. She turned them in a circle as the singers crooned a poignant "Silent Night."

His family. His heart swelling with love, he gave himself an additional moment to watch them. Because love was what Christmas was all about.

One-on-One

A vignette featuring Daegan and Gideon of Vampire Mistress *and* Vampire Trinity, *from the* Vampire Queen Series.

Originally Posted 9/15/2008

Background: *Near the end of Vampire Trinity, Anwyn set three conditions on Gideon's service to her and Daegan. One of them was that he prove he'd accepted Daegan as his Master, as much as he'd accepted Anwyn as his Mistress. To do this, Gideon had to feed the male vampire and let Daegan take him to his bed, without Anwyn having to be present. This vignette focuses on how Gideon went about meeting that condition.*

Round 1

Gideon twisted off the top of his beer, braced a booted foot on the edge of the coffee table and took a swig, waiting for the DVD player to juice up. Eyeing the bag of pork rinds next to him, then the artsy decorative bowl on the coffee table, he leaned forward, snagged the bowl. It had a base shaped like a beer can, and the bowl top, though shallow, had as much capacity as he needed. He tucked the base between his thighs to hold it and dumped the bag ass-over-end into the bowl. Easier for him to grab a healthy handful at a time. Plus, no crackling plastic to disrupt his *Sons of Anarchy* marathon.

It was the first time since he'd stumbled into this unlikely arrangement that he'd had the living quarters at

Club Atlantis to himself for a prolonged period. Daegan had left earlier in the week to fulfill a Council assignment. Gideon had stayed with Anwyn at the club, because Daegan felt better knowing he was watching over her. Bastard didn't think about the two of them worrying about him.

Of course, he'd be fine. He was always fine. Except for that time he wasn't, and he'd have been tortured to death, drained and killed if Gideon and Anwyn hadn't gotten to him in time. Daegan liked to point out that was about as likely to happen again as a lightning strike on his way-too-confident ass.

That aside, it was better that Daegan wasn't here. When Anwyn had decided, a few weeks back, to go off on this girls' weekend, Gideon couldn't help thinking about what would happen with him and Daegan hanging here together, alone. It was a good thing neither of his vampires latched onto his concerns, because vampires were like damn cats—the least bit of unexpected movement in their servant's mind and they pounced on it like a tinfoil ball.

Even if Daegan was here, it really wouldn't matter. The vampire probably wouldn't...usually it was about the three of them together, though on occasion Anwyn might take her pleasure with Daegan or Gideon alone. It actually wouldn't be so bad if Daegan was here. It would sure make the apartment less empty, and maybe Anywn's lingering female scent less distracting.

Damn it, was he turning into a complete pussy? Before the two of them had come into his life, Gideon had been used to being by himself pretty much all the time. Had told himself that was the way he preferred it. Alone, he didn't have to worry about getting someone killed. Or, even worse, having to express his feelings.

Here he was, by himself for the next thirty-six hours, no one to tell him what to do or how to do it, and he was missing them. Anwyn had given him the first three seasons of *Sons of Anarchy* for his birthday. He was going to laze like a bear in his den and be perfectly happy in his solitude. Beer, pork rinds and a marathon of shows about hardcore bikers. And since those bikers ran a porn studio—Season One or Two, he couldn't remember—there was going to be gratuitous female nakedness. What else did he really need?

Ice for your testicles, when Anwyn clamps them for scratching her coffee table with your boots. And submitting her Swarovski bowl to the blasphemy of your greasy snacks.

The elevator to the lower level made the humming noise that said it had been engaged and was on its way down. Oddly, Gideon wasn't too surprised to hear Daegan's voice in his head, and knew he'd subconsciously sensed his approach before he got there. He'd been thinking about him, so he hadn't realized his awareness was also linked to his physical proximity.

What were you thinking about me, vampire hunter?

How nice it was to have you out of my grill for a couple days.

Sorry to disappoint.

"I'll live."

The elevator opened. Daegan was dressed in slacks and a pullover, and it was raining outside, because his dark, ankle length duster was spattered with it. Then Gideon's nostrils flared and he realized the spatter wasn't rain. "What the hell happened?"

"A cadre of young rogue vampires who have watched Highlander far too many times. One of them even tried to give me the 'there can be only one' speech. I cut it short." Daegan shouldered his bag of weapons and glanced toward the television with a flicker of interest. "They run a porn studio? Anything worth seeing?"

"Girls with nice racks and very little clothes hanging on them."

"A day's worth of ball clamping is definitely in your future," Daegan observed, heading toward his rooms.

"Only if you run and tell Mommy, you squealer."

Daegan flashed his devastating grin. "I can be bribed, vampire hunter. Just offer me something I want, more than seeing Anwyn punish you. I'm going to grab a shower."

As he disappeared into his room, those words were a cinch of barb wire, drawing everything into a tight ball in Gideon's lower belly. It was a familiar feeling, that mixture of anxiety and anticipation. And he wasn't sure how the hell to feel about that.

When he'd committed to be in Anwyn's service, she had required him to prove it with over six weeks of intense 24/7 servitude. Hell, she hadn't let him wear clothes in the apartment for forty days. At the end of those days, he could practically become hard on demand, responding to their desires with mindless intensity. But *their* desires. Or hers. Never just his. Daegan's.

But despite that frisson of apprehension, it wasn't his top concern at the moment. The spatter on that coat wasn't the blood of other vampires. It was Daegan's. And the clothes he was wearing weren't his usual hunting clothes. He'd changed before he got here. Hearing the shower switch on, Gideon rose and went to their laundry room, where Daegan had dropped his bag. Squatting, he unzipped it.

"Shit," he muttered. The smell of blood was strong, despite Daegan having rinsed the clothes out somewhere. Lifting out the thick black cotton shirt, Gideon eyed the eighteen-inch slash that had cut through it. Someone had gotten him pretty good. There was a puncture tear in the jeans. Damn, the Council had sent him into a nasty nest. By himself.

It pissed Gideon off about ten different ways, because he knew there were still those on the Council who'd rather just not have Daegan around, but Daegan believed in what he was doing. He'd thought about leaving it for Anwyn's sake, but Gideon and Anwyn had convinced him what he did was too important to give up, knowing he really didn't wish to abandon it.

Maybe they should rethink that. Gideon stuffed it all in the laundry, dumped in detergent and got it started. They needed to wash it out before they threw the ruined clothes away, because cops got a little suspicious about blood-soaked clothes in a dumpster. And if they tested those clothes, the physiology of vampire blood could cause some complications.

Gideon went back to the kitchen. He kept a couple extra bottles of blood in there if Daegan or Anwyn wanted to take it that way instead of fresh from the throat. Anwyn rarely did, preferring to curl up in his lap and tease his throat with her fangs. Or stretch him out on the bed, arms and legs chained, and draw from his thigh, her hair brushing against his hard cock, the straining muscles of his thighs. But unless the three of them were tangled together, Daegan took it this way. He'd never taken it from Gideon one-on-one, except that one bleak day, months ago, when Gideon wasn't sure where he belonged. So he guessed that sort of didn't count, or at least wasn't the same situation as the sensual, lazy teasing of Anwyn's tongue tracing his jugular, her soft breath on his flesh.

Though he tried to dispel it, he couldn't help imagining what it would be like if Daegan came up behind him when Gideon was on the couch. The vampire's skin would be damp and heated from his shower. Strong hand curling in Gideon's hair, the other sliding across his throat, tilting him back with that demanding touch, his fangs punching into Gideon's flesh. Daegan would lean over further as he drank, hand cruising down Gideon's chest, into his lap to grip his cock, work him like a damn gear shift, revving him up from zero to a hundred in a—

Gideon closed the refrigerator with a decided snap and went back to the couch. Damn it, why did Daegan have to come back early? And damn it, why did he have an overwhelming urge to march straight to that shower, yank open the door, and inspect Daegan head to toe, make sure everything was all right? He'd seemed to be moving okay, but Daegan healed with lightning speed. No matter what, he'd need blood. More than a couple small bottles. But for some reason, Gideon didn't move back toward the kitchen, toward the knives and crystal tumblers he could use to slice a vein and work up a visceral crimson cocktail for Daegan. It was almost as if he didn't want Daegan to have options other than him. It was almost as if he wanted him to...

Sitting back down, he pressed play on the DVD and turned up the volume, drowning out his thoughts with the opening riff for *Sons of Anarchy*. Porn, bikers, trash talk. That was all that mattered today.

§

He knew exactly when Daegan returned. The scent of freshly showered male reached him a moment before the vampire came into view in faded jeans and a shirt buttoned a careless two buttons, just enough to hold it on him. Bare feet, his dark hair still damp. He took a seat on the opposite end of the couch, finger combing his hair, which fell attractively over his forehead. Anwyn had asked him to grow it longer these days. It only barely brushed his collar, but being vampire, that was all the length it took to make him twice as irresistible as he normally was.

At least that was what Anwyn said.

Gideon put the bowl between them with the pork rinds. Daegan couldn't chow down on them, but he might want a bite. "There are a couple bottles of blood in the fridge. You want me to mix them with something?"

Daegan gave him a sidelong look. "You were prying where you were not invited."

"Didn't realize your laundry was a state secret. You okay?" Gideon asked it straight out, with a touch of impatience. Daegan shrugged.

"I lost a good amount of blood, but their advantage was numbers, not skill. I've been hurt worse. I suppose you will tell Anwyn."

"Not if you take the blame for anything I do to the bowl and coffee table."

Daegan's lips curved, a distracting effect. "A fair trade. I'll take a beer first, and think about the blood later."

Gideon automatically rose, went to the kitchen and brought him one. As he handed it over, Daegan considered the crystal bowl, a quirk on his lips. "Her birthday is coming up, you know. Any ideas? Other than getting you a proper chip bowl so you won't use her table decor?"

"There are a couple plastic bowls in the kitchen. Just didn't feel like getting them at the time. She went pretty sappy over that puppy Chantal brought in with her niece. Maybe we should get a dog. Make our Christmas card family complete."

"Hmm. While her bloodlust attacks are getting more manageable, I'm not sure a pet is a good idea. Killing you by accident, she could probably get over. Killing a puppy, not as easily."

Gideon narrowed his eyes. "I could still let a thought slip about your Highlander geeks, you know."

"Only if you like testicle clamps. I'm pretty sure I already see a scuff mark from your boot there at the end.

"If we had a puppy, we could blame things like that—and rips in your clothing—on him."

"Good point." Daegan pursed his lips. "But since she's off with Lyssa, doing female things like shopping, we could instead ask Jacob what Anwyn particularly liked, something she didn't buy for herself. When is she coming back?"

Catching the impatient edge to his voice, Gideon felt a little more on solid ground. On that, he and Daegan were on the same page. This was the first time since she'd been turned she'd been off without the both of them. Though Gideon couldn't speak for Daegan, he felt like a parent letting his child go off for a sleepover for the very first time, a nameless anxiety moving in his gut that he'd been trying to coat with pork rinds and beer.

"Sunday. Unless Lyssa finds more for them to do than can be covered in a weekend." He gave Daegan a considering look. "Truth, I was kind of surprised you didn't play the Ma—Sire card with her on this."

Technically, Daegan was Master to them both, though Anwyn was a vampire and also a natural Mistress. However, Gideon felt funny drawing attention to it without her there to be a buffer. Okay, it was official. He was being a chickenshit. And there was no way Daegan wasn't hearing all this crap.

Unless he was pale and tired and not into picking Gideon's brain at the moment, which appeared to be the case. So he needed to take the reprieve and banish this stuff from his head. Act like he was just hanging out with a fellow vampire hunter, as he'd done in years past. That was all this was.

"You wouldn't have been so surprised if you'd been there when Lady Lyssa asked me if I thought her incapable of protecting a fledgling," Daegan said dryly.

Gideon winced. "Let me guess. The cold-as-death voice,

and the I-could-laser-off-your-testicles-with-a-look gaze?"

Daegan tapped his bottle against the neck of Gideon's. "Yes. Besides being rather un-manfully intimidated, I was quite reassured about Anwyn's well-being in her care."

Gideon chuckled. "That is one scary bitch. And I mean that in the most respectful way."

"I still wouldn't suggest using the term around her, or Jacob."

"I can handle Jacob. Big pussy."

Daegan gave him an amused glance. "I notice you didn't say anything about handling Lyssa." He sobered then. "In truth, I realized we are both being overprotective and Anwyn needs to have a sense of freedom to continue to gain confidence."

"Yeah, but it still sucks. She's close enough to tune into our heads. She could at least send a mental postcard. 'Wish you were here so I could torture you with endless hours of shopping and girl talk.'"

"If she did that, she'd already know about her coffee table and bowl."

"Yeah, yeah."

He missed her, had gotten used to being her shadow. It was pathetic. He was a vampire hunter who was now a vampire's servant, two vampires' servant. But truth, he didn't like being away from either one of them. It never felt right. So he had to admit it felt better, at least having Daegan here.

Feeling the vampire's gaze on him, Gideon became interested in the DVD remote, futzing with the buttons.

"Tell me about this show," the vampire said at length, "so I can catch up."

Relieved to do so, not wanting to think about what Daegan was thinking during that pause, Gideon spent the next few moments explaining the basic premise, and they settled into a companionable silence to watch.

He'd only left on the kitchen light, so it made the couch area dim. After a time, he noted that vampires apparently were not immune to the narcotic effect of a TV's glow in semi-darkness. Daegan's eyes were closed, his hand loose on the beer he'd given him, and he'd only drunk a couple swallows. Leaning over him, knowing that Daegan would go on battle alert at unexpected movement, Gideon murmured, "Just moving this next to you until you're ready for it."

Daegan made an amenable noise and Gideon drew it from his hand, putting it on the side table. He had to curve over Daegan to do it, and his fingers brushed the other male's as he took the bottle away. Looking down at him, Gideon had a sudden impulse, one he almost followed. What if he brushed those dark strands of hair over his forehead, an easy caress, combing the damp hair aside? He could almost see himself doing it, but hell, what kind of can of worms would that open?

He sat his ass back down on the other end of the couch. After taking off his boots and propping his socked feet on the table.

It was the damnedest thing, the way he was about this guy, because no other guy turned his crank like that. Yet other than Anwyn, no woman had ever successfully pulled the Mistress routine on him, either. With her, he craved it. They'd taught him not to agonize over the why so much, just to accept it was what he was with them. But there were times when something unexpected happened, where it came back full force, putting jagged glass in his gut.

Daegan had propped one bare foot on the table, his other folded under him, pulling off a male warrior's sensual grace with ease. The two buttons allowed a lot of visual, the smooth terrain of chest and abdomen, the sleeves stretched over the well-defined shoulders. It was unusual not to see him in his tank and cotton drawstring *gi* pants, his usual pre-dawn attire. It was the outfit he wore to work out, which he did every single day, even if he'd just come back from a hell of a fight, like now. Gideon understood the routine. A soldier always did everything he could to prepare himself for his enemies, never letting himself get slack.

Daegan was more conscientious about that than most, and these days he was hyperaware of how much Anwyn needed his protection. He had a family now. Gideon was included in that definition, though he'd never asked for that. It stirred things somewhere between Gideon's heart and gut to think about it, about how Daegan watched over them both.

Big. Ass. Pansy. For the love of God, just watch the fucking show.

Gideon sent himself the deprecation at the same time he made the determined resolve *not* to look toward the other end of the couch again. He succeeded, mostly.

After a time, Daegan stirred with a grunt. Opening his eyes, he shifted enough to focus his attention anew on the television. He stretched his arm along the back of the sofa, reaching for a pork rind with the other hand. Sniffing it, he took a measured taste, his fangs slicing through the crisp skin. "So what did I miss?"

"A pretty good gun fight. I'll take it back." Gideon rewound a couple scenes, put the remote back down on the sofa arm, and slouched down.

He'd seen the show before and was watching scenes he'd viewed only moments before. So it made sense that his attention was elsewhere. Already hyper-cognizant of Daegan being only a couple feet away on the couch, now there was the proximity of his arm across the back of it. He was acting like such a girl. *Jesus.* But still...

Daegan's fingers were about even with Gideon's neck. If Gideon decided to put his head back, he'd have his head right on that hand. So he wouldn't do that.

"You know, I was watching that gun builder's show the other night," he said casually. "They modified a 1940s machine gun so it could be used as a shoulder weapon. About twenty-five pounds, too, which wouldn't be that much for you at all. Pretty cool."

Daegan's gaze flickered to him with interest. "Did you record it?"

"Yeah. That same episode, they put together a door breacher with a precision rifle. It was awesome. Thought we could take a look at it, see if we'd be interested in ordering one."

"Anwyn will fuss. She says we have an arsenal now."

"What's her point?"

Daegan smiled, a quick flash of fang. Gideon felt his

fingers brush his nape, a passing caress as he returned to watching the show. But it didn't stop with that fleeting brush. Daegan started to fondle the back of his neck absently, letting his fingers tug through the short strands of Gideon's hair.

Do you really think I would ignore your thoughts, vampire hunter? Particularly when you're thinking them so loudly, it's like you're shouting them at me?"

Gideon tensed, but Daegan made a calming noise in his throat. He just kept sliding his touch over Gideon's nape, a trailing sensation that spread through Gideon's shoulders and arrowed downward. The vampire's fingers slid with devilish knowledge along the occipital bone, then down the back of his neck again, following the track of those parallel tendons, coming to rest on the top bump of the spine, a circling motion over his collarbone, then back up. It was an idle path that felt anything but idle.

"When you came back to us, a few months ago, your Mistress set three conditions on your service to her. Do you remember?"

If you wish to stay with me, you accept three things. You accept me as a vampire, not as a victim of one. You accept yourself as a servant, with me as your vampire Mistress...and you accept Daegan. Feed him, and let him take you to his bed, without me."

...You will submit to Daegan taking you to bed, without me there. I'm too greedy right now to let you out of my sight, but I won't be forever.

Yeah, Gideon remembered her words all right. Hard to forget since they'd been knocking around his head ever since he learned she was going to spend the weekend with Lyssa, which meant Daegan and he would be here without her. Yet those words had been niggling at his brain even before then.

Why it should still be uncomfortable, he didn't know. Daegan had fucked him, often and hard, with Gideon inside of Anwyn. Or while she was doing other crazy shit to him. Was it really so different to do it, just the two of them?

Yeah, it was. He didn't know exactly how to explain it, but it had something to do with looking at Daegan, tired and too pale, but still so capable of kicking anyone's ass who messed with his family. Anwyn *and* Gideon.

He was so not going down this road. "I remember. And I told you, when your day came, you better bring your A-game. You don't look up to an A-game."

"You'd be surprised what I'm up for, vampire hunter. I have enough left to run you to ground...and into the ground."

With another slight shift, a sharpening of those dark eyes, Daegan had gone from casual circling to zoning in on his prey. But Daegan wasn't the only hunter in the room.

Giving the male a look of solid challenge, Gideon angled his jaw, letting Daegan's still wandering fingers graze his jugular. Just the contact made him start to get hard—or rather, harder—but slowly, he tilted his head, so those fingers could follow the line of his throat up and down, like the stroke of a feather. Gideon locked gazes with the vampire.

"Maybe you should go ahead and have some blood first," he suggested. "I want it to be a fair fight."

Round 2

Daegan's fingers stilled. In fact, all of him stilled, in that eerie, dangerous way that vampires had, that Gideon suspected had been picked up by horror films somewhere along the way. *Camera pans across what's supposed to be an empty room, and two to three clicks later, you realize something's not right with the living room décor. Bam, there's the axe murderer, standing patiently right next to the potted palm.*

Only Daegan's stillness—at least in this instance—didn't herald the attack of a psycho serial killer. It meant he was about to make a move, so fast and strong, so irresistible, that anything but surrender was pointless.

Except Gideon didn't know the meaning of surrender. His body had automatically shifted gears. It was alert, battle ready, well-trained instinct kicking in.

Which was why he was surprised when, instead of pouncing on him like a wolf, Daegan resumed his motion, stroking his fingers along the pulsing vein in Gideon's throat. "Just how strong are you, Gideon? I know you can fight like a lion, but are you strong enough to remain utterly still?" His gaze flickered to the side, down. "Your fingers are curled, tense. Straighten them, relax your palms."

Okay, easy enough. Sort of. As Gideon complied, Daegan's attention wandered up Gideon's legs, the splayed angle of his thighs, lingering over the groin area so Gideon felt heat build there. Then he was back to Gideon's face, those dark eyes pinning Gideon's own midnight blue ones. "Can you stay still until I tell you to move, vampire hunter? Are you that tough? Fighting is easy when you want to fight, when you *need* to fight. At such a time, finding stillness, embracing it, that's the most difficult thing any warrior can do."

Didn't matter how many times he told himself he was ready for whatever Daegan brought to the table, the bastard always managed to turn the ground to quicksand. Hell, yeah, he'd prefer to wrestle this out. They'd done that before, with Anwyn there. It'd been fun, rough and dirty. But Gideon didn't have any doubt this was way different.

Daegan was challenging him to remain in place. Could he do that? It sounded easy, but Daegan had already called that for the bullshit it was. Gideon wasn't going to be a pussy about it, though. It was just sitting still. *Jesus.*

"Mind if I keep watching the TV, while you do whatever it is you're about to do? Jax is about to get it on with his old lady in the bathroom. Don't want to miss that."

In answer, Daegan shifted closer. It didn't seem rushed, yet suddenly he was much closer. His hand turned, thumb passing along Gideon's jaw, other fingers spreading along his throat to hold him in that position, chin raised. Gideon kept his eyes fixed on the vampire's face, though it was tough. For some reason, he was having an incredible urge to look away, look down. Forget that. He knew the laws of the jungle. You didn't avert your eyes from another predator unless you were conceding dominance. And Daegan himself had just said Gideon was a lion. King of the jungle.

Yeah, him and Tarzan. Right there together. *Sans* prissy loincloth.

His heart rate had increased. He wasn't aware his hands had clenched again until Daegan noted it.

"Fingers relaxed, vampire hunter."

He forced himself to comply once more, though it seemed that tension transferred to his spine. Daegan's thumb passed over his cheek, once, twice. His face was close to Gideon's so the dark eyes dominated his vision. Daegan's clean shower scent washed over him, the damp hair so close, tempting touch.

"Stillness, Gideon. Utter stillness. You are not permitted to move unless I tell you to do so." *That includes any part of your mouth, inside or out. It is frozen until I indicate otherwise.*

No part of him was frozen, not this close to Daegan's heat. His core quaked with uncertain anticipation as Daegan closed the gap between them and put his mouth on Gideon's. It wasn't a girly, soft kiss. His tongue demanded entry right away, yet once there, explored Gideon's mouth with lazy devastation. As he took his time about it, Daegan tightened his grip on Gideon's jaw and throat to remind him to stay still, but Gideon thought it also conveyed the vampire's own reaction.

When Daegan made a low growl in the back of his throat that vibrated against Gideon's lips, his stomach coiled up tighter than a virgin ass. He certainly remembered having one of those, didn't he? Daegan had fucked him there first. Anwyn had done it since, creating some shamefully pleasurable memories, but Daegan had been the only male, ever. And Gideon didn't want that to change, as unrealistic as that might be for a vampire's servant. Two vampires' servant.

Your desire to have your ass taken only by me pleases me, Gideon.

God, how did he do this? As Daegan's tongue continued to stroke and tease his, Gideon had to employ all his focus to remember he wasn't supposed to move his tongue or mouth in reaction, tease and tangle back, press against or bite at that sensual mouth. It wasn't that he was obeying the vampire; he just wasn't going to give Daegan the satisfaction of saying Gideon wasn't man enough to do something as simple as stay still beneath an assault like this.

Always the games with you, Gideon. Do you remember what I told you about games, not too long ago?

Of course the bastard would bring that up now, while Gideon's body was spiraling toward hard, throbbing need.

It had been a few weeks ago. On a rainy, cold night, Anwyn had initiated a game of Truth or Dare in the upstairs suite after she finished her paperwork. Whenever it was Daegan's turn to demand something of Gideon, both vampires noticed that Gideon always chose Truth versus Dare. Later in the evening, when Anwyn was answering a question from her floor staff, Daegan had fixed Gideon with a steady look and said, with deceptive casualness, *"It doesn't matter whether you choose to accept a dare from me or not, Gideon. As your Master, I can require you to do anything I command, without game or challenge. The day is coming, very soon, where you and I will resolve this between us once and for all. There will be no more games."*

Coming back to the present, Gideon realized he'd closed his eyes. Daegan seemed okay with that, though. He moved from plundering Gideon's mouth to cruising across his cheek bone, taking a sharp nip at his jawline, the five o'clock shadow rasping against the vampire's mouth.

Two years ago, you broke your hand during a hunt. You had to learn to shave with your other hand.

Over time, Daegan had picked up many of Gideon's memories from being a vampire hunter. Now he used that one against Gideon. The vampire was right. Gideon had damn near slit his throat a couple times, because he shaved with a barber's wicked straight razor to keep his reflexes sharp. Daegan interjected himself in the vision now...or maybe Gideon was imagining it himself. He couldn't really tell; their minds were so close.

In the vision, Daegan was standing before him, bare chested, wearing slacks not yet fastened so they hung low on his hips. He was touching Gideon's face with firm purpose, like now, angling it so he could scrape that blade over Gideon's jaw, down near the vulnerable throat... An act of mutual care and trust.

Gideon met Daegan's gaze. The dark eyes flickered, then Daegan dipped his head. When his fangs grazed the carotid, Gideon shuddered, forcing his fingers to stay flat with tremendous effort. Daegan's hand closed on his thigh, inches from his cock, cramped in his jeans.

Do you know what I was imagining, Gideon, when you thought I was dozing?

Playing dress-up with Anwyn's clothes? "I know you've been eying those silver latex pants of hers. The ones that lace up the sides."

A smart ass answer was *so* the wrong tactic here. He was going to push this to a place he didn't want it to go. Or maybe he did. Hell, that was the problem with Daegan. Gideon couldn't figure himself out when it was like this.

"Because you are fighting yourself. I can take you down in a heartbeat, vampire hunter, and you know it. That's all too easy. Forced submission has its place between us. We're males, and we need that challenge. There are times your resistance makes me harder, all the more determined to take you down and fuck you. But this is not that time or place. Because of your nature, I know you will fight me like this, again and again tonight. Each time, I'm going to bring you back to stillness, shut down your avenues of escape, until you have to accept what lies in that stillness, and surrender fully to it."

"You're talking during all the good parts," Gideon said, but his throat was constricted. Daegan's grip increased on his thigh, and the vampire tilted his head, the hair on his forehead brushing Gideon's cheek. He found the beating pulse of Gideon's artery where it columned down from behind his ear, nuzzled that sensitive region, his mouth suckling, tongue flicking along that line. As he moved down, his fangs brushed Gideon again, his breath hot on his throat.

What good parts, vampire hunter? On the TV, or this?

Gideon bit down on a moan as Daegan moved his hand and cupped his testicles where his splayed legs revealed their swollen curve against the denim. Daegan's thumb rubbed with sure skill against the base of Gideon's hardening cock. The male's fangs pierced flesh, puncturing the carotid at last. Gideon convulsed, his hands flexing in reaction, but then he pushed them flat into the sofa again, mashing hard. He was going to leave handprints in the resilient foam.

"What were you imagining?" His voice was hoarse. "When you were dozing?"

Daegan's lips curved against him, his tongue flicking across Gideon's skin, taking the fast rush of blood with precise skill. Gideon felt lightheaded, but there could be a variety of reasons for that.

I imagined opening my jeans, pulling out my cock. I command you to go down on me, suck me off while I watch television and drink my beer. I'd curl my fingers in your hair, push you down harder and harder, make that smart mouth of yours work for it. I'd hold off for quite a while, tiring your jaw and throat. You'd be too stubborn to give up, sucking, licking and occasionally biting to test me. When I came, vampire hunter, it'd be so thick and fast, you'd gag, but you'd fight to take every drop.

His hand withdrew from Gideon's cock, fisted instead in his shirt. *When you fight* for *something, you are just as determined as when you fight against it.*

Using that hold in his shirt, Daegan kept him steady as he drank from his artery. He'd been worried about Daegan's blood loss, so Gideon was glad the vampire was taking what he needed, but he noticed how aggressive the vampire was being about it, the strong pull on the throat, the clamp on his body. Usually, Daegan went with a gentler, more courteous approach than Anwyn, as if he knew Gideon had an innate nervousness about letting a male vampire drink from him.

The couple times Gideon had been captured, the male vampires who'd taken him had torn into his throat or thigh with maximum pain without inflicting death. While he wasn't some whiny therapy case, he had enough bad dreams about it that he still tensed up if Daegan came at him a little harder than usual, even with Anwyn present.

Apparently Daegan wasn't so worried about that today. He had those fangs driven in so deep, was pulling on that vein so hard, he'd be leaving a blood hickey there, a visible mark of how he'd tasted Gideon.

My purpose exactly, Gideon. One of several marks I intend to leave on you tonight.

Daegan lifted his head, replacing his lips with his thumb, holding pressure on the puncture marks. "Clean my mouth, servant. With your own."

Those dark eyes were implacable. This wasn't going quite as Gideon had expected. But before he could question his own response, he was leaning in, remembering that kiss, and knowing now he had permission to move his mouth. Putting his over Daegan's, he sucked the blood away from the firm lips, used his tongue to trace the seam, tasting himself and Daegan together. Daegan's hand shifted, a collaring that caused pressure against the larynx, keeping Gideon at a certain distance, keeping him from deepening that kiss. Damn if he didn't want that, because he kept pushing against it, reminded again and again by the force on his windpipe to ease back.

When Gideon was done, he'd cleaned every trace of blood, inside and out, and his heart was racing as if he'd just run a race. Daegan's eyes showed traces of crimson fire. Okay, this might be going into really dangerous territory. He wondered if it was too much to hope that they'd just start watching TV again. Or maybe Daegan would want a quick fuck. He could do that. God knew, he was more than ready for it.

"Stand up, Gideon. I want you to strip. Take everything off, here in front of me. Then go into Anwyn's personal supply room and put on the cock harness I've laid out on the desk there. Then come back here."

No. He couldn't do that. Anwyn had done stuff like that to him, and her and Daegan together, but put himself in those kind of trappings with just Daegan, for Daegan? It made things somersault in his chest and stomach. Gideon couldn't determine if the reaction was pleasant or unpleasant, but he recognized a gut-level, won't-cross-that-line apprehension. He wasn't going to call it fear. He wasn't afraid of Daegan. But he didn't need to do the psychoanalysis crap. Just no. N-O, hell no. Daegan might be able to force him to do it, but no way was he going to do it willingly.

"So you are refusing your Master?"

Gideon rose from the couch. He faced Daegan, hands now fully clenched, the whole "relax" thing off the table. "Look, you can fuck me, all right? I can handle that. Maybe even handle the going down on you thing after I get in a few beers. But it's just not that way between us. I don't...I can't."

"Your cock says you can. Your pulse leaped with every demand I made. You want to do all of it and far, far more, Gideon. You're just afraid of yourself, of what that means."

"Quit the psychobabble. Look, it's just the two of us. Why does this shit have to be part of it?" He reinforced that admonishment mentally to his body, and the various other parts of him that were yearning to do exactly as Daegan had ordered. Well, fuck it, no. He wasn't going down that road, going to become some sniveling, weak thing like some of the guys he saw up in Club Atlantis, being led around like cowering dogs on leashes behind other guys, their junk trussed up ten different ways.

"That's not what you fear." Daegan studied him, then extended his empty bottle. "Very well. I need another beer. Get it, and we'll watch the next episode."

Just like that. Gideon took the bottle, waiting for further reaction, but Daegan's expression didn't change. He didn't seem mad or anything. On the contrary, when Gideon went to the kitchen, the vampire was fiddling with the remote, rewinding the DVD to the point they'd been at before the whole disturbing conversation had started.

Which meant the jagged rock in his lower belly should start to dissipate, right? Only it hadn't become a jagged rock until a second ago, when he'd refused Daegan. Gideon pulled out two more beers, popped the tops, brought them back. His cock hadn't settled, and the vampire's languid gaze slid over the tight fit of the jeans, but he made no comment, merely leaning forward to take his beer from Gideon's hand. He gave him a nod. "Thanks for the blood, vampire hunter. I prefer it fresh from your throat."

"Hey, one of the things I'm here for." See, he could be useful. He didn't have to do those other things to be appreciated by the male. Unbidden, Gideon remembered those forty days once more, when Anwyn had forced him to stay completely naked in the apartment. She and Daegan had used him in every conceivable violation of biblical tenets, short of coupling him with a farm animal. At times, he'd gotten so lost in all of it, he didn't even recognize the mindless, lust-driven creature he'd become, willing to do anything for them, to please and sate them. That was what a vampire could do to a human servant. He became all about serving his Master. Whatever the Master desired brought the maximum amount of pleasure to the servant.

He meant *her*. Mistress. Whatever *she* desired brought the maximum amount of pleasure to him. To Gideon.

Sitting back down on his end of the couch, Gideon tried to resume the same relaxed position. He knew it wasn't going to work. Daegan had flipped a switch. He could argue that he'd flipped it right back off, but that wasn't what his revved body and mind were saying, the ache in the middle of his chest. And Daegan was right. It wasn't all about lust. But Gideon wasn't as comfortable with that part of himself as Daegan was, not when it came to the feeling part. All he knew was a sense of irritating wrongness had settled over him.

Hell, it was what it was. He stared hard at the TV, watching without hearing or seeing it, all-too-aware when Daegan finally rose after about thirty minutes. He mentioned something about catching up on his reading Gideon barely heard. A few minutes later, the vampire re-appeared from his room, a couple books under his arm. He headed for the elevator. Once it passed dusk, Daegan liked the panorama of windows in the penthouse living quarters, the heated pool and all the greenery Anwyn had up there.

"If Anwyn calls, let me know," the vampire said, giving Gideon a half-smile as the elevator doors opened. "We'll find out how much of her fortune she's blown in the underground malls."

"Yeah, there goes my hope of being a kept man. I'll have

to get a part-time job to supplement my servant gig."

Daegan chuckled, stepped into the elevator. "If you—"

"Stop." Gideon rose, setting down the beer. "Don't."

As if the chuckle and half-smile had been mere masks, and Gideon guessed they had been, Daegan's casual body language vanished. The predator was back. He cocked his head like a raptor, his hand on the control panel. "Don't what?" he asked softly.

"I'll do what you asked."

"I don't recall asking, vampire hunter."

Gideon swallowed. Daegan kept his position in the elevator, not yet ready to change course. He was waiting for something and Gideon was all too aware of what it was. He knew it like he knew how to breathe. He knew how to serve a Master, just as he knew how to serve a Mistress. They'd taught him. All he had to do was grasp at the lesson, and it would be there. No matter how it conflicted with his image of himself. What he wanted was stronger than that, right?

"I'll do what you...ordered. Commanded, whatever."

Daegan still waited, but that charged silence increased. Tightening his jaw, Gideon pulled off his shirt. The vampire's gaze followed the motion, appraising the expanse of Gideon's chest, his scarred, broad shoulders. Opening his jeans, Gideon pushed them off, got his socks free, then kicked it all to the side. There. He stood before the dressed vampire completely stripped. Even though he had a feeling he'd taken off way more than his clothes.

Daegan took his time covering all the exposed terrain, lingering on Gideon's cock that was getting hard again, the skin over it taut as a drum. "The cock harness, Gideon. I marked the holes so you'll know how tight I want it. Don't change any of the adjustments."

Gideon nodded. He moved across the room, trying not to be self-conscious about it, even while feeling the weight of that growing erection pulling against every step. In Anwyn's personal dungeon, there was a supply room. Just as Daegan had said, a cock harness had been laid out. Jesus. It was the one with the prongs that went around the base of the cock. The stiffer a guy got, the more they dug into him. It also had a nice, big ring in back so if Daegan wanted to put his sizeable dick through it and fuck Gideon's ass, it would be accessible.

He'd said not to change any of the adjustments, but Christ. The prongs were already tight, enough to make Gideon wince. When he reached full erection, it would be excruciating, leaving marks. *One of several marks I intend to leave on you tonight...* Sure enough, that wide-assed ring was positioned in back right where it was supposed to be. Another strap fitted around his testicles, and the cinching around them was likewise going to turn his balls blue before it was all over. But all those uncomfortable sensations made him even harder.

During those forty days, he sometimes craved punishment, pain, the lash. Anwyn told him he was purging a lot from his soul, and that was a good way to do it. His response was she'd turned him into a fucking happy lunatic, an answer that earned him one of her amused, beautiful smiles. And another flogging.

He moved back into the other room. It wasn't easy walking this way, but those forty days had given him the training of a runway model. He could get right up there with the Victoria Secrets' angels. Hell, he could outprance them any day, because *he* knew how to walk with a thick, six inch dildo up his ass. Thank the gods Daegan hadn't added that to the arsenal tonight. Yet.

But man, those prongs hurt. Didn't seem to dim his cock's enthusiasm, though. Soon as he got back to the main room in Daegan's line of sight, it got thicker. A drop of semen had collected at the tip, was smearing the slit. Daegan's attention swept over the harness, confirming its fit, but then he zeroed in on that response. As an anticipatory hunger suffused his expression, it honest-to-God made Gideon's cock convulse right under his gaze.

The vampire had stepped out of the elevator, but left the doors open, his books propped on the rail inside. The latest Michael Connelly novel Anwyn had gotten him, and what appeared to be an ancient volume of Greek poetry. The guy was eclectic, you had to give him that.

"You owe me an apology, Gideon."

"What, this isn't enough? My dick is in the jaws of a

Rottweiler."

"That is what I commanded you to do at the beginning, no more, no less." Daegan continued to regard him steadily.

"I'm sorry," Gideon muttered. Didn't Daegan realize how screwed up he was over this kind of thing? He had no clue why the need to say he was sorry, to make amends somehow, was overwhelming him, as if he'd really done something unforgivable. But it was making him whine like a girl. *Jesus.* The really pathetic thing was that he wasn't pissed off, wanting Daegan to be gone again so he could be by himself, watching SOA and propping his feet on the coffee table. He wanted Daegan touching his neck, hell, feeding from him. He wanted things to be okay, enough to do pretty much anything. But he didn't know how to fix it.

"That's because you are looking to the wrong person to fix it."

He tuned back in to Daegan's expression. He saw the implacability of a Dominant vampire, for sure. Gideon knew that look. When it was on the face of any other male vampire, it just made him want to reach for the nearest stake. With Daegan, it twisted his guts into further knots. Below that implacable expression was something important, something Gideon wanted. He just didn't know if he could do all the right stuff to get it. He was like the kid that kept putting his hand on the stove time and again, just because he was told not to do it. It was his makeup.

"And that is also part of what we appreciate about you."

"What, that I'm a clueless dumbass?"

Daegan's lips twitched, easing Gideon's gut. Some. "No. That you stay who you are, even as you desire to be ours. Mine." His gaze intensified again. "Because you *are* mine, Gideon. My servant as much as hers. The only one who refuses to accept it is you. I'm done waiting for you to figure it out. So again, what is wrong in your gut now is not yours to fix. Say the words, and I will make it better. But you must say the words."

His. All his muscles were tight, Gideon's feet digging into the floor. But he wasn't a coward. Daegan had told him that countless times as Gideon faced moments like this.

Moments he and Anwyn knew were more terrifying to Gideon than any vampire who'd ever tortured or tried to kill him.

He did know the words. The gestures. At the beginning, he expected them to feel so awkward and unnatural. But now, his leg bent, and he put himself on one knee. And he did what he hadn't done on the couch. He bowed his head, eyes settling on Daegan's bare feet. His Master's feet.

Wow. He felt a strong reaction from Daegan from that thought, so strong he almost lifted his head, but he didn't. Instead, it gave him the courage to clear a dry throat and speak.

"I disobeyed you. Mouthed off." He wasn't sure where to go from there, but thankfully, Daegan stepped in.

"Do you deserve punishment?"

"Yeah. I mean...if my Master thinks I do." Another revelation, the sudden understanding that it was Daegan's decision to make. Gideon always said "if my Master and Mistress", because he was used to addressing them both, but now there was only Daegan. It was alien to everything he'd ever expected himself to want or need.

"You do deserve punishment." Daegan left the elevator doorway, because his feet moved toward Gideon. They stopped beside him, and Daegan pressed his hand into Gideon's shoulder, passing almost gently over the bump of his spine at the base of his neck. "Keep your head down."

Gideon felt that quake in his lower back, his gut, down to the soles of his feet, as Daegan spoke again. "Thirty strikes with the punishment strap should do."

The punishment strap was a foot-long rubber strap, folded over and bound to an eight-inch knobbed handle wrapped in metal twine. Anwyn had used it on Gideon in play—her personally sadistic version of play, bless her dainty little heart. Even holding back, it had hurt like hell. She was a tough Mistress, one who knew how to focus her servant with just the right dose of pain and pleasure.

Daegan was male, a Master who'd been directly challenged by a servant he knew had extreme resistance issues. What was Newton's third law of motion? Something about mass exerting an equal and opposite force on the object? In Daegan's case, maybe it was exerting excessive force, to take the object down and keep it down.

You've read a book. I'm shocked.

Hey, I remember a few minutes of high school.

Gideon let his gaze flicker up to register the brief amusement in Daegan's gaze. But when he looked down again, Daegan's hand tightened in his hair, a brief pull on the scalp. "Follow me, Gideon."

God help him, he obeyed, rising to his feet, ass tight and cock stiff as a board. He wanted Daegan to do it. To beat the crap out of him with that strap. He wanted forgiveness from his Master, even as some part of him knew when it was over, it would merely be the starting bell for another round.

There was too much shit going on in his gut, and he was in completely over his head. Everything in him told him to resist, to fight. With quiet despair, he knew he would, just as soon as he could get past this hurdle, make this right. He didn't know how to handle Daegan alone, just the two of them. That same craziness was hoping the pain would open up the solution, a way to figure all this out. To make it okay once and for all. Of course, after thirty strikes from that strap, he might be ready to soak his ass in Epsom salts and call it a day.

Unfortunately, in this contest, Daegan was more than his opponent. He was the damn referee and judge, the only authority who could call off the match. Or declare a winner.

Round 3

Daegan took him into Anwyn's playroom. Since Gideon had been with her, she'd added some diabolical-looking things to it, including something she called The Spider Web, a series of crisscrossed manacles, ropes and other suspension equipment that would allow her to hang a submissive in a variety of poses for her viewing pleasure. She hadn't really done much with it yet, but she'd been poring over books of Japanese rope bondage and suspension techniques with the fervor most women saved up for interior decorating catalogs. Daegan had glanced at them with her, pointed out things here and there that Gideon tried his best to tune out, but he hadn't seemed as enthusiastic as she was about it.

Now, as he moved toward that area with a purposeful air, Gideon wondered if what he had taken as lack of enthusiasm was actually confident familiarity. Stopping in the center of the platform, he gestured to a manacle hanging at eye level. "Put your left wrist in this, Gideon. Latch it."

His dominant hand. "Not sure you can handle me if you do the right instead?"

Daegan didn't smile. Just waited. Gideon moved to the steel cuff, stared at it and the forest of other ones around it. He didn't want this shit to be about other things, but he couldn't help it. Something seemed to be holding him frozen in front of that manacle. Sweat, darkness. Cruel laughter. A lash, hitting him over and over again, fangs scraping his nipple...

"Easy, vampire hunter." Daegan was right behind him, the denim of his jeans brushing Gideon's bare ass as he settled a hand on his shoulder. Daegan's breath was at his ear, so Gideon closed his eyes and made himself grasp the manacle, though he stopped there, just holding onto it until Daegan spoke, a sensual murmur.

"I will give you pain, Gideon. Pain that you desire. I will restrain and bind you in ways that free so many other things. You are my servant, my slave. I cherish you, and will never abuse the gift of what you are to me. Do not let the past take away from that. And those two vampires? The ones who had the audacity to torture you? If you had not killed them yourself, I would do so now, with or without Council decree, because I take care of what is mine. I will exorcise your demons. Put your wrist in the manacle."

Gideon tightened his jaw. He wasn't a pussy; he could do this. Cognizant of Daegan's hands still resting on his shoulders, he seized the manacle, slapped it on his wrist and latched it. He was trapped now. That cuff, the chain that held it, were built to hold a fledgling vampire, like Anwyn. Most of the restraint systems in this room had been beefed up to help her if she was having a really bad day. It offered some variety in how she had to be restrained until the seizure passed, and hey, life was all about variety, right?

When they'd made that overall design change to her playroom, Gideon remembered the sadness that had been in her eyes. Occasionally despair would take her, the worry that she'd always have to deal with a control problem. Gideon had knelt at her feet, taking her hands as Daegan slid his arms around her from behind. While Gideon kissed her palms, her wrists, making the pulse trip a little faster, Daegan had put one hand over hers on the catalog page and spoken against her ear. *I like this change. If I want to tie up the strong Mistress who submits to me as her Master, I know she won't be able to get away while I do as I wish to her. Or when I order our servant to lick her pussy until she screams.*

She'd pushed him away with a smile and a swat, but her shoulders had eased. Daegan was good at that. At reaching into their heads and making things better. But this was admittedly a tough one.

Gideon tried to shrug it off, telling himself it would be okay. Once Daegan started walloping him with that punishment strap, his mind would pretty much phase out. That was the weird thing about it. When Anwyn punished him, at a certain point...he was just all about her and nothing mattered. He'd experienced it before, when they both decided to flog him or inflict pain in some way, but he wondered if he could lose himself with Daegan that way, given that all he could feel right now was his heart beating like a damn conga drum and his breath shortening.

"We talked about how you have difficulty simply staying still. Even with one hand tied like this, you could kill a human, perhaps even an equal third marked servant. You probably know a few tricks against vampires as well, else you wouldn't have gotten away from those other two."

"They thought I was done, that they'd taken the fight out of me."

Gideon heard the fierce smile in Daegan's voice. "They obviously don't know you. You'll be dead long before the fight goes out of you, Gideon Green. You'll arrive in the afterlife, fully armed and swinging your fists."

It eased the tension in him, a little. "That last vampire, I got away when he took me off the rack, planning to move me somewhere else."

To an iron maiden. It would have killed him, an agonizing claustrophobic death, impaled on short spikes arranged strategically to puncture areas that resulted in terminal blood loss...eventually.

Daegan moved around to his front now, fingers caressing his hip, Gideon's ass. His dark eyes flickered, a hint of crimson, revealing a more intent emotion. "You were ready for him."

"He wasn't ready for me. And I got lucky."

"Be still, Gideon. Show me that you can stay still, and just feel."

Daegan slid a hand in his hair, stroked it. Gideon moved his gaze to the male's shoulder, the smooth line of biceps. He couldn't look Daegan in the eye when he was doing that. But Daegan touched his jaw with the other hand and guided his face back up. "Look at me, vampire hunter. Watch me when I touch you."

His knuckles moved to Gideon's nape, as they'd done on the couch. Then he slid that hand down Gideon's chest. He flicked a thumb over Gideon's nipple, teased him there, his dark eyes lowering to watch the cock Gideon could feel stiffening, despite the dampening of enthusiasm it had felt during the manacle part of things. He breathed through the discomfort, quelling the instinctive panic as his cock swelled enough to press harder against the prongs. Anwyn had taught him that as well. That you could breathe through pain, find pleasure on the other side of it.

Daegan descended to the abs. As he traced every individual muscle, he was unhurried, watching intently as each quivered and flexed with Gideon's breath. Then his gaze flicked upward, noting Gideon's hand closing into a fist in the manacle.

"Loose, Gideon," he reminded him. "Keep your fingers loose, every part of you loose. No fists clenched around me, not ever. You'll add to your punishment if I see that again."

"You think I'm scared of that?"

"No. But I don't think you want to disappoint me." Daegan moved to the other side, started doing that tracing thing again. Once again different from the violent passion of their times before, a continuation of the same disturbing lesson, apparently. Daegan was studying Gideon's body, not jumping right into the fucking, hot kissing or grabbing hold of his cock. It made things swirl strangely in Gideon's belly. The male's head was bent, focusing on what he was doing. He touched the scars Gideon had brought with him, before he was turned into a servant. Daegan knew what had caused each one, and now the memories moved through Gideon's mind. Bullet, knife, burn...the knife fight was the bad one. Not the scar in front, but the back one. That had nearly lost him his kidney.

"You know, I've got a line from *Pretty Woman* going through my head," he said, trying to ignore the odd feelings rising in him. "The part where she says 'I appreciate the whole seduction scene, but here's a tip – I'm a sure thing.'"

"Hmm." Daegan moved to the work bench on the side of the room. Instead of drawers and drawers of manly tools, it had bunches of nifty stuff Anwyn had collected, a Mistress's weapons cache. Or in this case, a Master's. When Daegan turned back around, he was carrying a thick butt plug, still in its wrapper, one she hadn't yet used. He stopped in front of Gideon. "Open your mouth."

Gideon nodded. Then he slammed his head into Daegan's, put his weight against the manacle and hooked Daegan's right leg, pulling it right out from beneath him.

It was pure instinct, no thought. The only thought he had came right after. He was fucking crazy. No idea why he'd done that, except he was trapped and needing to feel something different from what Daegan was making him feel. Damn it, he'd agreed to the punishment. So why was Daegan doing this other shit instead?

He wasn't surprised that the vampire rolled out of it faster than he could follow, and was back behind him. He steeled himself for whatever Daegan would choose as his retribution. Probably shoving that butt plug in his ass with the force of a jackhammer.

Instead, Gideon suppressed a frustrated moan as

Daegan started doing the same thing behind him that he had done in front. Light trails of his fingertips over Gideon's shoulder blades, then the muscle groups of his back, resting on that kidney scar. Daegan moved in. When he was close enough, his breath soft on Gideon's neck, Gideon tried to hook and tangle his legs again. Daegan evaded the maneuver and managed to curl his fingers around Gideon's cock. Or rather, that cock harness. And squeezed.

Holy fuck. As a distraction, it worked wonders. Gideon bit down on a near scream at the pain that lanced through him. Shit, he had to have broken skin. He had to be bleeding. Looking down, he was surprised to see that wasn't the case. The damn thing was just engineered to dish out a lot of pain without maiming. Daegan eased his grip, fingers moving down to circle the part of Gideon's cock without the harness. He stroked, pulling the skin up toward the head, pumping in that way men knew so well. Gideon's cock got even more turgid, which meant the painful pressure of Daegan's fist was replaced by something else just as devastating. The prongs bit in anew.

"Jesus."

"You will not pull any more shit like that. Easy, Gideon." Daegan moved in front of him. Cupping the side of Gideon's face, he made him look at him once again.

"Fuck you," he muttered weakly. Hell, he was a broken record, wasn't he? *I don't know how to do anything but fight. Don't you get it?*

"That's why I'll teach you how to do something different. Still, Gideon. Just stay still."

He had to close his eyes, he had to, but this time, Daegan was okay with it. At the last moment, as Gideon's eyes closed, Daegan's mouth settled on his. Not hard and punishing, not demanding. This was a tease of tongues, an almost playful nip with fangs, a slow, sensual rub of mouths coming together in heated, moist intimacy. Deep, languid, the way he'd seen Daegan kiss Anwyn. There was tenderness, quiet passion, enduring care...love.

He chose a dirty defense this time, snapping down on Daegan's lip, biting as hard as a vampire would ever think to do. When he yanked back, he intended to take flesh with him. But Daegan had a hand at his nape and pressed on the hinge of his jaw so it reflexively opened, just like a horse being made to release or take a bit. He'd probably learned that in his billion years of life, the bastard. Gideon tried to wrench his head back, but Daegan held him so he could only manage a few inches of space between them.

"Let go of me," Gideon said. "Stop."

As Daegan licked the blood off his own lip, Gideon noticed the darkness of his eyes had expanded, taking up most of the sclera, a trait unique to the vampire, likely because of his unique parentage. It told him the drawing of blood had roused Daegan's warrior instincts. His blood roared eagerly in answer. Rough, violent sex, that's what it needed to be. Pain, punishment, lust and passion.

"I'm going to kiss you again, Gideon," the vampire said in a low voice. "And you will remain still through all of it, no fighting. Look at me. Meet my eyes. Don't be a coward."

That snapped his gaze right up, and what he saw in Daegan's eyes was terrifying. He wasn't pissed. He was patient. Patient as time itself. He would go at this all night if needed. And probably intended to do just that. "Now, lick the blood off my mouth."

He came closer, no hesitation, no apparent worry about what Gideon might do next, even though so much of it so far had been fight-or-flight instinct, little thought passing through his head to tip Daegan off about his next move. But the guy was an assassin. He anticipated things.

Gideon licked the blood off his lip. It tasted like Daegan, hot and sweet, and since it was still seeping from where he'd bitten him, it made him want more. He suckled it from that wound, feeling Daegan's hand curve around his nape once more, then Daegan tapped his chin, made him lift his mouth, and began the kiss again.

The same, devastatingly tender warmth. Tongue slowly tangling with Gideon's, a lazy penetration and exploration, Daegan making an approving noise as some of the tension went out of Gideon's shoulders, even while things below the waist got way more rigid. Jesus, he hoped Daegan knew his adjustments, because it was possible those prongs would impale him like an iron maiden in truth before this was over.

I am very familiar with the diameter of your cock, Gideon. Never fear.

Gideon leaned forward against the chains, realizing belatedly he was leaning into Daegan's body. The vampire had an arm around his back and waist, was holding him against him in a full embrace. His palm descended, cupped Gideon's ass, fondled and squeezed. Fingers dipped in between, rubbed the rim and made him clench there in need. He needed to fight. Needed to get away from this feeling. But his eyes were closed, and he was feeling that kiss.

Other hand in the air, Gideon.

Lifting it, guided by Daegan, he felt the vampire close a manacle over his other wrist. It still sent an uneasy tremor through him, but he pushed himself in that kiss, tried to push the darkness away. Then Daegan eased back from him. He was still close enough to continue the kiss, but Gideon's eyes sprang open as the vampire hooked the corner of his mouth with a finger and pushed the plug into his mouth. Gideon tried to expel it, but of course Daegan had his hand on the back of his head. "Take it, vampire hunter. Take it the way you've taken my cock."

It slid in deep, stretching his mouth at the flared base. Daegan adjusted the strap, cinching it around Gideon's head to hold the gag in place.

What the hell does this do? I can still talk in your head.

Daegan didn't answer him, didn't acknowledge him, though Gideon was sure he'd heard him. But it underscored the point. There was an inexplicable sense that being able to speak was an advantage, a requirement to be noticed, to have one's rights taken into account. Daegan had just taken that away. And more than that. Daegan had gone back to the work bench and now returned, carrying a full head mask.

No. Don't.

Gideon tried to jerk his head out of range, but of course he couldn't. Daegan fitted it on, and the world disappeared into darkness, the close material hugging Gideon's face, blinding him. Daegan positioned the ear pieces so his sense of hearing was also dulled. He was taking away all the senses he used to protect himself.

Gideon thrashed, fought, panic rising in him. Daegan caught him around the chest from behind, pressing his body full length against Gideon's naked one once more. He had his head right up next to Gideon's, his hand stroking his chest, palm pressing over Gideon's racing heart. He still didn't speak in his head, but he used his warmth, his presence, to remind Gideon his Master was here, was close. Those powerful hands that could kill in less than a second were almost tender, easy, petting his chest, his abdomen. Daegan's lips pressed against the side of the mask, and the material over the cheekbones was thin enough for him to feel the pressure. Daegan's very aroused cock, a hard, impressive package under denim, pushed against the seam of his buttocks. The vampire pinched Gideon's nipple, a rough caress, making Gideon's cock flex in its pronged cage.

His feet were still free, he reminded himself. But more than that, Daegan's calming touch was helping him steady, breathe. He was here. And now Daegan was putting pressure on his back, telling him to walk, pulling those cuffs along their track with him. Daegan stopped him a couple steps short of where Gideon knew the wall was, and put a different kind of pressure on his back, making Gideon bend forward. It was a move that made his balls tighten, wondering if Daegan was about to give him that hard, rough fuck. Somehow, he already knew it wasn't going to be that easy. Not that anything about this ever seemed easy.

The manacles came down toward the floor with him, so the vampire must have the remote that activated the pulleys in the ceiling, paying out slack in the chains. Daegan kept up the weight on his back until Gideon was bent over in a full fold, chest to knees, feet spread out so he was like a triangle, his ass the top point. Gideon had felt the crown of his head brush the wall as he bent toward the ground. Now Daegan had his hands on Gideon's hips. In one unexpected and impressive show of strength, air slipping under the soles of Gideon's feet, the vampire closed the distance between Gideon's body and the stone wall, putting his upside-down back firmly against it.

As the slack in the chains disappeared, and panic made a leap in his chest, Gideon realized what Daegan was doing. By then it was too late. As the chains retracted to the ceiling, they pulled his arms back up, increasing tension on his shoulders, as well as decreasing the angle of his bent over position. With the wall pressed into his back he couldn't flip over, especially now. His fingers scraped stone as Daegan locked a manacle around his left leg. He tried to move, but Daegan was too damn fast. The right one was manacled in a blink, and then he felt those chains draw taut. His feet were short-tethered to the floor, his wrists drawn up to counter balance, his body doubled over so his chest pressed against his knees. His head was upside down, face practically pressed into the open space between his spread knees, thanks to Daegan's ruthless angles on those chains and the pressure of the wall against his back.

That also meant his ass was fully exposed above his head and his cock and testicles in their shiny choke collar were just hanging out there, vulnerable. And he couldn't see a damn thing, could barely hear. Couldn't speak, because that thick phallus pressed down his tongue.

You do not need to hear or see, Gideon. I am here, and I am taking care of you. Your mind is not necessary, because you are my slave, serving my pleasure. That is your only purpose right now.

Daegan curved his palm over his right buttock. *Your balls are swollen up, your cock so hard, dripping. Your ass offered to me, however I want it. First, though, there's the matter of punishment.*

When his captors had made him helpless, he'd been fortified by rage. He had a rage boiling through him now, but it was different. A weird, self-hatred kind of thing, mixed with fury at feeling afraid, because he didn't really understand what he feared.

Daegan had to be squatting, resting that fine ass on his heels, because he'd reached between Gideon's thighs and was now touching Gideon's face. He opened the mouth zipper on the head mask, pushing it to the outside of the flared base of the gag so he could touch Gideon's lips, stretched around it. Gideon's hunger for that touch was so exponentially stronger he knew the sensory deprivation had to be heightening the craving. His mind didn't seem to be able to think beyond Daegan, because all he could imagine at the moment was how it would look if Daegan pulled out the gag and replaced it with his own dick, stretching Gideon's mouth with it, letting his slave serve him, deaf and blind to anything else. Jesus, this was crazy.

You are getting the way of it, Gideon. I would say don't resist it, but I know that automatically makes you try to resist. But I am not concerned about your resistance. You are utterly dependent on my will right now. And for my pleasure, to see your dick get harder, I'm going to let you see how this looks through my eyes.

It was another invasion, one that was perilous and irresistible at once. Daegan reached into him, opened up that window. At first, though, Gideon didn't see himself through Daegan's eyes, because Daegan had turned away, walking back to the opposite wall to pluck the punishment strap off it. He tested it with an experimental slap against his hand that almost made Gideon wince, anticipating it. But when he turned around to look at Gideon, Gideon swallowed hard against the gag.

He was folded over, muscles of his arms and legs rigid, his head covered by that mask, underscoring his status as a slave. His balls were a swollen angry red, his stiff cock following the center line up his belly, already marking his abs with pre-come. The pucker of his ass was there, plain to see, practically begging to be fucked. He supposed Daegan would have to take him down to his knees to do that because of the angle, but he was sure the vampire would figure it out when the time came. If it ever came, please God.

Daegan looked down then. Gideon suppressed a groan as he watched Daegan run his hand over his own erection, so prominent against the jeans. He gave himself a good rubbing, flexing his thighs against the stimulus. Gideon felt his rectum contract involuntarily, wanting it. Wanting him there.

In time, vampire hunter. If you beg.

Yeah, that would happen. Not. Maybe. At this point, he wasn't sure of anything. But when the scene went dark, Daegan plunging him back into the isolation, he knew what he really wanted was Daegan to talk some more in his head. He couldn't handle silence.

I might help my slave with that. If he says the magic word.

Asshole, Gideon muttered mentally.

I'm fairly certain that's not the magic word.

It almost wrested a desperate chuckle out of Gideon. Daegan could be like that. Interjecting that dry humor at the most unexpected moment. Steadying. Reminding him that...well, reminding Gideon that he didn't have to be his enemy. That Gideon was his own worst enemy.

Beautiful, servant. You are getting there. But you still have not said the right word.

If you keep talking to me, I guess it won't be needed, will it?

The first strike hit then, before Gideon was expecting it. Holy Mother of God. He'd forgotten Daegan was holding the punishment strap. But he was right about challenging a male vampire. As hard as Anwyn hit, he had no doubt that after thirty of Daegan's stripes, his ass was going to be running with blood from broken welts.

Do you remember why you are being punished?

Because...I mouthed off, to my Master. And I wanted...I wanted to make that right.

Gideon strangled on a cry as the strap popped his ass twice more. Jesus, this hurt. When it licked up and caught his balls on the next strike, also getting his chest beneath his chin, he howled against the plug. The pain ricocheted and vibrated through him, making him rock back and forth against the chains. Sweat broke out along his chest and back.

Daegan had paused, thank the gods, except Gideon wasn't sure if what he really wanted was for him to keep going. To get it over with. Or to help him lose himself in an oblivion of pain where emotions couldn't torment him with a far worse agony.

Have I punished you enough, Gideon? Is five enough?

Gideon squeezed his eyes shut. *No. No, it's never enough.*

But he still hadn't figured this out, was still fucking it up, the proof in Daegan's cool response.

You are wrong, servant. It is for me to say when it is enough.

He jumped when Daegan touched him, expecting the strap. Instead, he was surprised when Daegan removed the plug from his mouth. He was squatting on his heels again, his foot pressed against the side of Gideon's, his knee touching his calf. This time when Daegan's mouth closed over his, Gideon was so hungry for him he practically impaled himself on the vampire's fangs. Daegan controlled his reaction, holding him steady. Gideon moaned against his lips as Daegan reached up, caressed his turgid cock above the prongs, squeezed his balls. He was rubbing him, slow, and then his other finger slowly sank into Gideon's ass. One finger, two fingers, three. Even more devastating, Daegan's mouth went up above Gideon's, that small distance to his aroused cock, and he strangled on another cry as Daegan licked his shaft, playing around those prongs.

No, don't. Oh, Jesus...

Daegan pulled back, straightening to his feet so he could thrust his fingers in at a better angle, plus get out of the firing line for his diabolical intent. He milked Gideon with those three fingers, shot him into a climax so fast, there was no resisting him. Gideon screamed hoarsely as his cock convulsed, the prongs biting in like the jaws of a Rottweiler in truth, but there was no stopping the inevitable. He writhed between agony and ecstasy, his aching balls convulsing, pumping semen out against his chest and throat. He was sure it was hitting the wall as well as the mask, painting him in his own come. His legs quivered and, if they hadn't been anchored and countered with the arm manacles, he would have fallen over like a ton of bricks.

Truth, he was pretty sure he blacked out a little bit. He sensed Daegan though, about the time some consciousness returned to him and the reminder he was helpless, alone in the dark.

Not alone, vampire hunter. I am here. I am with you.

Daegan removed the pronged part of the harness, making Gideon grunt at the relief and momentary fire of the prongs pulling from his flesh. He probably had deep red marks in a decorative band around the base of his cock. Anwyn would hate she missed that, he was sure. Gideon made a futile noise as another thick plug, lubricated, was worked into his ass through the ring of the cock harness, then strapped down. He jumped against his bindings as it started to move and vibrate, deep inside. A low setting, but it kept him moving the small amount he could against those chains, grunting like an overtaxed animal.

I am going upstairs now, Gideon.

Say fucking what?

Daegan's fingers trailed through the wet tracks of semen on Gideon's chest, slicking it over his nipples. He was doing that idle pinching, a bit harder at Gideon's insolent reaction, making Gideon's balls twitch. He continued to paint Gideon's abdomen with his come, then moved over the smooth bare pubic area over his cock. Anwyn bound Gideon down once a week to enjoy shaving him. Every once in a while, if he'd been a particular pain in the ass that week, she took him upstairs to the public playroom and had one of the staff submissives do it. She'd sit in a chair and watch, idly masturbating as Gideon got harder and harder in perilous range of that razor. The delicate, pretty subs she chose would giggle over him, slap at his cock and scold it, telling it to behave. But Anwyn was always there, watching.

What, I'm boring you? He struggled to contain the panic that was returning in full force.

I'm going to go read awhile. When you have come several times, I will be back down to see where else this takes us. Daegan's hand gentled on the side of Gideon's face, a thumb tracing his jaw. He spoke then, but Gideon also heard the words in his mind. "To clean you up, care for you. And decide if I will finish your punishment with the strap. I know you want me to speak in your head, and I may do that, if I feel that's what you need. But do you know the right word to sway my decision?"

He was leaving him in darkness, bound, helpless. He was going away. Gideon wanted to be stubborn about it, but something about that climax, Daegan's words, left him so raw, torn open. His ass was killing him.

He pressed dry lips together and couldn't speak the words, even without the gag. But he knew Daegan wouldn't take anything less. He forced out the words, knowing they had to be hoarse from his abraded throat. "Please, Master." *Don't leave me alone in my fucking head.*

That is the lesson, Gideon. The one you need to be thinking about while I'm upstairs, even if I choose to say nothing to you for the next hour. Daegan was silent a moment, and then he spoke, his breath caressing Gideon's mouth, making him hunger for what was so close but held just out of reach.

"A servant is never alone."

Round 4

One of the vampires who'd captured Gideon during his vampire hunting days had talked incessantly, like the villain of a cheesy superhero flick. Gideon had suggested the asshole puncture his eardrums as the appetizer of his torture menu, hoping he'd comply so Gideon wouldn't have to listen to him anymore. Instead, the vamp had stuck electrodes on his testicles. Vampires didn't handle constructive criticism well.

But ceaseless diatribe wasn't nearly as bad as being put in solitary like this. No, this was worse than solitary. Not only was he alone, but with the mask, he had no eyes, and muted hearing. He could talk to himself, but that was kind of crazy and pointless. A few minutes ago, he'd considered reaching out to Anwyn, begging for a thought from her. A playing-mommy-against-daddy kind of thing, for sure, showing his level of desperation.

He was going insane in his head. He should have known Daegan would do this. That plug kept vibrating, stimulating his prostate and all the associated nerve

endings that were way too familiar with what Daegan felt
like when it was his cock there, instead of a plug. Gideon
had already come twice, grunting and writhing in the
chains. When he'd groaned from the power of the orgasm,
some of it had splattered his lips, making him taste that
salty fluid. His nostrils flared, unable to escape the musky
smell of semen, drying on his skin.

He felt Daegan's presence, because the third mark
allowed that. He was close, but not close enough. Probably
stretched out on one of the couches on the penthouse level,
reading one of those goddamned books. But he knew his
Master. The vampire was tracking his every reaction,
thought and movement. Gideon was alone in his head, no
one talking to him, but he wasn't alone. Ironically, the
certainty of that kept him hard, as much a stimulant as that
damn plug. As much as his vulnerable position. His mind
kept flashing back to the view Daegan had offered, Gideon
bent over double, ready to be fucked and used by his
Master however he wished.

God, had it been an hour? Was that how long he'd said
he would be gone? He had no idea, because on that second
climax, he'd blacked out. He thought Daegan had been
closer then, maybe checked on him during that hazy time.
In that dream state, Gideon had turned his face into
Daegan's palm, kissed him hard there, needy, a physical
plea. But he'd probably imagined that, because when he'd
come back to consciousness, Daegan was on that upper
level again. After all, there was no reason to check on him.
A third mark couldn't be killed by standing on his head
during multiple climaxes, but of course it did stress the
body enough to make him pass out.

Fuck, fuck, fuck. Please talk to me. Master?

Under the mask, he squeezed his eyes shut hard, his
fists even harder, then he remembered, loosened his
fingers. *Sorry, sorry, sorry. Daegan?* He hated being alone
in his head like this, too many emotions choking him, more
with every passing moment. He couldn't breathe.

Oh, shit. Another climax was boiling in his balls, getting
close. *Three times, really?* Sometimes being a third mark
could be a pain in the ass, that fast recovery time. Of course

it was a source of delight to their vampire masters and mistresses. Fanged sadists.

Gideon bucked against the chains as his cock convulsed, thumped against his abdomen and then jerked like those electrodes were back on it. Ropes of come spurted out. All the veins running along his inner thighs knotted up with the intensity of it, his balls drawing against the base of his cock.

He cried out, fighting those chains until it began to recede. Even then, as he came down, his muscles continued to tic violently. Like the aftershocks Anwyn had after they gave her a claw-the-skin-off-their-backs climax. She might do those sexy little twitches for up to fifteen minutes afterwards. Sometimes it got them all so revved up, Daegan would initiate it all over again, because he alone could override her will. That's what a Master did. He controlled it all, knew how to make you give beyond what you knew how to give. He and Anwyn both did that to Gideon, had done it even more intensely together. Now Daegan had proven they could do it singly as well. Which meant something pretty important, if Gideon had the brain cells and the desire to wrap his mind around it.

"Don't tax yourself, vampire hunter. Your brain capacity is very limited."

Gideon shamed himself with a noise that sounded suspiciously like a sob. The vampire squatted in front of him, because he touched his mouth. "You *did* kiss my hand after you blacked out. I won't let you forget that, I promise."

At least he hadn't kissed his foot or some stupid shit like that. Of course, the moment he had that thought, Gideon mentally punched himself in the head. You never, never, *never* had thoughts like that around vampires. They immediately put it on their to-do list, the bastards.

"I could make you beg to kiss my foot, Gideon, but that's not my purpose today. Easy." Daegan's voice dropped to a soothing murmur, and when he stroked Gideon's arm, his tense stomach, the line of his shoulder, Gideon realized he was shaking again.

"Why did you..." Gideon swallowed on a dry throat, his

tongue swollen from lack of fluid and screaming. "Why did you stay so quiet?"

He knew the answer. What he was really asking was: "Why did you do that to me, knowing how it fucks up my head?" Again, probably a self-answering question.

"There are things in your head you need to hear. You got close to it a few minutes ago. At least..." Daegan paused, an odd note to his voice, "I hope you did."

He closed his hand over Gideon's cock, idly stroking. Gideon stifled a groan, his ass clenching against the plug. *Bad idea.* He held onto control by his fingernails as Daegan continued in that mild tone, as focused in his intent as a laser.

"You look entirely fuckable, vampire hunter. I think I've waited long enough for my pleasure. Let's make sure you're ready." He made an adjustment, despite Gideon's futile protest. All of a sudden the vibrator was on a more intense setting, one that had Gideon rearing up in reaction.

"Be still," Daegan said, that commanding edge in his voice that had Gideon fighting to obey, to prove he could. But then he wished he'd kept writhing, because Daegan restored the pronged part of the cock harness. The edges bit into him as Daegan hooked it closed, Gideon's cock thick as hell.

"Want to...see you..." He wanted the mask off.

"You'll have to wait on that." As Daegan refused him, Gideon heard the rustle of clothing. A zipper opened, then what had to be Daegan's jeans hit the floor with their tantalizing thump. Another rustle said they'd been kicked away. The pulleys in the ceiling hummed, loosening the chains holding the arm manacles. Daegan's hands were on his ankles, freeing the short chains that anchored his feet to the floor.

The vibrator was going like a damn train engine in his ass. Gideon couldn't stop the involuntary jerks, despite Daegan's earlier admonition, but now that he'd gotten those prongs around Gideon's dick again, the vampire didn't seem to mind him jittering like a puppet on crack.

"You follow my lead," Daegan reminded him. He moved Gideon back, enough steps that he could clear the wall, straighten and stand upright. Gideon wasn't steady enough to get there before Daegan knocked his legs out from under him. He would have landed right on his head or face, except the vampire's arm was around his chest, taking him down to all fours on the cool stone. He re-anchored his ankles to another set of eyebolts, snapping his knees down with an additional set of metal straps affixed to the floor. The hand pressed to his back told Gideon to stay in the all-fours position. As he sensed Daegan moving around to his front, Gideon gasped for air against the continuing massage of that plug. He wasn't going to come. He wasn't.

"No, you aren't. Because your Master says you can't."

He felt like a wild animal around the guy, entirely unpredictable. Gideon assumed Daegan was about to anchor his wrists the same way as his knees, so he couldn't take advantage of the slack of the chains even now brushing his shoulders. Probably a good idea. If he could lift up, he'd probably try to wrap them around Daegan's neck.

"That would be foolhardy."

"Foolhardy?" Gideon panted out the words. "You were reading...the Greek poetry instead of the...Connelly, weren't you? Pansy."

"*O love, thou art victor in fight: thou mak'st all things afraid...thou passest the bounds of the sea, and the folds of the fields; to thee the immortal, to thee the ephemeral yields. Sophocles.*"

Gideon swallowed, pushing down the feelings that rose in his throat at that sensual voice, so close to him. "Yeah, but you can't put it to music. Great big gobs of greasy, grimy gopher guts, chopped up parakeet, mutilated monkey feet..." He swayed with the nonsense tune, even though he knew he sounded as hysterical as a girl. Fuck. "It's what I look like right now. Especially the disgusting, greasy part."

"Greasy, yes." Daegan's fingers trailed briefly over Gideon's shoulder, making his cock flex and his body shudder. "Disgusting, hardly. You taste like pleasure."

His rectum clenched over the plug at the vision of Daegan tasting his come. The vampire did anchor his wrists, bringing his scent and heat close. Gideon breathed him in, imagining him there naked, within touching distance, though he was prevented from that by the chains. It made his gut ache. Then Daegan put his hand on the back of Gideon's neck. "Use your mouth to get me slick again. Do it fast. I want to fuck you now."

He heard it in the roughness of the male's voice. Gideon wanted it fast as well, such that he lunged blindly for him. Daegan steadied him, guiding the head of his cock to Gideon's eager mouth. Gideon didn't want to come with that plug again. He wanted Daegan to make him come, Daegan's hard, irresistible cock. Apparently it was mouthwatering as well, because he found the saliva to suck it good, had the vampire gripping his neck with bruising strength. He did his level best to test his control. If Daegan lost it, came in his mouth, Gideon would consider it a victory, even if it meant he lost in other ways.

The male pulled back out then, despite Gideon's attempt to clamp his teeth down and hold him there. Daegan let out a grim chuckle, did that little maneuver with the hinge of his jaw to free himself, and gave him a not-so-pleasant thump on the forehead. "Nice try."

Gideon heard another chain drop. The steel manacle fit his throat snugly as Daegan locked it. Putting a collar on him always had the strangest effect on Gideon, making his breath shorten and his dick harder. When Daegan retracted the chain attached to it so he had to lift his head, and keep lifting it, back toward his shoulders, like a horse with the reins severely shortened, Gideon had to fight that plug vibration even harder. *No, no, no. Not yet.*

"You crave a permanent collar, Gideon. One from both your Master and Mistress. One that locks and only we can remove. We know. We're going to take care of that."

He wanted to beg, plead for it. Plead to be fucked. But he couldn't. And not because he was being rebellious. If he spoke one word, he was going to go off like a geyser. It was a close thing when Daegan removed the slippery plug from his ass, the friction making him fucking insane.

"Now beg me, servant. Beg for what you want. Get it right the first time, no games, or I swear to God I will make you suffer."

Gideon got it out on a strangled moan, working so hard not to come, not to clench his hands. Oh, fuck, those prongs hurt so bad, but his mindless cock didn't seem to care that it would only get worse. "Please, Master. Please fuck me. I want your cock...in my ass. Please."

It didn't matter how tirelessly he claimed not to recognize this side of himself, he was getting really familiar with this dark, needy creature that was his soul. And he was getting too damn close to the heart of it all, the yearning ache that went beyond the physical, that had other words hovering on his lips.

"In heaven-high musings and many, far-seeking and deep debate; Of strong things find I not any, that is as the strength of Fate. Euripides that time." But Daegan's voice had that hoarse touch in it again.

Please, Master. I need you. Gideon couldn't force that through his lips, but it resounded through his broken soul. He needed Daegan; no games, no artifice. He needed his Master to fill him, to bring balance. To help him figure it out.

"Ah, vampire hunter. You destroy me." Kneeling behind him, Daegan put his hands on Gideon's ass, fingers flexing against the cheeks. "Tighten up. I want to push in hard, make you feel the burn. It will help you last longer."

Gideon complied, grunting with the exertion as Daegan shoved in through the harness's wide ring. The tightened muscles held against his entry for a blink, but once he was at a certain point, it all gave way. Gideon lost control, welcoming him so Daegan slid in deep, his balls slamming up against his own, a sensation that spurred his reaction into the red zone.

"Fuck..." He wasn't sure which of them said it, but maybe both. Daegan hadn't been kidding. He was in the mood to give Gideon a rough ride. He pistoned into him, only his powerful hold on Gideon's hips keeping him from being thrust forward against the collar's hold so his air was cut off. Gideon lifted his ass up to him, cognizant of the restraints on his ankles and knees keeping him in place for that punishing, soul-level fuck. *Jesus...God...*

His balls drew up again. *Master...coming...*

"Come for me, Gideon. Come now."

"You too," Gideon grunted it out, a strangled sound. "Aw, fuck..."

His cock spurted. While a third mark could come far more often, after they reached a certain point, they would dry-come, like a normal male. Gideon experienced the incredible intensity of that, because after the streams of hot semen splashed against the floor beneath him, against his wrists and knees, he kept coming, his body jerking, humping air. Daegan fucked him thoroughly, slamming in again and again, burning and stretching Gideon's ass to the point he thought he might be bleeding in among the pleasure of it all. His cock was in agony and still hard as a rock, those stainless steel teeth biting down on him. It didn't matter. The vampire's breath got harsh and rasping and Gideon clamped down on that irresistible cock inside him. Daegan's balls slapped rhythmically against Gideon's, an incredible sensation that just goaded him further.

Come on, come for me, let me feel it.

Daegan let go with a snarl, those fingers tightening until Gideon was pretty sure his pelvis was in danger of being snapped beneath that strong grip. He didn't care. Daegan could break every bone in his body, and he'd just beg for more. He moved with him, not caring that the pressure of the collar against his windpipe increased until black spots started to fill his vision and his breath started to rasp and wheeze against it.

Slowing down. Slowing. The chain eased, the slack pooling in a cool weight between his shoulder blades. Gideon necessarily went down to his elbows, breathing hard, swaying back and forth. Daegan dropped down over him, his arm sliding around his chest, his face pressed into the back of Gideon's neck. The vampire's lips touched him there, the graze of his fangs, and then they punctured skin. He'd fed earlier, but this was different, a possessive marking. A vampire's idea of cuddling, because Anwyn did it pretty often after sex as well. Though her fangs were more like a kitten's, whereas Daegan's were obviously cousin to a mountain lion's.

Daegan's lips curved against his neck. They didn't move for a while, just stayed melded to one another like that. Probably literally, because between the blood, sweat and come, Gideon was probably like one of those sticky frogs that Velcro'ed themselves to glass surfaces on Southern summer nights. Of course most of that stickiness was on his front. His back was all about Daegan's sweat, because the vampire had actually worked himself up to a light perspiration that made his muscles slide pleasantly against Gideon's back as he shifted. He cruised up to Gideon's ear, nipped him there. Then he reached beneath him and deftly unlocked the prongs, as well as the cock harness, pulling it all free as the vampire himself pulled out. Gideon groaned at both the loss and the agony of relief, pressing his cheek to the floor to steady himself.

He was able to lift his head enough to let Daegan unlace the head mask and pull that loose. Air touched his cheeks, his forehead, his hair matted against his temples and neck. Daegan released all his chains but that first one, the one on his wrist. Cracking open his eyes, Gideon saw Daegan squatting before him, a pleasurable view of his bare thighs, the still somewhat-erect cock, his sizeable testicle sac. Gideon had never been one to eye a guy's junk, but everything about Daegan's body got him aroused, even that.

It wasn't the physical. It was Daegan that aroused him.

There was that uncomfortable thread again. He still didn't have the brain cells—or maybe the guts—to follow that thread, but another instinct drove him. Reaching out with his free hand, he curved it around Daegan's calf, just above the ankle, before the male could rise. If Gideon touched Daegan voluntarily, it was usually the precursor to an attack, so Daegan visibly went on alert, ready to counter him. But Gideon was acting on pure feeling, no thought to give him away. As a result, something entirely different took over Daegan's expression as Gideon shifted enough to press his mouth to the vampire's bare foot.

He stayed there, eyes closing, fingers tightening on his Master in a sudden fierce need to hold him like this, stay like this, until he could bear to move, to handle the tide of emotions washing through him. Emotions that weren't all his own. The vampire bent over him, sliding his arms under Gideon's body. He laid his cheek on the curve of his back.

"It's all right," Daegan murmured. "I've got you, Gideon. Everything you give is safe with me, remember? Everything."

Gideon nodded, not sure how to respond, throat to raw to speak. He wasn't sure what was happening, what he was feeling, but something had changed in this moment. Something significant.

At length, Daegan eased back. He put Gideon into a seated position, his back against the wall, the one hand still manacled, his knees bent and feet flat on the floor. Daegan rose. "Stay there."

Gideon managed to roll his head toward the manacle and arched a brow. "Where d'you think I'm going?" Hell, his voice was slurred like he was drunk.

"I never underestimate you, vampire hunter." Daegan flashed that devastating grin, and moved away to the next room. Gideon got way too good a view of his perfect ass and muscular body, the grace and power with which it moved. It would stir the libido of a dead man. Even a dead straight man.

When Daegan came back, he had a basin, some soap, a wash cloth and other items. "I can clean myself up," Gideon protested weakly, but Daegan ignored him and dropped to one knee at his side.

"It is my right as your Master. I don't have to bind you to do this, do I? Will you obey me, be still for me, Gideon?"

Be still. It was how this had all started. Learning stillness under Daegan's touch. Gideon gave him a nod after a long moment, his jaw tightening. It was still strange as hell to watch Daegan's capable, male hands moving over him, wiping the come off his chest, making him lift his chin to get to his throat, using the soap on his arm pits and then working his way down to sore cock and balls. Daegan was thorough, firm but gentle, and it made Gideon feel so odd, sitting there silent, watching him do it all, moving only when he ordered him to adjust. Daegan even stroked his hands through Gideon's hair, loosening it from where it had matted, combing it back with his fingers.

He balked a bit when Daegan had him rise and commanded him to grab his ankles so he could shoot some soothing herbal crap into his ass, but Daegan patiently waited him out again, giving him that implacable look. When Gideon complied, he listened to the soft splash of water as Daegan caught most of it in the basin. The vampire mopped the rest off his thighs and buttocks with the towels. As he did all that, Gideon realized he was back in that floating trance state. Happy to...just be.

Daegan took him back to a seated position and brought him a bottle of water, opening it for him. Then he really unsettled Gideon by sitting down himself. Against the wall, right behind Gideon, pulling him up between his thighs. He adjusted him so Gideon could slouch down, his tired head resting partly on Daegan's chest and shoulder, his one arm draped on Daegan's knee, the other loose across his own abdomen. His naked body was sprawled out for Daegan's view, but he was essentially cradled in Daegan's arms, held between his thighs. The male stroked his knuckles down Gideon's sternum, teasing a nipple as he directed Gideon to drink, even closing a hand on his wrist so Gideon had to bring the bottle to his mouth.

"Drink, vampire hunter. This night is far from over. I'm not through with you yet."

Round 5

Author's Note: *Thanks to a reader winning a walk-on part in this vignette, we're happy to introduce our readers to "Shan" in the next two segments of this story. Whenever we've offered this "walk-on" giveaway, I've always found it contributes greatly to the ongoing storyline. So a thank you to all our winners of this kind of prize for their willingness to work with me. I hope you enjoy the results in these two segments as I did!*

§

Gideon drank long and deep, emptying the water bottle in one go. He fumbled it toward the end, but Daegan kept holding his wrist and hand, anticipating his servant's lack of coordination. When he was done, Gideon realized he was still thirsty. But not for water.

Setting the bottle aside, Daegan unlocked the manacle around Gideon's wrist, freeing him, at least in one sense. Laying his palm on Gideon's forehead, Daegan kept Gideon's head resting on his shoulder and chest, even while Daegan played with the strands of hair there, a drifting caress. The languorous strokes, Daegan's intriguingly bare-ass naked body behind him... It reminded Gideon of lying on a raft in quiet surf, being okay with the tug of the current, wherever it took him, because the sun was warm, the breeze was gentle, and the ocean was so much larger and more powerful than himself. There was a comfort to that.

His head moved with the motion of that hand, slow increments, until his face was turned into Daegan's neck, mouth an inch away. His nostrils flared, taking in the vampire's scent. He wanted to taste. To bite. To drink. Since he'd become Daegan's third mark, he hadn't really asked for that. Not from the male vampire.

Daegan was silent, but his fingers continued that caress. Gideon realized his hand had fallen on the male's thigh, just below his knee. He kept his face pressed toward Daegan's neck, but he looked down at his hand as if he wasn't entirely sure what it was about to do, and maybe he wasn't. He curled his fingers, touched firm skin. No hair of course. Vampires had no hair below the neck, but that didn't make Daegan girlish at all. He was like one of those Roman statues, all smooth muscles that Gideon had never considered arousing until he compared them to Daegan. Jesus, he was turning into a fucking fairy.

Daegan's lips pulled into a smile against his temple. *I don't think you have to worry about a guest appearance on* Queer Eye. *Except as one of the very straight, poorly dressed, utter slobs they are trying to rehabilitate.*

He'd let that smartass remark pass. One, because he'd have a better chance of getting even when Daegan was off-guard later. A nice right jab to the testicles would do. He'd also point out to the antiquated fanged fossil that the show had been off the air for a few years now. But right now he had something else capturing his attention.

Gideon watched his own fingers slide a few inches down that thigh, as far as he could go before his own armpit got in the way, then back up toward the knee. Daegan was all lean strength, and stroking the lines of it was...mesmerizing. He did it again, and became even more aware of where lots of other muscle was touching him. Daegan's chest against his shoulder blades. His ridged abdomen against his lower back. His cock, pushed against the top of his ass.

Technically, the cock is not a muscle.

Gideon huffed out a half chuckle, and was amazed to see a ripple of gooseflesh cross Daegan's forearm. His breath on Daegan's neck had caused that reaction, as well as a stirring of that beast at his lower back.

It made him think about touching Anwyn. There were few things in the world Gideon loved as much as touching his Mistress. Sometimes, she'd withhold that permission, knowing how the denial aroused him, but he knew she liked his hands, his mouth on her. While he savored every taste, the way her skin felt, he loved the little noises, the caught breath, the movements that betrayed her desire. Women reacted with their whole bodies to stimulation, from violent undulation to a simple pressing together of their lips. But until this moment, he hadn't noticed that a man could react in such subtle ways as well.

He did it again, this time deliberately. A heated breath against that major artery. Daegan's fingers twitched against his sternum, thumb doing a pass over his nipple that made Gideon's lower gut tighten. Wow. Fucking hell. He brought his mouth closer, but before he made contact, Daegan caught his hair in one strong hand and held him off, tilting his head until they were eye to eye. His eyes had done that startling thing, where the dark brown color had taken over the whole eye, no whites, so it was like Gideon was looking into a pitch dark room, wondering whether it was a good idea to step blindly over the threshold.

Fuck it. He wanted that darkness. But then Daegan's other hand came up, caught his throat. Reflexively, Gideon's hand landed over it, tightened, and they were locked there, teetering on that prelude to physical combat. Gideon could turn it into that, Daegan could squelch it, they could start from square one again. Or...

"Let go of me, vampire hunter," Daegan said, his voice holding that dangerous edge. He wasn't in the mood to play. Normally, that would be the trigger Gideon needed to ignore him, test the limits, do whatever the hell he wanted and see what Daegan would do to override him.

He didn't do that this time. But he didn't let go, either. Closing his eyes, Gideon eased his touch so his fingers spread, settling over Daegan's on his throat. He felt the heat and strength, the taut tendons as his touch slid to Daegan's hand, then the wrist and forearm, all the way to the biceps. When he reached that point, he gripped and held, not in struggle or defense, but to connect. And then he spoke, direct to the vampire's mind.

I'm still thirsty. I want...to take it from your throat.

He opened his eyes, stared into Daegan's. Because of that freaky snake charmer eye thing the vampire had going, he couldn't really tell what Daegan was thinking, but he knew the male was a hundred and fifty percent involved in this moment, in Gideon's every move, his expression, the slight, not-the-least-bit-unmanly break in his mind-voice.

The intercom buzzed.

While it wasn't unusual for Anwyn to receive a call from upstairs, she had a very competent staff and those interruptions were minimal. Since they'd been made aware she now had a "health problem" that sometimes indisposed her, their competence had only increased. They also knew she was gone for the weekend, so the only reason they'd be buzzing down was if they had a security problem. Gideon backed up James, the head of security, when needed. As such, Daegan's eyes immediately returned to normal, his hand dropping from Gideon's neck, both of them going on alert.

"Intercom on," Gideon called out, since the speaker system fortunately responded to voice commands. "Yes?"

"Gideon? It's Ella."

Fortunately, the staff submissive sounded nervous but not too rattled. "Yeah, Ella. What's up?"

"We have a problem with one of the sessions planned for tonight. We need a favor. Um...the other girls didn't think I should bother you, but I thought it was something you might consider. Can I come down and ask you something, or would you be willing to come up?"

Realizing it wasn't a security emergency, Daegan had decided to entertain himself. He closed his hand around Gideon's cock in a firm squeeze, fingers stroking with diabolical purpose. Though Gideon had twitched in his arms when the intercom first buzzed, Daegan hadn't allowed Gideon out of his seated position between his thighs. Gideon had been sort of okay with that, but he didn't know how he felt about his dick being fondled while he was talking to Ella.

Jesus. The vamp had a skilled touch. His dumbass cock shouldn't be asking for more after this many orgasms, but Gideon was hardening. Though Ella couldn't see him, it still felt...disturbing. While he had a friendly relationship with most of the subs on staff, she was the submissive toward whom he felt most protective. A few weeks ago, he'd helped James pull her out of a sticky situation with a Dom who shouldn't have gotten through the door. A guy who'd been vetted when Anwyn wasn't on her game the way she usually was. So Ella knew Gideon as an alpha guy who sometimes helped James with security, not some...

Daegan squeezed harder, uncomfortably tight. *Slave?* His mind tone was heat and coolness at once, a warning and a withdrawal. While it raised the hackles on Gideon's neck, unexpected regret speared through his gut, given where they'd been a moment or two ago, on the edge of...something. Now he'd done something to turn Daegan off.

Wrapping his fingers back around his throat and jaw, the vampire turned Gideon's face so his mouth captured Gideon's, raw and hot. *You can piss me off, Gideon. You couldn't turn me off if you tried.*

"Fuck," Gideon muttered. Daegan let go of his mouth,

but his hand down there got even more insistent, fist-pumping him slow and sure. He closed his hands on Daegan's thighs. He knew better than to try and stop the vamp. Though of course he could if he wanted to.

Of course you could. Not.

"What was that?" Ella had apparently picked up Gideon's expletive, but she also had something else to get out, so she didn't wait for a response, thank God. "Oh, and if you're agreeable, it-might-involve-Mr.-Jones-too."

That rushed finale stopped Daegan. His fingers flexed, making Gideon go cross-eyed. In just that short time, his thighs had started to get drum tight, his ass rising off the floor in tune with that firm stroke. Hell, he shouldn't have had that thought. Wouldn't want Daegan to get smug.

I know exactly what effect I have on your body, Gideon.

Gideon glanced back at that little stress, but Daegan shifted, pushing him off so they could get up, though at least the shove had the tone of roughhoused affection. "Yes, Ella," Daegan replied for both of them. "You can come down. We'll punch up the security code."

Gideon imagined Ella had blanched at that unexpected voice. The Atlantis staff knew Anwyn lived with two males, but Daegan kept a pretty low profile with them, not difficult since the guy could move way faster than any human could detect. James and a few of the staff had met him, but Anwyn made it clear that "Mr. Jones" preferred his privacy. Since their business was all about discretion, the staff respected that.

The pseudonym might be a decidedly unoriginal name, but generic names served a purpose. They didn't stand out, and emphasized that Anwyn didn't invite questions about him, though anyone who encountered Daegan was unlikely to forget him, even if his name was John Fucking Doe. Even at a distance, he'd made enough of an impression Ella was probably rethinking her audacity.

Come to think of it, Gideon himself was pretty surprised Daegan had spoken up. But Daegan didn't offer an explanation, just a hand to pull him off the floor. The vampire picked up his own jeans and yanked them on bare-assed. "You might want to get dressed before she gets down here," he suggested. Moving to the wall, he punched in the security code to open the elevator doors one level up.

Gideon retrieved his jeans and pulled them on, glad Daegan had cleaned him up with the sponge bath. Else he would have had to perform a lightning fast shower between the time Ella stepped into the elevator and the ten seconds before the doors opened, which was beyond even a third mark's enhanced abilities. Though maybe not Daegan's. That was one thing Daegan never rushed. The guy loved a hot shower and, from his own violent career path, Gideon knew it helped wash off the sense of blood, though nothing got rid of it entirely. Not once you'd been immersed in enough of it, way too many times.

Apparently his libido still hadn't settled, because that serious thought couldn't erase the visual of him and Daegan in the shower together, Daegan giving him an even more thorough washing, pushing him down so the heels of his hands were on the tub edge as Daegan lubed himself up and sank deep into him again, the hot water beating on both of them, steam swirling over slick, rippling muscle...

Daegan lifted his head and met his eyes. There was something a little dangerous in that expression, just like when he'd caught Gideon by the throat. "I'll consider that, vampire hunter," he murmured.

Gideon concealed the hot flush that swept over his upper body by pulling his T-shirt over his head. As he did, the elevator made the noise it did right before it opened. The double doors parted.

Ella had an hourglass Marilyn Monroe figure with lush curves. Along with her long red hair and a doe's dark brown eyes, she could get a guy hard in a blink. She had a unique grasp of her submissive personality, such that she could tailor it for the needs of different clients. Whether she was feisty brat or docile servant to the paying Master or Mistress, her underlying nature, the desire to serve, was deep, true and real, and made her a valuable asset to Atlantis.

She was also well liked by the team of long-term employees who considered one another family, thanks to Anwyn's intuitive hiring skills and the fact she was a damn good boss. Good professional subs were as valuable as good professional Doms, due to the exceptional talent both required to handle an ever-rotating client base. At least, that's what Anwyn said. While he didn't know about that, Gideon knew he liked Ella, liked her forthrightness. Her only drawback was she was often all intuition and feeling. Which was a double-edged sword, because what made her popular with clients could also endanger her, in the wrong situation. Like many subs, Ella could get lost in her head and the Dom's desires and forget to protect herself.

As a result, Anwyn particularly screened the clients who requested Ella, making sure they were the kind who never forgot a Dom's responsibility to care for a sub, no matter how deep or intense a session became. His Mistress had the right touch not only for vetting clients wanting to hire a sub for the night, but for pairing them up to the right staff member.

The night Ella had needed to be bailed out from a Dom who stepped over the lines had been a bad night. It had shaken Anwyn's confidence in herself deeply. After ensuring Ella was all right, that consequence had been Daegan and Gideon's primary concern.

But it was also that night which had won Ella a permanent place in Gideon's heart. When Anwyn was falling to pieces over it in her office later, Ella had slipped in at that key moment. She'd gone to her knees in front of his formidable Mistress and put her arms around her.

"I love you, Mistress," the young woman had said, calm and clear-eyed. "The very first day I was hired, you told me that mistakes are *always* going to happen. The key is keeping them to a minimum and being prepared when they do happen. You were prepared. James and Gideon came. You keep us safe. I'm never afraid here, and we don't want you to be, either."

Other staff members had come in then, hugged her as well. It wasn't just Daegan and Gideon who wouldn't let Anwyn back away from being who she was to Atlantis. She was its heart, and they all knew it.

Remembering that moment now, he gave her a look of warm reassurance. From her wary expression, he knew she wasn't sure what to make of Daegan being actively part of the conversation. As she stepped out of the elevators, her eyes went right to the vampire, leaning against the couch in her direct line of sight. Since he wasn't wearing a shirt, just those jeans and bare feet, Gideon was already in motion. He caught her as she pretty much stumbled over the threshold. Yeah, Daegan had that effect on women. Okay, sometimes men, too.

No, I'm not going to feed your ego and say it, Gideon thought testily as Daegan gave him the expected raised brow and ironic glance.

The vampire's eyes glinted, but he rose to his feet. "What may we do for you, Ella?"

Daegan took the leadership role, surprising Gideon, but Ella seemed to take that in stride. Of course, she was a skilled, professional submissive. It probably took her three seconds to realize "Mr. Jones" was a formidable Master. So what did she think Gideon was?

Slave. The word echoed in his mind again. Gideon tightened his jaw, firmly deciding to focus on Ella. She might faint if Daegan took a couple steps toward her, so he better be ready to catch her.

Fortunately, she displayed the fortitude he'd come to expect from her.

Her lashes swept down as she inclined her head to Daegan, a deferential gesture. "I'm so sorry to bother you both, but I think this is pretty important. We have an appointment scheduled tonight that's hit a snag. The Dom, Aaron, paid for a session for his fiancée Shannon. It's for her birthday. She's loved vampires since she was a little girl, so he's been working with Anwyn for a couple months to engineer a fantasy where she surrenders to a vampire and his servant."

Gideon wondered if Daegan was having as much trouble keeping an impassive expression as he was, given that Ella was unknowingly facing a vampire and his servant right now. However, Gideon did telegraph a confirmation to Daegan. Anwyn had vaguely mentioned something about a fantasy of that sort. All types of scenarios were choreographed for clients, some for exorbitant fees, depending on how elaborate they were. She didn't always mention all of them to Gideon, but this one had come up briefly, a humorous topic, for obvious reasons.

"It's a test run for them," Ella continued. "They're both pretty new to the scene. It's the first time she's been part of a BDSM session in a club environment like this. The fiancé is still learning the ropes about being her Dom. He planned to watch, and then come in toward the end, take over. Two birds with one net." Ella's glance strayed to Gideon, probably seeking a little encouragement, because so far Daegan's expression wasn't revealing whether he was going to be affable or try to eat her.

Gideon wasn't sure he gave her what she needed there, because she accelerated the dialogue in that fascinating way women had—dumping a huge load of information in less than ten seconds.

"Richard and Dave were supposed to do the honors, but Richard came down with a twenty-four-hour flu, and Dave of course only works with Richard. Unfortunately, Richard has been so sick, he forgot to call it in, and Dave thought he already had. We don't really have any other male Master/sub pairings used to working in tandem with each other on the floor tonight, and this is a complicated role playing scene. Aaron and Shannon are driving in from a couple hours away and we can't get in touch, because they've already left their hotel. They're on a month long trip in the States, visiting from Australia. This is the last week of the trip, the grand finale. We have the info on all the boundaries and limits for the session—"

"Okay, we're getting the situation," Gideon interjected. "But what is it you need from us?"

Ella turned toward him with relief, though the tension in her shoulders said she was well aware of Daegan's unwavering scrutiny. "Forgive me if I seem a little direct about this"—a flick of her gaze toward Daegan indicated exactly whose forgiveness she was soliciting—"but a few weeks ago, I saw you two together, in the corridor outside the elevator. The way you were with each other... I've seen you with Mr. Jones a couple times since then and..." She gave a helpless little shrug. "Perils of the job, I'm afraid. It seems pretty clear that he's your Master, and you serve him, as well as Mistress Anwyn. So I didn't know if you'd even consider it, but I had this feeling, maybe. The fiancé doesn't want actual sex. Just playing around the edges, give her release... But if you're not at all interested, I'll go back upstairs and see what we can figure out. And please don't get me fired."

Gideon blinked, spoke slowly. "So, based on seeing us together a couple times, you think we can roleplay vampire and servant in a paid session with a woman we've never met? While her fiancé watches?"

Ella beamed brightly. "Yes. That pretty much sums it up. There's a dramatic tension between you...it meshes. I thought you could pull it off really well, if you're comfortable with it. Since you're with Mistress Anwyn, and have been staying at the club awhile, I know you're pretty experienced."

Triple scoops of irony on a banana split sundae. Fuck. No one on staff except James knew what Daegan was, after all. Hell, they didn't even know Anwyn was a vampire.

"You see *him* as a vampire?" Gideon hooked a thumb in Daegan's direction. "Really? I think that's kind of a stretch."

"Him, no stretch at all." Ella arched a brow, apparently more sure of herself now that he was teasing her. "You, as a servant? *That* would be the stretch." She sobered. "And you're not, not really. Except with him, and Anwyn. It comes out real strong with them. I notice things." Ella shrugged, sighed. With visible effort, she turned back toward Daegan, but kept her eyes fastened to his chest. Or perhaps wandering over it was more accurate.

"Mr. Jones, I don't want to offend you, so if this is completely inappropriate, I'm sorry. I'll go back upstairs."

Daegan shifted, lips pursing in a very distracting way. It even made Ella's glance flicker up for one brave moment. "Do you have the paperwork with you?"

"Yes, definitely." Ella slipped a folder out from under her arm. She was closer to Gideon, but when he reached for it, Daegan made a quelling noise that brought their attention to him. He extended his hand. "Give it to me,

Ella."

She handed the file to Daegan, who was ignoring Gideon's narrowed glance. Planting his fine ass back on the edge of the couch, he looked through it, silent. Ella shifted her attention to Gideon during. As she gave him a questioning look, he shrugged, trying to act casual.

"You want a soda or anything?" Gideon asked, though his mind was whirling.

Was Daegan really considering this? Why wasn't he telling her no fucking way, sending her back up? Gideon didn't want to see Ella called down for it, though. And truth, Anwyn likely wouldn't chastise her, because she appreciated staff initiative to make their clients happy, but that didn't mean that this was doable.

You are very doable, Gideon.

Bite me.

Before Ella interrupted, I believe your desire was to bite me.

Gideon chose not to respond to that, increasing his concentration on Ella to laser fierceness. "Soda?" he prompted again, through gritted teeth. "Or chocolate milk and cookies?" He really wasn't entirely comfortable, even in his mind, dealing with this side of Daegan and him in front of her. Hell, he still had trouble with it when it was just the two of them.

But it didn't seem to bother Ella at all. She made a face at him and stuck out her tongue the same way she'd do if he was picking on her upstairs. She apparently didn't even consider it a bump in the road, thinking of him as Daegan's submissive.

What would it be like if it wasn't such a problem for *him*, if *he* could let go of this nagging self-consciousness about it when he was around others? It was an oddly wistful, unexpected thought.

Ella moved a stepped closer, tilting her head up to study Gideon's face. Wetting one of her long-nailed fingers, she smoothed a stray strand of his hair at his temple. "You have head mask hair," she said, with a teasing smile.

He caught her wrist, lightly pushed it away. "Brat." He'd gotten used to the girls petting and teasing him. The

Mistresses did it, too, but in a kind of a different way. It all made him feel good. Like he was part of the family Anwyn had created here. Like Atlantis had become his home.

"Ella?"

She immediately turned her attention to Daegan. "Yes, sir?"

"While I agreed to let you come down to see us, you interrupted a session. I think that's obvious."

She colored about three shades of rose and stepped back from Gideon as if she'd been hit by a Taser. "My apologies, sir. I shouldn't have touched him."

What the hell? Gideon looked between them, but it was as if he wasn't even there, Daegan's total attention on Ella and hers on him, though her gaze was lowered. She looked ready to kneel if Daegan ordered it.

"Not without your permission," she amended.

"Hmm." Daegan handed the folder back to her. "Your behavior toward him is fine; you merely should have asked first. How long before they arrive?"

"A half hour. It'll take about thirty minutes to get them set up. Shannon knows what her fiancé is giving her, so that part's not a surprise. But she doesn't know any details. Just that tonight her Master is turning her over to a vampire and his servant. And that he's given us her limits and boundaries, and he'll be watching from an observation room."

"All right. I'm going to step into the next room to contact Anwyn and discuss this, because he belongs to her as well." Daegan shifted his glance to Gideon, nodded, and then pivoted toward his bedroom. When he did, Gideon gave Ella a pinch that made her jump. She shot him a mischievous look and stepped a safer distance away.

"Sir?" When Daegan stopped and looked back, Ella dimpled. "Do I have permission to resume touching?"

"Within reason." His lips quirked. "Gideon knows his limits."

Gideon bared his teeth in a feral grin that made her giggle. But when Daegan disappeared down the hall, Ella turned to him, giving him a flurry of smacks against his arm that had him backpedaling, fending her off.

"*Shit,*" she whispered. "I thought I'd be talking to you alone, Gideon. Running this by you to get your take before we sprang it on him. I am *so* dead. Anwyn's going to put me on closing shift for the next millennium."

"No, she's not. It's fine." Looping an arm around her neck, he pulled her to his side and drop a kiss on her head. Then tugged her hair. "I'm sure she'll just have you publicly flogged and then paraded around in a stock for a month or two."

Ella sighed. "Maybe you *aren't* experienced enough to do this. Around here, that's the reward for *good* behavior."

"Sick bitch."

She gave him an answering pinch and shoved away. "I'll take a swallow of that soda. God, my mouth went dry as a bone, seeing him right there. He's like a thousand kilowatt Dom, you know? If I was Anwyn and had the two of you in my bed, I'd stay in it until I had bedsores the size of pancakes. I'm lucky I didn't spout complete gibberish in front of him."

"Actually, you were on a pretty good jabber roll there..."

"You..."

Gideon laughed, sliding toward the kitchen before she could get in another punch. It was good to play with a girl. It helped ease things up inside him. And made him miss Anwyn more.

§

Daegan knew how he felt. Gideon wasn't dead, so he could enjoy flirting with Ella, but Daegan knew his heart as he knew his own. Anwyn was the only woman they wanted.

There were other things Gideon wanted as well. Though Daegan had regretted Ella's timing, Fate intervened for particular reasons. He found Ella's idea...intriguing, for his own intentions.

He closed the door, so Ella wouldn't know that he wasn't dialing a phone, but reaching out with his mind. He and Gideon had made a pact they wouldn't "dial" Anwyn; they'd wait for her to reach out to talk to them directly when she had time and inclination. One didn't interrupt a visit with a vampire queen, and Lyssa had low tolerance for hovering. Of course, Daegan had employed the occasional subconscious mind touch to make sure Anwyn was doing well and wasn't under stress. Since she didn't typically block Gideon out of her mind, he'd done the same thing, such that they'd received an amused playful "push" back at least once or twice, an acknowledgment of their protective natures, both Master and alpha servant.

It felt so damn good to actively call out to her on that link, to feel her respond, turn to him. He savored that first touch, the feminine shape of her in his mind, her intelligence and attention, the warmth and love she gave so generously. When he gave her the situation, he saw her immediately recall all the details she'd set up for the couple. He also saw her weigh the idea, while simultaneously being amused by Ella's intuition and audacity. It made him smile.

So what about it, cher? Are you okay with this?

Yes. I hate for Aaron and Shannon to be disappointed. He's been emailing me for weeks, working out the details, making sure it will be everything she wants. He loves her so much. Damn it, I'm going to shove vitamins down Richard's throat. I keep telling him he needs to quit smoking and get healthier. Every virus knocks him down. A mental pause as she considered, and then he felt a stroke from her mind, a smile. *I assume this doesn't disrupt the one-on-one you have going with Gideon. He's still taking direction from you, same way he'd be doing at a vampire affair, interacting with another servant under our combined or individual command. So it's merely a continuation of the training we've been giving him. Plus, I suspect you already have an idea of how to twist this toward your objective.*

You know me well. As I know you. Daegan's lips curved. *You're more comfortable with him touching a sub, or her touching him, under the command of two Masters. A Mistress would be an entirely different matter.*

You have no proof of that.

He sensed her mental sniff and chuckled. *I've seen your staff subs treat him like their big adopted pit bull. Ella's wrestling with him now. Whereas the Mistresses treat him with courteous warmth...and no touching.*

I have nothing to do with that.

Mm-hmm. You're possessive of your servant, and they know it.

Our servant. And before you get too smug, I'd like to see your reaction to another Master touching him. Fucking him.

Daegan had no conscious response to that, but he was sure she was aware of the predatory heat that rippled through his blood. He chose the graceful way out—introducing an entirely different subject. *How long do you think he'll continue to believe it was a spontaneous decision, rather than a carefully engineered plot, the two of us here alone this weekend?*

Her delicate snort echoed in his mind. *I expect he's already figured it out, but being Gideon, he's just ignoring a lot of things. You know how hard it is for me not to be tuning in to what you two have been doing? I expect a play-by-play detail when I return.*

"It will just make you wet, *cher*. Wet and hot for both of us. We'll have to fuck you for hours to sate you." He spoke the words, knowing it increased the timbre of it in his mind. When he felt her shiver of reaction, he ached for her. God, he hated it when she wasn't here, and he knew Gideon felt the same way. But he knew she needed this weekend. And he had his own goals to accomplish here, some essential training they both knew their servant needed. He made his tone more teasing.

Go back to your shopping and girl talk. You know Gideon is fervently hoping for some girl-on-girl action to report.

Her laughter wrapped around him, and he held onto it, closing his eyes. But she knew him too well. She left a lingering whisper in his mind.

He's getting there, Daegan. It's there already, just waiting in his mind.

He's stubborn as a castle wall.

While you are as relentless as time itself. I know who will prevail. And we all will win. I love you.

She was not a creature of great sentiment, one who gushed *I love yous*. She was a Mistress, after all, so he held the words like the treasure they were.

Try to get into a little trouble. I want to have a reason to punish you when you come back.

Her laughter again, the lightness of it a good sign. She was having fun, she felt safe, wasn't worried about seizures. All was well. If she could have that, he wouldn't begrudge her a couple days away from him and Gideon. Much.

Breaking the link, or at least turning the volume down, he turned to leave the room. Time to tell Ella that Shannon was going to get her vampire and servant fantasy.

Already looking forward to the vampire hunter's reaction, Daegan grinned, imagining his response: *We're going to fucking do* what?

Round 6

Gideon paused at the security view window, but didn't look into the private playroom. He wanted to take a second. He still couldn't quite believe they were doing this and, to be honest, he needed to be sure this was what Anwyn wanted, no matter how much of a pussy Daegan thought he was for checking.

The vampire brushed behind him, a shadow among the shadows, but Gideon felt his hand slide along his nape. *You think I would tease you about your oath to your Mistress, Gideon? If you ever fell one inch short of total devotion to her, I'd flay you alive.*

Same goes. Even if I had to sell my soul to Satan for the superpowers to kick your ass.

He sensed Daegan's grim smile, then he flushed like a damn girl as the male gripped his buttock and squeezed hard before his hand slid away.

Anwyn. Just speaking her name in his mind, a deliberate reach toward her, loosened the weight around his chest. It was amazing how much he fucking missed her. In some way, everything he and Daegan had shared today was a striving for that connection, an extension or part of it. He couldn't really explain it, so like most things he couldn't vocalize, he chose to focus on this one thing. *I need to know what you want, sweetheart.*

He winced. He had a habit of forgetting, using the endearments instead of the honorific, but as she wrapped her thoughts around his, she only gave him tender amusement. Fuck, he missed her.

You're a creature of intuition. Feel what I want, Gideon.

Her desire unfurled in him, way beyond gut level. She wanted him to get lost in this, wanted to see him pleasure this female sub, to let primal male lust, his drive as a sexually confident alpha male, take him over in the face of a trembling, aroused female. It would please Anwyn because he would be acting upon her will and command. It was an act of service to *her*, his Mistress. Every ecstatic cry he wrested from the woman behind this door would be a tribute to her.

Anwyn locked it into place with a caressing whisper. *I trust you, Gideon. When I return, you will convince me of your devotion. I will chain you to the bed, straddle your face. You will replay your time with her in your head, moment by moment, while you bring me to climax with your mouth. It will be very...stimulating.*

His cock hardened, like he needed that area to be any more noticeable. According to the specifications of the fantasy, he'd changed into nothing more than a pair of black snug brief shorts that covered his ass and upper thighs, barely, and made it clear he had enough of a package to make a woman happy. He'd felt a little foolish until he saw Daegan's expression. A shot of heat had gone through those dark eyes, making Gideon feel...well, a little cocky, no pun intended. Ella's jaw had dropped at the sight of him, but Chantal had pushed it closed. Then she'd handed the young woman a light oil to spread over his upper body, to make it gleam.

Maybe it had been Anwyn's command, what she wanted from him, but he felt differently toward Ella than the usual affection, laced with harmless flirtation. When she approached with the oil, he had a predatory restlessness, knowing she was going to slide slick fingers over his body.

She'd sensed it as well, because instead of teasing him, she'd kept her eyes lowered, her lips pressed together, a little nervous. Daegan's focus stayed on him, picking up that heightened sexual aggression.

Once Ella had her hands cruising over him, though, she got less nervous. Her own nature stirred, such that she deliberately lingered over his biceps, his pectorals, stepping in close enough he knew she could feel his breath on her hair. With every passing moment, the stretch of those shorts got more of a workout. He was close to letting out a growl. When her fingers slid a little low on the abdomen, cruising toward the waistband, Daegan *did* growl.

Gideon lifted his head, met the male's weighted stare. Daegan slid that stern glance Ella's way, sending her scampering. Before she slid from the room, Gideon caught her mischievous smile, flicked his way.

But now he returned his attention to the present. Daegan was dressed in his signature black, but uptown sharp. Silk shirt open at the throat, belted slacks, all dangerous elegance. Though Chantal was conferring with him on some final details, he gave Gideon a nod.

Go on in and get it started.

Gideon moved to the door to the private playroom, but when he put his hand on the doorknob, he paused. He couldn't go in yet. He didn't have everything he needed.

What Anwyn had given him was part of it, but not all. The realization was unexpected, but then a lot of things were taking him off guard tonight. Something sexy and perilous moved in Daegan's dark eyes, seeing his dilemma. Leaving Chantal with a murmured word, he came to Gideon and put a firm hand onto his shoulder. He brushed his mouth over Gideon's.

"I do not doubt your devotion to me, either. Everything you do in that room will be the will of your Master and Mistress. Do not doubt yourself. We don't." *Unleash that part of you Anwyn loves. The male animal that will not be tamed.*

Gideon had his hand curled in the fancy silk of that collar before he realized it. His next move was pure response to what was building in him, a domino effect of

Anwyn's thoughts, Ella's teasing touch, the challenge in Daegan's eyes. When he slammed his mouth on the vampire's, Daegan was ready for him, already digging his fingers into Gideon's hair, tugging, giving him a cut of fang that drew blood on his lip and had Gideon drawing away with a feral sound of his own.

The urgency of the kiss reminded Gideon of everything he and Daegan had done tonight. Particularly that confusing edge they'd approached several times, each near miss increasing the demand in his gut. What they were about to do, it was still part of it. He felt that from Daegan, the same way he'd felt it from Anwyn. They'd said it outright. With every breath, every act, he served their will. There was no thinking to it. He knew it, because they were in his soul.

That brazen edge died back, leaving him a bit overwhelmed. But he wasn't going to turn all chickenshit now. He managed a casual shrug, one that put a wry, knowing curve to Daegan's lips. Then he turned away. He could do this. Hell, he'd hunted vampires and stood fast before the Vampire Council. Pleasuring a beautiful, willing woman, making her sexual fantasy come to life—no way he was going to admit that could make his stomach flipflop like a trout, merely because he'd gotten used to belonging exclusively to two people.

Everything you do in that room will be the will of your Master and Mistress.

Gideon stepped into the room.

The gray stone floor and stone façade for the walls, illuminated with dim electric torch light and candles, gave the room a sinister look. There were weapons mounted on brackets embedded in the stone. The weapons were mostly fake, but they looked pretty good, the metal caught by the gleam of the candles. Chains and various types of restraints hung from hooks at key points among the weaponry. A wooden stock in one corner and an iron maiden in the other were the obvious Martha Stewart choices to flank the unlit fireplace. But there were other, different choices. A couch draped in silk and pillows, several viewing chairs. A faux bearskin rug soft as the real thing, because Anwyn had one in her playroom, and she'd taken him on it more than once. It had felt pretty good on his ass, to tell the truth.

The room focused its occupant on power and pleasure...and the dangerous edges of both. The main feature of the chamber underscored it—a steel, freestanding frame anchored to the center of the floor, with a variety of hooks and eyebolts to maximize restraint and suspension options.

Since Gideon could scent the arousal and nervousness of the woman currently positioned in a vertical spread-eagle and cuffed to that frame, he'd say the room was doing its job in spades.

Shannon was an attractive woman, about five-seven, slim but with the kind of generous curves that attracted his gaze, particularly when she was stripped completely naked, as she was now. The entry door was behind her, so as he closed it, Gideon took his time, something lazy and dangerous unfolding in him as his gaze coursed down the line of her raised and stretched arms, the hint of breast he could see at this angle, the slope of her back, the flare of her ass. He did like a nice ass, especially one tilted up and framed like this one was. That was the effect of the stilettos and waist cincher she wore, respectively, and the way her legs were spread and cuffed.

Velcro straps held the shoes on her feet, wrapped over the top of them and beneath the soles. Damn if that kind of foot bondage wasn't hot. His cock was staying hard as steel, keeping him appreciative of the genius who had come up with Lycra shorts. He'd be strangling in denim, no matter that it was his usual preference.

Across the room was a large mirror. Aaron, Shannon's fiancé, was behind that glass, watching everything as it unfolded. Now that the game was in play, Ella would be with him, ready to help him understand things from a submissive perspective, as Shannon reacted to what happened in this room. But a lot of what Ella planned to do involved standing quietly against the wall of that small room, so he could get as lost in the experience as they hoped his fiancée would.

You were listening to the strategy session with Ella and

Chantal. I thought you were too busy freaking out to pay close attention.

He decided to ignore that smartass remark from the world's most arrogant vampire in favor of some better things. As such, he also dismissed the other viewing room from his mind. If he had the choice of paying attention to a naked, bound girl or thinking about some guy he'd never met who was getting to see him in tight shorts with a huge cockstand, he'd take Door Number One, please.

Shannon had smooth tan and olive skin, evidence of her mixed Maori heritage. *See, I did listen to Ella's book report.* Somewhat. Experiencing it firsthand was nice, though. Shannon's waist length brown hair was wavy, curling a bit. The way it brushed against her skin made a man want to wrap his hands in it, use it to hold her fast as he fucked her from behind while pushing her down on all fours.

Jesus, had that come from him? Well, it was hardly his fault. She was all tied up and obviously hugely turned on by it. She had that little trembling nervousness, a mixed-signal, 100% aphrodisiac.

Was that why Anwyn and Daegan had given him his head here? Anwyn had affected him like no other woman had, taking him over, commanding his submission, but before her, and even now, it was the delicate ones, the submissive ones, like Ella or this woman, who could call a different side of him, an alpha who might not be a Master, but who definitely knew how to hold the reins in the bedroom. He had a compelling, implacable desire to make a woman lose her mind, claw his back to shreds and beg him for more.

They wanted to see that side of him, wanted to see him do it. They'd taken off his leash, somewhat literally, and wanted to see what their pit bull would do in a room with a sleek, lovely female trussed up and helpless to his animal nature. They wanted to feel it as it happened, a performance for them.

And fuck, what a stage. Thirty minutes earlier, two other staff subs had brought her here. They'd worn head masks that hid their faces from Shannon, and gags that prevented any conversation with her. While they made her stand on the bear skin rug, they massaged her with a vanilla warming oil from neck to toes. They'd slipped fingers inside of her, oiling her anus and pussy as well. The massage was intended to relax and arouse her, while the intimate handling of her body, and their inability to offer any spoken reassurances, would increase her anxiety, that interesting line between arousal and fear.

She'd been hooked and laced into a deep blue-grey corset-style waist cincher, one of his personal favorite types of women's garb, given that it left all the good stuff bare and emphasized it tenfold. In the mirror's reflection, he could see the solid round weight of her breasts, the taut nipples. Her ass's tempting heart shape was enhanced to the point his palms itched, wanting to take a good handful. They'd added a matching tiny thong to it. He could hook a finger into it and tug, putting that pressure on the pussy women loved.

Given how she was tied up, she was a gift just waiting for a man. He wasn't sure how her fiancé was restraining himself, but if there was one thing Gideon had learned from his Master and Mistress, anticipation just made it all the sweeter and edgier for them. And though the subs suffered from the wait, he knew it made it deeper and more intense for them as well. Wouldn't catch him admitting that anytime soon, though. Not verbally, at least.

As he'd noted when he came in, they'd cuffed her hands to the frame, above her head and outward. They'd done the same to her legs, making her body form an X. They'd also placed a corset collar on her throat, lacing the front snugly so it made her hold her head up and kept her neck rigid. This particular steel frame had an additional set of restraints to it, a modification Anwyn had made. Two pairs of steel bars could be unfolded from the tracks in the vertical sides of the frame and locked into horizontal positions on either side of the bound slave. Those bars could be hooked to a waist strap or collar to enhance the sense of being utterly immobilized. That had been done to the corset collar, so Shannon could only see as far as her straining peripheral vision could take her.

The other set of bars were attached to a thick strap that had been buckled on her waist, over the waist cincher. Two chains ran down the front of the strap and between her legs. The subs had positioned those chains on the outside of her labia, increasing the psychological sense of her cunt being spread open.

She was trembling even harder now. She'd heard the snick of the door. Ten minutes ago, they'd left her alone, deliberately, and from direct experience in this situation, he knew ten minutes could seem like an eternity. She was straddling that line between terror and anticipation. But she was also violently aroused. That quivering wasn't all fear, not by a long shot. Her pussy's honey was a thick perfume to someone with his senses. His nostrils flared, taking it all the way into his gut, into his balls. And just like that, what he was, who he needed to be, kicked in. No more freaking out.

When he started to move, her head jerked, an involuntary reaction since she couldn't turn to see him. As he drew closer, he picked up the more finite details. Her ears were pierced, but they'd taken any jewelry away, leaving her entirely vulnerable except for that collar.

He heard her audible swallow, her voice rasp. "Who's there?"

In answer, he put his hands on her shoulders. She jumped, but then settled, taking a shaky breath as he made a reassuring noise. He wasn't ready to talk yet. Instead, he slid his touch along the base of her neck, following the edge of the corset collar. Gathering up all that long, thick hair, he worked his fingers through it. It was thick as it looked, beautiful, spilling over his hands. He delved deeper into it, found her scalp and stroked. Then tugged. He didn't want to pet her hair like a soothing girlfriend. He gave her a man's touch, stroking deep, pulling, giving her sexual demand coupled with the strength of a male caress. Like the subs' prep of her body, it would keep her worked up and wet. He savored that.

"Are you...the vampire, or the servant? Please talk to me. I'm getting a little freaked out here. I've never done this."

She had a pretty voice, that New Zealand accent with a desperate touch of wry humor that told him she knew how to laugh and play. Though he'd lost that ability a long time ago, he liked a woman who had it. Anwyn had it, even with the challenges she faced as a vampire. It was a nice thing.

"Mmm." Noting a ripple of gooseflesh over her skin, he closed the small space between them. It brought his body right up against her. Even nicer. Her ass and thighs against his thighs, the ache of his cock. Her bare shoulder blades against his chest. The smooth olive skin was as soft as it looked. When the silk of the waist cincher slid against his abdomen, he ran a finger over the edge of the cincher, just below her shoulder blades. "Are you cold, darling?"

"Some." When he rubbed the hardness of his cock against her buttocks, nice and slow, there was an audible quiver in her tone. It felt good, so he did it again, even slower. Not being too aggressive about it, but letting her know it was going to happen, that she had to get used to having it around. And hell, it wasn't just strategy. It felt damn good to rub a cock against a woman's backside. The catch in her throat was suggestive as hell.

The heat of a third mark body would warm her up pretty fast, so he kept the rest of himself pretty close as well. He didn't like it when a woman was cold. "I'm the servant."

"Okay... Can I...can I talk?"

"For now. You're going to be gagged soon, and then there'll be no talking. We'll blindfold you, so there'll be no seeing. What...my Master does to you...it will make it more intense."

Okay, if she kept gulping air like that, she was going to dehydrate. He noted a pitcher of water had been left on a table by the couch. He'd make use of that when needed. Idly, he wondered if there was any ice in it and what he could do with that.

"They put this collar on me. Seems...odd, if he's a vampire. You know, wanting to bite my neck and all. Should we...ah, take it off?" A little chuckle wobbled on her lips.

She's trying to top to gain a sense of control, Gideon. Direct the situation. It's a common thing new submissives try to do. And some high-powered ones.

The ironic tone told him exactly who Daegan meant with that little dig, but Gideon decided to let that go. He'd already recognized what Shannon was doing, mainly because Gideon *had* tried things like that. Acknowledging that to Daegan would just make the fanged bastard smug.

Her brown hair was still spilling through his hands as he kept up his stroking and tugging. When she tried to tilt her head into his touch, it almost made him smile. But he leaned in to speak against her temple. "Your neck belongs to my Master. No one else. That's why it's collared that way. The rest of you, though..."

Bringing his lips down, he nuzzled the shell of her ear. "He's given that to me to enjoy. Would you like that?"

Round 7

Shannon didn't know what she'd been expecting. Aaron had told her he was doing this for her birthday, that it was time to go beyond the tentative first steps they'd taken at home, the experiments and ideas, and try them out in a full-fledged D/s scene. He'd called it a test run. She'd imagined it like a rehearsal, with lots of laughter, missteps, do-overs and none of the expectations and anxiety that came with the real thing. This was *way* beyond expectations. She was scared, aroused...intrigued. With one breath along her ear, this male sent sensation straight down to her curling toes. While she couldn't see him, he was all powerful muscle. The scent of heat and danger to him, along with that impressive bar of steel that was teasing her ass, had alarmed her. But she hadn't freaked out. Not quite, thank God. The servant seemed to have a knack for knowing just how hard to push. Literally and figuratively.

She had to quell a snort at the thought, but the rest of her wasn't laughing. The hands curled in her hair suggested he could pretty much do anything he wanted with her. Break her neck, fuck her twelve different ways. But the way his stroking felt, and the slick slide of his body against her, confused her, made her *want* to see what he would do with her.

It was undeniably frightening, to be bound and at the mercy of strangers, but she had to remember she wasn't, not really. Aaron was watching. He would keep her safe, no matter what. Beyond that, even though this man was unknown to her, the press of his body, the sound of his voice...they were reassuring. Oddly, she felt that while he might demand things from her that stretched her limits, he also wouldn't let anything harm her.

Such an entirely unfounded, fanciful thought would normally amuse her, but this moment didn't call for her usual brand of humor. Later she'd wax philosophical about all this, and Aaron would laugh at her, fully expecting her to dissect all of it that way—but in this second, a lot of other deeper, simpler and more primal things were happening. As well as a few smallish concerns.

She wanted to let loose, savor, but she hadn't been expecting such a devastating assault on her senses. Did her fiancé really intend for her to completely let go, enjoy the fantasy to the nth degree? How far was too far?

Aaron had commanded her... Commanded, imagine that? It gave her a sexy shiver, just remembering it. He'd commanded her to just feel and react, not analyze. *There are no wrong responses. I want to see you get lost in the fantasy.* Wow. Could she trust that? The stranger had said "just feel" as well, so he must be keyed into the script.

She took a deep breath. She'd take the leap, and assume her fiancé was totally fine with her enjoying...well, everything, including this male. Worst case scenario, Aaron could punish her if she was *too* bad.

"That's a devilish smile." She heard amusement in the stranger's voice. Butterflies returned to her stomach as his hands left her hair, skimmed along her shoulders, then up the length of her bound arms. He was testing the strain on her joints, and then the tightness of the cuffs, sliding his fingers beneath to caress her wrist pulse. "I expect you're a handful and a half for your Master."

"I bet you are, too."

The servant's dry chuckle sent a ripple of sensation over her skin again. "He just said, 'you have no idea.'"

She closed her eyes, clutching the cuffs as he pressed his mouth to her shoulder. His touch dropped to her hips, fingers molding low to touch flesh, but only after he'd followed the line of the waist cincher, learning her shape.

"So he can talk in your head," she said. It was all role playing, but she wanted to get into the fantasy, just as Aaron had said. Being a little afraid was part of it, but she didn't want to be too scared to ask questions. This might be a once-in-a-lifetime experience, after all. "Would you...tell me more about being a servant?"

There was a long pause, and it was almost as if he was searching for an answer in himself that he might not have ever articulated, not to another person. It reminded her of her early struggles to tell Aaron what she felt, her desires to be a submissive. The vulnerability that came with those conversations...she sensed it in the male's response. Maybe she was making things up in her head, but it made her feel closer to this stranger, a common, vital bond between them.

"You serve your Master," he said at last, slowly. "Whatever he desires, whatever he needs. Sometimes you know what he needs before he does. Mine sometimes needs an ass kicking."

She swallowed on a chuckle as he moved to trace her abdomen, up, up. "Ah..." She quivered as he cupped her breasts. Didn't touch her nipples, merely held the weight. It was the most incredible feeling, to be handled this way, a body restrained to be used for the pleasure of two men she didn't even know. Aaron was watching. Was he getting hard, imagining it was his hands on her breasts? Or was he imagining what he would do to her when they were done? Reasserting his claim on her, that deliciously male territorial nature. The savagery of it scorched her blood.

"What do you do for a living?" The servant followed the outside of her breasts with his knuckles. Her nipples were drawing up, hardening, begging for contact now. Though he kept away from them, he was looking over her shoulder, staring at them. In her peripheral vision, she had a vague impression of dark hair falling over the brow of a strong face, vivid blue eyes, a warrior's serious expression. She knew from tactile, real time experience that he was wearing nothing but a pair of tight brief shorts that left nothing to the imagination. She swallowed against the incredibly arousing hold of the corset collar.

"Books. I do...books." They weren't going to need to gag her. She was losing the ability to talk.

Her sexy tormentor grew serious. "Shannon, my Master requires a clear answer to a question. Focus."

The sexy rumble, the edge of command in the servant's voice, did exactly that. Aaron knew this about her. A command could steady her, help her find her center. This was the most amazing experience ever. She wasn't sure she ever wanted it to end. "I work in a bookshop. They call me...a book pimp, because I love books so much."

"My Master likes books as well. You'll have a lot to talk about. When he wants you to talk. First, he prefers to hear you scream."

Okay, there went her focus, like a baby elephant slamming his arse onto a down pillow, a volcano eruption of feathers.

"What else do you like to do?"

She let out a whimper as he finally touched her nipples. A brush of sensation with his fingertips, then another. Back and forth, back and forth. "Oh..." She was writhing in her tight bonds, not able to move enough, and the stimulation was immediate and intense. "Oh, God..."

"We asked you a question, Shannon. Answer it."

For a servant, he was pretty damned masterful. And relentless. "Music," she gasped. "Oh, God, that feels good. I play...guitar. Love to dance."

"You're dancing now." His touch slipped away from her nipples, then he gripped her breasts again, squeezed and kneaded. As she was undulating against that touch, it was rubbing her ass against him. Aaron and she had talked about this fantasy. She didn't want any other male inside of her, and she still didn't, but it was a titillating sensation, to have an aroused cock so near, knowing it was more than ready to fuck her. Knowing she was helpless, if this male wanted to break the rules. Something was taking her over; thinking of this as a fantasy was getting tremendously harder.

"Love the tongue stud," the servant murmured, his mouth teasing the corner of hers. "Saw it when you were panting with lust there, wiggling that hot little ass of yours against me. Put that tongue out here, so I can play with it a minute."

She did, and was amazed at how provocative *his* tongue could be, rolling over that metal stud, caressing the corners of her lips. "That would feel fucking good against my cock. I bet your Master loves the way you go down on him."

She didn't know how to respond to that. Her senses were being overwhelmed. A sexy stranger's hands, her fiancé's eyes on her, and the sense that they were waiting for one more to join the party.

Or maybe not. Maybe he was already here. The servant said his Master could read his mind, but of course that was role playing, right? He had to be within earshot.

When she shifted her gaze as far as she could in both directions, she didn't see anything. It was so unnerving, to have her head immobilized and only a limited sight range. But then she glanced left, as far as she could, and started under the servant's hands. A tall male stood there, though she was absolutely sure no one had been there a moment before. No one could move that fast. Maybe there was a hidden panel in the wall. It was an impressive effect, but even more impressive than that was the "vampire" himself.

He was all in black, leaning against the wall. And he wore an incredible mask, shaped like a raptor's head, complete with a sharp curved beak. Sleek brown short feathers layered the upper part of his face, but left his jaw and sensual, cruel mouth visible. Where longer feathers folded into the sides of the mask, she could tell he had short dark hair. He had his arms crossed over his chest. The male behind her had more of a brawler's build. This one had a lean physique that nevertheless emanated even more power.

She jumped as the fire started in the grate with a pop of noise and flame. "More heat," the servant murmured at her ear.

"Magic," she managed.

"Well, a gas log remote," he offered, showing it clasped in his hand. She snuffled on a hysterical giggle. Then that creature against the wall moved, claiming her full attention again. When the flames caught the glint of dull metal, she realized the vampire wore two pewter talons, on his middle and fore fingers. One had the head of a dragon on the largest knuckle, the other the head of a wolf. The tips were wicked sharp points, and, even more disturbing, curved razor blades arched over the heads of the dragon and wolf.

"He's your Master," she said on a really dry throat.

"Mm-hmm. He has a different kind of magic for you now. Time for you to be quiet."

"No." Alarm surged in her chest, making her choke out the protest.

The servant caressed her hip, then he slid down, parting her labia. Shannon bucked up against the stimulation, not expecting it, not expecting that knowledgeable caress of her clit. "You know you serve your Master here," he said. "Will you trust him?"

"Can I trust...either of...you? Oh...fuck." The hoarse, animal sound that came from her throat startled her.

"Oh, us you definitely can't trust." The servant pushed inside her pussy with his thick fingers, just a little, but it jolted her. It had been a long time since anyone's fingers but hers or Aaron's had been there. "But do you trust your Master?"

She lifted her eyes toward the mirrored window. Aaron had given her this, this ultimate fantasy, more than she'd ever anticipated. But beyond that, he'd been willing to take this journey with her, figure out what she truly wanted. As dangerous and out of control as this felt, if she said she didn't want this and truly meant it, he'd be in the room in a minute, taking care of her. He was taking care of her now.

"Yes, I do."

The vampire shifted before her. His eyes, visible through the mask openings, were like a raptor in truth, all darkness. Jesus, they did a good job with special effects at this club. "Gag her," he said in a voice of velvet sin. "Her voice no longer matters. She's here for my pleasure."

She was afraid of being gagged. Maybe she could talk

them out of it. "But your servant said...the things I could do with my tongue..."

Those solid black eyes flashed. Pure, piercing command, and a rebuke that didn't require words. The servant's fingers gripped the tight fit of her waist cincher, enhancing the sensual restraint it offered and ironically reminding her of the terms of her submission.

"You're trying to control things, darling. Are you panicking?"

"A little."

"Hmm." He nuzzled her shoulder, well outside the area the vampire commanded as his non-taloned hand wrapped around her throat, putting pressure on the corset collar. She gasped at the sensation, the way the male pinned her in place with just a gaze and that weighted silence.

"Don't play with him, Shannon," his servant murmured against her skin. "He's a predator, and he takes it as a challenge. I promise you're not up for that. Not this first time. Remember—just feel."

Okay, she defied any woman *not* to panic—a lot—when overwhelmed this way. Before she could make another sound, the servant had drawn back from her to retrieve something outside her range of vision and come back with a ball gag he pushed gently into her mouth, situating it firmly on her tongue, holding it down. He followed it up with a thick wad of cloth that further stretched the inside of her mouth and would absorb unsightly saliva. Finally he held it all in place by situating a wide strap between her teeth and cinching it against the corners of her mouth like a horse's bit, buckling it tight behind her head to hold it in place.

The vampire had kept his hand on her throat throughout, his dark eyes tracking every expression on her face, his mouth set in that firm line. She was breathing fast, the thin skin of her nostrils flaring. As much as being rendered completely voiceless alarmed her, she was twice as aroused now. The more helpless she became, the hotter she was getting. Aaron knew that about her, too.

When the servant drew his touch back to her waist, the raptor mask cocked, the direction of the beak helping her follow the vampire's gaze. He was looking at her breasts, though she couldn't tilt her chin down to see what he was seeing.

A moment later, she let out a strangled noise as the tips of those talons scraped her right breast. They had her nerves so worked up, she was sure it felt far sharper than it was, but she couldn't see what he was doing, couldn't look down, and those things had razor blades. She could feel that point moving toward her vulnerable nipple.

The servant cupped her breasts, held them up for his Master. When that sharp point dragged over her nipple, she cried out into the muffled wadding, but she was arching toward the sensation, not away. Her pussy was wet, dripping against her leg. She was helpless to them.

"Blindfold her." The vampire was implacable. "And remove the collar and side bars attached to it. I want access to her throat." Those stern lips curved in treacherous intent. "If I want her to keep her head still, I'll use my hand as a collar and remind her."

"No, no..." She didn't know why her mouth was making that muffled protest, when every part of her was saying yes. Now she knew why "oh God, no, no, no" were never chosen as safe words. Regardless, she would have to fully trust, fully surrender to all of it, because that was what Aaron knew she wanted, needed, craved. Somehow being brave enough to face that was honoring this gift, and his willingness to be her Master. All three of these implacable men—including the one behind the window watching— knew it. In her dreams, she'd hungered to serve as a submissive, but never had the reality of it. *This* was the reality. Part of her ready to bolt screaming, another part reaching, wanting, her mind whirling and about to break free of something that might be good or bad to leave behind. But it was all out of her hands at this point. Almost.

The blindfold was a soft silk, and fit like a glove against her eyes and temples. The servant smoothed it over her face, petting her. As the world went completely black, she tried not to let her teeth chatter with nerves.

"You feel this?" The servant pushed something soft against her palm, his fingers caressing her bound wrist above the cuff. Reflexively, she closed her fist over what felt like a rubber ball, maybe another ball gag, a smaller one.

"Vampires are much more sadistic than humans," the servant said. "My Master doesn't believe in safe words."

The grin in his voice held a taunt, a challenge directed entirely toward the vampire, not her. It gave her a chocolate sweet taste of the erotic undercurrent between the two males. Suddenly, she could envision the fierce vampire, his eyes still hidden behind that mask, pushing the male servant to his knees. He'd fuck him on the floor right before her for the impertinence. Blindfolded, she'd hear the hoarse grunting of a man being punished and pleasured at once, both sensations so intense they'd almost be unbearable. But he'd have to bear it, because it was his Master's will.

Holy God, it just made her hotter and wetter. She had to struggle to focus on the servant's next words.

"Fortunately for you, *your* Master has a touch of mercy. If something becomes too much, you drop this. Don't worry, we'll ask if you dropped it by accident, in case something my Master is doing affects your motor skills." A wicked note of pleasure entered that rough, sexy voice. "Nod if you understand."

She did, a quick jerk.

The vampire spoke now, not in the stern tones he'd used thus far, but in a sensual voice that caressed her ears. "It was almost a shame to put a blindfold on her. She has beautiful eyes. The colors of the ocean during a storm."

"She's beautiful, period. Totally fuckable." The servant's voice became a feral growl that made her quiver anew. "That's what your Master will do when we're done. We'll wear you out, make you scream. Then he'll come in here, fuck you hard, remind you that you belong to him. Probably work over this fine ass of yours, put some stripes on it. It's what I'd do." When he cupped her buttocks, squeezed hard, it set her to rocking against him again, a shameless, involuntary reflex of lust. She panted through the gag, thinking of Aaron coming in with a strap or cane...or just spanking her with the flat of his hand. He had strong hands.

She was robbed of voice and sight. She was just a body to serve them, as the vampire had said. And she'd never been so turned on in her life. Everything was throbbing. Those chains digging into the outside of her labia were wet, she could tell by how it felt, the air caressing her cunt. It clenched in reflex as that talon passed over the top of her breast, perilously close to her nipple again. Then gooseflesh rose as the feathered mask followed the same path. The vampire had taken it off, was teasing her nipples with the feathers, back and forth, relentless stimulation like the constant brush of the servant's hands. She swayed, gurgling against the gag, panting.

"You've fantasized about vampires since you were a little girl," the vampire said. Though the servant had that tough, deep timbre, there was something about this one's voice that compelled strange, crazy things inside her. She could listen to him talk for a few decades and never move from this spot. "But I bet the little girl didn't imagine anything like this," he continued. "A vampire requires absolute submission and surrender from his servant, but from his food...he demands whatever he wishes. Your blood is only part of it. You are feeding his pleasure, his desire, his demands. I'm strong enough to take anything I wish from you and make you offer your life to me for more."

She sucked in a breath as the razor blade bit into her right breast. Just a tiny, tiny cut, that quick sting like a paper cut. She cried out, though, as the vampire pressed his mouth to it. He was so close to her nipple as he suckled that taste away. He could probably do all sorts of acrobatics with that tongue, things that might make her lose consciousness.

When he slid behind her, she realized the wall of muscled support the servant had provided was gone. Now it was just the vampire.

No, the servant was back. His presence steadied her, oddly. However, as he unlaced the corset collar from the front, just as the vampire had ordered, it was a powerful, almost dizzying sensation. She had the freedom to move her head, but before she could, the vampire had placed a hand over her forehead and used that hold to pull her head back against his shoulder at a straining angle. He held her fast. Those dual talons moved down her sternum, avoiding her neck. She could hear her pulse hammering so close to that sensual threat.

I'm strong enough to take anything I wish from you and make you offer your life to me for more.

Mentally, she was just gone. There was no Club Atlantis, there was no carefully planned fantasy. In her mind, she *was* in a room with a vampire and a servant, delivered to their demands and desires, her Master watching all of it with still eyes and pounding heart. His hands would be clenched and his cock hard, seeing what they were doing to her, his property, making her crazy at his command. This was no fantasy. This was the reality she wanted, she craved, no matter if she died from fear, longing or the power of the desire building in her.

"I want to suck on her tits," the servant muttered. "Jesus, those nipples are practically begging for it."

"Ask me."

A hesitation. For some reason, even blindfolded she could sense the two males' gazes meeting over her restrained body, that lingering challenge arcing between them. But the servant didn't push it. Not this time.

"Master, let me suck on her nipples. Let me give her pleasure. Let me give you pleasure by doing it."

A nod against her head from the vampire, and then the servant's callused hands framed her breasts. She sensed him going down, the pressure of his hip against her inner thigh as he planted a knee between her spread feet. She screamed against the gag as he covered one nipple with his mouth. So much sensation... He was right, she was dancing in truth, because she jittered as much as she was able against that devastating assault. Then the vampire clamped his hand on her neck, collaring it. What felt like really, really large, curved fangs slid hard and wet against her carotid.

My, what big fangs you have... Her sense of humor really had the oddest sense of timing, but it was swallowed by the intensity that rolled over her as her whole body yearned toward that base, most primal fantasy, a vampire's fangs piercing her, possessing her, feeding off of her. His servant had a mouth made for sin, suckling, nipping her. He moved to the other nipple, making sure they received equal attention.

"Eat her pussy. Make her come. I want it to rip through her while I'm feeding." The vampire's voice was a near hiss, impossible to disobey or deny. She struggled, though again she had absolutely no idea why. She was being assaulted on all sides, and cried out as the vampire's other hand slipped down her back to her buttocks. He slid his touch intimately between them, playing with the rim, gave one cheek a sharp pinch. "Behave for us, perform well, or your Master will decide you need a good ass fucking to remind you of your place."

Dirty words, sordid threats. They just made her want this even more. Those talon fingers tightened over her throat. She realized he was keeping her head tilted up so high because that razor blade would be right below it. But she wasn't afraid of that. The vampire emanated such utter control, she knew any cut would be deliberate, done with utter precision. Those fangs slid along her carotid again.

Then the servant's touch shifted to her upper thighs. He'd gone down to both knees, because she felt them pressing against the insides of her spread feet. Bracing himself on her thighs, fingers exploring her flesh, he started by lapping up the arousal on her thighs, his hair brushing her clit and labia, teasing them as he got closer and closer to her core. She moved more violently against him, restless demand. His hands replaced the vampire's on her hips and ass to hold her steady for what he wanted. The vampire went back to her breasts, alternating between sharp jabs, the occasional kiss of the blade, lingering caresses and writhing pinches. He didn't draw blood with the blades again, simply kept her nerves on high alert with the delicious threat. When he slid his fangs along her throat once more, his other hand tightened in her hair and she knew he was getting ready to bite her. Everything in her stopped, waiting, like a rabbit in the hands of a hunter, strangely trusting and terrified at once.

"Gorgeous hair," he murmured. "Irresistible. Just like

my *cher's.*"

She wasn't sure what that meant, didn't have the brain to wrap around it, because his servant's mouth found her pussy then. *Oh, God...* How many times had she invoked God tonight? Hopefully, He'd forgive her, because this kind of skill called for reverence.

Lips played with her clit with total authority, tongue easing inside, swirling, suckling her juices and playing with the pleasures of those slick petals. She was rocking again, held fast at the throat by the vampire as her lower body moved as much as the servant allowed. And as overwhelming as all those incredible sensations were, the two of them kept adding to it. The servant parted her buttocks, his fingertips playing there like the vampire's had done. Throughout, he kept teasing, suckling, nipping and scraping her cunt, only now he started to apply himself in earnest. She could hear those sexy wet noises his mouth was making, feel that delicious rough sandpaper of his upper lip and jaw against her thighs.

She was wailing against the gag, and then she shrieked as the vampire's grip tightened and his fangs pierced her artery. It hurt, *God it hurt,* because he did have large fangs, but it was overwhelmed by the rush of endorphins matched by the raging pulse between her legs. They were going to meet somewhere in her chest and make her heart explode. The metallic scent of her own blood filled her nose. A vampire was drinking from her, his servant eating her pussy, and an orgasm was about to overwhelm her, one she couldn't stop, even if she wanted to try.

"Please..." She was incoherent against the gag, but she kept saying it. Then, like the voice of a beloved fallen angel, she heard Aaron's voice. He was in the room now.

"You can come, Shannon. Come for me."

She let go on the last word, helpless to do otherwise. It was like nothing she'd ever felt, an incredible chaos of pleasure, agony, yearning and sheer ecstasy. She screamed herself hoarse, the waves of sensation pounding her, spinning her. She was held between two points, those two powerful sets of hands, and they didn't give her a moment's respite. The servant kept his mouth working between her thighs, the vampire feeding from her throat, as she came and came.

Even when she went limp at last, she was aware of the vampire's feral, hungry growl in her ear, the ease of his fangs as he finished his meal and began to lick her throat instead. She convulsed, making small cries against the gag. No matter how many nerve endings existed in pussy, breasts and nipples, she was pretty sure—at least in this moment—her neck was her biggest erogenous zone. The more he nuzzled it, the more she kept experiencing those jerky, bleating aftershocks. It was incredible.

She knew now why submissives couldn't be trusted to use their safe words. She would have happily died from whatever the three of them wanted to do to her. She was still making those little noises. Vaguely, she realized the vampire had reached up toward her bound hand to pry the rubber ball out of her palm. "You didn't let go."

She could argue with him, because she'd let go on so many levels, but she wasn't sure how to get back to coherence. Her mind was a fog, no control over her limbs. More funny sheep noises as the servant licked her clean, nipping her to make her jump. He hummed, a very satisfied male chuckle against her flesh. "You'll do, darling," he murmured.

He was this vampire's servant, for certain, but there was a different Dom/sub dynamic here than between her and Aaron. They'd acted as two alpha males pursuing the same goal—her utter surrender—with relentless synchronization. This male might submit to this vampire, but she couldn't imagine him submitting to any other male. Perhaps a woman...

She didn't know where that thought came from, but with her mind drifting in that heavenly subspace, so many things were clear and made sense. She could almost feel the presence of a third. The servant had a tentative tranquility backed by the presence of healthy female energy, an energy that had to be a vital part of the equation between these two men. And for tonight, she'd gotten to be a part of it. She was in a drifting state of bliss, never wanting to come down.

"Oh yeah, she's gone." The servant was caressing her face now, her shoulders. He stroked her body, using his touch to ground her to earth, whereas moments before he'd used that same contact to cut her loose, help her fly. When he shifted behind her, she realized the vampire was gone.

The servant pressed a soft, sweet kiss to her shoulder. Loosening the gag, he removed it, but he left the blindfold. A bottle was brought to her lips, giving her a needed drink of water as he cleaned around her mouth with a soft cloth.

"Your Master wants you now, darling."

Her senses reeled as the servant fitted that corset collar on her once more. She couldn't possibly...but maybe she could. Someone else's hands took over the snug lacing, the restriction that reminded her she was owned by another. Remarkably, that simple thought tightened everything in her body. She could become aroused again during this delicious floating feeling. Who'd have thought it? She had no shields, no reservations, no self-consciousness right now. She wanted Aaron inside of her. She needed him. She would beg for her Master's cock, to be taken, to have that sense of total connection, the only thing that had been missing in the whole remarkable experience. He hadn't overlooked it, though. He was here.

She felt Aaron's hands, his lips brush hers, and tears sprang to her eyes. "Thank you," she whispered. "Thank you. I love you."

As the kiss deepened, her fully open heart spilling into his waiting touch, she felt the servant's hands slip away. The place on her neck throbbed, her body vibrated, and all of her yearned to continue the gift they'd started. Aaron had brought her to the starting gate of this new journey between them. But the vampire and his servant, whoever they really were, had launched them.

Based on such an unforgettable experience, she knew the possibilities going forward were endless.

Round 8

"Well, as much as I like *Sons of Anarchy*, I've got to say that beat the hell out of an SOA marathon."

Daegan chuckled. In mutual accord, they'd decided to take a little air, strolling around the warehouse district where Club Atlantis was located. There wasn't much activity this time of night except the occasional sighting of a security guard or homeless person. Here and there they caught a glimpse of a more unsavory element, clinging to the shadows, but nothing of the caliber—or stupidity—that would bother two males capable of dismantling a human body one cracked joint at a time.

"Look at that." With easy strength, Gideon hiked himself up onto a loading dock and reached behind the stack of empty pallets there. Pulling out a football, he tossed it a few feet in the air and caught it. "They must throw it around when they're waiting on deliveries. Hey, go long." He smirked. "Reasonably long, like thirty yards. Not thirty miles down the road."

"You can't throw it that far? I'm disappointed."

Gideon threw, and of course Daegan was already waiting where he'd aimed it, catching it out of the air. "I think mindreading is against NFL rules. Toss it back."

Daegan paused, considering the ball. In about two blinks, Gideon realized he must be replaying it in his head, how it had been thrown. Analyzing it. "You're shitting me. You've never thrown a football?"

"The game has not been around that long."

"Yeah, if you're ancient." Gideon grinned at Daegan's slightly defensive tone. Something the vampire didn't know shit about. Now there was a Red Sea miracle if ever he'd heard it. He walked across the parking lot to him. "Here, let me show you."

When Daegan passed him the ball, Gideon palmed it, showing him where to wrap his hand, the L-shape that brought his fingertips along the lacing. "Now, when you throw it, you want to get some spin on it. The key's the release point, top of the throwing arc, and your footwork. You want to step into it."

Daegan studied him closely as Gideon made the motion. "Being a vamp, you can probably sling the thing halfway across the universe, with enough force to bypass the rules of physics, but if you're working with the elements, this helps."

"All right." Daegan took it back from him, positioned his hand as Gideon had shown him. Almost.

"A little further under. There it is." Gideon helped adjust his grip, stepping into alignment with him. After a brief hesitation, he employed the movements of his own body to put the vampire through the proper form. Taking hold of Daegan's wrist to bring the ball back, Gideon used the pressure of his chest and thigh to demonstrate how he needed to pivot and come back square with the ball's direction. It put Daegan's ass up against his pelvis. Gideon's hand dropped to his waist, his fingers curving loosely into the belt loop of Daegan's slacks, his thumb on the rise of his ass. All to help him throw the ball right, of course. But it reminded him, vividly, of what they'd been doing before they'd been role playing for Shannon and her Master.

He was feeling pretty good and loose right now, but the proximity reminded him that neither of them had found release in that chamber. He was tempted to take a bite out of Daegan's neck, press his cock harder against his ass. He could feel Daegan's stillness, his awareness of the desire, but before anything could come of it, Gideon stepped back. "I think you got it. Let's see it."

"Go...long?" Daegan arched a brow at him. Giving him a tight grin, Gideon took off across the parking lot.

It was a decent first attempt, but Gideon had to use his third mark speed, because it went a little wide and wild. He talked Daegan through it a couple more times, and of course the vampire was a quick study. He was doing an acceptable spin by the time they took a seat on the loading dock and set the ball aside.

"We need some beer," Gideon noted. "I think there was a place—"

"Thirty seconds."

Gideon opened his mouth, but Daegan was gone. Thirty seconds? Jesus. He'd time the guy, but wanted to give him the latitude to buy Bubble Yum or Pop Rocks if he wanted to do so. That made him think of the age old sexual use for Pop Rocks, the candy's fizz on the flesh, tingling against the mouth of the person covering them. He adjusted himself in the jeans. If he thought he could get away with it, he'd jack off so his mind wasn't so much on sex. Food would help.

Hey, some Twinkies would be great if they've got 'em. The yellow cake kind, not the chocolate. And some Fritos. Barbecue flavor.

Eleven seconds later, Daegan dropped a grocery bag next to him, giving him a sardonic look. "Anything else?"

"Did you steal those?"

"I left money by the cash register. Probably overpaid."

Gideon grunted, started on the Fritos. Daegan tried one, then leaned back on one arm, lifting the beer to his mouth. He'd sat down close, such that the arm was positioned just behind him, his hip brushing Gideon's, and it didn't bug him. Truth? It kept him kind of revved.

"Which is why I did it, vampire hunter. We're not done yet, remember?" Daegan gave him that heavy-lidded look. "And no, you wouldn't have gotten away with it. Cock getting harder?"

"Not going to tell you if it is."

Daegan bared fangs, that wicked, dangerous smile that sent another shot of arousal straight to the place in question. Gideon decided he'd move it off that footing for awhile, one, because his curiosity was getting the better of him, and two, because he really did want the snacks. He gestured with the Twinkie. "You can't throw a football, which is the most pansy-assed thing I've ever heard. But *sometime* during X times a hundred years you had to take advantage of your super-fast, super-hard-to-detect mad skills to peek in a really hot girl's bedroom. Or hang out in a sorority for a Girls-Gone-Wild video-in-training. If you give me details, I'll let the football thing slide. I won't accuse you of being a total girl. Or tell James, because it's just more satisfying to make fun of someone if you have help."

"I haven't been involved in any sports in the past several hundred years," Daegan shrugged. "It's difficult when you can lap the field before anyone moves."

"Yeah, yeah. That's a lame excuse. You're just a big pussy nerd with fangs."

"Sports used to be about testing combat skills; they weren't for million dollar contracts that put you above the law if you killed your pregnant girlfriend or got caught with illegal drugs."

"So you're saying Lancelot didn't get all sorts of groupie sex because of the way he handled his lance?"

"I'm not going to dignify that with a response."

"So now we can add sanctimonious, self-righteous and pretentious to the list. Oh, I forgot, they're all the same thing. *Pansy-assed.* Isn't there a Latin word for that? *Pansius Assidus.* I'm sure someone who spends more time reading than watching TV would know the right word."

"If there was, I wouldn't waste the knowledge on a Neanderthal who only reads cartoon books or magazines with center tri-folds of naked women."

"Now you're just trying to hurt my feelings. And you totally blew off the Girls Gone Wild thing."

"I might be inclined to share a few stories, if you share another Frito."

Gideon offered him another and Daegan took it. Vamps could eat small bites of things without it messing up their constitution, and Gideon felt absurdly pleased that Daegan seemed to like the taste of something he'd chosen.

"I'll like tasting it on your lips better." The idle observation, the way Daegan's gaze lingered on his mouth, gave Gideon that restless feeling, but the vampire was in a similar mood, willing to be lazy about it, take his time. Of course, that altered Gideon's interest, perversely ramped it up, but he sat on it, played it cool. Didn't matter if Daegan could read it from his mind or not, because Gideon knew Daegan wasn't as cool as he was pretending to be. His cock wasn't the only one getting hard, and that gave Gideon an unexpectedly pleasant feeling, with the right edgy bite to it. No pun intended.

Daegan shot him an arch look, leaning back again as he took another swallow of beer. His gaze automatically flickered over the area, doing a sweep as he always did. Always watchful. Always protective.

During the lull, Gideon replayed the football lesson in his mind. The crease of concentration on his fine brow as

Daegan figured out how to do something he'd never done before, something Gideon could show him. He hadn't ever really thought about Daegan's childhood, but he guessed it was pretty strange. Not a lot of tossing around the football with Dad or other kids.

"Your father taught you how to throw a football?"

Gideon slanted him a glance. It was odd, sometimes, how Daegan would follow his thoughts like that and then just come in as if they were having a conversation. He kind of liked it. "No, that was my coach. My dad was a bookworm, a teacher. But he came to my games, found me books and clippings about top players and winning strategies, things that made me a better player."

Daegan made a quiet noise, then Gideon yelped as the vampire caught the back hem of his T-shirt, pulled it up and swiped the cold beer bottle along his lower back. Twisting around, he tried for a punch, and his arm was caught, Daegan using the momentum to turn him, roll him to his side. The vampire had him pinned, arm twisted to his back, the other hand on the back of his neck. Gideon went still. He could struggle, try to break the hold, but when Daegan lowered his mouth to his nape and held the contact there, Gideon found himself waiting, wanting.

"You just rolled me on the other bag of Fritos," he said. "Asshole."

"When you showed me how to throw the football, you wanted to fuck me, Gideon. I saw a glimpse of it in your mind." Daegan's grip shifted, going from the back of the throat to the front, holding tight, a Master's threat in the grip. "You want me to surrender to you, the way you do to me or Anwyn? Top me?"

The smartass response—though not really the smartest answer— was, "Yeah, what you going to do about it?" But that wasn't the truth, was it? Watching Daegan's absorption with throwing a football had reminded Gideon of the handful of times he'd caught the vampire watching him and Anwyn, almost like someone who'd stood outside the candy store all his life looking in. Which was crazy, right? He should give the smartass answer and take the consequences.

But they were teaching him not to lie. Well, not to lie about the unexpected things. They indulged a certain level of bullshit about the expected things.

He waffled on it and, as he did, Daegan levered him back to a seated position, releasing his arm. Shifting to sit beside him, shoulder to shoulder, he pinned Gideon with those dark eyes. Gideon couldn't tell if he was reading his mind or not, but he had a feeling he wasn't. Sometimes Daegan did that, wanting to hear it straight from the lips first. "I'm waiting, Gideon."

He thought it through serious, no wise cracking. When at last he spoke, he did so slowly, working on it.

"Yeah, I do want to fuck you, but not the way you're thinking. You've been in control for so long...I figured you'd like the chance to let go sometime. Not just to me. I'd want Anwyn there, that's important. I wonder if you could trust us enough to take care of you. Like you do when you sleep."

It was ridiculous, how much that meant to him and Anwyn, the few times Daegan had slept deep, letting down his guard, trusting them to watch over him.

"It's not like I'm...topping you, or whatever they call it. It's like I'm still serving you, a different way, a way you can trust me to do, because I am..." He cleared his throat. "Your servant."

Daegan's eyes had gone full dark, elevating Gideon's heart rate, because that always meant the vampire was pretty worked up, on a lot of dangerous levels. His lips barely moved. "Say the word that was in your head, Gideon. The one you were almost brave enough to say."

"Not sure if I can. It goes against a lot of things..." Hell, it was the truth. He swallowed, hard. Really hard. "Your slave."

That blackness in Daegan's gaze caught fire. Gideon saw it, accepted it, burned in it. Jesus, he'd follow him into Hell if that's where the Devil said this guy needed to go. He and Anwyn, they'd link arms with him and go anywhere, do anything to be at his side, take care of him. To be chained to him. So yeah, slave fit. Slave actually felt pretty damn good. Though he sure as hell wasn't going to say it in front of anyone else, ever.

Daegan's lips curved then, acknowledging the challenge. But he ran his knuckles along Gideon's cheek, a surprisingly tender gesture. "Perhaps we will do this fantasy of yours one day. I like it when you open your heart, Gideon. It takes a can opener of monstrous proportions, but when it happens, you always surprise me." His mouth got firm, taut, making Gideon want to bite his lips. "In there with Shannon, when you called me Master, I wanted to eat you alive. I want to eat you alive now."

The docks were pretty deserted, and there were a lot of shadows. Gideon wouldn't deny him, he knew that. Not now, probably not ever.

"No, not this time. I want you in the place you belong. My bed."

Gideon met his gaze. "The dungeon might make more sense. I still owe you five strikes with that strap."

"That you do. But we'll hold that for later. As much as I enjoy punishing you, right now, I want this far more."

§

Daegan's bed. He didn't sleep there with Daegan, not without Anwyn. When they came into the room, Daegan put his hand over Gideon's before he could snap on the light. Instead, he tangled their fingers together, put his mouth on the juncture of throat and shoulder, where the stretched collar of the T-shirt allowed him access. As he sank his fangs into Gideon's flesh, just the tips, Gideon's brain scrambled with lust. It was demand, passion, but it wasn't rough and violent. There was no fight here. This was pure, overwhelming seduction, Daegan taking everything out from under him. A continuation of the lesson Gideon realized the vampire had been hammering into his head the whole time.

Yes, Gideon. This is you and me. I want my servant, my slave. I want to take him down, be balls deep inside of him, hear his cries of pleasure, his plea for release, and know he's all mine.

Those capable fingers were removing the T-shirt, opening his jeans with a deft tug, but the words created an overpowering set of wants in Gideon as well. He twisted in Daegan's grasp, caught his mouth with his own. He locked his other set of fingers around Daegan's, so it was like they were wrestlers, facing off, about to begin. Or dancers, if Gideon was willing to admit he danced. Which he wasn't, but if he did dance, Daegan was clearly leading now. He was moving them toward the bed while Gideon did his level best to devour his mouth. When Daegan's fang speared his lip, Gideon cursed, even as he embraced the pain, his cock becoming even more of a steel bar when Daegan suckled that blood off him. Thank God he'd unzipped his jeans or he'd be in pain. Jesus, the guy was so bloody strong. He maneuvered Gideon back to that oversized bed, spun him and shoved him down face forward. Gideon caught the covers in his fists as Daegan's mouth landed on his bare spine, his hands inside the open jeans, gripping Gideon's ass, fondling, kneading.

All the way up on the bed, Gideon. Get in the center on knees and elbows. I want to see your submission to me. It will make me so hard, I might stand over you and come against your back, your fine, fine ass. Perhaps it, and the lashes I will give you later, will remind you that you do not have the right to jack off whenever you have the craving. Your seed, your release, belongs to me and your Mistress.

When Daegan reached between Gideon's spread thighs and gripped his cock in his strong hand, Gideon groaned, fisting the coverlet again. Then he remembered, letting go, spreading out trembling fingers.

"Good man," the vampire whispered in the darkness. "Good boy. My good slave."

It was dark, dark and quiet here, like the inside of a womb. One of those crazy montages was playing through Gideon's mind, the things that led to this moment. Anwyn, curled up between them in the bed at night, but turned face first into Gideon's chest, holding him close as Daegan held them both, his fingers trailing Gideon's back, his forearm resting on Anwyn's hip. Daegan, standing for him at the Council meeting. The vampire had come to find Gideon when he'd run from Anwyn and the male vampire. She and

Daegan had welcomed him home with the joy of people seeing a loved one coming back from the grave.

Finally, more of that montage tonight, everything that had happened. But especially Daegan being not so proud he wouldn't let Gideon teach him something as basic as throwing a football, underscoring he was interested in what Gideon had to offer. That odd candy-store look on Daegan's face as he watched Gideon teach him.

It had always been easier for Gideon to believe Anwyn was the glue that held the three of them together. And he loved his Mistress with everything he was, but now, with Daegan's mouth trailing over his spine, his fingers caressing him and sending his mind spiraling, he was getting a really off-the-wall, crazy thought.

Maybe *Gideon* was the glue that made things work for all three of them, and the only thing standing in the way of it being Super-Glue, not Elmer's, was his refusal to embrace that, what it meant.

He'd do anything for Anwyn, but that wasn't the end of it. Standing separately in his mind was how he felt about Daegan. He'd die for the guy, fight to the last drop of blood for him. He'd wanted to tear apart the young vamps who'd gotten the jump on him tonight. He needed to go fight them now, rather than fight the way this felt, unfolding inside him.

"Gideon." Daegan's touch softened, stroked his hair. "Easy, vampire hunter. You're shaking. It's all right."

Gideon shook his head. In the darkness, there was nothing but truth. *I love you. I love you as much as I love her, damn it. I don't want to fight that shit anymore. I want you to have everything.*

Stillness. Utter weighted stillness. Daegan's fingers shifted, curved around his throat, brought him up so his ass rested on his heels. The vampire was suddenly on the bed right in front of him, those eyes containing some crimson flame, because Gideon could see their flicker.

"Say it to me, Gideon." Daegan's voice had a rough quality. Gideon could make out a strain to his handsome features, an intensity that made him want to touch Daegan's firm mouth, much as he touched Anwyn's face when he knew she needed him. So he did. Reached out to touch. He wasn't at all surprised when Daegan caught his wrist and stopped him. It broke Gideon's heart open even more, because of what it said to him.

"I'm going to touch you. Only way you're stopping me is if you break my arm."

Daegan's jaw flexed, and then his hold loosened enough that Gideon brought his knuckles to the male's face and slid his fingers into his hair to tighten, tug. Daegan had opened the silk shirt, and so Gideon let his fingers slide down his sternum, aware of the thud beneath the firm flesh. Daegan curled back a lip, showing a sharp fang, but his eyes kept their intense lock on Gideon's face.

"Say it to me," the vampire repeated. "Can you?"

"Yeah. Not sure if I can say it more than once, though." But that was a lie. His heart had been saying it for awhile now, with every other thump, the in-between beats for Anwyn. "I love you. Master. I mean it. And everything that means to me."

Daegan nodded. "I want you take your hands off me now, Gideon. Lock them behind your back, lift your chin. Show me your devotion by obeying. For once."

That made Gideon grin, no help for it, but the wry twist to Daegan's lips said he'd intended that response and was giving him a chance to ease up. He knew how hard the emotional could be for Gideon. But Gideon didn't feel overtaxed by it right now. It felt...peaceful. Right. And overwhelming.

He swayed, but Daegan's arm slid under his, palm flat on the center of Gideon's back, steadying him, bringing him close to Daegan's chest. The vampire pushed Gideon's face down into his shoulder before he leaned over him, punctured his throat from the back, sinking the fangs in deep as they could go as he held a tight grip on his nape, an excruciating physical and emotional demand. Gideon was held fast, curved over in that submissive posture to his Master.

His fingers locked together, biceps flexing with the effort of resistance. He wanted to touch him. Needed. *Fuck...Master. Let me touch you.*

Instead, Daegan moved off the bed, shrugged out of the shirt, opened the slacks. In a tantalizing moment, he was completely naked, showing a damn impressive erection, already tipped with fluid that Gideon's enhanced sense of smell detected and inhaled like a cocaine fix. For all that he was pale, the guy had a body meant for fucking. Daegan got back on the bed, his gaze on Gideon's.

Eyes down, servant. And keep your hands behind your back.

Gideon fought the overwhelming urge to disobey, to simply tackle him. His muscles were quivering with the strain of self-deprivation. When Daegan moved against his body, his heavy, aroused cock dragged across Gideon's thigh, making the long groin muscle twitch. He had to resist the overwhelming desire to push against Daegan, insist, demand, hell, beg. Especially when Daegan reached behind him, teasingly close to Gideon's tangled fingers, and gripped his ass, a tight hold as he nudged Gideon's jaw to the side and sank his fangs in at another spot. It made Gideon curse and draw in an aroused breath at once.

But then he got the keys to Heaven. Daegan's touch moved over Gideon's clasped hands, loosened the fingers, a tacit approval for him to do as he desired. He didn't need a second invitation. His fingers bit into Daegan's ass as the male suckled his throat. He felt Daegan's cock brush his belly again, the damp tip marking him. Gideon ran his hands up the male's back, over the architecture of powerful muscle, lean, perfect, invincible. And all his, in a way that few understood, particularly when it was him who was the servant, taking the orders. That didn't matter. He knew what he knew.

Sliding his fingers back into Daegan's hair, Gideon clutched as the male pulled blood from his throat. His chest pressed against Daegan's, and the slide of a nipple across his own was enough to send fire jolting down into his balls. He pressed into that cock aggressively now. He wasn't some girl, willing to wait. He wanted to be fucked, wanted his Master to take him down, take him hard. But he also didn't want to give up this contact.

You will have the chance again. If you deserve it. Back

down on knees and elbows, vampire hunter. I want to take what's mine. Don't make me force you. I command you to do all this willingly, surrender the same as you started.

Gideon managed it, though he knew Daegan understood just how difficult it was to give up the contact, as well as resist the need to fight. Somehow he swallowed it down. It was worth it. When Daegan's body slid over his, covering him, his arm braced along the outside of Gideon's, he felt something powerful and overwhelming move inside his heart. Putting his forehead against the powerful biceps, Gideon closed his eyes. He bit into the male's flesh, hard, as Daegan slid his lubricated cock into Gideon's ass, coming in, and in, and in, until he was fully seated, ever the demanding Master. His Master.

"Fuck, you feel so good. Hold me tight, Gideon. I want to feel you come all the way to your soul." Daegan began to thrust, and he knew just how to do it. Strong and relentless, hitting the right spot inside, so it was an insistent squeeze, stroke and push all together, making Gideon's world spiral out of control within five strokes.

"You beg when you want to come. I want to hear it."

"Fuck..." Gideon muttered it, and Daegan caught his hair, giving him that delicious edge of pain in amid the crazed pleasure.

"All mine, vampire hunter. Your fine, fine ass is mine. Say it."

"Yours. Fuck, all yours. Please..."

He never thought he'd beg. Never thought he'd love one vampire, let alone two, with this all-consuming fire and need. But with them, his soul was split wide open, every dark fear and wish exposed, and the scariest part was, he trusted them with all of it. Anwyn and Daegan. Together or apart, they both owned him. He'd serve them with everything he was, whether they needed him to be a wiseass, give them his challenge and resistance, or this, proof that all of it meant the same thing. He loved them. And nothing would ever change that.

"Keep begging."

"Please..." He was grunting with every thrust. Jesus, the

guy could use that cock, and his strength, to take someone right to the edge of agony and ecstasy at once. Daegan's balls slapped against his, and then Daegan took his elbows out from under him. With his arm banded across Gideon's chest, he pressed him down in the quilts, his pelvis tucked in flush to Gideon's, working him hard against the mattress, pummeling him. He was trapped, overwhelmed by the vamp's strength, and knew Daegan was making it clear he was completely overwhelmed, submitting to him utterly, no fight. Gideon thrashed beneath him, but the climax was taking him. He humped up against Daegan's thrust, trying to reach that point, knowing he couldn't until Daegan said so, but he wanted Daegan to feel the clutch of his muscles, the flex of his ass, and make him come along for the ride as well. That was half of it, right? He might surrender, but he was never going to be docile.

"Never in this universe. Thank God. Come for me, Gideon. Come now."

"You, too...come too."

They came together, a hot release of seed, male groans of satisfaction. Slick bodies moving against one another, hard muscle giving way, then arching and flexing once more. In that last moment, Daegan's hand found Gideon's, and he was staring at their interlaced fingers, the way they clutched and held on, then convulsed as the male vampire's body bucked and moved with ripples of sheer power against every inch of his. He could break Gideon's fingers, but he didn't. He protected, even as he gave him everything.

When the world slowed, Gideon felt overcome, conquered. Willingly conquered, at least for this moment.

Daegan's lips curved against the back of Gideon's shoulder. "I always expect that caveat, vampire hunter. But there are some lines you can't back away from, not once you've stepped across them."

"I don't want to." Gideon was flat on the covers, trapped beneath the vampire, and okay with that, particularly when Daegan nuzzled his throat, gave him a nip and worked his hips against his ass, setting off some low level tremors. "What the hell are you doing?" His words were slurred.

"Enjoying my slave. I plan to fuck his ass several more times before his Mistress returns. I want her to see I used him well, made him sore." Daegan slid his arm under his waist and brought him back to the all fours position, pushing him gently to his elbows. "We're going to take care of those five strikes, then I'm going to fuck you all over again, vampire hunter. I want you exhausted by dawn, so I know you won't leave this bed while I sleep."

"Only when I...go fetch your newspaper and...slippers." Gideon struggled to hold the position Daegan had ordered. His cock was throbbing in response to that threat, Holy Mother. He guessed before this was all done, he'd have a better idea how much stamina that third mark actually gave a servant. But no matter what, he had a feeling he wouldn't outlast Daegan. And that just didn't sit right. He'd figure out how to keep pace with him. Or make the vampire give out first.

He heard Daegan's soft chuckle, then the vampire had left him. Gideon stayed on his elbows, forehead on the covers, and knew his mind was drifting in that place Ella talked about. He was in the state where it didn't matter what his Master or Mistress wanted; he would provide it, be it, do whatever they wished. If Daegan wanted to shove rebar through his chest right now, Gideon wouldn't stop him.

"But I would stop anyone who thought they could do such a thing." A paddle teased his buttock, the curve of testicles. His Master had decided to change out his weapon of choice, though Gideon knew the paddle could be just as excruciating. "Your Mistress is on her way home, Gideon. She just told me."

Pleasure spiraled up in his chest, his lower belly, and he knew Daegan felt it as well. They instantly wanted her here right now. With the sex still ripe and sharp in the room, the idea of plunging her in the middle of it, seeing how she'd twist and sculpt it for her own pleasure, filled the brain waves between them in a heartbeat.

"Soon. She'll be here soon. She has a special gift for you," Daegan added. "A surprise. I just made a call upstairs to be sure the preparations are in place for it. And no, I won't tell you what the surprise is."

"What am I? Eight?"

"Only in maturity." Gideon yelped as Daegan spun the paddle, gave him an unexpected smack with it. "Count them off, Gideon. Last five. At least until you need discipline again."

"Asshole. Maybe you ought to add a few in, start a credit for me."

"That's Master Asshole, and you shouldn't tempt fate, Gideon."

Round 9

Daegan was as good as his word. He gave Gideon ten, left his ass on fire, then tied him down spread eagle to his bed. He put his mouth on Gideon's cock until he was hard and aching, his ass abraded from clenching against the covers. When he was nearly spurting, Daegan released his legs, but only to hook the ropes under his knees and pull them up to the level of his chest so he was spread like a woman, an incredibly unsettling experience.

"What the—don't—"

"You don't get the luxury of refusing your Master, Gideon." Daegan stood over him on his knees, put his cock up Gideon's ass while staring down at him. Gideon clenched his jaw, his body shuddering, trembling as Daegan slid deep, withdrew, slid deep again, all while facing him, looking down at him, tied and helpless. "You'll come this way, upon my command."

And he did, but it fucked up his mind enough that when Daegan released him, he sprang, tried to wrestle him down. The vampire met him strength to strength, hand to hand, and then pretty much smothered him in the bedclothes as he fucked his ass once more.

But that was okay. It was all okay.

Especially when he woke a couple hours—Gideon couldn't remember the last time he'd slept so deeply—and realized Anwyn was home. He could feel her.

She wasn't in their apartment, but she was upstairs, in the club. He felt the caressing touch of her mind, the sense that she'd be coming to him soon and he needed to wait on her. It wasn't fair, because Daegan was with her, but since he wasn't yet sure he had any feeling in his limbs, and he probably needed to take a shower and make himself a little more presentable once he could crawl to the bathroom, that would be all right. It was all good.

A glass of ice water, so cold the condensation dripped on his forearm, appeared in front of him, held by a familiar hand.

"Rough night?"

As much as he wanted to see Anwyn, it was a pleasant surprise, though a bit weird, to have his brother sitting on the edge of the bed, giving him an amused, understanding look. His tone was dry, the voice of experience, and Gideon couldn't deny it, not with the tangled sheets, his obvious dehydration and nakedness, and the room smelling of sweaty male fucking.

"Yeah." Gideon cleared his throat and sat up to take the water. "But okay."

"Hmm. They're good at that. Taking us way beyond our threshold, but making us okay with it, every fucking time. Even when our heads stay a bit screwed up about it."

"Yeah." He was aching and sore in all the right ways, so redundant and monosyllabic were the best he could do.

"Daegan said she'd be down pretty soon. He went up about a half hour ago."

"Where's Lyssa?"

"She went to take the tour. Probably picking out a room we can use for a few hours." Jacob's lips tugged in a wry smile. "So I'm not going to be too smug. God only knows what will meet her fancy here. You know, it was a little strange, talking to Daegan, knowing he'd basically wrung you out like a dishcloth during the time we were gone. He looked pretty damn satisfied, though."

Gideon grunted. Fortunately, his brother was used to that. His brother was used to all of this, too, and there was a comfort to that, to not needing to say anything else about it. Hell, he'd come quite a ways. At one time, he'd believed his brother would be better off dead than bound to a vampire mistress.

Hope you don't feel that way about your binding to me.

And there Anwyn was, leaning in the doorway. All sexy and perfect in jeans, heels and a tight T-shirt with sparkly things on it that etched out a red heart with a silver dagger thrust through it. Since she'd essentially been out on the town having a fun girls' night, she was carrying that appealing aura of the unattainable and available at once, which just roused the hunter in him more.

Her sensuous lips curving, she sauntered into the room, the jut of her breasts and casual sway of her hips enough to draw both males' gazes. Jacob's eyes flickered with renewed amusement.

"Can you give us a moment, Jacob?" she asked.

"I think you'll need more than a moment, but sure." He rose.

Gideon glanced at him, feeling a twinge of guilt at how much he wanted his little brother to scram so he could have Anwyn to himself.

"You heading out before I even get a chance to catch up on what's happening with my nephew?"

"We'll have time later. Your Mistress's company takes precedence over mine."

"Damn straight. She's a lot prettier."

"No argument there. So is my lady. She's found what she wants and is calling." Jacob gave him a friendly shove that set everything to aching again, but Gideon managed to cover it with a stoic grimace. When he was even with Anwyn, Jacob paused to give her a nod, a slight bow. "Remember," he said quietly, a trace of seriousness in his gaze, "You never ask a servant to leave the room. You tell him."

"I know. But I'm not so much a vampire yet that I'll be high-handed with family." She pressed his arm with fondness, then let him go. After he left, Anwyn turned her gaze back to Gideon, studying him from head to toe, the naked body sprawled and barely covered by the sheet, the mussed hair. He knew she'd scent the semen that had dried on his chest and abdomen after Daegan brought him to climax on his back like that, as well as what had dried on his balls and in the folds of his cock. She'd smell Daegan's seed as well, because he'd been as good as his word, pulling out one time to come over Gideon's ass, a primitive marking.

"You object to being fucked like a woman, Gideon? Like me?"

He lifted a shoulder. "Didn't really mean it like that."

"Sure you did." When she took another step toward him, she was close enough to run a nail along his shoulder and tip up his chin. As she let the sharp edge drift over his jugular, she held his gaze with those blue-green ocean-colored eyes. "But you liked it when he did it. You came harder when he did that to you than any of the other times."

Bending down, she brought her mouth so near to his he could feel the sweet whisper of her breath. He gripped the sheet, but knew he wasn't going to be able to keep from touching her another second, no matter the consequences.

"You haven't welcomed me properly."

It was all the encouragement he needed. Lunging, he caught her by the waist and pulled her onto her knees on the mattress. Laughing, she knocked him down to his back, holding him there with a hand on his chest as she straddled him.

"You don't worry about being high-handed with me," he said, recalling her comment to Jacob.

"You need high-handedness. Quite often."

He propped his knees up behind her, forming a back rest. When she leaned against that support, they hooked hands so she could rock side to side, comfortable in her male cradle. "You miss me?" she asked.

"Not a bit. Watched *Sons of Anarchy*, drank beer, said women are icky and who needs them." He wondered what Daegan was doing. There was a sense of expectation to her, as if she had something of major import to tell him. It made him a little nervous, wondering if he needed to be up and moving, finding weapons or at least something pointy. She read it from his mind, and caressed his palm with her fingers.

"No, love. Nothing like that."

"What's going on?"

"You'll find out soon enough." She cupped his face as he stroked her hair, her arms, a familiar touch she didn't deny him. As he did, he got the myriad scents of a night out on the city. Coffeehouses, maybe a nightclub and a bakery. He hoped she'd brought some bear claw pastries back.

"Do you ever think of anything other than sex, food or fighting?"

"What else is there to think about? I missed you," he admitted. "A lot. More than beer or bear claws."

"I'm glad. But I wanted you and Daegan to have time together."

She had her sable locks down, so he twined a strand around his wrist and felt it stroke every nerve ending to life. "What was this all about? Really."

"You think it was planned? You and Daegan?"

"I may be thickheaded and stubborn, but I'm not dumb."

She cocked her head, giving him a smile. "Not about everything, I'll give you that." Then she sobered. "If I was killed, what do you think would happen, Gideon?"

He pushed himself upright immediately, sliding his arms around her hips and slim back. "Nothing's going to happen to you. Not while either of us is alive." He was ready to fight without a stitch on, with teeth and nails if needed. "What's the matter?"

"Sshh." She put her hands on his face again, but this time he closed his hands over her wrists. There was the side of him that was her servant, and the part that was her protector, and when they came in conflict, his priorities were never confused.

"Don't *sshh* me. What—"

"This isn't about me. I know you and Daegan would move Heaven and Earth to protect me. But it's an uncertain world. If anything does happen to me, you won't die. Daegan's mark on you is stronger than my binding."

He met her gaze, held there. And it clicked. The thoughts he'd been having about Daegan, the vulnerability, the childhood... "Did you plant those things, lead me to them?"

She shook her head. "You're not as emotionally closed

off as you once were, Gideon. You've been noticing things about him, opening yourself up to the details about who and what he is, the way you were doing with me all along. You came to it yourself."

"So you arranged this because...?"

"For several reasons. One, because it was a requirement of your service to me. I set the terms, and you've been procrastinating."

"Well, not to sound like a girl, but it wasn't my job to initiate." At her level stare, he shifted. "Yeah, I was avoiding it some. It's not so easy."

"Actually, I suspect it *was* easy, in a lot of ways, and that was what made you avoid it, avoid confronting that truth. But you did it." She softened, touched his face. Then she dimpled, that mischievous spark in her gaze. "The second reason was pretty straightforward. Once I have you rewind every detail in your mind, I'll be ravishing you both every second for about a month."

"I have absolutely no objection to that."

"I didn't figure you would." Catching the hand sliding down to cup her ass, she squeezed it in reproof. Then she sobered once more. "We're a trinity, but I wanted to make sure the bond between you and Daegan is as strong as what lies between you and me."

"I'm not that important. As long as you have each other—"

He knew he'd made a mistake the second the words left his mouth. Her gaze turned to frost, chilly enough to make him wonder if Lyssa had taught her that Jedi ice trick that could transform a room into the North Pole. Anwyn slapped him upside the head, though when she tried for a double play on it, he caught her arm, a warrior's defense. She glared at him.

"You've accepted the truth, Gideon. So why do you keep backing away from it, lying to yourself? He doesn't love easily. In his hundreds of years, he's never let anyone in his heart, until the two of us. So if anything happens to me, he'll need you. I need to be sure you won't quit on him. The way you feel for him has grown into something as strong as what you feel for me. The past twenty-four hours proved it.

Tell me I'm wrong. Call me a liar. And undermine your own worth once more and I swear I will put my high heel all the way up your ass."

Whereas Daegan being pissed off could just raise his hackles, her ire always struck him straight in the chest and forced him to admit truth, no matter how it chafed. Putting his head down on her shoulder, he pressed his lips to the rise of her breast under the snug T-shirt, a quiet apology. When she sighed, her arms going around his shoulders, he wanted her to take the shirt off, let him rub his lips over the silky pillow of her breast, rising above the scrap of bra he knew she was wearing. Instead, he gave her honesty. "You're not wrong. I'd take care of him, Mistress. You know I would."

She lifted his face, her fingers caressing his jaw. "You'd take care of each other. That's what's important. You're so vital, Gideon. You matter so much, we want the world to know you belong to us. You've fantasized about a collar, haven't you?"

The shift of topic was unexpected, and definitely back out of his comfort zone once more. But hell, most things with them were. He tried to look away, but of course that slim hand, those sharp nails, dug into his face, threatening puncture. "Haven't you?" Her voice was silk over thorns, telling him he'd better answer.

"Yes. But—"

"You think we haven't longed for the same? We only needed to be sure that you felt bound to us both emotionally as well as physically. And you are, aren't you?" That touch caressed his throat, sent a wealth of sensations radiating out from it. It brought his gaze to her beautiful eyes, and he knew he could never lie to her. Especially not about this. He'd told Daegan he loved him, and even if he never said it again, he didn't have to do so. He meant it.

"Yes, Mistress. I'm bound to you both."

She nodded, a triumphant expression crossing her face, happiness and pleasure intertwined, along with a fierce, arousing possessiveness.

"We're going to collar you. A permanent sign of our ownership of your body, your heart...and every inch of your soul."

§

She had him rise from the bed and go to the shower. She chained his arms over his head, manacled his ankles to the floor, and then she stripped down, thank the gods. However, her purpose apparently was to drive him crazy, not fulfill her own lust. She washed him with the vigor and thoroughness he'd expect to see in a stable when a horsewoman was preparing her mount for show. It painfully aroused him, how she kept her body out of reach, though he watched all those rivulets of water tighten her nipples, follow the curves of waist and hip, the folds of her bare cunt when she bent over in front of him to pick up one of those scrubbing sponges. She used that on him, rubbing it over his testicles and cock, a mild abrasion that, with the soap, had him struggling not to jerk against her touch, particularly when she bade him be still.

As she stretched up to do his hair, she had to lean into his body, so he got his chance to take a nip from her shoulder, suckle the beads of water on her throat, and feel the sexy little quiver go through her as she adjusted her stance and trapped his hard cock between her thighs. When she handled his shampooing, it moved his cock in that channel, her inner thigh muscles stroking him as his breath got shorter and his heart pounded.

But she backed off before he could coax her further into it. She shut off the shower, released one of his hands so he could do the rest, and tossed him a towel. He shot her a feral grin. "Don't trust yourself too close, Mistress?"

She gave him her mysterious look, elusive seductress that she was. "Get yourself free, dry off. Don't put anything on. Come up to the first level, kneel outside the elevator. I'll come for you soon. I want that cock to stay hard, but you do it without touching it. I expect you at that elevator in five minutes."

Staying hard wasn't a problem. All he had to do was watch the twitch of her ass as she put on a light silk wrap, tied it snug and disappeared. A few minutes later, he knew she'd left their apartments. He dried off, ran his fingers through his hair and gave his face a quick glance. Three and a half minutes for a decent shave, and then he was in the elevators.

He didn't give himself a chance to think about who he might meet, though Atlantis was closed for a few more hours. Thank all the gods, when he stepped off, he didn't see Jacob, but his brother was probably off with Lyssa, enjoying free run of the club's diverse bondage equipment. Or rather Lyssa would be using him for *her* enjoyment of it. The idea of his brother stretched out on some of those torture devices that Anwyn and Daegan had used on him was a little odd, so he put that out of his head.

Though he wouldn't mind seeing Lyssa stretched out naked on some of those things. If Anwyn ever read *that* from his mind, he expected he'd be in for a world of hurt. Thank goodness his Mistress was choosing to ignore it—or planning to exact retribution later.

When he heard the tap of those heels, he remembered the first night they'd met, when he couldn't see her, could only hear her coming up behind him. She touched him now, fingers whispering over his bare shoulder, caressing his jaw. "Follow me."

Rising, he obeyed. She stayed several steps ahead of him, giving him the pleasure of watching her walk in that thin robe, and distracting him from his own nakedness. He was surprised when she took him to the Rose Room, a room of all mirrors on ceilings and walls. It was the place she and Daegan had first come together. But instead of a center pedestal holding a vase of roses tonight, there was a mid-sized iron fire pit, which appeared to be filled with red hot coals, irons and tongs. Next to it was a silver chalice, like the ones he'd seen in churches, holding wine, wine that represented blood. Only his enhanced senses told him he *was* smelling blood.

He was surprised to see Daegan back in the silk shirt and slacks he'd worn with Shannon and Aaron. The mask was missing though, so he could see the dark eyes and fall of black hair over his forehead. And the shirt was open, underlining the fact Daegan was six foot plus of pure sex.

The vampire leaned against the far wall, his arms crossed. The way his gaze coursed over Gideon, taking his time and pleasure in the view, made Gideon remember everything they'd done. Particularly that last moment, when he'd been almost unconscious, but felt Daegan's lips brush his temple, his hand glide with possessive pleasure down Gideon's back, over his ass.

Sleep, vampire hunter. You've earned it.

Anwyn made a pleased noise. "Lovely images, Gideon. I want you to kneel now. By the fire pit."

He did, some swirly crazy things happening in his chest as he guessed at what was about to happen. His cock jumped when her fingertips trailed over his shoulders again. "Arms held out to your sides, chin up, back straight. Sit on your heels."

He did it, feeling his testicles press against them. She tugged on his hair. "You're a warrior, Gideon. Fierce in your loyalty, almost savage with it at times. We've talked about it, Daegan and I, and we know a collar that can be removed won't do. We want something that permanently shows your servitude to us, something that can't be taken away, given back."

Yes. He tightened his lips at the involuntary thought, the fervency of it.

"So that is what we are going to give you. And hereafter, if you accept this binding, you also accept what it means. What you mean to us. You never question it again. You *are* the glue, Gideon." Her tone was soft. "Do you understand?"

That swirly quality became thick, hard to speak around. "Yes, Mistress."

"You are not speaking only to me." Her tone was sharp, snapping his back to a straighter stance. She could do that with the badass routine, tighten up his balls, harden his cock. He had no idea how she did it, when any other woman would just make him want to pat her head and call her cute. He was unsettled, restless and anxious. Alert, almost battle ready. But he obeyed her directive and amended his response.

"Yes, Master and Mistress."

"Good. There are no restraints in this room, Gideon.

Daegan will hold you steady when the time comes, but part of the challenge of accepting this is your accepting the pain of it." She moved to the chalice, picked up a paintbrush with bristles that almost matched her sable hair. Soft looking. "Hold your position."

He did, watching her dip the brush in the blood. As she stroked the brush over his throat and wrists, he felt the slick slide of warm blood, sensuous, like the silk of her tongue. It was her blood and Daegan's, mixed together.

"There are three sets of irons. Each one has two curved metal pieces, like tongs. When brought together they form a fitted circle, a tight manacle over your wrists or throat, measured to make that tight fit. *D* is cut into one cuff, *A* into the other, for our shared ownership of you. The trinity, the servant's mark you bear, is cut into the collar, so the scarring you experience from our blood will reflect those symbols."

Any wound inflicted on a servant became a permanent scar when it was marked by his vampire's blood. There was a strange feeling sweeping through Gideon, a heat over his skin, a tingling and almost light headedness.

"You've worn him out, love," Anwyn said with amusement, but her eyes were intent on Gideon's face, he could feel it. "He might need some of our blood when this is done."

"I worked him hard," Daegan agreed, pure male satisfaction in his tone. "But he's strong as an ox, and just as stubborn." His voice became rougher. "And I'll hold him up."

The vampire came across the room then, taking a knee behind Gideon, his hands closing over his forearms, leaving his wrists clear. As he did, it put his front against Gideon's back, the pleasure of that hard bare chest pressing into his shoulder blades. The position reminded him of how he'd shown Daegan how to throw the ball. *Go long, go far. Go forever.*

"Are you ready, Gideon?" Anwyn asked, her eyes full of emotion. Her hand hovered over one pair of the irons in the fire pit.

He glanced back at Daegan, met his dark eyes, then

shifted his attention forward to his Mistress. *For the two of you, I'm always ready. For whatever you want and need.*

"Do you accept our love and ownership of you completely, with no doubts and full surrender?"

He swallowed, knowing he always had to be honest, even if it ruined the moment. "It's hard for me to accept the way you feel about me. But not because I don't want it. It's everything I want...so no matter how hard it is for me to understand or accept the way you both feel about me, I'm yours, in every way. And I hope to God you'll always want me."

"Good enough." She reached out with her free hand, a gentle brush of fingers over his face that briefly closed his eyes as she touched his lips. When he raised his lids, the Mistress took over, the direct stare that told him to lower his eyes, and damn if he didn't do it. She didn't require that often, but he could see she wanted his focus to be internal right now. He moved into that state pretty quick, almost a shallow-breathed trance, knowing what was coming. God help him, he wanted it. It didn't matter that—

Holy fuck. Daegan's hands locked down on his forearms in an unshakable grip as the first set of tongs closed around his wrist. Anwyn had branded humans for Atlantis's more extreme activities, and knew the limits of the human body, what amount was needed for the brand to scar and yet not cause medical emergencies. A third mark had more tolerance, but also needed the metal to stay long enough to sear the blood into the flesh, activate the chemical reaction that would make his Master and Mistress's marks permanent. He was making a strangled scream, tears of exertion overflowing as he tried not to rely on Daegan so much, to hold still as possible, but his Master had him, held him steady.

When the tongs were taken away from that wrist, he was gasping.

"One down," she said, and picked up the other. No time to brace for impact. That was the way his Mistress wanted it. Daegan's power was definitely needed his time, because it didn't matter how badass his mind wanted him to be, his body reacted on instinct to the smell of burning flesh, the excruciating pain of it. He twitched and jerked, a hoarse cry tearing from his throat and face muscles working as the second wrist cuff stamped its mark in that location.

D on the right, *A* on the left. He could see it, see how it would heal up enough to make those initials more precise, always there, now and forever. At the moment they hurt like a son of a bitch. But it was okay. Adrenaline was pumping crazy through his system, and his cock was staying high and hard as a tent pole, because he knew what was coming, the most important one of all. He lifted his head to Anwyn again, gritting his teeth and staring at her through those stress tears. *Please...*

"You want the collar, love, don't you?"

He nodded. Daegan brushed his mouth against his shoulder, his body pressing in closer. Gideon felt him right against his ass, his clad knee next to Gideon's bare calf.

"Lift your chin higher," she commanded. "Let me see your desire. I'm going to put the collar over the area I bite you to feed. That way those marks will be part of the scarring pattern. Will you like that?"

"I like any mark either of you leaves on me," he said, his voice a determined rasp.

"Good answer."

She lifted the iron. "Hold my gaze, Gideon. Watch it happening."

The mirror made that possible, though he preferred to look at the object, not its reflection, because then he could see her, something the mirrors didn't provide. He wished he could see Daegan, but he was there, body so close, a vivid reminder not only of the physical demands he'd placed upon Gideon earlier, but the emotional ones as well.

Daegan slid his arm around Gideon's chest, his other hand curved over his forehead, holding him steady as Anwyn lifted the last set of tongs, the one whose two curved metal pieces were intended to clasp around Gideon's neck, hold there against the painted blood so he was permanently marked by his vampires. Her hand didn't waver, and he loved her for it, her understanding of what his soul wanted. Something permanent, that couldn't be removed. It was too easy for this dog to break his leash.

With this, there was nothing to fight. It was there, embedded, his willing submission to them.

It took all he had not to fight Daegan's hold, the body's involuntary and sensible reaction to being burned in a way that would likely be terminal if he was human. He smelled his flesh burning, heard his scream and, after a short blackout, became aware of Daegan still holding him fast. Anwyn had pulled the metal pieces away and dropped the iron back into the fire pit.

Daegan let him fall forward to his hands and knees, though he stayed kneeling behind Gideon, knee brushing his hip, hand lying in a light caress on the valley of his spine. Gideon breathed hard, working through it, staring at the red, abraded bands around both wrists. *D* and *A*. As a vampire hunter, he'd fought for the memory of his lost fiancé. Throughout his life he'd always kept his goal just ahead of him, never attainable. Now the goal was in this room. He'd never expected to end up here, but this was where he wanted to be.

Anwyn knelt in front of him, lifted his face and brushed her mouth over his, once, twice. Sweet and gentle, where she'd been brutal moments before. Feeling the tremor in her hands, he automatically lifted his to close them over her wrists, though he thought he might be shaking more. "It's okay," he said.

She nodded, eyes luminous, lashes so thick he wanted to kiss them, breathe on them, watch them close and fan her silken cheeks. "The brands will feel better soon," she said.

"It feels better now." He coughed, flinched at the agony to his skin. "Really."

"I can tell." She stroked his brow, his temple, his jaw. He saw her gaze resting on his wrists, then the collar, her attention clinging to it, and it swept through him like heat. He was all hers. The trinity mark did that, but this was something she'd chosen as a Mistress would, and she'd been a Mistress well before she'd been a vampire. The two together made this moment all the more significant.

He wanted her. Wanted to pleasure her and his Master, while still riding the pain.

Her lashes lifted, her eyes meeting his. "Please," he said

thickly, and he knew there was a fierceness in his eyes that straddled the line between demand and desire.

She straightened, slipping the sash of the robe. Somewhere along the way, she'd donned a scrap of bra and a tiny thong panty, thank the lingerie gods. As he watched, the robe pooled around her, and she gracefully folded herself to the floor, then lay back in a supine position before him. Spreading her legs, she teased the crotch of the panties with her long fingered nails, drying up any saliva he had left in his mouth. "Down to your elbows, Gideon. Put your mouth on me and serve your Mistress as you should."

The smell of her pussy was nectar. She was aroused, but she'd been aroused for awhile, the heavy musk telling him she'd been worked up well before this minute.

"You've been cheating, *cher*," Daegan murmured, proving he was catching it, too. "You've been listening in."

"There isn't a woman alive who could resist watching the two of you in that bed," she said, her lips curving. "And Lady Lyssa will take extra pleasure in her servant, thanks to me sharing that vision. It's never a bad thing for a vampire queen to feel she owes us a favor."

She reached out, tugging on Gideon with impatience. "Now."

He dropped to his elbows, ignoring the pain in his wrists as he slid his hands under her, cupping her buttocks to angle her up to his mouth. She had a beautifully shaped ass, firm and soft in all the right ways. It made his cock even more eager, that conflicting message between physical agony and intense arousal. She'd marked him, collared him, they both had, and now they were demanding he serve them as required. It quite frankly made him insanely aroused, no matter how lightheaded he felt or drained from what he'd only recently given Daegan.

"Drink, Gideon." The rest of the blood in that chalice was in front of him, and Daegan tipped it, so it ran down over her mound, into the channel and crevices of clit and labia. Anwyn sighed in pleasure, then gasped as Gideon began to clean her and take in the blood at once. She writhed under the stimulation while he suckled, nibbled and licked, and then made a noise of helpless pleasure himself as Daegan's well-lubricated finger teased the opening of his sore ass. He pushed in slowly, testing that ground, telling Gideon he was going to get well and truly fucked once more, as often as his Master demanded.

He let go, lost all sense of who he was, pulled into what he was for them entirely. Servicing his Mistress, his Master, the burn of those collar and cuffs on him. It was when he entered this state of pure and perfect service that he didn't doubt what he was to them. Daegan's fingers withdrew, the head of his cock replacing them, and Gideon pushed back against him, welcoming him in, flinching only slightly as the flare of Daegan's broad head pushed through the inner ring of tight muscles, sank deep like a fucking drill.

The vampire's satisfied grunt of pleasure, her soft, seductive moans, they sent him spiraling. He worked his mouth over Anwyn, getting every bit of that blood and tasting her honey at the same time. He dug his fingers into her ass, an anchor, as Daegan increased his thrust, bumping Gideon's mouth up against her, working her clit harder. She was crying out, arching up, arms over her head, scratching at the tile floor, seeking purchase.

I want you inside her, Gideon. Take her into mindless climax, while I do the same to you.

He lifted his head as Anwyn's wild eyes found his. She wanted him to keep going with his mouth, but he understood what Daegan was wanting, and Gideon knew she'd like it as well. Daegan ruled them both when it came to this. That, too, could cause an odd feeling in his chest, and it was one matched by Anwyn; he could tell by the way her gaze fastened on him, her lips moist and eyes bright.

Shifting, Daegan moved with him, staying in his ass and making Gideon cross-eyed with the friction of that angle. Sliding up her body, Gideon guided his cock into her wet pussy. She arched up to him, her arms banding around his shoulders, forearms making contact with the abraded skin on his throat. He didn't care. He started to thrust, Daegan's hold on his hips setting the pace, and he grunted himself, cursed as the vampire worked his cock with devilish knowledge.

Better get to work, vampire hunter. She will be very

displeased if you lose control and come before she does. She's even more cruel than I am.

"Well...she's a girl." Gideon managed and earned a tight squeeze of her pussy around his cock, a stroke that damn near sent him over. "Jesus."

He set his jaw, went the rougher, harder route, knowing she was already pretty hot and worked up. Setting his lips to the quivering pale tops of her breasts over the enticing bra, he licked, finding his way into the cup and to the nipples, squeezing both breasts hard in his large hands.

"Love your tits," he murmured, knowing she liked the crude talk at the right times, and this was a right time, if her unintelligible sounds of pleasure meant anything.

I've got you, Gideon. Everything you give is safe with me, remember? Everything.

He remembered Daegan saying that, and knew they both meant it, especially as Anwyn's gaze swept back over him at the thought, emotion filling her eyes once more. He meant it, too. They *were* that perfect trinity, each one caring for the other two, forming a solid triumvirate capable of handling anything, based on the strength of the bonds for each other.

He stroked inside her, deep, loving the feel of her, the arch of her body, the beauty of it. She was a goddess, an earth bound, blood bound goddess, and he would do anything for her. But, oh, fuck, Daegan was too good at what he did. He'd dug his hands into Gideon's hips, his thighs flush against him, and Gideon was going to die from the pleasure of it.

Anwyn let out a cry of release, and Gideon snarled, the frustration of holding back as she spasmed around his cock, but then Daegan's hand landed on the back of his neck, outlining that collar of flesh as she reached up, even through her climax, and clasped it from the other side, their fingers overlapping, thanks to the size of Daegan's hand. The pain of it shot through Gideon, pushing his climax back, but the meaning of it, them squeezing down on that collar of ownership, was overwhelming at an even deeper level than a balls-level climax.

Daegan released then, and Gideon gritted his teeth, bore

down on that pain, held onto it even as he reveled in them using him for their pleasure and holding his out of reach until they gave him permission. Just when he thought he couldn't hold back any longer, the gate to heaven was opened.

Come for us, Gideon.

It was in both of their minds, resonating between them. Their fingers tightened on that collar, spiraling him over the edge in a wild jerking intensity, tearing him between overwhelming pleasure and excruciating pain. He came, growling, groaning, cursing. Anwyn caught his mouth with hers, let him cup her head with his hands, dive deep with teeth and tongue. He made another soul-deep sound when her hands left his throat to clasp his wrists, putting her touch on those burns as well.

As he bucked between them, she milked his cock to the very end and beyond. Daegan kept stroking inside of him. They showed their love of every moment of his helpless, passionate violence, holding him between them, keeping him going and savoring their slave's reaction.

He saw that in their minds, that shared delight. Then, at long last, like the aftermath of a summer storm, there was a deep, clean satisfaction as they came back to earth, all twined together. Daegan's mouth was back on the valley of his spine, and Anwyn was still holding him in her kiss.

They loved him. It gave his throat that thickness again, because he realized it was the first time he'd really, truly believed it, all the way down to the soul they'd claimed with their third markings. Maybe he wouldn't hold onto it, maybe it would come and go, because it was an incredible, hard-to-believe thing, but he had it in this moment, and the seed had been planted deep this time. Maybe it would take root, such that one day, none of it would be difficult, accepting this. Accepting their love as a fact, not as something to avoid or push away for fear it wasn't real. He had their collar, the cuffs, sign of their ownership, and he'd never felt so...right.

They truly loved and wanted to keep him.

As long as you don't start peeing on the carpet and chewing up my very expensive shoes.

Anwyn chuckled as Daegan sent that thought through their minds. The vampire eased back, catching Gideon's arms to lift him. "Off your Mistress, Gideon. I want you both in my bed."

Gideon rose, and though his legs were shaky as hell, he would have been happy to carry Anwyn. Instead, he was a bit mortified to find the two of them flanking him, guiding him, underscoring how unsteady he felt.

"You need more blood, love," Anwyn observed. "We'll take care of that."

He was going to deny it, say they didn't need to worry about him, but for now he just wanted to be, was floating where words weren't needed. He was just theirs, to do with as they thought best.

They took him back to Daegan's bed. Always before, he and Daegan had put Anwyn in the middle, but tonight, they put him there. Anwyn curled up in his arms, Daegan spooned behind him, brushing his neck with his lips and putting a familiar hand on his ass. Gideon's cock was nestled against her hip, her leg insinuated between his. Daegan stroked his hair. Gideon felt drowsy, not sure if he'd ever let his guard down so much.

"I trust you when I sleep, vampire hunter. You can trust me."

"You'll probably...tie me up and shave my head."

"I could do that while you're awake. And listen to you curse me the whole time."

"You could try. Anwyn...I taught him to throw a football."

"I know." Her fingers stroked through his hair on the other side as her eyes met Daegan's over Gideon's shoulder. "You teach us so many things, Gideon. You always will."

A small smile appeared on his firm lips. Anwyn had told him he didn't smile enough, so he'd work on that. Now that smile stayed, as he let himself fall asleep in the arms of the two vampires he served with all he was, all he would ever be. They'd give him blood in a little while, but for now, there was nothing more he wanted. Not tonight.

For once, Gideon gave himself to slumber *and* peace.

The End

###

Afterword

Did you enjoy reading this? Was it a true pleasure to spend time with Joey's characters? If you feel it was, then she asks that you do one simple thing in support of her future work. Please share that experience with at least one other book-reading friend who hasn't read her. Or mention her on a Facebook page, at a book club meeting or online forum, on Twitter, in an Amazon or GoodReads review, or wherever you feel comfortable. You, the pleased reader, are the best marketing strategy an author can have. If you do just one of those things to spread the word about her work, she will be very grateful! And thank you again for taking the journey with her characters.

Ready for More?

Check out Joey's website at storywitch.com where you'll find additional information, free excerpts, buy links and news about current and upcoming releases for all of her books and series.

You can find free vignettes and friends to share them with at the JWH Connection, a Joey W. Hill fan forum created by and operated for fans of Joey W. Hill. Sign up instructions are available at storywitch.com/community.

Finally, be sure to check out the latest newsletter for information on upcoming releases, book signing events, contests, and more. You can view current and past editions and subscribe to receive upcoming editions at storywitch.com/community or click the link under the Community menu.

About the Author

Joey W. Hill writes about vampires, mermaids, boardroom executives, cops, witches, angels, housemaids...pretty much wherever her inspiration takes her. She's penned over forty acclaimed titles and six award-winning series, and been awarded the RT Book Reviews Career Achievement Award for Erotica. But she's especially proud and humbled to have the support and enthusiasm of a wonderful, widely diverse readership.

So why erotic romance? "Writing great erotic romance is all about exploring the true face of who we are – the best and worst - which typically comes out in the most vulnerable moments of sexual intimacy." She has earned a reputation for writing BDSM romance that not only wins her fans of that genre, but readers who would "never" read BDSM romance. She believes that's because strong, compelling characters are the most important part of her books.

"Whatever genre you're writing, if the characters are captivating and sympathetic, the readers are going to want to see what happens to them. That was the defining element of the romances I loved most and which shaped my own writing. Bringing characters together who have numerous emotional obstacles standing in their way, watching them reach a soul-deep understanding of one another through the expression of their darkest sexual needs, and then growing from that understanding into love - that's the kind of story I love to write."

Take the plunge with her, and don't hesitate to let her know what you think of her work, good or bad. She thrives on feedback!

Find more of Joey W. Hill's work by following her on Facebook and Twitter, and check out her website for more books by Joey W. Hill.

Twitter: @JoeyWHill

Facebook: JoeyWHillAuthor

On the Web: www.storywitch.com

Email: storywitch@storywitch.com

Also by Joey W. Hill

Ice Queen

Mirror of My Soul

Mistress of Redemption

Rough Canvas

Branded Sanctuary

Divine Solace

Worth The Wait

Naughty Bits Series

The Lingerie Shop

Training Session

Bound To Please

The Highest Bid

Naughty Wishes Series

Part 1: Body

Part 2: Heart

Part 3: Mind

Part 4: Soul

Vampire Queen Series

Vampire Queen's Servant

Mark of the Vampire Queen

Vampire's Claim

Beloved Vampire

Vampire Mistress

Vampire Trinity

Vampire Instinct

Bound by the Vampire Queen

Taken by a Vampire

The Scientific Method
Nightfall
Elusive Hero
Night's Templar

Non-Series Titles

If Wishes Were Horses
Virtual Reality
Unrestrained
Medusa's Heart

Novellas

Chance of a Lifetime
Choice of Masters
Make Her Dreams Come True
Threads of Faith
Submissive Angel

Short

Snow Angel